DARKNESS AWAKENING

Books by Lisa M. Green

The Awakened Series

Dawn Rising
Darkness Awakening
Midnight Descending

Standalone Novels

The First

See the rest at *lisamgreen.com/books*

Newsletter

Sign up for updates and information on new
releases at *lisamgreen.com/newsletter*

*The truth is often more complicated
than a lie could ever be...*

DARKNESS AWAKENING

AWAKENED ~ BOOK TWO

LISA M. GREEN

TRIDENT PUBLISHING

ISBN: 9781952300035 (hardcover) / 9781952300042 (paperback) / 9781952300059 (ebook)

Library of Congress Control Number 2020916320

First edition published in the United States of America in November 2020

Trident Publishing
Atlanta, Georgia
tridentpub.com
contact@tridentpub.com

For my readers

You're either going to love me or hate me by the end of this one.
HAHAHAHA!

Love all of you!

#sorrynotsorry #evillaugh

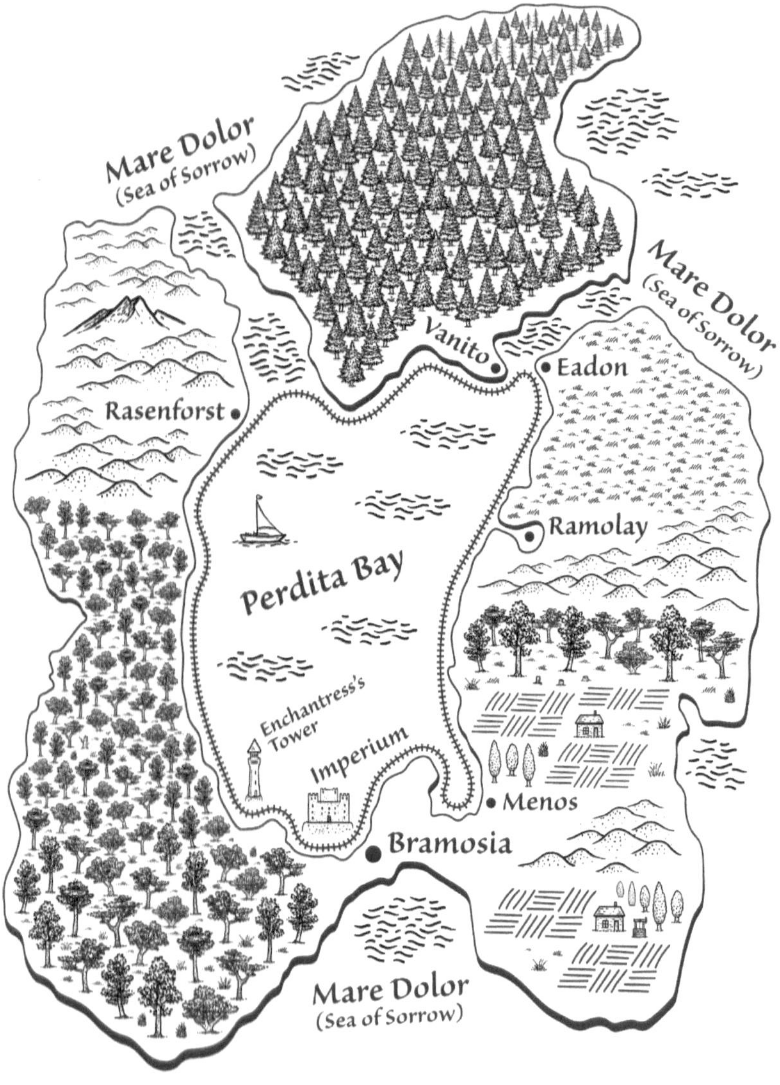

A glossary is located at the back of the book.

Awakened

In waking dreams I glide on thorny paths
Trampled upon by those who wish to harm.
The briars all but broken in their haste
To rid the world of what must come to pass.
The roses dying, dying in their bed;
A thankless death to purge the unseen past.
An unknown path I take through the darkness
To reach the grail I do not wish to seek.

Through sylvan screen, I know he's waiting there,
An unwilling specter in my dark thoughts.
Never seeking, always finding, poor soul.
He does not want this, a burdensome crown
Upon his weary head, crushing down hope
And freedom from what he knows he must do.
This fearful dance will set the world ablaze;
Embers ignite, dreams fading into dust.

But dreams are shadows of the waking world,
Weaving a web of whispered promises.
In the end, pricks may sting and thorns may bite;
The spell was cast, but death did not take me.
Fumbling, stumbling, crumbling mind.
In death I'll not be someone's rotting corpse.
In sleep I lie in dreams that do not die,
Awakened by one who knows my true name.

PART ONE

AN UNWILLING SPECTER

Through sylvan screen, I know he's waiting there,
An unwilling specter in my dark thoughts.
Never seeking, always finding, poor soul.

Chapter 1

AURIANNA

The walls, the floor, the chairs . . . they were all just as Aurianna remembered. But the house was silent, her aunt nowhere in sight.

"Larissa?" she called into the silence. Darkness poured from every corner, shadows lurking in wait.

Something wasn't right.

"Larissa?" she said again, a little louder. Still no answer. Gingerly, Aurianna picked herself up off the floor and opened the front door.

The palpable blackness of the night hid the moon from her searching gaze, not the slightest glimmer of moonlight peeking through. Why was it still so dark? If she had indeed succeeded in stopping the catastrophe the prophecy spoke of, all of this should be different, the Darkness—that mysterious entity that pervaded the air and stole both mirth and magic from the world—no more.

Eresseia was a small world, but far vaster than she had ever imagined. Her world, growing up, had consisted of one small community in which she and Aunt Larissa lived. Aurianna had feared her actions in the past she had just returned from would erase the people of this future community, but she had refused to think too much about that. Now, as she stared into the black void of the night, she knew that the thing to fear was staring back at her. The Darkness was a danger to all—past, present, and future.

The past might have been where she was born and where she now had friends, but the future was the home she had always known. Everything she had done was to protect both past and future. And apparently...she had failed.

Many Kinetics had traveled to the future to escape a war between Kinetics and non-Kinetics, only to be captured and drained of their powers by the leaders of this time. It seemed she had done nothing to prevent their horrible fate.

As she peered out into the dark, confused and forlorn, she noticed a shadow pass in front of a dimly lit window. A figure appeared to be moving in the direction of what had commonly been known as the Imperium in the time from which she had just returned. Despite her hopes, despite her efforts, the structure appeared to remain as she had known it in this life—empty and deserted.

It was strange to see it dark and abandoned, since she had grown used to seeing it full of people and activity. In the past, the place had been the home of Kinetics, those with elemental powers, like herself. When she had traveled to the past, the Imperium—and indeed all of Eresseia—had been vibrant and teeming with life. Now both the building and its surroundings sat ominously silent and shrouded in Darkness.

When Pharis had traveled into the future to bring her back to fulfill the prophecy, he had been shocked and saddened to see his home like this. At the time, she had been bewildered by everything that was happening to her, uncertain of her future and unaware of what lay ahead. But now, as she squinted into the dark and hastened to follow the shadow that loomed up ahead, Aurianna felt those same pangs of grief hit her heart. She now knew what that place had been like, and seeing it deserted and forgotten was a punch to her chest. The friends she had made and subsequently left behind—

No, now isn't the time for that. I have to figure out what went wrong.

She could only barely make out the moving form in front of her. But she was afraid to call out too loudly for fear of drawing the attention of the Praefects—who shouldn't exist any longer. The Carpos, Praefects whose sole job was to arrest Kinetics, would surely have noticed her return to the middle of town via magic.

Nothing made any sense. None of this should still be here. She had stopped the singularity that would have sparked a war. The Darkness should be gone. The town should be different.

Her aunt should be at home, waiting on her as she'd promised. For Aurianna, their last words to one another on the night of her twentieth birthday had been a few moon cycles ago, but for Larissa, only moments should have passed.

Lost in thought, Aurianna didn't notice the figure had stopped in the middle of the street. When she collided with a solid form, she started to cry out, but a hand quickly slipped over her opened mouth. Looking closely, she saw Larissa's worried frown, and her eyes widened in surprise.

The two women grasped one another in a fervid embrace. Aurianna was mumbling in her aunt's ear, trying to be quiet, but beyond excited to see the older woman's face at last.

Larissa pulled back, looking her over, checking for signs of injury. "Child, I thought… I happened to be looking out the window and saw a light at the Imperium, and I just thought maybe you'd been brought back there instead of the house for some reason."

"Oh, Auntie! I'm so happy to be back. I know it doesn't seem like it for you, but it's been ages since I last saw you." She paused, absorbing her aunt's words. "Wait, what light?"

Larissa nodded toward the building up ahead. "Just across the bridge, there, inside the building. A bright light fell from the sky and landed just inside the entrance not a moment ago. I ran as fast as I could. I was worried the Carpos—"

Aurianna stepped back. "Larissa, why are there still Carpos?"

Her aunt's eyes held a knowing sadness. "It doesn't matter. We need to check on the Imperium, find out—"

"Why are there still Carpos? Tell me!"

Eyes glistening, Larissa finally said, "Nothing's changed. Not yet, at least." She placed a hand on Aurianna's arm.

The woman didn't seem surprised by the fact, nor did she seem as upset as Aurianna thought she should have been.

"I don't understand!" Aurianna exclaimed, shaking off the woman's touch. "You said I could fix it, and I did! I fixed it. I…I thought I fixed it." Her words ended in a breathy whisper, and her head felt heavy as her vision began to darken at the edges.

Larissa grabbed her as she began to sink weakly to the ground. "Get up, child, before someone sees us. We must get to the Imperium. Something is different, and maybe that's a good thing." Steadying Aurianna on her feet, she dragged the girl onward.

"Wait a minute." Aurianna tried to free herself from her aunt's grasp, but the older woman was stronger than she looked. "What do you mean *different*? Different from what? Everything seems the same to me, and that's the problem, isn't it?"

"Hush, girl. We have to get across the bridge before the Carpos show up."

"But why is this happening? Do you know?"

Larissa continued to ignore her questions, marching across

the bridge and through the crumbling entrance to the building Aurianna had only recently begun to think of as a second home.

Once inside, Aurianna again attempted to break free and face her aunt. There were too many unanswered questions. Just as she managed to pull her arm loose, from the other side of the main hall, a familiar voice said, "Let's go."

Pharis.

"Pharis? What the hell are you doing here?" Pointedly, she added, "Again!"

As he walked up to them, he said, "I'd like to know the answer to that myself. I didn't exactly volunteer."

"Volunteer for what?"

He threw a sideways glance at Larissa, his nostrils flaring. "To bring you back."

Aurianna took a step away from him, trembling, her insides filling up with a weightlessness that threatened to take her away up through the ceiling and into another life, another world. It was happening all over again, her life reduced to its utility within the scope of some destiny she had never asked for, never wanted.

Larissa touched her arm, saying, "I know this is hard, dear, but you did something while you were there, right?"

Aurianna nodded, still grasping for a handle on her inner turmoil, a way to steady her nerves and the rising flood of panic. "Yeah, I did do something. I stopped the woman they said I was supposed to stop! Then they let me come home. So why is everything still the same? Or is it? You said something is different. What do you mean by that?"

"I just meant something feels different, is all. Everything here still seems the same. But something is headed in the right direction."

Pharis interrupted. "This is really fascinating and all, but I'd love to get back home so I can rearrange the faces of those Arcanes who made me come here." He paused, looking at each of them in turn. "Obviously it didn't work. Something's still wrong. But I'm not waiting around again. We are leaving. Now." He grabbed Aurianna's arm. "Where is it?"

"I . . . I don't have an Aether Stone. They disappear when you use them. You know that." Her body trembled in anger and fright simultaneously, and Aurianna heard the tremor in her voice, ashamed of her weakness. Pulling away with a hard yank of her arm, she glared at the man before her.

He was glaring right back. "Your pocket."

"My pocket? Pharis, that one doesn't work, remember?" To emphasize her point, she pulled the dull stone from her pocket and held it up.

He sighed. "Not the stone," his voice dripping with condescension and bitterness. "The lighter I gave you."

"Oh." She produced the metal box from her pocket and put the non-functioning Aether Stone away.

At that moment, a not-so-far-off whistle pierced the silence of the night. Voices trailed behind the sound, too far away to make out the words, but close enough that the three bodies inside the building froze. The owners of the voices were perhaps as close as the opposite side of the bridge, causing the priorities of the moment to shift . . . drastically.

Pharis snatched the lighter from her outstretched hand, grabbing that same hand as he pulled her off into the darkness within the building.

Aurianna didn't give herself a chance to think about what was happening. Again. A quick glance around was the only confirmation she needed that things were not okay. She yelled to her aunt, her voice strained with the adrenaline of the moment, "Don't let them catch you! I promise I'll be back soon."

They disappeared into the shadows of the stairwell and, as the sound of multiple sets of boots pounding across the bridge reached Aurianna's ears, they set off on a new journey.

* * *

Pharis was moving at a speed that left them both breathless, though he seemed better skilled at hiding his discomfort. Despite his firm grasp of her wrist, Aurianna struggled to keep up. But she was determined not to let him see her as weak. Not to mention, if they stopped, even for a moment, the Carpos would overtake and capture them. The thought of what they would do to them was enough to keep her moving.

They entered the underground tunnels, Pharis holding the lighter with his other hand but unable to use it. They needed to lose their pursuers before they reached wherever the Aether Stone was buried. Without the stone, they would not be able to travel back to the past where she needed to fix whatever was wrong with her world.

Again. Properly this time.

After a while, the sound of pursuing footfalls grew fainter until it was gone. The Carpos were lost somewhere in the tunnels but could find their tracks again at any moment.

They slowed and a spark flared in the dark. The flame of the lighter only partially illuminated the passage, but it was better than nothing.

"Are we near the other stone you buried?" Aurianna asked.

"What makes you think *I* buried it?"

"Whoever, Pharis. That's what we're looking for, right?"

No answer as they continued down the corridor.

She tried again. "Why is this happening?"

"I don't know."

"What do you mean, you don't know?"

"I *mean* I don't know."

"What did the Arcanes tell you?"

"Nothing."

"Nothing?"

"Nothing useful," he barked. "Stop talking to me."

Pharis had slowed, and she was able to keep up. Aurianna huffed, irritation clouding her mind. "What is your problem?"

In a whirlwind of motion, Pharis caught her up, her forearm gripped tightly and the wall of the tunnel against her back. His mouth was on hers in an instant, hard but not ungentle. Her thoughts raced faster than she could piece them together.

That was in the first second. After that, all thoughts fled her mind.

His lips were warm and soft, despite the roughness of the kiss. Pressed against the wall, she started to lean into the kiss just as he pulled away abruptly. The connection had lasted mere seconds.

His eyes were focused on the ground, his face still inches from hers, but the sentiment written there wasn't pleasant. Neither were the words that followed. "What is my problem? My problem is you! I told you the last time we were down here to shut your mouth, or someone would shut it for you." His breathing was still ragged—whether from the kiss, or the exertion of the journey, or his fury and frustration, she wasn't sure. "Stop. Talking. You . . . and your stupid bloody prophecy are ruining my life and my attempts to get anything of value done in my world." He turned on his heels, walking off at a brisk pace into the dark corridor ahead. "I suggest you keep up, 'cause I'm not waiting on you."

The wall was cold against her back, but not nearly as cold as his demeanor. Aurianna felt her eyes well with tears of bewilderment as her mouth slackened in shock. Then she hurried after, afraid he'd leave her behind. She couldn't believe what had just happened— he'd kissed her, like it was nothing, like she was nothing.

He'd kissed her. Why? To make a point?

Something had made him incredibly angry. But none of this was *her* fault. The little part of her heart that felt sorry for him withered. He had no right to touch her, especially like that.

But she had let him.

She knew better than to trust people. Slowing her steps, she wrapped her arms around herself, trying to comfort and soothe the miserable sensation of his callous disregard for her feelings.

Eventually, Pharis stopped. This time, they had no map and no torch, only the faint illumination from the lighter. She desperately wanted to know what the plan was, but she refused to initiate a conversation with the man.

He stood there, scratching his head as he stared at the ground in front of him.

"Is this it?" he asked, voice gruff but subdued.

"Is this what?" Even as she spoke the words, she looked down and realized where they were. Half-exposed rings of blackened dirt covered a small section of the floor and walls, almost erased by time. Almost, but not quite.

This was where she had exploded—quite literally—back on that first official day of Fire training. The day she had scared a Void and her instructor half to death. Suddenly, she realized what Pharis was saying.

"So, it's buried here, then? They knew I'd recognize this place."

"I take it that's a yes?"

"Yes."

"Fine." He knelt on the ground and began digging with his bare hands, right in the middle of what used to be a large circle of black. With a sigh, she finally joined him. They would never get out of there if they didn't work together.

The Aether Stone was in a shallow grave, one of its pointed ends sticking almost straight up. Pharis grabbed it and spoke the words needed to take them back to the past once again.

"In the name of the Essence, we ask for safe passage back to our time," he unceremoniously spoke into the silence. He held out his hand, only hesitating for a moment before reaching out to grasp hers. She had no choice but to allow it, as bright purple sparks shot out from the stone, filling the room with a blinding light that flashed brighter and brighter.

He placed her hand just above his on the stone, checking to ensure she made contact with its surface. "Take us back, and we will neither disturb your realm nor attempt to stay." Those were the words she'd forgotten to say when she had taken the journey here on her own. As ridiculous as she knew it was, Aurianna began to worry about having left that part out, concerned it was somehow the reason everything was still messed up.

However, there was no time to dwell on her thoughts as the world around them disappeared in a flash of light and sound.

Chapter 2

AURIANNA

Aurianna had prepared herself for the icy rush of cold water hitting her from all sides as it had the last time.

She wasn't expecting a hard landing on the ground to knock the breath from her lungs.

Light flashed behind her eyelids, the pain an overwhelming presence within her as she rolled onto her side, gasping for air. She looked up.

Pharis was standing beside her, no pain registering on his face. If anything, he looked bored and impatient.

Right, she thought. *The Air power thing.*

Most fully trained Kinetics had a tiny reserve of Air power they could use to slow or cushion their landings.

Lucky him.

He didn't bother offering her a hand up—not that she would have taken it. Rolling onto her side, she regained her breath then pushed herself onto her knees and gingerly tested her legs. She swayed slightly for a moment, but she didn't have time to adjust further as Pharis had already taken off across a grassy meadow. She could see the Imperium in the distance.

Night had fallen, making footing uncertain in a field of random holes and vines which continued to trip her up.

"I don't understand why we landed there." She had finally caught up to him, but his spine was stiff and his body ramrod straight as he marched forward to their destination.

No answer. That was fine. She'd figure it out herself.

He led her into the building, up the wide steps at the far end, and through the doors to his father's audience chamber. Entering the room, Aurianna gaped at the tableau before her. The five Consils huddled in a semi-circle to her left, next to the dais. The Magnus sat in state on the dais. No one looked pleased in the slightest to be there.

The Magnus spoke first. "Well, well, well. Here she is." His face looked haggard, but his eyes shone with an intensity that filled his gaze with... something. Something dangerous. Something deadly.

"Yes. Here I am. Could someone explain to me why that is?"

One of the Consils cleared his throat exaggeratedly. "You lied to us."

Taken aback, Aurianna stared at him for a moment, her mouth slightly agape at the accusation. "Excuse me?" she finally managed, her blood beginning to boil.

The Magnus glared at her, sitting up straighter in his grand seat that was clearly meant to resemble a throne, even though the Kinetics insisted he wasn't a king. His behavior and attitude, however, suggested otherwise, so she had begun to refer to his chair as his *not-a-throne*.

Aurianna had to admit that her concept of royalty and other such fantastical things was limited to stories she had read as a child. Where the concepts had come from was beyond her, perhaps some long-forgotten history of the world that predated even the Arcanes.

Was that possible? The Arcanes—in some form or fashion—seemed to have been around since the beginning of time, considering their connection to the Essence and the history books. Come to think of it, how many generations of Arcanes had lived down among those dusty shelves? How were they even chosen for the position? They didn't seem to have families or any connection to others outside of their rooms. Aurianna's mind began to blur at the direction her thoughts had taken.

She suddenly realized the Magnus was still glaring at her, the violence behind his eyes unmistakable. "You told us you destroyed that woman. You said it was done."

"And I thought it was! Clearly something went wrong. All I know is I got back home, and nothing had changed, nothing was different. Your son here dragged me back, once again, and if it weren't for the fact that we were being chased by people who would have most likely killed us both, I would have stopped to ask more questions—"

"You were being chased?"

"Yes. By the people who torture our kind in my time." She shook her head, chewing violently on her bottom lip. "Now it's my turn to ask questions." When the female Consil from Vanito, the one who had seemed particularly unkind the day after the train had exploded, started to protest, the Magnus waved his arm impatiently to signal her to be silent. The woman glared at him, her icy gaze boring holes into the side of his head, but he paid no attention.

He was looking at Aurianna, waiting for her to continue.

She stepped forward. "First of all, what day is it, and how did you know I'd be arriving today?"

The Magnus looked puzzled. "What do you mean?"

"I mean, how long ago did I leave this place? For me it was only hours ago. But we didn't land in the same place as before. So . . . What. Day. Is. It."

"We had no idea what day you would be arriving. The Consils are here to discuss a separate topic with me, one that is of no concern to you or your mission. It's been about two moons since you left. I told the Arcanes it was a bad idea to let you go, and now we know why."

"What does that mean?"

"It means, my dear, that the Enchantress is still sitting up in her tower, completely unharmed as far as we can tell."

The room began to spin, floor and ceiling sliding into one another, blending into one solid mass that threatened to reach out and choke the life from her.

"Unharmed? But that's impossible. She must be dead. Or extremely burned at the very least."

Pharis walked over to stand in front of her. "Like you?" As he said the words, his eyebrow shot up in mocking question.

"Well, I…I mean…"

"Was the woman even on that train?" His accusing words matched his angry glare.

Now it was her turn to be angry. "Yes! I saw her! Or I saw someone that looked like her, with powers that only someone as you have described her could have. How many fire-wielding Enchantresses do you have around here?" Her chest heaved, exhaling breaths in loud bursts.

Pharis stared at her for a brief forever before turning around in a huff and stomping to the back of the room. He exited through the door leading to his personal quarters. His father called after him, but he didn't stop.

After a moment of staring after his progeny, the Magnus sighed and turned his attention back to Aurianna. "Look, girl, it's simple. That wasn't the singularity. She's still alive, and she still plans on destroying the world as we know it. The Arcanes have said the prophecy speaks of war and destruction. She is bent on destroying us all. War is on the horizon."

"How do you know that?"

"When people started claiming she was still alive up there, we sent soldiers to scout the area around the tower. There is no way in as far as we can tell, but they did see her pacing high up on the ramparts."

"How do they know it was her?"

"No one else can get in. She lives there alone. And besides, like you said, her physical appearance is very striking." He added, "It was definitely her. And the Arcanes have confirmed it."

"I want to speak with them." Aurianna thought about Simon, the Arcane who, despite being vague and cryptic in his remarks, had, ironically, been her greatest source of information so far. She would visit him and his fellow Arcanes who resided in a set of rooms amidst the underground tunnels below the Imperium. They might have more insight for her on this Enchantress, considering they were tasked by the Essence—the supposed deities who resided in the realm of the Aether—to maintain the history of records of all of Eresseia, including any prophecies.

Prophecies like the one given on the night of her birth—which supposedly pertained to her, though she couldn't understand how—and which had inspired her name, which meant Dawn in the old language.

"Be my guest. But for the time being, you are to continue your training and . . . find a way to make this prophecy thing work." He waved a hand at her dismissively.

"And how do you propose I do that? No one understands the prophecy, and no one can tell me what I'm supposed to do other than a vague 'fulfill the prophecy.' If you lot can't be bothered to figure it out, how the hell can you expect me to?"

The Magnus's nostrils flared as he matched her glare and said through gritted teeth, "If you truly are the one mentioned in the prophecy, I have been assured that things will play out as they are supposed to. The Arcanes have insisted that we leave you to forge your own path. As frustrating as that may feel to you, it is the will of the gods. Your purpose here has not changed. Find a way to stop that woman…and do it as quickly as you can."

Aurianna bit back a stinging retort and said simply, "I make no promises. I thought I already had. This prophecy is proving to be more ridiculous by the day. I want some answers." When the Magnus started to interrupt, she raised a hand. "I mean some *real* answers." She whirled and left the room. Just before she reached the door, she turned back. "And I'm certainly *not* going to be marrying your son, just so you know."

Smirking to herself, she spun around and left. It couldn't hurt to gently remind the Consils about the Magnus's power plays, his attempts at going behind their back to use her to gain more power. Pharis's father had thought he could get away with forcing the union, despite the obvious objections of his son—not to mention her own. The man was clearly too used to getting his way.

As she reached the staircase, she heard one of the Consils address the issue with the Magnus.

"Yes, Magnus, about that…"

Serves him right.

*   *   *

Her time away had been negligible in her own experience, but the two moon cycles had been a long wait for her friends. Not that they'd been expecting her to come back. No one had told them she'd be returning, so when she walked out to Sigi's post by the cliff, the girl practically knocked her over in her excitement.

"You're here?! Oh, Essence you're here you're here you're here I can't believe you're here I've missed you so much!" The string of squealed words swirled around them as the girl grabbed her into a fierce embrace. Sigi pulled back abruptly. "Wait." Tilting her head in puzzlement, she asked, "*Why* are you here, Aurianna?"

"Didn't they tell you about the Enchantress? That she's still alive?"

"Well, yeah, but . . ." An odd look crossed over the girl's face, making Aurianna's stomach twist in knots.

"What?" she asked.

"Nothing, it's just . . . Things have been pretty calm around here since . . . all that."

"Then why did Pharis bring me back?"

"Phari—oh." Sigi stepped back, rubbing her forehead. Then, "Oh."

"What's the matter?"

"It's just . . . we all thought it was over, you know?"

"You want me to go back home?"

"What? No! I'm just worried is all. Of course I'm happy you're here. Everybody will be. Especially Javen." Sigi waggled her eyebrows as her smile widened.

Aurianna rolled her eyes and changed the subject. "It's only been a few hours for me since I last saw you."

Sigi visibly started. "Are you serious?"

"Yeah. What time is it? It's getting close to dinnertime for me. I haven't eaten since I left."

"You could probably go bat your eyes in the kitchens and get something to tide you over until breakfast. My shift isn't over for another hour or so, but I can go straight to bed and get up a little early to have breakfast with you before class. Wait, do you have classes now?"

Aurianna sighed, chewing on her bottom lip. "I honestly don't know." She froze as a sudden thought hit her. "I'm not even sure if I'm supposed to use the same room. I'll have to find someone to ask. But, either way, I guess I'll be down at breakfast early too, just in case. See you then?"

"Of course." Sigi nodded and gave her a reassuring smile. "Get some rest."

Aurianna made a beeline for the spiral staircase in the corner that connected the Imperium's ground level down to the tunnels beneath and up to all the other levels. The second level had the chambers and residence of the Magnus and the Regulus, an area not accessible from this particular stairwell. The dining hall was on the third level.

She had never gotten used to calling Pharis "Regulus" and still called him by his name, though for different reasons than Javen did. Aurianna had met Pharis before she knew who, and what, he was.

Javen hated him, and the feeling was clearly mutual. Aurianna wondered how Javen had come to hold such a deep disdain for the "ruling family," despite being a Kinetic himself. And was it only that which had convinced Pharis that Javen was in league with the resistance movement? The resistance was rumored to be somehow involved in the disappearance of Pharis's twin sister, Mara.

The dining hall was deserted, save for a small group of people who had clearly finished eating but were chatting into the night. Their trays had been cleared away, and they all looked up at her when she entered. She thought she could detect both surprise and perhaps fear on their faces.

Trying to ignore them, Aurianna made her way to the back of the room and into the upper kitchens where the food was served to any Kinetics who either made their home at the Imperium or were just traveling through. A few Voids were cleaning up, putting away food and clearing the counters.

Voids were those who had exhibited Kinetic power as children, but once they began training, they displayed no further control over the elements. If they made it through all the years of training with no indication of Kinetic power, they were deemed a Void, destined to work in disgrace at the Imperium, and never allowed to return to or start a family. The whole idea made Aurianna sick, but she didn't know what she could do about it. The people here claimed that a family who sent a child off to be a Kinetic would be ashamed if that child came home as a Void.

For a culture where not everyone seemed to hold Kinetics in high regard, the implication seemed strange. Did people really care that much, enough to never want to see their loved ones again?

Aurianna edged closer to one of the Voids, hoping to catch her eye without drawing undue attention to herself from the others. When the woman looked up, she froze, staring at Aurianna as if she'd seen a ghost. She probably knew the story of the Void to whom Aurianna had almost given a heart attack when, during a Fire training session, Aurianna had spontaneously combusted, leaving the ring of scorched rock where they'd found the Aether Stone.

Trying to stay invisible wasn't working, as every Void in the vicinity had looked up—including one she recognized. He'd been sweeping in the corner, his back to her, but now that he was turned to face her, she recognized him immediately. The Void who had continuously freaked her out the last time she was here. Though they had never spoken—not encouraged between Voids and Kinetics anyway—she had noticed him staring at her every time she'd seen him. Staring at her with an intensity that rattled her.

And here he was, less than twenty feet away, once again boring a hole through her like no stranger ever should. She had no idea who he was, but the staring made her want to turn and run.

She chose to ignore it, as usual. She tried to, anyway.

Aurianna cleared her throat. "I'm sorry to bother you," she said, addressing the female Void before her. "I just got here, and I haven't eaten in a while. I was wondering if you might have some food left over from supper?" When the woman didn't respond, she added, "Anything at all will do. Some bread perhaps?"

As if coming out of a trance, the Void shook her head to clear it. "Yes, yes of course. We have some bread and cheese on the shelf under the table over there." She pointed to a table beside…

It was *right* beside the creepy guy.

Of *course* it was.

Nodding, Aurianna expressed her thanks. The woman told her to help herself, so she scuttled ungracefully over to the corner, grabbing whatever she could as quickly as possible, and trying to keep her eyes down to avoid the stare of the man currently within reach.

Sitting in that empty, open space while people stared at her was not an option she relished. So she hustled her snack to the dorm levels, hoping to eat in her room.

When she reached the door to her room, she hesitated. Someone else might be in there now, even though she was still wearing the bracelet that allowed her access. No one, including herself, had thought to take it from her when she had left, two moon cycles ago by their time, to return to the future. They might have created another one, though, so she gingerly knocked on the door. No answer came, so she knocked louder. Still no answer.

Deciding it was safe to enter, she held her wrist up to the pad by the entrance, unsure if it would even work. Thankfully, the mechanism stirred to life, moving pieces of the door around and opening to reveal her old room.

It looked like someone had been in to clean at least once, as the bed was made, and fresh towels were on the shelf in the bathroom. Aurianna wondered if they'd kept it clean and empty for her, somehow expecting her back. But that was impossible. No one had known she'd be returning until recently. It must have been done when Pharis left to retrieve her.

The small space had a soft familiar glow, wrapping her up in a warm cocoon of some forgotten memory. Despite having so recently left, it felt good to be back in this place, in this room, and with these friends.

Even though she'd been thankful and anxious to return home to Aunt Larissa, this had become another home, a different kind of home. She wished she could reconcile the two. She wished her aunt could be with her here to make the scene complete. She might never feel the need to go back if that were the case.

But the woman was insistent that she could not come here, could not follow Aurianna to a time and place one hundred years in the past, even though both of them had originally been from this time. She needed more answers. About her aunt, the woman's life here in this time. And about her parents, as she still had no idea who or where they were, only that her mother had died in childbirth. Leon had promised to use his network of contacts to find out what he could but had found nothing in the short number of moons she'd lived here before. Perhaps he was still looking or could start again.

As she walked into the bathing room, Aurianna remembered another thing she loved about this second life. The shower was a luxury she had never known before coming here, and she decided to take advantage of it immediately. Laying her food on the bedside table, she rushed into the bathing room to luxuriate in the heat and steam.

The steam trailed her out of the room as she exited many minutes later. She assumed they had an endless supply of hot water, as the water was reused and manipulated by Hydrokinetics, who controlled Water, and heated through by Pyrokinetics, who controlled Fire. There were more than enough of them—and enough resources—to provide a level of comfort she had never known during her previous existence back in the future.

Forward in the future? Time travel was complicated. Best not to think too hard about it.

She sat on the bed, nibbling her bread and cheese as she lay back on the pillows. When her eyes finally began to droop, Aurianna wiped the crumbs from her chest and rolled over, falling into a sleep filled with dreams of shadows and darkness, hair made of flames, and the persistent feeling that things were about to get very, very dangerous.

CHAPTER 3

LEON

The waves lapped at the sides of the small skiff, lazily mocking his pointless journey back into the depths of hell.

Hell. Home. What's the difference? Leon thought to himself, a sardonic smirk gracing his full lips. The movement almost succeeded in knocking the cigar from his mouth, but he managed to clamp onto it with his teeth. Pursing his full lips around it, he pulled a puff from the end, relishing the heady taste and smell of the gift he'd received from a friend the night before.

Friend, sure. She'd been his *friend* on more than one night recently. Catarine was a walking volcano of irony, her name a testament to exactly the sort of life her parents had dreamed for her. Her profession was a virtual slap in the face to the name and to her parents. Catarine was a Vanitian name that meant "pure" in the regional dialect. And she was anything but.

Pale, creamy skin topped with a smattering of small freckles, long silky legs that defied logic. Full red lips that stirred his memory of what she may or may not have done with that cigar before handing it to him as if passing along a gift from the Essence themselves.

Madam Trudel must be making a fortune off that girl. She was fairly new, but everything about that lifestyle came naturally to her. And she'd quickly become one of his favorites, though with all the available options—just as talented, just as pretty—he wasn't sure exactly why he was so drawn to her in particular.

The water around him had started to kick into gear, the lagoon trying to hitch a ride in his skiff. Cursing his wondering thoughts, Leon grabbed the bucket beside him and dealt with the puddle that had trickled in over the sides, heaving it back into Perdita Bay where it belonged.

He sighed and threw the bucket back into the bottom of the boat. Picking up the oars, he continued rowing his way across the enormous expanse of water. The water was fairly calm, but he couldn't help thinking that it might have been easier just to take a horse through Menos to get to Ramolay. The train and track repairs were progressing but still had about a week to go before they'd be back in service.

He hated horses. Well, not the horses, just the riding part. So, Leon had chosen to take the skiff from Bramosia all the way to his hometown of Ramolay, a decision he was now half regretting. The journey was exactly the kind of tedious monotony he despised.

Home was the last place he wanted to be right now, but it was the first day of a new moon—just after payday—so, that was that. His life was far too complicated sometimes. Life should not be complicated.

Leon craned his neck to look behind him. The main pier was finally coming into sight. He was nearly there, a thought he wished made him feel all warm inside.

Instead, his heart was empty, his insides cold with dread.

Docking at the far end of the pier, he waved to a couple of men he had known as a child, still recognizable owing to his regular trips back every moon. But they were virtual strangers to him. Leon's powers had developed around the onset of puberty—like most Kinetics. The Imperium had snatched him up at ten years old, just after his teacher reported having witnessed him demonstrating Kinetic power at school one day.

It had happened as he'd been washing his hands in the classroom sink one morning. The water simply arced off to the side as he touched it. The shock had frozen him in place, but the teacher had come up behind him, a cruel look of glee on her face. She hadn't hesitated to inform the Imperium, eager to show her loyalty to the hand that did the feeding. They had sent representatives to his home that very evening. That was the last time he'd seen his friends as children.

They remembered him, but as he was a Kinetic, some of them also feared him a little. Or resented him in some cases.

And no one resented him more than his mother.

Already embittered from the losses in her life, she had never forgiven him. She hadn't been able to see it from his perspective—the loss of his childhood, the loss of his mother. She had just felt abandoned. Her husband had abandoned her by dying, and then her son had left her.

It wasn't Leon's choice, however. It was never a choice for any Kinetic. Hiding a child with powers had serious consequences for families. He had tried to keep it from everyone. He didn't want to leave home. His mother had been a housewife but, due to a debilitating bone disease, was unable to get around much without help from her two sons. She needed him.

Once he'd actually graduated and taken on a permanent job as a Hydrokinetic, his paycheck had been his way of trying to make up for . . . everything. He didn't need much money, to be honest, as a lot of things were given on credit issued by the Imperium. And as an adult Kinetic, he got a paycheck on top of it, a fact his mother had latched onto the first time he had come to visit her with money.

Leon ambled down the pier to the gondola station, hoping his one true friend was around. He smiled and waved as he saw Emile down at the far end, sitting at the water's edge as he waited for a passenger.

Approaching with his usual swagger, Leon tipped an imaginary hat to his friend. His customary top hat was back in Bramosia, an article he never wore on the open water lest he lose it to a rogue wind. He loved that hat.

Emile, on the other hand, greeted his friend by wrapping his arms around Leon in a friendly hug. Leon was a giant of a man, the reality of which was never lost on him as he constantly found himself stooping over or leaning down when anyone else was around.

"My friend! 'Tis a new moon already, eh?" Emile exclaimed, twirling his finger in the air as he pointed a mock-accusatory finger in Leon's direction.

"Ah. Yeah, I'm back. Just headed home, you know?"

Emile's smile turned into a grim frown as he said, "Perhaps you want to stop by the pub on the way?"

"And why is that?"

His friend sighed, the sound echoing across the channel that led through to the waterways of the city beyond. "I just worry for you, Leon. There's no need to do this." Emile hesitated. "And your brother's home as well."

"Really." *Great.*

"Yes, well, I just think you should spend your visit here enjoying yourself. I can drop you by the pub. Then, when I get off work, I can come back to pick you up, and we could have a drink together . . . ?"

Leon shook his head, looking sad and yet determined.

Cringing, Emile asked, "Can't you just . . . send it to her?" His eyes brightened. "I could do it, yes? I could take her the money and tell her it's from you."

"You and I both know that won't satisfy her."

"Why not? She just wants the money."

"Yes, but she wants to *pretend* for everyone, for her neighbors. Let them think her son is this exotic entity who travels the world and returns as the prodigal son now and then."

"But the money is all—"

"I know that. You know that. She knows that. Hell, I'm pretty sure her shitty stuck-up friends know that." Leon had to work hard to force another smile onto his face, dread of the encounter ahead already pulling on his features, his limbs, his entire body. "But this is how I keep her happy."

"Why do you care, my friend?"

"You always ask me that."

"And I will continue to do so until you give me a satisfactory answer. The woman is . . ." Emile's voice trailed off as he noticed the dark look on Leon's face. "I know, I know. She's your mother."

"Let's just get this over with."

"Yes, all right."

They climbed into the gondola—Leon sitting on the bench in the middle and Emile standing on the back end with his rowing oar—and slowly made their way into town. Ramolay consisted of water, docks, and buildings, and not much else. To travel anywhere within the city, you had to go by water. No land roads existed, and very few sidewalks, aside from the piers that lined the major waterways.

His home—no, his *mother's* home—was located on the outskirts of the busiest section of town, nestled between buildings that all had a similar facade. Apart from the occasional size differ-ence, the color was the only major variation among many of the houses. Their house was, and always had been, an ugly muted pink. The inside decor was standard for Ramolayan residents, but the woman standing on the dock in front of the structure was anything but standard.

She was waiting on him. Knew he would be here like clockwork.

Damn that woman, he thought with bitterness, instantly regret-ting it. Despite everything, she was his mother, the only parent he had left. She was leaning on a cane, her legs unable to hold up her form on their own. And she was beaming.

He realized she was staring at the bag of money he held in his hand, her line of vision barely registering his existence. She would put on her show, nonetheless. She always did. Especially when his brother was here.

Jumping out of the gondola, he went straight to her, arms out in expectation. He didn't need to ask Emile to wait on him. His friend knew how this always went down. He would receive his customary forced embrace, put his arm around her shoulders, and lead her inside the home.

Once there she would snatch the bag from his hands and talk nonstop for ten minutes about how horrible her life was and list everything wrong with the town . . . and him. Always, everything that was wrong with him. Especially if Derrell were there.

He accepted the hug, pulling her tight to him as he said, "Hi, Mom," with a sad longing catch in his throat.

She didn't return the greeting, merely saying, "You wouldn't believe what they're planning on doing to the pier here. Come on inside. Your brother is here. He has so much to tell you."

Leon sighed, trying to mask the noise with a yawn. "I bet he does."

The woman turned sharply to him, the daggers in her eyes speaking every unsaid word she was holding in as they made their way inside. Once behind the closed door, she slapped him full force in the chest, his face thankfully no longer within her reach ever since his growth spurt during the years he'd been training at the Imperium.

Despite her petite size and brittle bones, the attack knocked him back a bit, more from the shock of it than anything. Why he was shocked, he didn't know.

"How dare you, boy! Don't speak ill of your brother, especially when people could be listening. What's wrong with you?"

He sighed again. "Dunno, Mom. Sorry."

"You better be sorry. Here I was, waiting all morning for you, and your brother here and all, and—"

"You know what time I get here."

"What is that supposed to mean? How can I ever be sure you'll even show?"

"Of course I'll be here, Mom."

"Damn right, you will. Now come through here and say hello to your brother. Derrell!" She yelled her other son's name as she shuffled down the hallway and into the sitting room. "Derrell!" his mother yelled again, her cheeks flushed with the exertion of dragging her deteriorating body around.

Derrell. Whatever she didn't spend on clothes or redecorating or on lavish dinner parties with her fake friends and casual acquaintances went to Derrell.

Ah yes, there was his brother.

Derrell was clumsily sitting up on the sofa where he'd most likely been napping. Not bothering to stand up in greeting, he said, "You're late."

"Nice to see you too, brother. Yeah, I am. About thirty minutes late, in fact. I had to gauge the time as best I could, considering the train's still out. I took a boat over."

"A boat?" his mother exclaimed. "You spent good money on a boat rental?"

"Didn't have a choice, Mom. It was either that or rent a horse."

"Horse is cheaper." His brother's eyes were shining with amusement. Derrell wanted to start trouble, but Leon wasn't in the mood. Not for any of this.

"Not by much," he told the room in general, knowing his argument would go unheard.

"That's very irresponsible of you, son. I'm disappointed," their mother scolded.

"What's new?" Leon mumbled, but his voice was too loud, too deep to hide in a confined space. Too late, he tried to move out of the way, but the woman had him backed against the wall in the blink of an eye, her cane wobbling under her trembling arm.

Her fist was tiny but powerful, perfected from years of blows, years of anger and resentment. "You are just like your father, you overgrown son of a bitch!" she screamed, her voice hoarse and full of rage. "He left me. You left me. You run off and do gods-know-what. I hear about it from all my neighbors. You are your father's son, through and through."

Squeezing the bridge of his nose between his index finger and thumb, Leon remained silent. Any other course of action was pointless. He'd tried arguing before, tried defending himself, but the woman had fallen into self-delusion a long time ago. Changing her mind was out of the question. Dysfunction was all his mother had left, and the one person who she really wanted to blame wasn't around. He took the brunt of it, just like he took the beatings and the verbal lashings.

His father was probably rotting in hell. And Leon would be

joining him one day. Not soon, he hoped, but one day when the booze and cigars got the best of him. And the girls. The girls would probably kill him too.

He'd be sure to punch the asshole in the face when he got there.

His mother was still yelling. "—don't know who you think you are. A shitty death just like his is what you'll have. Running around drinking, gambling, sleeping with every whore in Eresseia. He deserved what he got, and you will too, you ungrateful piece of shit! I clothed you, fed you, and you done run off and left me and your brother here with no way to provide for ourselves."

"Derrell has two working legs, two arms, two hands. They're good for more than holding up cards. Pretty sure he'd be fine if he actually looked for work."

His brother piped up. "I tried looking for work. I've told you that a million times. Nobody wants to hire me. Think we're cursed or something after what happened to Dad."

"There are other towns, Derrell. You could go to Menos and get work on one of the farms real easy."

His mother punched him in the chest again, harder than before, pulling a grunt out of him. "You want *another* person to leave me? Is that it, boy? You *want* me to be left here alone! That's it, ain't it?"

"He could work there during the day. As you said, horses are cheap to rent."

And he knew it was a mistake the moment the words left his mouth. Her eyes widened in fury at their own words being thrown back at them, and she reared her arm back to smack him closer to the face.

Enough. He'd had enough.

Dodging her attack, Leon lunged away and made a beeline out the front entrance as quickly as he could. She screamed in pain, and he assumed she'd ended up punching the wall. He wanted to not care, wanted to say *to hell with her*, but he knew he couldn't. She was his mom.

And she was mostly right. He was following in his dead father's footsteps. The pub and the escape it offered was an irresistible siren he had no will to resist.

Leon hurried over to his waiting friend, and Emile poled them away from the pier without a word. They made their way in silence to the nearest pub, and while Leon ordered his first of many pints of beer, he could not keep from poking at his conscience and scarred-over wounds.

The current sad state of his family *was* his fault, and for more reasons than his mother even knew. His father was dead and gone, and he'd tried to make it up to her. But it was never enough. Despite her attitude, he wanted to help his family, to take care of them. Derrell had been too young to truly understand everything that had happened back then. The venom their mother spewed in his ear had created what his brother had become—not what a man should be.

Not that Leon had any place to talk. But he tried to be a good man. Essence help him, he tried.

Derrell was eighteen years old. Plenty old enough to find steady work if he wanted to. The problem was, he didn't want to. Derrell was a gambler. Well, so was Leon, but there was a big difference. He had a job. Derrell didn't. And Derrell had a massive addiction problem.

So did Leon. But Leon rarely lost, *and* he knew when to quit.

Part of him hated them both, and part of him felt sorry for them. Their family had been tainted by that day, the day his inebriated father had died.

Leon's father had been a boat courier, delivering packages and shipments around the city. At night, however, he had been a drunk and a frequent visitor to the brothels. Eventually, the man had contracted a disease from one or more of the women he slept with, causing his health to worsen rapidly. Leon's mother had known about her husband's nightly activities, becoming more and more bitter over time.

When Leon was seven years old, his father had been leaving a brothel in the early hours of the morning, too drunk to even notice the horrible storm that was sweeping across the region. Just after leaving the establishment, he had been struck by lightning and had fallen into the channel. His father had drowned before anyone could get to him.

Leon's mother had said the Essence punished her husband for his wicked ways. Yet at the same time, she became even more bitter from the loneliness and isolation, and she never left the house.

He had tried to hide his powers so he could stay and help her. But his gift would not stay hidden. And he had visited her as often as he was allowed, but she continued to treat him like everything was his fault.

Maybe it was.

His father had been an excellent swimmer. That water had been out of control.

And Leon had been out of bed that night.

* * *

Sobriety was overrated. Or, at the very least, boring.

Leon leaned back in the seat of the gondola. He was already one or two sheets to the wind, having made Emile stop at the closest bar on the way to his destination, which was, of course, another bar—brothel, pub. They were all the same in his world.

He had paid extra for his friend to wait on him for the short amount of time it took to chug down an ale. Emile knew his pain, his misfortune. Even his secret.

But Emile was still on the clock, so he had agreed to take Leon to his next stop with promises to return when his shift was over in an hour or two. Emile was a good friend, and Leon could count those on one hand. Friendship was something he did not take for granted.

They were floating down the waterway with Emile softly humming a Ramolayan melody when Leon saw a little girl and her mother in line outside the post office. She was dancing—twirling her colorful dress in vivid circles—and singing her excitement for life at the top of her lungs.

Her mother scolded her. Loudly, and without a hint of humor.

Mothers, he thought. *Always sucking the fun right out of life.*

After stepping off the gondola and waving farewell to his friend, Leon simply stood outside the establishment, gazing at its exterior with an expression of disgust and fascination.

The pub…the brothel where his father had met his end. His last drink, his last whore, his last breath.

Glancing back at the waterway he'd just left, Leon conjured the scene in his mind for the millionth time. His father stepping—no, *stumbling*—out of the bar, the smell of booze and tobacco, perfume and desperation floating behind him, around him, on him. Never looking up, never taking notice of the stormy sky above him, the rage of ancient deities swirling in the cosmos, reaching down to exterminate the evil from the world.

Taking those steps, those three stumbling steps that would be his last. One, two, three.

The crack, the thunderous boom and flash that rent the darkness, shattering it with a blinding light, flashing across the heavens, and beaming down judge, jury, and executioner for a man who never saw it coming.

He'd been alive when he hit the water. Barely. Alive enough, probably, to know he was drowning, but injured and drunk enough to not fight back, much.

The bastard had deserved it. Leaving his family, his wife, and their two young sons. Leon had been seven then, Derrell three. A dependent mother was too much responsibility, too much burden for the shoulders of a couple of young boys.

Standing outside the pub, Leon felt a sudden longing for his arm cannon to blow the place to hell. He wanted to destroy the memories and the cursed life he now led—the legacy handed down by a wasted man, a wasted life that shadowed him, following him down every corridor, into every back room, and into the arms of the girls who waited there.

He was his father's son all right. But *he* didn't have a family waiting on him.

He had no one.

With a shake of his head, Leon trudged into the dingy interior of the building. He took a seat at the bar, nodded to the girl behind the tap, and ordered a shot of whiskey. No sense in doing things halfway, after all.

Two more of those, and some of the anxiety seemed to slip away into the recesses of his mind, little by little. He must have ordered an ale after that, as he found himself cheerily nursing one a short time later. It seemed like hardly any time had passed when a hand clapped him on the shoulder, and a voice he knew spoke his name. Emile had returned. Leon embraced his friend. "Good ta see ya 'gain. Glad ya showed."

"Of course. I told you I would. Now, I would offer to buy you a drink, but it looks like you've had plenty."

"Don' be silly, man! Always room fer more," Leon bellowed, banging his fist on the bar. "Drrrrrrrink fer my friend here . . . and fer me . . . an' he says he's paying, so it's on 'im."

"My friend, I really think maybe I should help you get a room, and we'll call it a day."

"Whatcha talkin' 'bout? It's barely noon."

"Exactly."

"Huh?"

"Look, I'll have the one drink, but then I think you should go take a nap somewhere."

"Sure thing, buddy." Leon slapped his friend on the shoulder and turned back to the bar.

An hour later—his vision hazy, his footing unsure—Leon allowed his friend to help him to a room. When they entered the small space, he exclaimed, "Wait! Where's the girl?"

"What girl?"

"The one I paid for."

Emile sighed loudly, his face no longer masking his concern. "No girls tonight. Just sleep, friend. You have a long journey back tomorrow, no?"

Leon wanted to protest, but the pillow had decided to jump up off the bed and nestle into the side of his face, so he decided to pass out instead.

His huge body sprawled across the tiny bed, he drifted into dreams of thunder and lightning, waves crashing against the cliffs as they reached up to pull him under, deeper and deeper into the depths of hell.

CHAPTER 4

AURIANNA

Aurianna stood glaring at the group of friends assembled around her in one of the common rooms on an upstairs floor.

My friends. Right.

Laelia glared right back at her.

Javen watched her, his eyes full of concern and something else.

Theron sat at the back, watching everyone.

Leon's eyes, when they were open, were red and glassy from what looked to be a massive hangover.

Sigi refused to even meet her eyes.

After their breakfast together, Sigi had dragged Aurianna up here, where the group had gathered to welcome her back and express their excitement over her sudden return. Javen seemed obsessed with watching her every move, almost as if he couldn't believe she was really there. The others showed their typical varying levels of emotion. Leon had simply grunted from his spot on the oversized couch.

After the initial exchange of greetings and embraces, the conversation had jumped to why she was back.

And she had no real answer to give, apart from the truth: the future was unchanged, and she had failed. Now they needed her to pick up the trail of her so-called destiny and stop the singularity from destroying Eresseia as they knew it.

But Aurianna's friends were doubtful. They were even skeptical about the future she had returned to when she left them.

Her breathing ragged from her sudden angry outburst, Aurianna continued to glare at them all.

Before she could speak again, Laelia said, "We get it. You wanted to be Little Miss Hero. But the issue was handled, the dragonblood is gone, the Enchantress is gone, and that's that."

"But she's *not* gone!" Aurianna's voice was harsh with frustration. "That's what I'm trying to tell you. The Magnus and the Arcanes found out she's still alive and plans to do something else. The Consils even agreed to have me brought back."

Laelia's face soured. "How do they know that?"

"I don't know. Because of the prophecy? The Arcanes have access to information in those books of theirs." She turned to Sigi for backup. "Tell them. You were there when Simon told us about them—the books that write themselves, or they're written by the Essence, or whatever. But those books keep a record of all events. And they say the singularity hasn't happened yet. The train was just—"

Leon's head snapped up. "Yeah, thanks for that, by the way." Grimacing at the sudden motion, he gingerly lay back again, placing his arm over his face.

Must have been some night.

Laelia interrupted them both. "The train was a distraction. The attack of the dragonblood-infected horde is the only thing that's been attributed to this Enchantress, and that has all been sorted. The Arcanes are being paranoid, is all."

Aurianna turned her icy gaze on the ivory-skinned girl, venom dripping from her next words. "So why, then, is my world not changed? Why is the future still a disaster?"

"I don't know. I just know that you can't trust those people. The Consils especially. They're all power hungry and have some agenda they aren't telling you about."

"That might be the case, Laelia, but I saw it with my own eyes. Kinetics are still being hunted. *We* were hunted on our way to find the Aether Stone."

"Where *do* they keep getting these Aether Stones?" Javen's question was curious but tinged with something else Aurianna couldn't decipher.

She shrugged, debating whether to tell them about her dream from the other night.

Of course, to them it would have been a couple of moons ago. The floating orb had led her somewhere in the underground tunnels, but the difficulty of convincing them to help her search based on what might have been nothing more than a dream left her feeling even more dejected. She wasn't sure she could trust anyone at this point, not even Sigi. Or Javen. If they were all doubting her about the woman on the train, about the future she saw with her own eyes, why would they listen to her about some dream she'd had about a glowing orb?

Aurianna sighed then threw a glance at Laelia. "I never said I wanted to be a hero—just the opposite, in fact. But I know what I saw."

"Maybe..." Sigi bit her lip and looked around.

Theron leaned forward, concern clearly written on his features. "Maybe the prophecy isn't about you after all. Maybe you're here for another reason. Or maybe they got it wrong. Either way, you're here, and you can take the time to train your powers and get better at controlling them."

Aurianna scowled at him, feeling attacked and betrayed by those she'd started to trust.

Sensing her defensiveness, he said, "Look at what happened with the train. Or maybe it wasn't you who did it. If that's the case, you still need to train since you don't have your power yet."

Aurianna wasn't sure how she felt. Weren't these all thoughts she'd had herself? She'd never felt like her destiny included saving the world.

"I think it's worth considering everything together. There may be connections." Theron spoke gently. Ah, the voice of reason. "There's also been some weirdness at the temples of late."

Sigi's face betrayed her confusion. "The temples? Why wouldn't I know about this?" She sat up, looking indignant.

He seemed ashamed for a moment, then a look of hurt flashed in his eyes for half a second. "Not the kind of thing the City Guard would handle. Weird stuff."

"What kind of stuff?" Javen asked.

Theron shrugged. "Just . . . weird stuff. Objects moving to different places, noises when no one's there. That kind of weirdness."

"Are you sure the clerics weren't drinking the sacred wine?"

"Please do not mention alcohol," Leon pleaded.

"Dude, what's up with you?" Sigi asked.

"Hard night?" Laelia asked. "Or perhaps not?"

He turned his head far enough to glare at her. "Jealous?"

"Um, no. I prefer my interactions with the opposite sex to be disease-free, thanks."

"*Interactions?* Wow, you must be a firecracker in bed."

"Bite me."

"No, thanks. I prefer my interactions with the opposite sex to be dis—" Leon stumbled abruptly to his feet when Laelia tried to push him off the front of the couch he was lying on. She was surprisingly strong for such a skinny girl. Laelia had an ethereal appearance—thin, and pale, with white-blonde hair—yet she was the tallest girl of the group, and she did have some lean muscle.

The sudden movement cost him dearly. Leon sank back down and leaned forward, grabbing his head with both hands.

No one spoke for a minute.

Finally, Theron said, "As I was saying . . . No, the clerics weren't drunk. And this has happened at different temples in multiple towns."

Javen asked, "How come none of us have heard anything about this?"

"None of you are exactly beating down the doors of the temples." He shrugged again. "I visit some of them from time to time, and I happen to be friends with several clerics who told me."

A frown darkened Javen's face. "Well, keep us updated."

Leon jerked his head up again and immediately regretted it, wincing as he gritted his teeth. "Before I forget . . . Aurianna, I did find something out about your mother."

She almost stopped breathing. "Really? I guess I just thought you'd stop looking when I left."

"Well, I did. But I'd already put the feelers out there, so to speak. One of my guys came back a few weeks ago and told me he heard she used to live over in Menos. But he thinks one of her parents was from Rasenforst." With a wink, he added, "Rasenforst is Fire, like our Sigi here. Could explain the disaster with the train."

She decided to ignore his last statement. "Does that happen often?"

"What?"

"People from different regions having . . . romantic relationships." Aurianna felt her cheeks warm.

Leon pursed his lips. "It happens sometimes, but not too often. Not outside Bramosia, at least."

Javen interrupted with a sigh. "It's not like it's forbidden or anything. Non-Kinetics can be with other non-Kinetics in whatever fashion they like. The Magnus doesn't have control over *that*. Yet."

Aurianna looked at him quizzically. "You think he wants to? Why? I mean, why would he care?"

"He just likes to be in control of everything. That's all. Kinetics control the lives of non-Kinetics in a lot of small ways. People just want to be left alone to do their own thing and make their own choices."

Sigi piped up. "Javen, that's not really fair. No matter your opinion of our leader—the man I *work for*—the rest of us are just doing our part to help. We provide things for those who weren't born with the abilities we have."

"You mean we do things for them, so they don't have to work it out on their own. So they come to depend on us for survival."

Sigi's mouth dropped open. "That's not what I meant." She and Javen glared at one another.

Aurianna felt uncomfortable at the change in tone and focus of the conversation. She cleared her throat. "So why then don't non-Kinetics from different regions intermingle more, if no one is stopping them?"

Leon looked up, frowning at her question as if it hurt to think. "Don't know really. I mean, I think people are comfortable with what they know. My situation is a little different than most. I'm only *here* because I was brought against my will, but even if I had been born without Kinetic power, I probably still would have left home." A dark look crossed his face. "You'd think more people would get the urge to travel more or move to a new location, but most seem happy and content where they are. I don't think that's a bad thing."

Sigi had finished her glaring contest with Javen and rejoined the conversation. "No, it's not a bad thing. Every region has its own customs and culture, and most people respect that. They don't disparage each other, but people tend to stick to what's familiar. My parents both grew up in Rasenforst, and they were both content with our region's traditions, like forging weapons and armor. They grew up in that environment, and they continued it with my siblings and me. If I weren't under obligation to the Imperium, I'd be back there now, working right alongside my father."

Laelia's voice was a whisper. "Yeah, me too."

Aurianna looked over at the woman who had been quiet for the last several minutes. "What do your people do? Vanitians, I mean."

"We have our traditions, same as Rasenforst, but they're a little more varied. My father…" Her voice trailed off. "Never mind."

Pain lived in those words, and Aurianna's chest burned with sympathy. Everyone was silent for a moment, no one willing to ask her to finish the statement.

Pausing to let the moment pass, Aurianna walked over to Leon and, careful not to jostle him, she hugged him awkwardly as he sat slumped on the couch, whispering in his ear, "Thank you for trying and for telling me. It means a lot. And it's a start."

Leon gave her a lopsided smile, his best attempt at one, anyway. "Don't listen to the naysayers. I know it was you who messed up the train. At any rate, it gives me someone to be pissed at." Grinning a little wider, he leaned back into the cushions, resting his head against the back of the couch as he closed his eyes.

A pregnant silence filled the room, and Aurianna felt her chest fill with all the insecurities she thought she'd lost through her recent experiences. They didn't believe her, and she felt at least some of them weren't telling her the whole truth themselves. She couldn't put her finger on who or what, but something didn't feel right.

She needed a plan. She needed action. "I'm going to talk to Simon." There.

Javen clasped her hand in his. "That sounds like a good idea." They waved to the others as he walked her over to the entrance to the spiral staircase leading down to the bowels of the Imperium. The Arcanes resided underground in a huge room. They left the room when necessary, but mostly they stuck to their own space.

Javen stopped. He grabbed her other hand, holding both between them. Leaning forward conspiratorially, he placed his lips right by her ear, hot breath sending tingles down her spine. "You know I believe in you, right?"

Aurianna narrowed her eyes at him. "Really? Where was that support a moment ago?"

He looked down at his feet, shaking his head. "They're just wanting everything back to normal, you know? It's nothing to do with you."

"Sure feels like it."

Javen gave her a small smile. "I know. Be patient with them, okay?" Placing a soft, chaste kiss on her cheek, his gaze dropped to her neck. His brow furrowing, he asked, "What happened to that necklace you always wear?"

It was an innocent question, yet her eyes welled up with the tears she had managed to hold at bay during the entire previous conversation.

Javen shook his head. "I'm sorry. I didn't mean to upset you." He pulled her into his arms.

She returned the embrace. "No, it's okay. Aunt Larissa said the necklace belonged to my mother. It just upsets me that I lost it."

"You lost it? When?"

"During the whole ordeal on the train. One of the attackers grabbed it, and it fell into Perdita Bay. So it's gone." She pulled back as she shrugged her shoulders.

"I'm sorry." He leaned forward and gave her another peck on

the cheek then turned and walked back to the others. She watched, satisfied for a moment that she had at least one friend who had faith in her, one person who was on her side.

* * *

The underground tunnels were a maze of confusion, but she knew how to get to the Arcanes. She knocked on the door, wondering if Simon or another Arcane would answer.

She wasn't disappointed by the face peering around the door frame as it swung inward. Simon smiled at her, but it didn't reach his eyes. He knew why she was there.

"Hello, Aurianna." The resignation in his voice put her on edge.

"Simon, we need to talk."

"Yes, I know. Follow me." He led her to a table on the far side of the room, past rows and rows of bookshelves filled with old books. Tomes of varying size and color graced the shelves, many of them covered in layers of dust. Several of the Arcanes—who were all men for some reason—were pulling books from shelves or perusing books laid out across the many tables in the space. Aurianna had no idea what they did all day. They were guarded about their role, keeping their secrets to themselves.

As she sat down across from Simon, the anger she'd felt upstairs in the common room rose back up in her throat like bile. "I want to know what the hell is going on. Am I supposed to be here or not?"

"Well, yes. Why do you ask?" Despite his words, the man was actually squirming in his seat under her intense glare. He wasn't being entirely truthful.

Trust no one. She already knew that.

"Because my friends are under the impression I'm no longer needed. Everything's apparently great, and I'm seeing things."

"What kind of things?"

"I'm talking about the Enchantress!" she yelled, causing a few Arcanes in the vicinity to jump. One dropped a book then snatched it off the floor, looking around to see if anyone had seen. He locked eyes with Aurianna, quickly looking away, then scurried off. ". . . and the future! No one believes me, Simon. None of my . . . friends." Her voice broke on the last word, the full force of the declaration a weight she had been unknowingly bearing all morning. The last word rang hollow in her own ears.

His jaw tightened, lips thinning as he reached out to touch her hand. When she pulled her hand away, he sighed and leaned back in his chair, studying her as if trying to read her thoughts. "People just want their happily-ever-after."

"Life doesn't leave room for happily-ever-afters. It's too busy tossing the *interesting* bits at you."

Simon's eyes lit up. "Yes, life is quite strange like that, isn't it? But everyone around here is eager for all of this to be over. The mess with the dragonblood-tainted water was a disaster across the board, and we're lucky it wasn't worse. But," he said as he leaned forward again, his voice taking on a hoarse whisper. "People died, child. A lot of good people."

She gasped. "You mean the ones in Eadon?"

"I mean everywhere. Some who died were victims of those under the influence of the dragonblood. Others were the ones who were crazed from the tainted water but couldn't be subdued into stopping their attacks. The ones who survived don't remember any of it. We're trying to keep it that way."

"So, they don't know what they did?"

"Well, we can't hide the details of what it did to them, but we have chosen not to tell them the details of what they themselves did. I'm sure someone will hear the grisly details from a fellow citizen, one whose family member or close friend was killed. But the local guards were given strict instructions for the town meetings. Everyone was asked to be kind and understanding, considering the ordeal these people went through—though I doubt it will stop someone with a grudge. We don't yet know the ramifications. But your friends have been here through this time of cleanup and rebuilding. They, like everyone else, just want an end to all of it."

"I keep having these dreams." She almost mentioned the one about the glowing orb but decided to stick with the dark, recurring one that had plagued so many of her nights in the Imperium. She hadn't wanted to mention it, but the dream had come back to haunt her repeatedly. "There's a shadow, a dark shadow like some horribly massive creature. And there are these other figures fighting it, all in shadow as well. I know it sounds like the Volanti. Maybe it is, considering I started having the dreams right after I'd first heard stories about them. But this shadow is different, bigger. And I keep having this same dream over and over."

The Volanti were monstrous creatures that invaded the towns randomly every few moon cycles. They would show up suddenly, attack violently, and leave just as suddenly ... *after* snatching whoever happened to get too close.

She had only personally witnessed the one attack. Monstrous creatures—massive teeth and claws, as tall as several grown men—Aurianna shuddered at the memory.

But they hadn't come again during the time she'd lived at the Imperium. Their existence was both enigmatic and horrifying. No one had been able to determine where they came from or why. Kinetic powers were useless against them, and kinetic weapons, even heavy-duty ones, barely put a dent in their hides.

Simon had the decency to look concerned. "You say it looks like the Volanti?"

"Well, sort of, but I'd never actually seen them the first time I had the dream. And the shape is different. I don't know how to explain it. Definitely bigger, if those other figures are normal-sized people. Which maybe they're not. I have no idea."

"How many figures?"

"Dunno. A pretty big group, maybe a dozen. Maybe more, maybe less. It's all very hazy, Simon."

"Yes, of course. I was just curious is all."

A thought struck her. "Theron mentioned something about the temples. Do you know anything about the weird occurrences?"

Simon raised an arm—scratching the back of his head—and refused to meet her eyes. "Odd things have been happening at the temples, yes. Objects moving, loud noises and such. The Essence are on edge. Something is stirring them up."

"You believe they exist because they supposedly use magic to write in some of your books, but how do you truly know what to believe?"

"It's not magic. It's . . . Aurianna there is much for you to discover, and I'm not able to tell you everything. The Essence have a complicated history, and their tale is not mine to tell. It's not my place."

"Whose place is it then?" she asked through gritted teeth, tired of having more questions than answers and having people refuse to tell her the truth.

He looked puzzled for half a moment before stuttering, "Why, theirs, of course."

"Theirs? The Essence? You want me to just ask them what's going on?"

"If you think it's the right thing to do." She stared at him in wonder, unsure if she'd heard him correctly. "I told you before, you need to follow the path that draws you. That's all you can do."

"And what if I feel my path leads to that bitch up in the tower?"

Simon winced. He hesitated as he nodded slowly. "If that's what you feel you must do. Though I'll warn you that you won't find your answers there."

"Oh, I'm not looking for answers from her. I'm just looking to stop the woman who tried to have me kidnapped. Not to mention blow up Bramosia. And since no one believes me, I guess I'll have to do it on my own."

*　*　*

Oracle, her mare, was beyond excited to be racing with the wind, legs pumping as she edged closer to the forest where nightmares and monsters seemed to lurk. A cool breeze edged along Aurianna's skin, her hair whipping sharply out behind her body. She felt a sudden onrush of clarity and crisp determination.

The closest she'd ever been to the forest outside Bramosia was the day the Volanti had come. Simon had mentioned they'd been back during the time she'd been gone. In theory, they shouldn't be anywhere around now.

She hoped.

The horse passed by the bridge to the Imperium then the entrance to Bramosia, never faltering. Only when they'd gone beyond the outskirts of the city did Oracle finally slow down.

The trees before them were clustered close together, their branches intermingling. Horse and rider crossed the woodland border into the forest, the one in a lather from the exertion, the other sweating with the fear that gripped her heart every time she pictured the Volanti.

A part of her wanted to shut her eyes, to close herself off from the reality of the world they were passing through. But her mind held still, coaxing her into a semblance of calm, convincing her she was braver than that. She had taken on the Enchantress atop a train filled with explosives as it sped through the night with no one to help her, no one to save her.

Compared to that, this was nothing.

Only here she was . . . alone yet again. It shouldn't matter if her friends thought she was mistaken. She knew the truth, and she had learned to live with a sense of isolation, even when surrounded by other people. She didn't need anyone.

The trees began to thin out, and the greenery became brighter, less cloaked in shadow. As the tree line came into focus just ahead, she saw it.

The tower.

The tower was somewhat cylindrical from top to bottom, the stones crumbling from age. A pointed roof covered the highest level of the tower—an open-air platform. She couldn't detect any doors or windows, not on the side of the tower she could see, anyway. The far side of the tower would only be visible from Perdita Bay. The tower sat just out of reach of the cliff's edge, nestled atop a rocky bit of land that looked like it grew up from the depths of the lagoon, completely separate from the rest of Eresseia, although it had probably been connected at some point in the distant past, a land bridge that had eroded over time. To reach it from here she'd have to sprout wings . . . or be an Aerokinetic, which she certainly wasn't.

From a distance, the tall spindle-shaped structure had seemed plain and unremarkable. Up close, the details told a different story.

An intricate web of vines crept up at least half the height of the tower, dotted with flowers the color of the sky at deep sunset, a haze of bluish purple. Thorns covered the vines, and the blooms seemed brave to Aurianna, careless of the sharp thorns they grew alongside.

The blossoms were beautiful, she thought—beautiful and

delicate and completely out of place in a remote location that leaked ominous shadows and a violent silence that shook the very air around her.

Aurianna strained her eyes to the topmost level, enclosed only by a wall no more than waist high. She hoped for a glimpse of the woman, despite the chances of her standing in that exact spot at that exact time being next to nil. But there was no one in sight.

Oracle was starting to show signs of bolting, loudly proclaiming her aversion to their environment. Aurianna shared the horse's anxiety but led her forward until they were slowly clip-clopping into the clearing beyond the forest, the area just before the cliff plunged down into the water below. She dismounted, approached the edge, and looked down.

The view was far different from what she had expected, however. Far down the side of the cliff, she saw the remaining portion of the land that had once connected the tower to the coast. The tiny isthmus stretched across to connect the expanse, as if the top half had simply been scooped out and thrown away.

It was too far down to reach without breaking every bone in her body, yet so tantalizingly close. But even if she somehow managed to get down there, the lack of an entrance still posed a problem. Across the gap, the tower sat, forlorn and empty by any visual account. But it was impossible to know for sure.

No way in or out. *Unless you have a dragon.*

Around the base of the tower were more of the flowers, exploding into shades of lavender and blue-purple iris. These were blooming among the tangled briars covering the ground. Someone had taken the time to create something sublimely calm and peaceful in a place of such evident malevolence. The effect was both beautiful and frightening.

Simon had said she would not find the answers she so

desperately sought here, and yet Aurianna felt drawn to the place. She needed to stop the singularity somehow. She needed to confront the Enchantress.

But *how*, if she couldn't get in?

CHAPTER 5

AURIANNA

"Hello?" Aurianna called as she stepped ever-so-carefully into the silence of the chamber, her voice echoing in the compact space.

The last time she'd been inside one of the temples, her clumsiness had almost gotten her into trouble. Metal trays had crashed together in a cacophony of humiliation, her cheeks aflame that others should witness her blunder. Of course, Pharis had been there to make matters worse, but—

No. That was actually one of the few times he had defended her.

This time Aurianna was careful with every movement of her body and limbs. She peeped around the corner into the area where the clerics usually retreated when no one was around or needing them in the temple.

Which was most of the time, sadly. She wasn't accustomed to the idea of a belief system, though she'd always thought there must be something out there, something that created everything, even if, growing up, her "everything" had been next to nothing.

She had spent her childhood in a simple yet rugged village which existed many years in the future. But she had been born less than a year ago from a linear perspective of time. If Aunt Larissa hadn't brought her eighty years forward in time to protect her from a terrible curse meant to end her life…well, she would be dead. Instead, the curse had been transformed, becoming a spell that bought her twenty years to grow up before she returned to her own time.

She reflected that, were it not for the curse, she would still be an infant now, since she'd been born perhaps six or seven moons ago. Aurianna tried not to dwell too much on these sorts of thoughts, lest her brain explode.

She had decided to visit the temple after her overwhelming failure at the thorn-covered tower. This was a different one from her previous visit, though the layout was basically identical.

One of the clerics, entering the main area of the temple, nodded in Aurianna's direction. "Can I help you, miss?"

He looked far too eager, and she felt a stab of pity for the young man and his fellow temple workers. Rarely did anyone come to visit anymore, let alone pray to the Essence or leave offerings at their respective altars.

Each temple was dedicated to one of the deities. Here in Bramosia, there were temples for each member of the Essence.

Outside the capital city, the other regions focused their worship on whichever element their people were aligned with—the element the Kinetics from their region would most likely show an affinity for, despite there being the occasional exceptions. Javen was one such, considering he was from Vanito and was expected to be strongest in Energy. However, he seemed to do best with Fire for whatever reason. And he was barely able to do anything even then. He had once confided in her he'd been afraid in recent years that they would mark him as a Void and force him out of training. Aurianna didn't understand why the Kinetic affinities seemed to be separated by regions or why there were exceptions. It was just more of the mystery surrounding the Essence that no one could or would explain to her.

The temple she had stumbled into several moons ago—though it had only been a few days to her—had been one dedicated to Caendra, goddess of Fire. But apart from the noise she herself had managed to make, the place had felt eerily empty and silent.

From what she understood, it wasn't as bad as the temples of Caelum, god of Air. Those had supposedly been completely abandoned by their benefactor. She wasn't sure what the real reason was since no one seemed to know or want to tell, but it explained why it was so rare to find a true Aerokinetic anymore. A tiny bit of Air power was granted to most fully trained Kinetics, but not enough to do much with other than soften a fall. Argo, the man who piloted the airship she had ridden on her first day here, was one of the rarities. He was the only one of the airship pilots she had met in all the time she'd been here.

This temple looked almost identical to that other, but the deity represented in this place of worship was Terra, goddess of Earth. Tiny stone statues of her supposed likeness adorned every flat surface of the room, including the top of each altar. In the middle of the room was the only other glaring difference between the temples. A large bonfire had filled the middle of the other temple, a hole in the center of the ceiling so the smoke could escape. She imagined the flames were intended to bring the worshiper closer to the element of Fire, the heat and the sizzle of its power. By contrast, the ceiling of this structure was intact. Dirt replaced marble flooring, and a jagged slab of stone, surrounded by mounds of Earth occupied the central place of honor within the temple.

Aurianna hadn't chosen this temple for any particular reason—other than proximity to the stable. When she had returned Oracle to her stall, the horse rubbing her face into her owner's side, Simon's words from earlier about following her instincts had wound their way back into her brain. The idea of visiting one of the temples refused to leave her, forcing her legs—against her rational judgment—to take her directly to the nearest one.

The cleric was still waiting for her answer, his face having taken on a look of wary concern. Clearing her throat, she said, "Um, no. I mean, yes. I just . . . I didn't bring anything." Her face heating in embarrassment at her sudden realization, she added, "For the altar, I mean."

His face lost most of its tension, easing back into a polite but detached smile. "No problem at all. An offering is customary, yes, but not required. The Essence are just happy to see someone who still acknowledges their presence in our lives." Even though he tried to hide the bitterness in his voice, Aurianna caught his meaning. They would take what they could get.

She nodded to the man before he exited the room then turned her gaze to the altars situated around the edges of the room. As she did so, she glanced over at the big rock right in the center of the temple.

And blinked.

What she had seen—*thought* she had seen—was gone the next instant. But Aurianna knew what had been on the rock just a moment ago.

It might have resembled a human, but there was no mistaking what it was.

A goddess.

She stepped forward, approaching the stone slab, shaking hands reaching out to the space just above it.

By instinct, Aurianna jumped back when the figure reappeared only seconds later, its form somehow managing to be equal parts corporeal and ethereal.

It looked like a woman, apart from the unnatural glow and slightly transparent appearance. Blonde hair framed a face of unquestionable beauty, and her graceful body was covered only by a thin gown, which sparkled in the low light of the candles placed around the room. Her skin had a luminous bronze tint, and light radiated from every inch of her form.

Aurianna forgot to breathe. Her mouth was flopping open and shut, and for the first time, she did actually start to question her sanity. She looked over her shoulder to see if the clerics had noticed the sudden increase of light within the temple.

The goddess shook her head. "They won't see or hear anything, so don't worry."

Aurianna's head snapped back. "You think I'm worried about *them?*"

An amused smile quirked the lips of the ephemeral image. Tilting her head to the side in an unnervingly human-like fashion, she replied, "We are outside of their time stream and, therefore, they are unaware of what we do or say."

"I don't understand. Who are you?" She already knew the answer but felt the question necessary, nonetheless.

"I am Terra. I am what your people call 'goddess'—a part of the Essence that binds the other realm together."

"Other realm?"

"The Aether is our realm, where my siblings and I exist outside of time. We are the Essence, and the Essence is us."

"So, you created the rocks, stones…the dirt?"

"More or less. Not exactly. You call me goddess of Earth, but I am more than that. This world was created by us all, by my brother and sisters alike. We each took on both a creator and a caretaker role for a portion to nurture, to help it thrive. Part of my role is to look after all the beasts that walk on the ground or crawl beneath it.

I created those creatures back when the world was young—before everything fell apart." She shook her head again, a melancholic edge straining her voice as she continued her story. "My brother Caelum, god of Air, created the winged creatures, those who use his winds to fly across the skies. Or used to. They rarely travel much these days, at least not any great distance."

"Why? Why did Caelum turn his back on the world?"

"He didn't, not intentionally. That story is long, and we don't have much time, though it would seem as if we have all the time in the world. What I came to speak to you about is our priority at the moment. The rest will come later." Terra stood, the goddess's height formidable, nearly reaching the low ceiling of the temple. "For now, I have brought you into the Aether with me. A pocket of it, at least. This is how your people travel through time, though that is not really an accurate description of how it works.

"Those men in the other room would appear frozen in place to you if you were to look around the corner. You are currently in a state of evanescence, a oneness with time. For you, it is only tempo- rary. My hold will only last a few moments." Aurianna strode over to the corner and peaked into the small enclave. The clerics did indeed appear to be frozen.

"We are walking on a different plane," Terra continued, "within a different realm from the world you know. This is the Aether, inter- woven with the Essence, with me and my siblings. We are one and the same. We have need to speak with you about what's to come."

"We?" A flash of a memory crossed Aurianna's mind. "Wait. It was you causing the mysterious commotions in the temples, wasn't it?"

The goddess nodded. "This is the only place we can speak with you, at present. We needed you to find us."

"What is it you want to tell me, then?" Aurianna's frustration was building along with her impatience for answers. "If we're so pressed for time, tell me what I'm supposed to know."

"I wish I could tell you everything, but this pocket will fade in a moment. My power is weaker than it once was. I need you to understand one very important thing. You must stop the singularity. You will, and you must. Time will continue to loop until that happens."

"Loop?"

The goddess sighed, an oddly human gesture. "The singularity is the moment when the loop either opens or stays closed. Your actions decide which way it goes."

"And what moment is that?"

"The moment you are forced to make a decision. A decision that determines the fate of both the present you were born into, and the future you come from. No one can help you with this. You have to make the right decision."

"Well, no pressure then, right? Why can't you just tell me when it will happen? Is it today, tomorrow, a year from now, or what?"

"We of the Essence are bound to let things play out as they will. Only you and those who live in your world can directly affect what happens there."

"But you're affecting it right now!"

"No, I told you, it is you who are being brought into another dimension. None of them are affected by this. This dimension exists outside of time as your dimension sees it."

"This isn't a game. Why not tell me what to expect?"

"Because I cannot affect the outcome."

"Why?"

"If the Essence tries to create any sort of change within the world before the loop is opened, both of our realms will cease to exist."

"But why?"

"For the same reason your world appears frozen right now. If we tried to intervene right now, we would create a connection between our worlds. But that connection would exist *within the loop*. Our worlds were connected on that level once upon a time. The singularity is outside of our power. Its creation is an anomaly. The loop, if connected to the Essence, would bring time into a space where time does not and cannot exist. And because the realms would be linked together, both would be lost, unable to break out of the loop. Do you understand?"

"No, I don't. It doesn't matter though. The problem is . . . no one will *believe* me. They don't think the prophecy is real. Hell, I didn't either, but here you are." Aurianna gestured resignedly at Terra, waving her hand at the goddess with a halfhearted attempt at a smile. "And the Arcanes say I'm destined to fulfill a prophecy because of my name and when I was born." With a derisive laugh, she added, "But Larissa would have heard the prophecy before escaping with me as a baby, right?" When Terra offered a hesitant nod, Aurianna asked, "So why wouldn't I just assume she named me after an ancient word for 'dawn' *because* of the prophecy's mention of 'red sky' and all that? Isn't that the more likely answer to all this destiny and fate nonsense?"

Instead of answering, Terra frowned and shook her head. "The Arcanes will guide you, but they are bound by the same rules as we are. They cannot help you beyond simple guidance. Follow your instincts. That's all you can do." The figure shimmered, fading in and out several times. "I promise to give you more of the story when next we meet. You simply must trust me for now." At Aurianna's pointed look, the goddess said, "Or trust yourself then, Aurianna. The Essence is slipping away from here." The vision vanished, the silence of the room filling up her ears. Then she became aware of faint noises from the men in the next room.

A goddess had pulled her into another realm, telling her to

follow a very unspecific prophecy and to let her heart guide her actions in the course of her destiny. Nothing unbelievable or hard to explain about that.

Fate had a sense of humor, at least.

* * *

"Aurianna! Over here." Sigi's sister, Hilda, was waving her over from the other side of the classroom. The girl wasn't quite into adolescence yet, but she had grown in the time since Aurianna had seen her last. The boy sitting beside Hilda looked familiar, though she couldn't place him.

Coming back to training meant figuring out her place in all of it again. She was far older than the junior Acolytes—those under sixteen who were known as Youngers—and had missed all the normal years of learning and practicing. As a result, they had decided the last time to have her train individually with each Magister. Now that she had gotten in more practice—and apparently managed to blow up a train, even though not everyone believed it was her doing—it seemed the Magisters felt she was better served by training with her fellow Kinetics. Since Kinetics graduated by the time they were twenty, finding a good fit for her was impossible. The Olders, including Javen, were closer to her in age, but she lacked the knowledge to keep up with their level of training.

Despite her discomfort, she could see their point. Kinetic training involved more than just explosions. In fact, the explosions were highly discouraged. She desperately needed to learn more control.

Even though she had resolved to curb her resentment and have a positive attitude, the underlying hurt refused to go away. Aurianna also wasn't oblivious to the truth that she needed to learn control as quickly as possible in order to do whatever was necessary to 'save the world.' She might give a mental eye roll every time the idea of her being a savior came up, but she did feel the heavy weight of responsibility very strongly. Aunt Larissa was counting on her.

As she approached Hilda and the boy, his face lit up with a disarming smile, and Aurianna realized why he had looked so familiar. It was the boy who had been unable to stop staring at her when she'd first begun her Kinetic training—the only other day she'd spent in the classroom before now. He was smaller than Sigi's sister, with sandy brown hair and freckles that almost blended together on his pale skin. He was skinny, with big hands he had yet to grow into. Warm hazel eyes reflected the grin that beamed across his face upon seeing her. She was flattered but a little unnerved by the attention from the young Acolyte.

Luckily, Hilda patted the seat on the far side of her. "You can sit here with us. My sister would never forgive me if I didn't take care of you." The girl was not quite thirteen years old, but she seemed mature and almost maternal in the way she wanted to look out for Aurianna. She was touched by Hilda's concern. Aurianna sat down as the girl introduced her to the boy beside her. "This is Sebastian, by the way."

"Hello, Sebastian."

With inflamed cheeks, the boy said, "Hi." His voice cracked a little and the blush crept down his neck as he gulped then added, "Nice to meet you."

Aurianna acknowledged the greeting with a friendly wave then turned away before her amusement could show and embarrass the poor kid.

Magister Martes, the instructor for Energy training, entered the room at that moment, his cloak swishing back and forth behind him as he hastened to the front of the room.

"Sorry about the delay, students. I was just having a word with another of the Magisters. Shall we begin?" On the table just behind the man, a small wire container held a ball of light which was emitting short bursts of Energy.

The instructor pointed to the container as he spoke. "As we all know by now, Kinetics contain just a tiny spark—if you'll forgive the pun—of one element or another, our bodies able to manipulate pieces of that element within the world as like calls to like. But it is just a small fragment, just enough to allow us this power to control. We cannot create the element out of nothing. No one has that power."

Unsure what she was going to say but unable to stop herself, Aurianna interrupted the Magister. "But… I saw orbs of fire appear in the Enchantress's hands. Not magma she'd pulled from under the ground, not fire from a fireplace, but fire that at first wasn't there, and then it was." Realizing everyone was staring at her after her frustrated and confused outburst, she insisted in a quieter voice, "I know what I saw."

Magister Martes nodded. "Perhaps so. But there must be an explanation. Simple tricks are not out of the question."

"So why do we have these pieces of the elements within us? What determines who does and doesn't develop Kinetic powers?" Aurianna could see Hilda and Sebastian out of the corner of her eye, their faces twin masks of concern tinged with embarrassment.

"Pure randomness, as far as we can tell."

"As far as you can tell? You don't know where it comes from?"

"We don't know much of anything when it comes to the nature of Kinetics." The Magister remained calm and detached.

"So, you've been using these powers for generations upon generations, but no one knows how they work?" The idea was frightening, and she was unable to hide her look of shock.

"Exactly."

"You're kidding, right? World-shattering powers, and everyone just accepts them without question?"

"We are always trying to better understand the world around us, including ourselves, but, as you yourself may have experienced, the Essence are not particularly helpful or forthcoming."

Aurianna couldn't disagree with *that*. "Isn't it dangerous to mess with things you don't understand?"

"I know all of this is new to you. It's difficult to understand in the best of situations. But what would you have us do? Try to stop children from using a power they suddenly have, power they have no ability to control? Teaching Kinetics to learn control over their power is the single most important thing we do here at the Imperium. If we were to ignore, or Essence-forbid, try to completely suppress our powers, the outcome could be most disastrous. That's why it is illegal to hide a child's Kinetic nature from the officials. It's not a punishment. We are trying to avoid a disaster caused by an untrained Kinetic." His meaningful glare did not escape her notice.

She bowed her head and nodded. Chewing her bottom lip, she said, "I see." And she did. Mostly. But the system still seemed flawed. Perhaps it was the fault of the Essence, or even the Arcanes, for not providing enough information. If they were truly unable to provide answers, she would just have to keep searching for them on her own.

Aurianna struggled to keep her thoughts on the lesson for the next hour. When it was time to leave, she approached Magister Martes. Clasping her arms behind her back, she said, "I'm sorry about all that. I shouldn't have taken my frustration out on you."

To her surprise, his mouth turned up in a grin. "No, it's good that you ask questions. That's the only way true learning happens."

Out of the corner of her eye, Aurianna saw Hilda and Sebastian waiting on her while trying to appear as if they weren't eavesdropping. "Anyway, sorry if I was rude."

The Magister inclined his head. "Apology accepted." He nodded in the direction of her young friends. "You don't want to be late for your next class."

Aurianna turned and walked out the door, Hilda and Sebastian following behind. They walked in silence down the hall to Water training, where Magister Jarden—not the kindest person but strictly fair-minded—would not tolerate tardiness.

Lost in thought again, Aurianna was jolted back to reality when someone aggressively knocked into her shoulder, causing her to drop her textbooks. A girl who couldn't have been more than sixteen years old was strutting down the hallway in the direction they had just come from. She was surrounded by a group of girls.

Hilda sighed and rolled her eyes. "And they say we're immature." She bent to help Sebastian as he gathered the dropped books.

"Thank you," Aurianna said, but she continued to watch the girl and her followers walk away. Nodding her head in the girl's direction, she asked, "What's her problem?"

"That's Belinda," Sebastian offered, as if that explained everything. Aurianna raised her eyebrows to show her confusion. He sighed. "She's . . . she's not very nice, and she pretty much hates any other girls not in her friend group. Actually, I'm pretty sure she hates them too."

Hilda laughed. "Yeah that, but I'm also pretty sure she likes Javen."

Oozing a casual disinterest, Aurianna asked, "So? What's that got to do with me?"

Hilda gave her a look that reminded Aurianna of her Aunt Larissa whenever the woman had to explain what she felt should be obvious. "Seriously? She likes Javen and has for quite some time.

He likes you and wasn't quiet about it. Clearly, she knows and is jealous."

"Isn't she a little young for him?" Aurianna's tone was amused.

Hilda replied, "No, seriously, don't underestimate her, Aurianna. She's one age group below him. Maybe sixteen or seventeen. He'll be twenty soon, I think, so it's not that big of a deal. Anyway, she may be young—"

"Young? Says you?" Aurianna tried to hide the smirk that was forming but failed.

Hilda pouted for a second but lowered her voice conspiratorially. "Says everyone. Even my sister talks about how ridiculous the girl acts. She's bad news and might do just about anything to get him all to herself. She already goes out of her way to find him, even outside the Imperium. He just ignores her, from what I can tell, but she's just crazy enough to do something stupid if she thinks you're with him."

Aurianna stared at the two children in front of her, shaking her head and muttering to herself, "I'm too old for games like this. She's a child. Actually, you are all children. What am I even doing here?"

"Hey!" Sebastian and Hilda both said indignantly.

"Sorry." Aurianna ducked her head and pursed her lips. "I didn't mean it like that. But compared to me, you are. And that's okay. We can still be friends, right?" When the two hesitantly nodded, she added, "You just can't understand how frustrating it is to be an adult but to be treated like a child." Realizing they were still standing in the middle of the hallway, crowds of Acolytes trying to walk around them, Aurianna led her friends on to the next class before they were late.

CHAPTER 6

AURIANNA

"Is there a reason why we're hanging around in the slums?" Laelia's voice cut like a knife through the noise around them. Aurianna had to agree but kept it to herself.

Leon tilted his head in Laelia's direction, a sardonic smile twisting the corner of his mouth in anticipation of whatever retort he was about to utter. "And here I thought you'd be right at home, sweetheart."

They were tramping through the unpaved, residential side streets of the town. Leon had offered to take them on a tour of the "real" Bramosia, even though Aurianna was the only one who was, in some respects, a stranger to the town. Javen, Sigi, and Laelia were with them, everyone having agreed an evening outside of the Imperium would be good for all of them.

Narrowing her eyes, the girl shot back, "I prefer to keep my life out of the gutter, thank you." Mimicking his smile, she said mockingly, "But by all means, don't let us interrupt what I can only assume is a typical evening for you."

Javen elbowed her before Leon could respond. "I think the point of tonight is to relax, Laelia. You two bickering is kinda defeating the purpose, don't ya think?"

"How the hell can I relax with . . . *whatever this shit is* that's getting on my boots?" Her eyes boring holes into Leon's back, she nevertheless directed her words at the group. "This better not be actual sh—"

"The recent rains caused some temporary flooding." Sigi was trying to help Javen play peacekeeper. "It's just mucky where there's no sun to dry the roads out."

"Yeah, just calm your ti—"

"Don't *even* finish that sentence, Leon." Sigi glared at him, drawing up every inch of her short stature as she put her hands on her hips.

Leon halted in front of a wooden door that looked like it was hanging on by a splinter or two and looked back at them. Lifting an eyebrow, he threw his hands up in surrender. "Just a joke, Sig. Anyhoo, we're here."

"And where is here?" Aurianna asked.

"Some friends of mine live here."

"We know what *that* means." Laelia wasn't backing off on the insults that evening, despite the looks everyone was giving her.

Leon rolled his eyes as he knocked on the door. "Yeah. *Friends.* As in people I like to spend time with." He shot a meaningful look back in Laelia's direction.

The street was filled with what Leon kept referring to as "the real people of Bramosia"— the poorest within the capital city, both Kinetic and non-Kinetic, though they did skew heavily on the non-Kinetic side. Some were alone or with friends, walking lazily around the alleys and small vendors who couldn't afford a spot on the main avenues in town. Others were clearly couples, enjoying an afternoon together as they strolled aimlessly down the street.

One of the couples had stopped at a well to refill the bottles they carried. The water in Bramosia contained herbs to prevent pregnancy. The citizens here were bound by the same rules about Kinetics using the contraceptive-infused water supply as the inhabitants of the Imperium or any Kinetics, no matter where they were living.

When Pharis had first told her about the mandated birth control measures, Aurianna had been angry at the thought of being subjected to contraceptive herbs without her knowledge or consent. But this wasn't her world, and she had no control over the rules that had been set in place. It wasn't like she was looking to get pregnant, of course, but she objected on principle to not having a choice. Indeed, the chances of her getting pregnant were nil anyway.

As they waited for someone to answer Leon's increasingly thunderous knocks, Aurianna suddenly realized something. She had felt, on other occasions, that something was missing in all the noise of the town, something inherent to her own world. She just hadn't been able to put her finger on what, till now.

Children. No children were running around or squealing in play. Of course, there wouldn't be any children if everyone was on birth control, but the reality of the complete lack of babies and children saddened her in a way she couldn't quite understand. She felt a sympathetic punch to the gut as she realized the full implications for the people who lived here. Kinetics were forbidden from having any children at all. Was fear of the power of such offspring what prompted the rule?

A thin man with weary eyes opened the door. He only looked a few years older than they were, but a tiny smattering of gray already sprinkled the hair at his temples. Drawing a deep breath, he looked from Leon to his little entourage. "And what is this?"

"These," Leon made a sweeping gesture in their direction, "are my friends." Then he added, "And Laelia." Aurianna could imagine the girl's narrowed eyes. Leon continued in a questioning voice, "We've come to visit the most gracious man in all of Bramosia."

Leon's friend turned his gaze back into his house, licking his lips. Then he turned around to face them. He shook his head. "Now's not really a good time, Leon. I just—"

"Who's at the door, Orion?" A soft voice from an adjoining room echoed faintly through the doorway.

"It's just Leon. He's brought friends."

A dark-haired woman in a flowing gown appeared behind Orion, her brown eyes wide with surprise. "Oh. Well, hello."

Leon said, "Hi, Juliet. Can we come in? Your husband seems to have lost his manners somewhere."

Orion's forehead wrinkled, and he turned to include the woman in the conversation. "We're kind of busy right now. It's just not a good time for us."

Juliet patted the man's shoulder and, in a comforting voice, assured him, "It's all right, dear. Leon can come in for a bit."

"But—"

She shook her head at him. "Any friend of Leon's is a friend of ours." Juliet looked back at the group standing outside, nodding and beckoning them to enter. "Come in."

They all piled into the house, one by one, as their hosts settled down on chairs in the small space. The woman, Juliet, struggled as she sat back into her tall padded chair. She placed her hands on her lap near her knees, leaning forward in an awkward position. Orion was watching her like a hawk, his gaze flitting back and forth between the woman and their guests. The girls found seats, but Javen and Leon remained standing.

The home did indeed exude an air of poverty, but also a sense of quiet dignity. These people were poor, but seemed kind and respectable, if a bit too tense.

Leon broke the silence. "Everyone, this is Orion and his wife Juliet. Both are Kinetics who work and live here in Bramosia. Juliet is a Hydron, and Orion is a Duster."

Aurianna felt confusion, as Kinetics rarely ever lived in poverty. Adult Kinetics, fully trained at the Imperium, received regular pay for jobs assigned to them based on their particular elemental affinity. Maybe this couple was sending the money to family back home?

Leon continued his introductions. "Juliet is from my hometown, and her husband, Orion, is from Menos."

Aurianna couldn't hide her confusion this time. "Husband?" Until now, she hadn't met any Kinetics who were married, and the idea that they couldn't have a child together saddened her.

A corner of Juliet's mouth lifted. "Is that surprising?"

"I just thought birth control was strictly enforced here."

The couple stared at one another for a long second, not blinking. "Yes, that's true. Doesn't mean we can't be married though."

"Oh." Aurianna didn't know what else to say. She was still working on adjusting to a different set of rules and customs.

Leon changed the subject. "What's got you two so busy these days? I haven't seen you in a while."

"We, um . . ." Orion's voice trailed off. "We've just been dealing with some family issues."

"Family issues? Is your father okay, Juliet? I mean, I know he was struggling there for a while, but I thought his health had improved."

"No, he's still improving." Juliet looked at her husband, clasping and unclasping her hands as she spoke. "Nothing like that. Just stuff."

"Well, we were heading over to the pub next. Did you want to join us?"

The tension in the air was palpable. Aurianna was unsure where to look, what to say. Perhaps they should just leave.

"Thank you, but no," the woman responded. "I'm not feeling very well. I was about to start dinner. Perhaps you'd like to stay and share the meal with us?" Her husband shot a sharp look in her direction, but Juliet pretended not to see it.

They looked around at one another, shrugging their shoulders at the invitation. No one else seemed to have noticed the exchange between Orion and Juliet. Finally, Leon answered for them. "Sounds good. We can head over for a drink later then."

"Um, we were supposed to meet Theron…?" Javen reminded him.

"It's a brothel, Javen. Girls. Booze. Cards. I'm pretty sure he'll find a way to entertain himself until we show up."

Aurianna felt awkward, but she needed to speak up. "Leon, maybe we shouldn't impose. They weren't exactly expecting to cook for an entire troop of people."

Leon's mouth opened as a look of hesitation crossed his features. By this time everyone seemed to have noticed the tension in the room.

But Juliet piped up, "Nonsense! It's no trouble at all." She glared at her husband then reached out a hand for Orion to help her up. She slowly moved into the kitchen. Laelia and Aurianna glanced at each other then followed. As she left the room, Aurianna heard Sigi and the men discussing the latest news and gossip around town.

Juliet's long flowing robes were very different from the practical, fitted look of the clothing most Kinetics wore. Perhaps it was a non-Kinetic fashion she had adopted. Or maybe she felt uncomfortable showing off her figure. It made Aurianna think of home, where the only clothing available was ill-fitting and colorless. Her allotted wardrobe at the Imperium had spoiled her, but she didn't care. None of it was extravagant or showy, just made with beautiful colors, comfortable, and tailored to fit just right.

"I was planning on making a vegetable casserole—nothing

fancy," the woman was saying. "I'll make a loaf of bread and throw in some cheese. Should be enough for all of us. Orion got some wonderful hard cheese on his last trip back home." Laughing, she continued, "I'm afraid my husband's hometown has rubbed off on my eating and cooking habits. Though I do sometimes miss the seafood I grew up with. Mom still makes it when I visit. Shrimp and fish, and the spices ... Mmmmm." Juliet closed her eyes, appreciating the memory. Then she gestured to the display of small wine bottles on a small wooden shelf. "Can I get you anything to drink?"

"Red wine, please," Laelia piped up without any hesitation. Aurianna nodded her agreement. Juliet grabbed a small bottle from a cupboard, along with two glasses. She poured them each a glass before turning back to where baskets of vegetables were laid out.

"You're not having any?" Aurianna asked.

"Oh, no. I'm not thirsty. Besides, as I said, I haven't been feeling well today." She started chopping, and the girls grabbed knives to help. Bread dough was already proofed and ready for baking, so between the three of them, the meal was ready in no time.

* * *

After a short but pleasant dinner, they said goodbye to their hosts and made their way to the pub. Every town had several pubs, and there were even more in Bramosia. The one Leon was leading them to was the grandest in town, not only in physical size but also in clientele not to mention the number of girls who worked there. The pleasure industry flourished in Bramosia.

When they walked in the door, the smells and sounds hit Aurianna in a wave of overstimulation. The sounds competed with one another—the clink of glass, laughter, shouting, coins jingling. The energy at card tables inhabited by aloof and arrogant men—and some women—was intense as they gambled away their hard-earned money. Girls—dressed in provocative clothing designed for ease of access—lounged on the laps of anyone who would let them, occasionally whispering something in an ear or stroking the side of a face.

Beside Aurianna, Laelia sighed. Loudly.

A flash of purple caught her eye, and a high-pitched squeal practically deafened her. Squinting as she backed up, Aurianna looked on as a girl in a plum-colored dress threw her arms around Leon's neck and planted her lips on his, nearly jostling his top hat off his head.

"Oh, dear Essence, help us all," Laelia muttered before sighing again and wandering off to the bar.

The petite young woman, who looked more like a child, pulled back—pouting a bit—as she said, "It's so good to have you back. Haven't seen you in days."

"Been busy, sweetheart. Need a table for me and my friends here. You seen Theron?"

The girl was still pouting but winked as she pointed to the corner. "Over there. Find me later?"

"Maybe."

Aurianna turned and looked at Sigi and Javen, who had been silent throughout the exchange. While Leon worked to pry the girl's grasp from around his neck, Sigi shrugged her shoulders and Javen grabbed Aurianna's hand as they walked over to Theron. Leon followed.

As they approached his table, Theron looked up from his cards and stared at Sigi, his mouth opening and closing a few times. Grabbing the mug in front of him, he took a swig and said, "Hey, Sig. Hey, guys. I'm almost done here."

A man across the table from him snorted. "Yeah, ya are."

Sheepishly, Theron scrunched up his face. "Not my day, it seems."

The group took a table in the back of the pub and waited for

Theron to finish his doomed hand. They ordered drinks from a girl who was slightly less scantily clad than the girls reclining on laps. She and her fellow waiters didn't serve the customers anything other than booze and food.

Theron walked over, his mug still in his hand, his pockets presumably lighter than they'd been before he stepped foot in the place. "Well, there goes my drink money for the evening." He hesitated before taking the chair beside Sigi, his body twitching in an attempt to find a position he felt comfortable with. When he stopped squirming, he leaned back and flagged down the waiter as she went to pick up their drinks from the bar. "Add another light ale to this order, would you please?"

Sigi said, "I thought you just said you were broke."

"I am. But seeing as I was invited here, I think Leon owes me at least one drink for making me wait so long."

Leon tapped his finger on the table. "We were over at Juliet's. Something weird going on with them. You talked to Orion lately?"

Theron shook his head. "No, but he's always been a little stand-offish with me. His folks are nice enough though, and I think my parents still talk to them from time to time in town."

"Hmm" was all Leon said.

Laelia, who had rejoined the group, rolled her eyes. "I think I'm going to have one drink then head on back to my room at the Imperium. I'm going home for a bit soon, so I need to take care of some things before I go."

"And by things, you mean—"

"By things, I mean *things*, Leon. It's none of your business, so shut the hell up, all right?"

Silence permeated the circle around their table until the girl arrived with their drinks. Taking a sip, Aurianna almost gagged. "What is this?"

"It's a lager," Javen replied. "Ordered you something lighter since you've never had ale or beer before."

"It's disgusting."

Sigi laughed. "Yeah, well, it grows on you." She lifted her own mug, the color of the liquid decidedly darker than Aurianna's.

"What is yours?"

Taking a long gulp, Sigi set the mug back on the table with a heavy thump. "Ale, same as Leon and Javen. Theron's got a pale ale. Same for Laelia. Yours is lighter, so not so strong."

"You mean to tell me yours is stronger than whatever I just drank?"

"Very much so. You work your way up, or you stick with lager. Either way, you'll get used to it."

"I don't think so," Aurianna said, eying her glass with a wrinkled nose.

"Relax," Leon said as he pulled a cigar from his shirt pocket and placed it between his lips. "We're here to have fun." He patted his pockets until he found what he was looking for—a small silver box. Aurianna recognized the shape as he opened it and flicked his thumb across the top. Metal hissed, but no flame appeared.

"Here. Use this." She pulled the lighter Pharis had given her out of her pocket and handed it to Leon.

He started to open it as he was inspecting the front. Tilting his head to the side, his deep brown eyes snapped up to meet hers. "P.J.? Who's P.J.?" Leon's gaze flickered over to Javen for half a second before returning to hers as he lifted his eyebrow at her.

Everyone at the table was staring at her, but she could feel Javen's eyes boring a small hole in the side of her head. "Pharis—I mean the Regulus—gave it to me. I've never really looked at it. Just keep it in my pocket in case I need it. I guess they're his initials?" Her voice had gotten very small by the end of the last sentence.

They all just stared at her with various emotions playing out on their faces.

Sigi looked surprised, but with a small twinkle in her eye.

Laelia smiled so widely it practically split her face.

Theron picked up his drink, pretending to take a sip. He looked like he wanted to disappear into the floor.

Leon was now looking at Javen in concern.

Javen looked like he was about to flip the table over.

"Pharis Jacomus just *gave* you his engraved lighter?"

"Yes. When I left."

"When you…" Javen's pale ivory skin was turning an odd shade of purple, the color creeping down his neck and under his collar. He huffed out a breath. "Why did he do that?"

"I don't know, really. It was kind of a joke between us." As soon as she said it, she knew it was the wrong thing to say.

"What kind of joke?"

"He was making fun of my ignorance about magic. When I first saw it, I thought the lighter was some form of Fire magic or some-thing. I don't know why he gave it to me, considering he was clearly angry with me when he did it. He handed it to me and stormed off. Next time I saw him, he was still angry, and…" The memory of the rough, steady kiss he'd given her in the tunnels sprang to her mind. She could practically feel it on her lips before she remembered what he'd said and done that day. He'd been a complete ass to her, for no reason she could fathom beyond the fact that he was being forced to retrieve her again. As if that were her fault.

Was it her fault? Perhaps. Not specifically that *he'd* had to come back to get her, but that anyone had had to. If she had just stayed where she was for a little while longer, been a little more patient, neither of them would have had to make the trip again.

Aurianna realized everyone was still staring at her, and she hadn't spoken for several moments. Clearing her throat, she said, "Like I said, I don't know. It's just a lighter."

Leon finally sparked the flame to life and lit his cigar, sliding the lighter back across the table to her. She hurriedly put it back in her pocket.

Sigi was shuffling a deck of cards that had appeared out of nowhere. She dealt them out to everyone but Aurianna, saying, "You should just watch the first round. Learn the rules first."

The others were pulling coin bags from their pockets to place on the table in front of them. Javen was still sulking, but he reached over and dragged her chair closer to his, showing her his hand and starting to explain the rules.

As they played, Leon finally spoke up. "So, Aurianna, do you know why our illustrious Regulus despises Javen here so much?"

Her eyes darted up from the coins being placed in the middle of the table as Laelia made her bet. "He thinks Javen had something to do with his sister's disappearance, right?"

Leon nodded. "But Pharis has always disliked him, and *us* just for being friends with him." He pointed to himself and Theron. "Apparently the girls get a free pass." He shook his head, ashes tumbling down from the end of his cigar to land on his crisp white shirt. He didn't seem to notice or care, throwing down a card and signaling for another one from Sigi.

"But why does he think you would hurt his sister?" She turned her gaze on Javen as she spoke.

Javen leaned back in his chair, laying his cards face down on the table. "I told you before. He thinks I have it in for his family. I may not like them, but I have better things to do than rebel against the people providing my food and shelter right now." A gleam in his eye said different. Aurianna knew he didn't like the way the place was run. Maybe he did have connections to the resistance movement, but Javen couldn't be involved in a kidnapping, much less a murder.

Leon took a pull on his cigar with practiced perfection, his hands never leaving his cards. "Point is, the Regulus is paranoid. He's hurt and he's taking it out on others. First his mom, then his sister." He blew the smoke up and away from them. Not that it mattered much, considering the amount of smoke already swirling around every inch of the room.

"What happened to his mother?"

"Died."

Aurianna felt the slightest pang of sympathy. She had never known her own mother, only that the woman had died after giving birth to her. Probably died trying to protect her from the curse that had threatened to kill her. The curse that Larissa had managed to transform into a spell, a spell that had sent them both into the future. That spell was broken on her twentieth birthday when Pharis came forward in time to retrieve her and awaken her to her destiny.

Setting aside her ruminations, she said, "How did she die?"

Leon shrugged. "Nobody knows. The ruling family likes their secrets. But some people say it was grief."

"Grief over what?"

"Dunno. This was before Mara disappeared, so there's no reason for it, as far as I can tell."

"Have you . . . have you found anything else out about my parents?"

Leon closed his cards, tapping them then leaned forward to rest his elbows on the table. "I'm afraid not. Sigi might can get her brothers to do some digging over in Rasenforst to see if anything shows up on your parents over there. Not sure there's much to go on, unfortunately." When her head dipped forward, he laid his hand on her forearm, adding, "I know you wanna find out, but maybe it doesn't matter. Family ain't all it's cracked up to be."

"Amen to that." Laelia muttered the words louder than she had probably meant to, considering the sheepish look she threw back when everyone turned to look at her. Shrugging, she said, "It's true."

Leon stared at her a moment longer than the rest of the group before looking back at his cards. The game continued until Leon won, and Aurianna felt she had a better grasp of the rules. As Leon started to deal another round, another girl, with a dark red dress and light blonde hair, appeared out of nowhere and plopped herself down on his lap. He squeezed the girl around the middle as she ran a finger down the front of his face in a teasing manner.

Laelia stood up suddenly, finishing off the rest of her drink. "Guess I better get going. I have to decide if it's worth paying to rent an airship all the way to Vanito next week, or if I should just take a horse to the ferry. Rumor has it someone blew up the train system." The pointed look she threw in Aurianna's direction before leaving was only mildly irritated.

After he managed to politely decline the "services" of the woman, Leon continued dealing the cards. The five of them played several more rounds, stopping between each one to order more drinks and talk about nothing in particular. Javen had a bag of coins for Aurianna to use, which she tried to refuse, but he insisted she could pay him back from her account. She still didn't know how to access it, but with his promises to show her all of that, she finally accepted. Theron had officially run out of money, so she split the coins with him, much to his delight and Javen's chagrin. It wasn't like she ever really used her regular allowance given by the Imperium—other than for Oracle and her upkeep. The look on Theron's face was well worth the gesture.

Leon and Sigi won most of the hands. Javen mumbled something about the two of them having the most practice, which they both ignored. Then the party moved out to enjoy their drinks on the rear patio and get some fresher air. The area was small—practically an alley—but the upper level had individual balconies off each of the upper rooms that faced the back of the pub.

A few patrons were out on the balconies, most with girls hanging on them, some with mugs of ale in their hands. Outside one of the rooms, two men were having a quiet, but heated, argument. A girl stood off to the side of the balcony, staring at them in mild amusement. Aurianna could guess what the argument was probably about.

Someone lightly grabbed her arm, turning her around. Leon stared at her for a moment. Her eyes instinctively went up to the massive hat he wore, its height adding to his already impressive form. She moved her gaze back down to his eyes, which had a gleam of uncertainty. "You okay?" he asked.

Javen and Sigi were talking with two of Sigi's coworkers, members of the City Guard. They were in uniform. Official business as opposed to a night on the town.

Theron leaned against one of the pillars holding up a balcony, sipping his drink as both he and Leon waited for her answer. "Yeah. I mean, Yes. I'm okay. It's just hard being back here without a clear purpose and all, you know?"

Leon waved the words off, gesturing with a lazy but slightly drunk hand. "Who needs purpose? Life is for living, sweetheart. That's the only way to find true happiness."

"Happiness is just a lie we tell ourselves to avoid reality."

"Reality, huh? And what exactly *is* reality?"

"Pain."

"That is ... depressing as hell. Get outta here with that bullshit." His words were harsh, but he was smiling as he spoke. "Life's too short. You obviously need to get out and have more fun."

"Isn't that what we're doing now?"

"This?" He looked around as if just noticing where they were. "This is just a relaxing evening. I'm talking about a night on the town. I can take you to my hometown! We'll eat some real food, drink some real ale. Get plastered." He placed a hand on her shoulder, gently squeezing. "You need it, girl. And, of course, my buddy Javen is welcome to come as well." Theron cleared his throat. "Yes, you too. Everyone. We should all go. Maybe next moon cycle after the train is—hopefully—fixed."

"You finally gonna introduce us to your family, Leon?" Theron asked.

A grim look passed over the other man's face. For a second, he seemed to sober up, his features reaching for a place to settle as they twitched in and out of a sad smile. Then it was gone, and his broad smile was back. "Nah. They'd be busy, I'm sure. Mom doesn't like company anyways. We can stay at one of the pubs in town. Somewhere that's got some music going or something."

Aurianna returned his smile. "It's a plan."

"Speaking of hanging out, I wanted to speak with you about something."

Theron emitted a sigh. She looked over to see the hunter rolling his eyes.

Leon ignored him and continued, "Javen, as you know, is a good friend of mine. I don't like to see him get hurt." Aurianna stepped back, wishing this conversation wasn't happening. But the man continued. "It's obvious he really, really likes you." She closed her eyes, willing him to stop talking.

One of the men arguing up on the balcony suddenly leaned back over the edge, his body tumbling to the ground just behind them.

"And I've never seen him so interested in a girl before," Leon continued, unconcerned, as though nothing had happened. He went on, oblivious to the fact that she was distracted, her attention focused on the man who had jumped up after the short fall. As he dusted himself off, he turned and met her gaze.

Aurianna knew that face. She knew those pale-green eyes. She'd recognize them anywhere. She'd watched the life leave them as he gasped his last breath. He'd died on a faded oval rug . . . only a short distance from the fire that would consume his body . . . one hundred years in the future.

* * *

She remembered the look of recognition on the dying Kinetic's face that day, like he'd seen her somewhere before. It had seemed impossible at the time, so she had dismissed it as nothing more than a dying man's confusion.

Had she not been staring at him so intently, perhaps he would have walked off without another thought. But as she continued gazing at this familiar stranger, he noticed it was more than a simple curiosity over his tumble from the balcony. The man approached their group, his attention fixed curiously on her.

No one was speaking. Leon had finally caught on, realizing something significant was happening.

"Can I help you?" the dead man asked. *Not dead not dead not dead,* she kept thinking.

It took her a moment to find the words and ability to speak. "I . . . I think I know you from somewhere."

He lifted an eyebrow, his mouth twitching in amusement. "I think I'd remember you, ma'am. Bright golden eyes like that aren't exactly common."

What could she say? *Well, you died in my arms after my people drained you of your power to within an inch of death. Yeah, I'm here to fix everything. Nice to see you again.*

"You look like someone I met once."

Javen came up behind the Kinetic and slapped him on the back before the man could respond. "I see you've met my friends, Sander." He was holding onto the other man's shoulder as if holding himself up, his face stretched into a drunk smile.

Theron chuckled, a soft sound that rattled in his chest. "Looks like you've had enough there, Javen."

"Nonsense, my friend. Sander here works at the Imperium. Surprised none of you have met him before."

Sander said, "Ah, well, I don't venture out much." Turning his gaze back to Aurianna, he suggested, "You may have seen me around. I'm a Duster down in the geothermal rooms."

"You're from Menos, then?" Theron asked. "My hometown as well." He inclined his head to his fellow Earth-wielder.

Sander replied, "Indeed. Surprised we haven't met."

"I spend most of my time outdoors. I'm a hunter."

"And a damn good tracker," Leon added, lifting his mug to Theron as if in toast before taking another swig.

"Well, then perhaps your services will be called upon."

"How so?" Theron asked, raising an eyebrow.

"We've been short a couple of Voids the last several weeks. For the equipment, you know. I mean, they sent us replacements, of course, but they have to be trained, and it's takes time away from our work. Maybe you could find out what happened to them."

"You use Voids? For what?" Aurianna was surprised. She thought Voids were only used in the kitchens and for other menial tasks. Most Kinetics seemed to consider them all but invisible.

"They run back and forth with things or move the equipment around for us. Stuff like that. We must focus our energies on the magma and rock, making sure a place as big as the Imperium stays warm and comfortable. Else the Magnus would have our heads."

"Have you informed the Magnus about these disappearances?"

"Hell, no. He wouldn't care what the reason was, only that we weren't getting the job done. We've been working extra hours just to keep things running smoothly. In fact, this is my first day off in a long time. And it's well deserved, if you ask me." He tipped an imaginary hat at them. "On that note, I must be heading back up to my room." Sander looked back at the balcony he'd fallen from, as if contemplating the idea. "It would seem my companions have gone back inside. Good evening to you all."

The man whose dying words had pushed her to seek out the truth, whose cryptic ideas had launched her on this journey, walked back inside and out of her life.

PART TWO

THIS FEARFUL DANCE

He does not want this, a burdensome crown
Upon his weary head, crushing hope
And freedom from what he knows he must do.
This fearful dance will set the world ablaze.

CHAPTER 7

AURIANNA

The contents of her stomach threatened to exit back the way they had entered as the train chugged down the track. Dizziness overwhelmed her senses, though she knew she was being ridiculous. Aurianna desperately wished for Laelia not to notice, not to see what the train ride was doing to her.

Taking a deep breath, she closed her eyes and willed herself to hide the reactions of her traitorous body. The gentle rocking of the train car could hardly account for the overwhelming feelings. She couldn't banish the visions which plagued her mind, images of the past which flashed across her mind's eye even as the scenery passed by outside the train window, mocking her as the memories shifted into something she didn't recognize. The truth should be simple and straightforward, yet her mind was trying to convince her she was remembering the events incorrectly.

The fight she'd had with the Enchantress on the train—a few weeks ago for Aurianna—was a bitter and terrifying memory, one infecting both her dreams and her nightmares. So much of it was hazy, but the parts she did remember clearly only intensified her fear of the newly repaired metal box she and Laelia now traveled in on their way to Vanito. Luckily or unluckily, the train system repairs had been completed sooner than expected, so things seemed to be getting back to normal around Eresseia.

She'd been surprised at the invitation, but Laelia clearly didn't want to travel alone, and Sigi couldn't get away from her guard shift.

They had all day to visit the town, and she was excited to see another side of the world which, for most of her life, she'd never known existed.

"You alright there?"

Laelia's question was so simple, yet the answer was so complicated. The urge to lie was strong, but it was useless to hide her feelings. "No, actually, I'm not."

"Anything I can do?"

The words surprised Aurianna, but she replied, "No. I'll be all right in a bit."

Her feeling of wrongness dissipated after about an hour or so, but Aurianna still felt uncomfortable, every little noise making her jump. She had no reason to think anything bad was going to happen this time, but she knew better than to become complacent, especially considering she was here, once again, to stop a catastrophe that could come from anywhere at any time. To make the right decision to break the time loop.

Follow the path that draws you.

She looked out the window to the left, the far-off coastline on that side impossible to see from this distance. A sudden thought occurred to her. Leaning forward, she asked her friend, "Why doesn't anyone just fly an airship over to the tower? Drag the woman out and lock her up?"

Laelia stared at her as if she'd grown an extra head. "Has no one explained to you about that tower?"

"What do you mean?"

"Aurianna, the tower is wrapped up in a spell that keeps anyone from entering. Well, anyone except the Enchantress, I guess."

"How do you know that for sure?"

"Because they *did* send people up there, right after you were born. They died."

"How?"

"The spell. It just killed them. I don't know. Their bodies were pulled from Perdita Bay that evening. Those who were watching from the ground said it looked like they'd been electrocuted."

"That's terrible."

Laelia nodded her agreement. They sat in silence for the rest of the trip, and after a time, Aurianna found she began to rather enjoy it. And Laelia wasn't so bad when she was on her own.

They arrived at the train station in Vanito. Aurianna eagerly took in the sights and sounds, the region a new and glorious adventure for her. Laelia had invited Javen as well, but he said he had things to do back in Bramosia.

"Where are we going first?" Aurianna asked.

Laelia shrugged. "Wherever you like. My plans won't come into play until much later, so we have all afternoon to screw around."

"What's there to do around here? I mean, I don't even know what my options are."

Tapping her finger against her chin, the other girl thought for a moment. "Well, there's the carnival?"

"What's a carnival?"

"Games, rides, food. You know." When Aurianna gave her a blank stare, Laelia seemed to reach a decision. "I'll just have to show you."

Laelia guided her through the streets and alleys to an out-of-the-way area of the town. In the distance, a giant metal ring moved slowly around in a circle. As they got closer, Aurianna gasped. "They're cages!" Horror gripping her heart, she yelled, "People are trapped inside!"

She started to run forward, but Laelia grabbed her arm. "It's okay. It's just a ride."

"What does that mean?"

"It's for fun."

"Fun? You get in cages for fun?"

Laelia laughed. "Yes, we do, believe it or not. Come on, I'll show you."

Half dragging her, Laelia got them to the entrance of the carnival, where a young man, who clearly knew her, waved them in. Laelia waggled her fingers at him as they walked by, a sultry smile hanging on her lips.

"Did you just flirt us in here?"

"Maybe."

Aurianna shook her head, allowing herself to be dragged further into the area. A plethora of colors and noises surrounded them, completely foreign to her senses. The intensity was intoxicating. Stopping at a small stall where a vendor was serving finger foods, Laelia procured them a meal.

Eating as they walked, the girls wandered through the maze of tents and people. Some were guests like themselves, but others were clearly part of the atmosphere. Enthralled, Aurianna couldn't take her eyes off a couple who were throwing objects up in the air and catching them with a finesse that seemed unreal. Mesmerized by the spectacle, she stood gazing until Laelia gently tugged on her arm to continue moving.

They reached an enormous white tent, a line of people snaking out of the door and into the surrounding space. Joining Laelia at the back of the line, Aurianna asked, "What is this for?"

"You'll see. It's one of the reasons the carnival is so specific to Vanito. We specialize in Energy, you know, so the workers at some of the attractions are Kinetics who were born here. Kind of a nod to the local pride and all."

"They're using Energy for entertainment? Seems kind of dangerous, doesn't it?"

Laelia shook her head. "No, it's just an attraction. The Electrokinetics are the only ones in contact with the Energy."

The line was long, but it moved swiftly enough, until they were finally inside the tent. Aurianna was anxious for a glimpse, and she wasn't disappointed.

The entire middle section of the tent was a concave sheet of metal. Small moving vehicles were careening around the corners, looping around the circle in a seemingly meaningless fashion. When three of the vehicles collided violently, she jumped, crying out in shock until Laelia shushed her into silence.

"But…"

"It's fine. That's kinda the point. It's just for fun."

"Fun? Crashing into one another?"

Her friend pointed to the top of the tent ceiling, the apex of it covered in metal bars cross-sectioned down the entire length of the central area. Long wires were attached to poles sticking up from the backs of the vehicles below, sparks shooting out from wherever the wires scraped across the bars.

"It's how they move. See those people over there?" As Laelia spoke, Aurianna looked to the far side of the tent at the group with their hands raised in the air. "Those are Sparkers, like me. Electrokinetics control the juice to get them going. Nobody can go any faster than they're allowed, and they can't leave the area. That's why they have the walls. You can only control the direction of the movement. The goal is to have fun. For some people, they just enjoy the thrill of driving around. For others, fun means slamming into one another." Laelia's devilish grin made it clear where she fit on that spectrum.

"I figured you'd head over here first." A familiar voice behind them rose above the noise of the crowd.

They spun and were greeted by the sight of Sigi pushing through the line to reach them, oblivious to the nasty glares she was getting along the way. "Glad I found you."

Laelia's brow was furrowed. "Sigi, what are you doing here? I thought you had to work."

"I did. Until it occurred to me what day it was, and then I felt really bad for turning you down."

"What day is it?" Aurianna asked.

"That's not why I asked you to come." Laelia's tone took on a hard edge.

"Bullshit. You want to pretend, that's fine. But I'm not going to." Sigi reached over, embracing the other girl in a tight hug. Laelia looked trapped, unsure of what to do or how to respond. "Happy birthday, friend."

Aurianna's head snapped up. "It's your birthday? Why didn't you tell me?"

Laelia pointed down at the petite figure still wrapped around her middle. "That's why."

"If you wanted to celebrate your birthday, all you had to do was say so."

Sigi released her friend, smoothing out her civilian clothes. "She'll never admit to it, even when she secretly wants it. This girl here is a walking conundrum." Laelia had turned around, facing the interior of the tent again, defiantly ignoring her words. Sigi shrugged. "Well, I found a replacement, and here I am. So, there's no getting rid of me now." She stuck her tongue out at Laelia's back before winking at Aurianna.

"How did you even get here? We haven't been here long enough for another train to arrive," Aurianna said.

"Took a horse. Two actually, when all was said and done. I exhausted the first one. Just barely made the airship ferry over from Eadon. Great timing, all in all."

"Isn't that expensive?"

"Yeah. But it's my friend's birthday."

The line continued moving until it was their turn. The girls chose different vehicles, or "cars" as Laelia called them. When the power from the Energy shocked them into motion, Aurianna was jarred in every direction. After a few minutes, however, she got used to the sensation and the feel of the controls, and she actually enjoyed herself.

The ride was over all too soon, the cars coming to a standstill just as she was aiming directly for Sigi again. The other girl laughed when they stopped two feet from each other, smirking in delight at the failed attempt.

They continued to explore the carnival, Aurianna in a continual state of amazement. Animals of all shapes and sizes—more than she'd ever seen before—roamed around or lounged in enclosed areas. A young man in skin-tight clothing held a long stick, the tip adorned with fire. She expected him to show off some Kinetic abilities. But the boy simply blew on the end, and a massive ball of flame erupted from it. Even those without Kinetic power could be part of the entertainment for the carnival patrons.

As the day wore on, Aurianna began to wonder if Laelia planned on visiting her family on her birthday. Despite her words the other day, it made sense that she had come here to see someone, or why else would she go to the trouble of returning to her hometown?

As they stopped at another food stall to get a snack, she decided to come right out and ask. "Are you going to see your family while you're here? For your birthday, I mean."

A dark look crossed the girl's face, the setting sun casting shadows on her features. "No."

"Why not? Why did you want to come here then?"

"Maybe because I enjoy the carnival? Can't it be as simple as that? I don't speak to my family."

Sigi attempted to keep things peaceful, diverting the conversation. "It's your birthday, and we can do whatever you like."

Laelia was busy eating, staring out to the horizon. Finally, she spoke again. "I do need to do something before we go. But I need you two to stay here until I get back."

"We can come with you, wherever it is."

"No. I want to go alone."

Sigi nodded as Aurianna said, "All right. We'll meet back here by the entrance. How long do you need?"

"Not long. Half an hour, maybe."

* * *

They waited for over an hour before heading off to look for Laelia. One of the workers at the gate told them she'd been walking north, out of town. They had no way of knowing where she might be.

"Where does her family live?"

"No idea. Probably in town somewhere, but that's not where she went."

"You don't know where her family lives?"

"I've never even met them. She doesn't talk about them, as I hope you've figured out by now." Giving Aurianna a pointed look, she gestured to the trees up ahead. "This is the direction they said she was going."

"But she could have turned off at any point. Doesn't it make more sense for her to be in town somewhere? She doesn't exactly strike me as the nature-loving sort."

Sigi nodded. "True, but this is the best lead we have right now."

"What if she comes back while we're out looking?"

"Then she'll have to wait. We'll just go this way for a bit and turn around if we don't find anything."

Aurianna had a sudden thought. "What about Javen's family? Does his family know her family?"

"Don't know where they live either."

Aurianna came to a dead stop. "You don't know where either of them live? Haven't you known each other forever?"

"Since we were kids, yeah, but that was back at the Imperium. We don't get to go home for the first few years of training, remember? Most of us haven't taken trips back home with friends in tow."

"But you have. Everyone seems to know your family."

"Some do, yeah. But that's just because it's how we are. My family ..." Sigi's voice hitched with emotion. She cleared her throat. "My family has always been close. And we're a big bunch, so having guests is no big deal." The pained look of grief on her friend's face inspired a surge of sympathy.

Aurianna reached out a hand to clasp her shoulder. "Family's a big deal. I get it. That's why I want to find out more about mine."

Sadness clouded Sigi's features as she sighed. "Well, let's focus on finding our friend, okay?"

The edge of the tree line was barely out of sight when they saw a flash of red—the color of Laelia's tunic—far across a field. As they got closer, they recognized where they were.

It was a cemetery, unkempt and in need of repair. The grass

looked to be knee-high in some places, the headstones and low walls crumbling. Rotting flowers lay decomposing among the gravesites.

Carefully stepping out of the trees, the two girls were unsure what to do. They looked at one another, shrugging. Finally, Sigi pulled on Aurianna's arm, dragging her back into the forest. Just as they reached the tree line, a voice half whispered, half croaked from behind them, "I can hear you, you know."

They turned back and saw Laelia sitting with her back to them, staring at the headstone in front of her. Fresh flowers adorned it—a small bouquet of white and orange blossoms.

Sigi walked up, tentatively placing a hand on Laelia's shoulder. "We were worried when you didn't show up. We didn't mean to—"

"How long have I been gone?" The words held a note of defeat, a sadness interlaced with resigned acceptance.

"When we left the carnival, it'd been over an hour. Not sure about now."

Laelia nodded distractedly. "We should get going. I think there's a train soon, unless we missed it already."

"Laelia, we can stay as long as you like," Aurianna said. "If you want, we can wait back at the—"

"No, it's fine. I'm done here, anyway."

The three of them sat in silence for several minutes. Just when Aurianna was thinking they should let their friend have some privacy, Laelia spoke. "My father was a good man. Everyone liked him. Almost everyone, at least." A sardonic smirk full of malevolence twitched the corners of her mouth up. It was gone a second later. "He died while I was an Acolyte at the Imperium. I didn't get to say goodbye, didn't even get to attend the funeral." Aurianna's brow furrowed, a swell of anger squeezing her heart.

The Magnus wouldn't let a girl attend her own father's funeral?

Laelia stood up without another word, stretching her back and limbs. "Let's go."

Sigi was staring at the ground to her right, her head angled to the side. "Hey, um...come take a look at this." Her tone did not sound amused.

"What is it?" Aurianna's voice filled with trepidation.

Sigi's expression hardened, and she walked over, squatting down to have a closer look. They were at the edge of the small cemetery that backed up further into the forest, the rusted and broken-down iron fence spanning the length of the area all but nonexistent on that side. As she stared at the spot where Sigi was pointing, two things became very clear.

The marks on the ground were clearly footprints, and they were very fresh.

They were also not human.

CHAPTER 8

AURIANNA

"You make it look so easy." Aurianna's focus was centered on the block of Energy pulsating in front of her. Try as she might, nothing was happening.

Sebastian and Hilda had stopped in their attempts, watching her intently as she continued to fail time and time again.

Sebastian, the same charming grin plastered on his face every time he looked her way, reached up and wiggled his fingers. After several tries, a tiny spark flickered off the side of the giant battery their class were practicing with down in the tunnels. The electricity hummed louder for a split second before curling back into itself.

"See? I can't do that." Even as she expressed her frustration, Aurianna heard a familiarly annoying voice enter the space. She looked up and saw Belinda walking around a group of Youngers on the other side of the room, pointing at their section of the battery and saying something she couldn't hear.

"But I'm not really doing anything. We haven't gotten far enough in our lesson. I just made it dance a little." Sebastian laughed at his own words, something he often did, and Hilda giggled along.

"Ha-ha. I'm glad you two find all of this funny." A muffled snort echoed across the space. Aurianna looked up and saw Belinda looking at her meaningfully.

"What's her problem?" Aurianna whispered.

"Isn't it obvious? She's kind of a bitch," Hilda said matter-of-factly.

"Hilda! Does your sister know you talk like that?"

"What?" The young girl looked offended. "I'm not stating an opinion. It's not bad if it's true."

"I'm not sure that's how it works, young lady." Still, she couldn't disagree with her.

"And besides, Sig would say the same thing if she were here."

"Why is she even over here? Magister Daehne's class is way over in the next tunnel. Shouldn't she be with her own age group?"

"Shouldn't *you*?" Belinda's voice was grating. Aurianna spun around. Belinda was standing directly behind her, much too close for her comfort.

"At least I have an excuse. What's yours?"

The girl smirked. "I'm helping some Youngers while my group finishes up with their magma loops. Seems I did so well on the first go, the Magister thought my talents should be put to use elsewhere."

"And what talents might those be?" Hilda asked.

Aurianna shook her head at the young girl, willing her to stop talking. Belinda might only be a girl herself, smaller and younger than Aurianna by a few years, but that didn't make her harmless. Aurianna knew all too well how vicious girls could be to one another. She rubbed the branded skin on her shoulder absentmindedly.

Belinda sneered at the little girl, increasing Aurianna's instincts to protect her friend's sister, no matter how stupid her words had been. "I happen to be an excellent Fire Acolyte, but I'm even better with Energy. The Magisters even think I might be one of the rare dual-wielders."

"That's great. Good for you." Aurianna turned her back on the girl, ushering her two young friends to the other side of the battery to avoid further altercation.

"Why are you letting her win?" Hilda said.

Sebastian's smile had dimmed with the look of concern he threw in his classmate's direction. "Win? It's not a game, Hilda."

"No, but it is a competition."

"It isn't though. You're just making it one."

Hilda crossed her arms, pouting. "So?"

Aurianna interjected, "So how about we focus on our own training right now?"

Sigi's sister continued to pout for several minutes, until the Magister called the time, and dismissed the class. Aurianna, Hilda, and Sebastian left Belinda and the tunnels behind to trek outside of the Imperium. Today was an activity day for everyone. While most of the Younger classes were based on bookwork and very basic manipulations, they occasionally had more hands-on experience to get them ready for their later years of training. No one expected much, if anything, from the very youngest Kinetics, and Aurianna couldn't help thinking it all felt like a regression for her.

She'd blown up a train, for Essence sake. Playing with tiny sparks or drops of water should be ridiculously easy.

If only that were true.

Even though she'd been back for several weeks, she was still unable to do much of anything with her power. Fire training had been going better than the other elements, and Magister Daehne seemed to appreciate her efforts more than he had the first time around.

But she was still struggling with the rest. The Magisters kept assuring her it was normal and would only take time, but her progress was too slow, and mastery seemed forever out of reach.

* * *

Magister Jarden was waiting for them, wearing a mask of her usual detached coolness. Water training was being conducted at the lake where some of Aurianna's individual training had taken place during her first visit to the past.

All around the lake, Magister Jarden had placed bowls for them to practice with. Aurianna, Hilda, and Sebastian found seats together near the center of the semicircle. Sitting on the edge of the water, they grabbed their bowls and scooped water into them. Aurianna sat with her legs crossed, the bowl nestled in her lap as she waited for instructions.

"Just like last time, I want you to practice swirling. Only swirling, do you understand?" The Magister's gaze landed first on one and then another of the students who had previously given in to the temptation to go beyond her explicit directive. "I don't need anyone trying to be cute and showing off. This is a very basic, but important, skill. It forms the basis of most of the movements involved in Water manipulation." She made a flourish motion with her outstretched hand. "Proceed."

Magister Jarden was a woman of few words, and despite her lack of emotion, Aurianna could appreciate the woman's no-nonsense attitude. Kinetic power was nothing to be trifled with, a fact she was keenly aware of after the incident with the train. Some students, especially the Youngers, had a habit of forgetting that all the elements could be dangerous, not just those like Fire that seemed to pose the greater risk. Aurianna needed no reminders that none of these powers should be taken for granted. Hell, no one even seemed to understand the full extent of the powers or their origins.

Lack of knowledge and understanding could be one of the biggest dangers of a society. She should know, considering the horrors the people of her time had perpetrated upon the Kinetics who had only been looking for a safe haven. Instead, those people had found death after being painfully drained of their power.

But that was why she was here now, or at least she hoped so. To prevent those sins in the future by fixing the sins of the past. If no civil war broke out, the future would be filled with all the things she now enjoyed. Her people would live like these people in the past did.

But who exactly were her people?

Did her loyalty lie with those she had known since childhood, or those who she now saw as friends—in the time when she was born? Could she risk the possibility of sacrificing the lives of the people in the future in order to better the lives of those in the past? Was the life she had led back home even worth saving? Could that existence be considered living?

Her head began to hurt just as Aurianna felt a sudden barrage of water slam into her face. Sputtering, she looked around, expecting either Hilda or one of Belinda's allies to be laughing at her predicament.

But everyone was merely staring at her in confusion. Magister Jarden merely looked perturbed. Hilda and Sebastian were both wide-eyed.

"Are you okay?" Hilda inched a little closer, careful to put her own bowl on the ground before moving. Sebastian followed—his eyes full of concern.

"Yeah, yeah. It's just water, right?"

"Well, yes, but you..."

"I...what?"

"You got this really scrunched up look on your face and then the water just…"

"Hilda, just tell me."

"It jumped up and slapped you. Hard."

"The water…slapped me?"

"I mean, it's the best description I can give you."

"You think I made the water in the bowl slap myself? Seems more likely someone is having a laugh at my expense."

Hilda was shaking her head wildly. "No, it wasn't from the bowl. The water came from the lake."

Aurianna looked out across the placid surface. Not a ripple in sight. She frowned. "Are you sure? I can barely make a drop of water dance, much less an entire lake."

"Please come with me." Magister Jarden had slipped up behind them without Aurianna noticing.

She sighed, dragging herself to her feet and following the woman over to the edge of the circle, away from the others. When the Magister turned back to face her, Aurianna blurted, "I'm really sorry. I wasn't trying to show off or anything." She stumbled over her words as she added, "I…I don't even know what happened."

"I do."

"You do?"

"Yes. You were clearly upset about something. I think this might answer a few of the mysteries surrounding your previous activities."

"What do you mean?"

"I can't be certain, but you do seem to struggle when there's nothing fueling your powers. Kinetics control the elements naturally. But your power seems a little different."

"How so?"

"I…I've only personally seen it once before but, if I am correct, it is likely you won't get much out of our traditional training methods."

"So, we're back where we started?"

"Maybe that's not a bad thing. Let's just see how things go. I still think the fundamentals are important to learn. Go have a seat back in the circle. But try to focus outside of your own thoughts for now, okay?"

"Yeah, okay."

Aurianna returned to her place on the grass and picked up her bowl. Staring into the water within, she could feel herself wanting to fall into its depths.

* * *

Oracle was being stubborn. Aurianna got her out to the fields near town, but the horse was irritable and kept trying to seize the bit. It was frustrating for them both, and Aurianna eventually dismounted and started walking the mare back to the stables in defeat. Perhaps the walk would give her time to clear her head as well as settle Oracle.

She'd needed to get away from the Imperium for a while. Her Fire training especially was progressing, but even though she was becoming quite expert, Aurianna disliked the class more than the others. It made her feel unsafe and insecure.

Ironically, Magister Daehne doted on her now that he was convinced she may have caused massive destruction to the train transport system. Either the man had a morbid fascination with violence, or he was just ecstatic to have a powerful star pupil on his roster.

But Aurianna didn't feel like a star. She felt like a pariah. Only Hilda and Sebastian would give her the time of day in her classes. Sure, the students in her group were all young children, but some company was better than nothing, especially considering how much time they spent in class most days of the week.

She was actually holding back in Fire training—afraid of her own power. And Magister Daehne knew it. Aurianna stayed in the middle of the pack, never showing off, just giving her instructor enough to keep him happy.

Earth training was another matter. She had never expected to enjoy it so much, but she was getting much better at manipulating rocks, and even slightly bigger boulders. The feeling came almost naturally to her now, but all her progress seemed to occur on her own time. Class was helpful, but she felt she could concentrate more when she was out on her own, the crisp breeze clearing her head on her rides through the countryside with Oracle.

After the incident at the lake, the Magister had spoken with her privately, suggesting that Aurianna spend some time at the lake outside of class—away from the other students—and work on focusing her thoughts. Aurianna was beginning to think that advice was probably good across all disciplines.

Electrokinetic training had been nothing but an exercise in frustration since the beginning.

It wasn't abnormal for a Kinetic to only excel in one type of elemental power. In fact, it was expected. But she wasn't supposed to be normal.

As they trudged on to the stables, Aurianna absentmindedly placed one foot in front of the other as she thought about her misadventures in training. Halfway to her destination, she heard a whinny from behind her. When she looked, she saw nothing for a moment, until finally a pure-white mane came into view, the horse nosing its way in her direction. On its back was the Regulus.

As horse and rider approached, Aurianna felt exposed, out in the open with no one else around for at least a mile. She tried to fake a smile as Pharis stopped beside her.

"A little backward, isn't it?" He sat ramrod straight in the saddle, his posture perfect and his bearing regal. Clearly, he had been trained to look pretentious in any and all situations.

"Pardon?"

Pharis nodded at Oracle. "I believe you are meant to lead the horse, not the other way around." To accentuate his point, Oracle threw her head back and shook her mane in a gesture Aurianna would have sworn looked like the horse was laughing at her.

"If you must know, we're tired from a long ride. I was just walking back to the stables to give her a rest."

Giving her a look that said he knew better, Pharis dismounted gracefully beside her. Aurianna was pretty sure she hated him just for the ease with which he slid down, making her own efforts look comical by comparison. He opened his mouth to speak but closed it again. They continued staring at one another for an awkward moment.

"Did you need something?" Aurianna felt exhausted and in no mood to play games with His Royal Highness.

For a moment, he looked nervous. "Well, I was actually heading back myself. Perhaps I could join you?"

"Does the royal stallion have his lodgings among the common horses, then?"

Pharis frowned and began walking his horse, leaving Aurianna little choice but to follow or stand there as he ambled off to the stables. "I really wish you would stop using that word. We aren't royalty. I've told you that. The Magnus leads the Kinetics. That is all. And yes, my horse is stabled there. Only one stable in town, Aurianna. I don't have some secret underground stable." His lips twitched.

Despite her irritation, Aurianna felt herself returning the quirky smile. They ambled along for a while then she offered, "I was actually thinking about looking for Leon to see if he could teach me how to cliff dive."

Pharis stopped so suddenly Aurianna had to step to the side to avoid colliding with him. He turned to face her. "You can't be serious?" His eyes had widened with a touch of both surprise and worry.

It was Aurianna's turn to frown. "Yes, I am quite serious. Why is it any concern of yours?"

"It's not. I just never thought someone like you would take that kind of risk."

Her eyebrows shot up at his remark. "Someone like me?"

Rolling his eyes, Pharis turned back to the field before them and continued walking. "I just meant you don't strike me as a risk-taker."

Aurianna pulled up alongside him, keeping pace. At his words, she barked out a laugh. "Are you serious? Have you somehow forgotten the fact that I blindly followed you into a damn *ball of light* on the out-of-the-blue insistence of my aunt and the promise of a trip through time?"

The Regulus scratched the back of his head, a sheepish grin spreading across his face. "Point taken. Of course. You are the epitome of impulsivity." He punctuated his words with a slight bow in her direction.

Aurianna chose to ignore his sarcasm. "You said you've never done it, right?"

"What? Cliff diving? No, I haven't. Couldn't if I wanted to."

"Why?"

"Because I'm the Regulus, the heir to the—"

"Throne?" Aurianna offered with a snarky smile.

"Stop that. No. I'm the heir to the title of Magnus. Can't risk anything happening to me, especially since . . . Well, it keeps things simple, anyway."

"And yet they sent you to fetch me. Twice." Her tone betrayed her confusion.

He rubbed the back of his head again. "Yes, that one is puzzling, I'll give you that. I will never understand their rules sometimes."

"So, the only reason you've never been cliff diving is because you're not allowed?" The thought rattled something inside her. Certain activities being forbidden because others wanted to control your life was something they had in common, it seemed.

"Well, I mean…yeah…" Pharis glanced at her through narrowed eyes as the sun bore down on them and a few drops of sweat beaded on his wrinkled forehead.

"So…let's do it."

He jerked his head in her direction. "What?"

"Cliff diving. Let's go. Right now."

"You can't be serious."

"You have got to stop saying that. Yes, I'm serious. Have you never broken a rule?"

"Well, yes, but—"

"Then let's drop our horses off and go down to the other side of town where there's never anyone about. If we're careful, no one will see us."

"What happened to your plan to get your friend to go with you?"

"I was only going to take Leon because he's a Hydron. And I didn't want to go alone."

"This is insane. You are insane."

"Is that a yes?" Aurianna waggled her eyebrows at him. "If you don't, maybe I'll just go on my own, and what would the Arcanes and your father think about the fact that you allowed their little savior to go and get herself drowned?"

"You…you are…" Pharis sputtered, his face turning red from more than the heat of the day.

"Yes, I know. Come on." Aurianna hopped on Oracle, who seemed to have gotten over her finicky mood and was happy to trot the rest of the way to the stables, with Pharis and his white steed following close behind.

Once the horses were untacked and safely stabled, Aurianna wasted no time making her way at a brisk pace to the cliffs far out of sight of the town and any prying eyes. The Regulus had to practically trot to keep up with her.

Puffing along at her side, he said, "I just want to go on record as saying I think this is a very bad idea."

"Duly noted."

"And I am not jumping into that freezing water. I have no desire to, and you cannot make me. I will stand by in case you drown, of course. Someone has to let the Arcanes know exactly what happened to you."

Aurianna chewed her bottom lip and shook her head. The man was so stubborn at times, yet he lacked the ability to put his foot down about matters in which he might actually enjoy himself. "Fine."

When they reached the spot she knew would be deserted, they searched for the access to the stairs that cut down the side of the cliffs to a lower ridge. Aurianna led the way down the steep decline, stumbling more than a few times over rocks and other debris. She was tempted to test out some of her Earth powers but thought it might be more sensible to save her strength for the task ahead.

She stopped a decent height above the water's surface but close enough to seem like a reasonable drop. Still, her heart hammered in her chest when she peered over the edge of the rock they stood on.

Pharis was staring at her intently, his eyes full of something she couldn't fathom. He said simply, "I still think this is a bad idea."

"Got it." Aurianna unlaced her boots and pulled them off unceremoniously, careful not to slip on the damp surface of the stone. She had her trousers halfway off before she realized the ridiculousness of the situation. She looked up, and sure enough, the Regulus was looking everywhere but at her, his cheeks stained a deep shade of pink.

Aurianna rolled her eyes and sighed. "We both know you've seen a lot more than this before. Many, many times over. Calm down and keep your shirt on, Pharis. Essence knows I am. I'm just taking off the pants so I can maneuver better in the water."

Instead of turning away again, his eyes met hers. "Do you even know how to swim?"

"No, but Leon says it's pretty easy to float as long as you don't panic." Without any further conversation, Aurianna stepped to the edge of the rock and brought her arms up like she had seen others do. She heard Pharis shout something, but the sound was lost to the wind as she jumped up and out over the water, leading with her outstretched hands.

In the scant seconds of her descent, Aurianna realized how absolutely unprepared she was for the enormity of what she'd gotten herself into.

She wasn't expecting to enter the water fingertips first in the graceful motion she had witnessed from others so many times at the coast. But she also didn't think her angle was so bad that she'd land flat on her belly. She was alarmed however by the speed with which she was hurtling toward the churning water below.

The force of the impact was like hitting a wall, but this wall bent inward. Aurianna had remembered to hold her breath at the last second. As she plunged further and further below the surface of Perdita Bay, she felt a rising panic in her chest as her velocity continued unabated. After what seemed like ages, her body did begin to decrease its speed, until finally a sense of stillness surrounded her. From what Leon had explained, Aurianna should have started to feel an upward sensation as her body's natural buoyancy returned her to the surface.

The burning feeling in her lungs intensified. She wasn't moving. Neither up nor down, nor side to side. It was as if her entire being were frozen in a state of suspended animation. Aurianna felt a rising panic, and in a blind instinctive movement she swept her arms out … and did not meet with the resistance she expected.

She opened her eyes. The water was just out of reach, her body cocooned in a bubble of air within it. Once she understood she would not inhale water, Aurianna let out her long-held breath, gasping in and out as her chest attempted to adjust to the feeling of inhaling and exhaling again.

Once the pain in her chest had lessened, she looked around in awe. She was trapped in a bubble made of air, seemingly sucked, along with her, into the lagoon from the world above.

The world above.

Aurianna realized Pharis was probably starting to panic, considering how long she had been beneath the waves. Unsure of how to control the bubble, Aurianna concentrated and willed both herself and the ball of air to the surface of the water.

She miscalculated. The bubble shot up into the air and froze in place, with her cocooned inside and a thin layer of water encircling her pocket of air.

Her surprise and shock were mirrored on Pharis's face, along with more than a little fear. His mouth had dropped open as he looked up at her where she was floating at least twenty feet above his head.

The air within the bubble was becoming stale. Aurianna willed herself and her sphere to the rocky outcropping, She landed with ease on its edge and reached out with a tentative hand, touching the thin layer of water with a fingertip.

It burst, and a waterfall flowed back into Perdita Bay below.

Pharis was still standing where she had last seen him, his jaw hanging open and his eyes alight with something she had never seen there before. She didn't think his fear was only *for* her. He seemed also to be afraid *of* her.

Aurianna spoke first to lessen the tension in the air. "So, that happened."

Pharis looked like he couldn't decide whether to yell at her or throw himself into the lagoon to get away from her. "What . . . was . . . that?"

"I've had some weird experiences with Water training lately, but I guess it's starting to work itself out."

Pharis shook his head violently. "No, Aurianna. Any Hydron worth his salt can form a water bubble. But you were *inside* it. Breathing."

She shrugged and couldn't hold back a nervous giggle.

"The thing is, though, you're not a Hydron. You're a Pyro, if Magister Daehne is to be believed. You blew up the train, didn't you?"

"That's what they tell me." Aurianna reached down to pick up her trousers then sat on a rock to get dressed. "I don't understand it any more than you do."

"Are you sure about that? Because I always feel like you're hiding something from the rest of us!" Pharis was yelling, his nostrils flaring as he spat the words at her.

"Me? I'm not the one with secrets!" She felt her own voice rising along with her temper.

"What is that supposed to mean?" His incredulous tone was mirrored in the confusion she read in his eyes. How could he not remember all the lies, all the reasons not to trust any of them?

Feeling her frustration deflate, Aurianna just shook her head in defeat as she finished lacing up her boots. She stood. "I just . . . I don't know. I need to go home now."

"Yeah, I guess we should." He shoved by her and began the journey back up to the top of the cliff.

The anger was welling back up inside her chest. Aurianna was certain he was intentionally trying to upset her. She remembered Aunt Larissa's lessons on keeping her emotions under control. She took a deep breath through her nose and exhaled slowly before speaking again, trying to modulate her voice to not sound accusing. "What is your problem?"

The Regulus didn't so much as look back at her when he spoke. "You mean, besides you and the insanity you get me involved in on a regular basis?"

Aurianna stopped with her foot halfway to a step. She looked at the beautiful blue sky and fought the urge to retort. Then she turned her eyes to the stairs, being careful of her footing, and followed. She concentrated on her breathing and counted to ten. Then twenty.

They didn't speak another word the entire way back to the Imperium.

CHAPTER 9

AURIANNA

Her days felt lonelier than they should have, considering how many people Aurianna had befriended since she first arrived in the past. But she didn't feel she could trust them. They didn't want to listen, or to really hear what she had to say. Her friends, like everyone else in this place, seemed content to believe everything was fine. But if that were true, she didn't know why she was still there.

Javen was walking with her through the Imperium, their destination the Kinetic library located on the topmost level. Javen had suggested she check it out after she mentioned her love of books.

But Aurianna had made it clear she didn't want company, a fact he seemed to be ignoring as he followed her up the stairwell like a lost puppy. He really was sweet, though, and his support of her feelings was commendable. Leon certainly thought highly of him, considering his drunken but heartfelt speech about her not hurting his friend. She had no intention of doing so, but her future seemed so hazy, and getting too close to anyone was a mistake, as she well knew. If you couldn't learn from past mistakes, what good were they?

Aurianna had been basically relying on Javen as her link to the group, since she didn't want to face them most of the time. They weren't speaking directly to her either. Javen reported to her with what little he could say to help ease the tension, hoping to clear the air between everyone. He was the only one who had let her speak her mind without dismissing her thoughts or changing the subject.

As he followed her up the stairs, he said, "The others still feel threatened by your presence here." When she shot a look of anger back at him, he hastened to say, "Only because they want peace, Aurianna. They aren't threatened by you, exactly."

"Just the idea of me." She had stopped halfway up a level and turned to face him directly, her arms crossed over her chest defensively.

"Well, yeah." Javen scratched his head and scrunched up his face. "I mean, no? Look, it's nothing personal. Nobody likes to think their home might break out into war any minute. Or blow up in a train explosion." His meaningful look only managed to anger her further.

No one was speaking to her about it directly, a fact that irritated her to no end. They weren't saying it to her face, but she could feel it all the same. And Javen's accounts of these conversations only lent credence to her feelings.

"Be patient" was all he would say whenever she expressed frustration over the lack of support.

With a huff, Aurianna turned back to the stairs and continued up.

She had never been to the library, but her irritation had been wearing her down, pushing her into bouts of silence when the others were around. She had always enjoyed reading back home, although the supply of books had been minimal. However, she had been told the library at the Imperium was immense, full of tomes accessible to any Acolyte or Kinetic who wished to read them.

They reached the top floor, and Javen reached around her to push the door open, allowing Aurianna to go ahead of him. His lopsided smile was as contagious as always, the twinkle in his eyes holding some secret. When he didn't follow her in, she raised an eyebrow.

He shook his head, his smile turning somewhat melancholic. "No, ma'am. You said you wanted some time to yourself. I just thought I'd walk you up here. See you at dinner?"

She beamed, her chest feeling lighter for the first time all day. "Absolutely." Maybe she was wrong to push him away so much. He really did seem to have her best interests at heart. "Thank you," she said as he waved and closed the door.

Aurianna drew a deep breath and took in the details of her surroundings. This place held many times the number of books as could be found in the Arcanes' library. The space had row upon row of bookshelves, each one crammed with books of all shapes and sizes. The shelves were twice as tall as she was, with wheeled ladders randomly spaced on each row. The further back she looked, the further the room seemed to expand. It was impossible, of course, because this level was the same length and width as the others, but the effect was still there. What made it even more impressive was the fact that the floor she was currently standing on wasn't the only one in the library. She could see three levels, her head tipping back to take it all in.

"May I help you?" Aurianna was startled by the whispering voice.

She snapped her head back down, tilting forward to see the tiny woman who had spoken. "What?" Aurianna asked.

"You looked lost. I work here. Did you need help with anything?"

"Oh, well, no. I just wanted to take a look around, if that's okay."

"Of course." She started to walk away.

"Wait."

The woman returned with an inquiring raising of her eyebrows.

"I was just wondering . . . are they categorized?" The school's bookshelves, back home, were arranged by the types of books. There were few books to be found elsewhere. Most people didn't own any.

"Of course. Something you're looking for in particular?"

"Adventure books, if you have any."

"Adventure books?" The Kinetic frowned at her. "We don't have many like that, but there are some upstairs." She pointed to a spiral staircase made of iron, one of many connecting the three levels. "Take the stairs up two levels and stay on the right side. They'll be at the far end of the room." Without another word, she walked away, leaving Aurianna feeling confused by her sudden change in attitude.

Aurianna shrugged to herself and followed the woman's directions, weaving in and out of aisles as she wandered down each row, stopping periodically to read the spines of some of the titles. Finally, she reached her destination and slowed down to peruse her options. Unsure how to determine which books would suit her mood, she started randomly taking them down and looking at the covers. Most of the covers were blank, or simply had a title, but she knew the ones she wanted typically had a picture painted on the front depicting a scene from the story.

Nothing stood out or seemed appealing, and she started to wonder if all she'd gained by coming here was time away from everyone.

No, she still wanted to escape into a story. As she continued down the rows, jumping onto the moving ladders from time to time to check out the upper shelves, a disconcerting sensation skittered down her spine, as if someone or something were watching her. Every shadow in every corner seemed ominous, but she kept moving, eyes darting in every direction in search of whatever was making her feel so unnerved.

She'd taken a step onto the first rung of the ladder beside her when she felt someone grip her shoulder. She opened her mouth to scream, but another hand clasped over her mouth.

Hot breath feathered across her ear, and someone said in a half-whisper, "Bit jumpy, are we?"

Aurianna felt her heartbeat pulsing in her temple as she wrenched away from the familiar voice. "Damn you, Pharis! You scared the hell out of me." Her breathing was ragged, and her skin felt clammy and sweaty from the sudden rush of adrenaline.

"Pharis? Is that the proper way to address me?" His mocking tone was punctuated by the infuriating smirk on his lips.

"It's not funny, *Regulus*. I almost had a heart attack. Why did you do that?"

"I tried to get your attention earlier, but you seemed a bit preoccupied."

"That's your excuse?"

"Well, that and the fact that I didn't want to announce my presence to everyone here."

"Why? How does no one know you're here? Perks of being special?"

"Something like that."

She narrowed her eyes at him as she slowly brought her foot down. Her gaze wary, she asked, "What happened to 'stop talking to me' and 'my problem is you'?"

He frowned but refused to step back, trapping her between himself and the ladder. "That was . . . unfair of me, I suppose. I guess I just thought you might still . . ." He forced a breath through his nostrils, the sound echoing in the silence of the large room. "My apologies."

The apology was unexpected. She wasn't sure how to respond, so she merely nodded and turned away to continue her perusal of the shelves.

But Pharis followed her. "Is there something in particular you're looking for? Maybe I could help."

She laughed. "And why is that?"

"Why am I able to help? I'm in here quite a bit, believe it or not."

"I meant why *would* you help."

"Oh," he replied. "I don't know."

She shook her head at his vague response and kept walking.

One step behind her, still trailing in her wake, he mused, "Perhaps because I don't know many people who read for pleasure."

"Not surprising, considering the sort of people you know."

"What is that supposed to mean?"

"I don't know." She was regretting saying anything. This could get awkward. "People talk."

"People can talk all they want." His stare was intensely focused on her, and his tone had an edge of warning. "I will begrudgingly admit I find you perceptive and quite intelligent, albeit overly talkative. But do not presume you know me."

"I wouldn't dream of it. And why is reading for pleasure so uncommon, do you think? Maybe it has something to do with the look the librarian gave me when I asked her where the adventure books were? They don't exactly encourage it, do they?" Her eyebrows shot up, daring him to respond.

"But that's where you made your first mistake."

"Oh?"

"Never tell a librarian you're here for anything other than something that sounds incredibly boring."

"You want me to lie?" A hint of a smirk tilted the corner of her mouth.

"It does make things easier sometimes. Adventure, huh?"

"Yes. You know, where characters go off into the unknown and explore the world?"

"You haven't had enough of that yet?"

"Even someone willing—even embracing—their own destiny, might need a harmless escape. To run away from everything, just occasionally." Crossing her arms, Aurianna felt her patience dwindling. Was he purposely taunting her?

"Why?"

"Why what?"

"Why would you want to run away from everything?" Pharis moved closer as the words left his mouth, his tone softening.

"I didn't necessarily mean it literally. I just meant it's nice to escape sometimes. In your mind, you know. Besides, no matter how much I might think about it, I can't run away. You wouldn't understand. I've tried getting away from my life before, and it keeps sucking me back." Subconsciously, her hand flitted to the mark on her shoulder for a brief second before she jerked it back.

His eyes trailed the movement of her hand, but he didn't say anything about it. "Yes, I do see what you mean. And understand more than you can know. Do you really think about that? About running away from your obligations?"

"Sometimes. It's not so bad here, though. At least I can travel places, do things. When I'm not preparing to save the world, that is."

"I'm not sure everyone here would agree with that." A note of bitterness had filtered through his calm demeanor.

"That I'm preparing to save the world? I was kind of joking, Pharis." Aurianna stared at him in bewilderment. *The man is infuriating sometimes.*

"No, I mean about it not being so bad here."

"Are you referring to the resistance?"

"What do you know about the resistance?" Pharis narrowed his eyes at her, looking around them hastily as he lowered his voice to a whisper.

"Is it supposed to be a secret? Everyone talks about it. You must know that."

"Yeah, I know about the gossip and rumors. I just wish I knew more about what's really going on."

"You're talking about your sister, right?"

"You know about my sister as well?"

"Like I said, people talk."

"Well, my sister is none of their damn business."

"If you're going around accusing people of kidnapping her, I think you've kind of made it their business."

"Ambrogetti." Pharis forced out a breath through flared nostrils. "He told you?"

"Yes, Javen mentioned it, as did others. I just don't see why."

"Why I blame him? Have you heard him talking about my family?"

"A little. But nothing to make me think he'd do something like that. Besides, you obviously have no love for your father. Why would you care what he says about him?"

"It's not just my father he's bad-mouthing. My family is my family, and one day I'll be sitting in that chair downstairs. I don't need my name slandered before I even begin."

"How old was she?"

"What?" He seemed startled by her question.

"Your sister. How old was she?"

Pharis's stare was piercing as pain entered his eyes. "I'd prefer you use present tense."

Aurianna felt her heart drop in sympathy. She uncrossed her arms and leaned forward a little. "I'm sorry. I didn't mean it like that. How old is she?"

"Same as me, twenty-four."

"So, you're twins?"

"Yes. We were—are—very close. She was smart and witty, and she had ideas that suited this role." Pharis didn't seem to realize he had also slipped into speaking of his sister in the past tense, but Aurianna knew better than to mention it.

"How does the whole succession thing work with twins?"

"She's technically older, so by law, she would be the Regulus. I took on the title after she ... disappeared."

"How did your father take it?"

Pharis let out a sardonic laugh as he raised an eyebrow. He lowered his voice further before responding. "My father? Have you met my father?"

"But she's his daughter. Isn't he worried about her?"

"He sent troops out to search, multiple times. No one could find a trace." He stared into the shelves behind her, his mind clearly somewhere else. After a few tense seconds of silence, he muttered through gritted teeth, "That's why I think it's the resistance movement behind it. And Javen Ambrogetti is a part of that movement. I'm quite certain of it."

Aurianna frowned. "I haven't seen anything at all to suggest that."

"Yes, well, I guess you two have become quite close, haven't you?"

"Why do you care? Afraid he's going to kidnap me and ruin all your father's machinations?"

Anger and something else flared behind his eyes as he invaded the small space between them and whispered, "First of all, I don't care. I just don't like him or trust him. I would advise you to be careful around him, that's all. And second, my father's plans are all but impossible to predict. I'm his son, and I only know the half of it."

"And which half is that? The part where he's still trying to marry me off to you?"

Quickly backing away, he at least had the decency to blush, considering they were both probably thinking about that moment down in the tunnels. No one had forced him to kiss her, but there had been blatant anger in his eyes when he had done it. "I think that ship has sailed, and I'm pretty sure he's aware of that. The Consils were quite clear on how they felt about that bit of scheming on his part."

"Oh, just that bit then?"

"You know what I mean."

"I'm not sure I do. You show disgust for the man—for reasons beyond just the obvious ones, like trying to force you into a marriage with a girl you don't even know. Based on the level of hatred you've shown for him, time and time again, you at least can recognize him for what he is. You can keep your secrets, *Regulus*, but do not claim a moral high ground over your father when you yourself throw baseless accusations at innocent men."

"Baseless? You speak of the obvious, yet you would ignore the truth right in front of your own eyes. Javen Ambrogetti is a liar and a schemer, and if you cannot see that, I take back what I said before about you being perceptive. Or intelligent for that matter."

Her face heated at his outburst, shock and anger over his hurtful words giving way to numbness. "I see." Turning back to the shelves, Aurianna pretended to look at the books she randomly selected and willed the man to leave before she started to cry in front of him. She could already feel angry tears welling in her eyes.

Behind her, Pharis was silent for a few moments as she made her way down the row, so she assumed he had left until his voice whispered down to her from the last place she had seen him standing. "That was . . . inexcusable. Certainly not the behavior of a future leader. I sincerely apologize for my rudeness."

She refused to acknowledge him, continuing her charade of

pulling books from the shelf to inspect. When nothing more was said for several minutes, Aurianna risked a brief glance.

The space where he'd stood was now empty, but as she strolled back to the ladder she had left behind, she noticed a book sitting on the second rung. Not understanding where it had come from, she picked it up. A painted scene of a woman with a sword and shield was emblazoned on the cover. The woman pointed her sword at a massive creature with flames shooting from its mouth—a dragon.

Despite the tears still threatening to spill onto her cheeks, Aurianna smiled and shook her head.

This will do.

* * *

"But I'm practically an adult now!" Hilda exclaimed.

Aurianna couldn't contain her snort of laughter, as Sigi stilled, jaw dropping in shock.

Her friend, still glaring at her little sister, said, "You can't be serious, Hilda? Really?"

"Well, I am. If Father could see me, he wouldn't believe how grown I am."

"And you think *Father* would approve of this?"

Sigi and the others had decided it was a perfect time to have a night on the town and show Aurianna more of this world and time she was practically a part of now. The idea of fun seemed so foreign to her, and she could learn so much about Eresseia from experiencing it firsthand.

Aurianna leaned forward, her elbows resting on her knees. "Which part are we talking about here? A Younger sneaking out of the Imperium, or cavorting around in pubs all night?" She tried to hold still as Sigi applied her cosmetics for the evening. "To be honest, I'd be more afraid of the former if the Magnus were to find out."

"It's not fair, though. She used to sneak out sometimes," Hilda countered.

Aurianna turned a gleeful eye on Sigi as the older girl gasped. "Hilda!"

"Well, it's true, isn't it?"

"You weren't even here yet."

"People talk." Hilda's words brought Aurianna's thoughts back to the conversation with Pharis a few weeks before. Keeping secrets was difficult with so many nosy people around.

"Well, it doesn't matter. I wasn't going out to pubs, and it wasn't all night. You are twelve—

"Almost thirteen!"

"Twelve years old. And that's that. Now, go back to your room." Hilda pouted as she got up from the edge of Sigi's bed and stormed out the door. Sigi grabbed the girl's arm as she walked past, stopping her. Reluctantly, Hilda looked up. "I promise, in a few years, you can go with us. Cross my heart."

Hilda was clearly not appeased, but she nodded at her sibling all the same. "Fine." She left the room in a quiet huff, bringing a smile to Aurianna's face. A twinge of jealousy stabbed within her chest. She had never had a sibling. Aunt Larissa was the only family she'd ever known. So many things she had missed out on, so many memories she might have had if not for . . .

"Ready?" Sigi's voice cut through her reverie.

Aurianna shook her head to clear her thoughts and looked at her friend whose full lips were highlighted in a bright shade of pink. "You're the one who took an hour to put on her face." Sigi had even used a glittery pink eye shadow around the top lids of her eyes, with multiple layers of mascara extending her lashes out to extreme proportions.

She has no idea how beautiful she is, even without all those cosmetics.

"I take pride in my appearance. What's wrong with that?"

Aurianna smiled as Sigi grabbed her cloak, and they were on their way into town.

* * *

Aurianna had been watching Theron closely for the last two hours, his awkwardness confirming her suspicions. The others might attribute his behavior to his poor card-playing skills, but she saw through it all. He wasn't even paying attention to his cards, slowly sipping his ale as his eyes darted to a certain guardswoman too frequently to be mistaken for anything else.

He was in love. With Sigi. And the girl hadn't a clue.

What was the deal with guys falling for her and her being completely oblivious to the fact?

The more nervous Theron became, the more he drank. The more he drank, the more awkward his staring became. And no one seemed to notice but her. Or if they did, no one spoke about it, nor showed any indication they were aware. Aurianna wondered how long he had harbored such strong feelings. Maybe it was so long-standing that their friends all knew and just accepted it. She knew he was close to her family, but only because of their mutual friends and his work as a hunter in Rasenforst and other areas.

"And why would I stoop so low? These girls might need the coin, but my face is fair enough. I don't need to sully myself like a common whore." Laelia was in rare form tonight, even more obnoxious than usual. Her mug had rarely been empty throughout the course of the evening, men around the pub constantly buying her drinks. They would probably all regret it before the night was over.

As would all her friends, most likely.

"Excuse me?" The high-pitched squeak came from the scantily clad young lady sitting on Leon's lap, her full lips pouting at him to address the insult made to her profession, and by extension, herself.

Leon lightly patted her outer thigh, throwing a hateful look at Laelia, who completely ignored the girl's outburst. "Yes, much better to remain an uncommon one," Leon murmured in a mock consoling voice.

Their back-and-forth banter always began this way, and never ended well. Aurianna, desperately tired of hearing it, attempted to change the conversation. "So, what's the plan for tonight?"

Sigi and Laelia, the only other females in their party, exchanged a look. "Already had enough?" Sigi said.

"What? No, I was just wondering."

Javen reached over, placing a hand beneath her chin as he lightly cupped her face. "And what would you like to do?"

"I don't know. I don't really know what my options are." Everyone turned to Leon, who had the decency to look sheepish as he removed his lips from the prostitute's neck, untangling his hands from the wavy mass of blonde hair.

"Sorry, what?" he asked.

Sigi leaned forward, putting her elbows on the table. "I think the question is whether or not you have any actual plans for the evening. Aside from your current project, that is."

Leon's confused look turned to one of devilish amusement. "Why? Care to join?"

She slapped him hard across his massive upper arm. "Gross. Real classy, Leon."

"And what kind of adventure are we looking for then?"

"Something new!" Laelia exclaimed with an eye roll at the occupant of Leon's lap.

"I've got a treasure map." Everyone turned to gape at Theron's quiet assertion.

After a few moments of silence, Sigi was the first to finally respond. "I'm sorry, what was that?"

"A map. I have one." His voice was already taking on the hint of a slur, so Aurianna wasn't certain if they were hearing him correctly.

"You have a map. A treasure map," Sigi deadpanned disbelievingly.

Leon's attention had completely shifted away from the girl on his lap. "Treasure, as in 'aargh'?"

"Aargh?" Theron's lazy smile turned to confusion as he tried to imitate the guttural sound.

Aurianna laughed loudly at the turn the conversation had taken. For once, she actually knew the reference, unlike so many things that felt foreign to her in this place. She leaned across the table. "Yeah, like pirates. Did you ever read adventure books as a kid?"

"Oh," Theron remarked. He was silent for a moment as his beer-soaked brain determined if it was that sort of map, before nodding enthusiastically. "Yes, like that."

"Would you care to elaborate?" Sigi was showing her annoyance.

Theron frowned, scratching the side of his jaw. "I don't know, really. My grandparents had this map they got from someone a long time ago. I don't know the details, but they framed it and kept it. Now my parents have it hanging up on their wall. Apart from some vague landmarks that look like trees, it just has some squiggles and an X to mark the spot for Essence-knows-what."

"And you chose not to mention this until now … because … ?" Laelia's attention had joined the others in staring pointedly at Theron. Her words trailed off in question, but he didn't answer. Instead, he picked up his spoon and shoveled an overly large portion of stew into his mouth. He pointed the utensil at Laelia while he continued chewing, punctuating each movement of his jaw by flicking the end of the spoon up and down through the space between them.

Finally, Theron mumbled around the meat and potatoes, "'S'not like you don't have secrets. That goes for all of you." He looked at each of them as his gaze went around the table, returning their stares.

"But you're talking about a bloody treasure map, friend!" Leon's focus had completely abandoned the curly-haired prostitute, who threw a final pout in his direction and stormed off to another table.

"An indecipherable jumble of lines at best. It's not like you're one for traveling. I can barely get you to leave a pub for long enough to enjoy the nice weather these days."

Javen had been oddly quiet for several minutes, simply listening to the conversation with a strange look on his face. The topic had attracted his full attention, and Aurianna could see a fixation forming in his mind. Why he would be obsessed with a map, she had no idea, although she had to admit it was an exciting revelation.

An excited glint in his eye, Javen spoke up in a hoarse voice. "How have I never noticed this in all the times I've been to your parents' house? And why haven't you had someone look at it? I'm sure the Arcanes might have some insight."

"It's really not that big of a deal. I'm sorry I even mentioned it."

"But—"

"Listen, I'll show it to you next time you're over. But I'm telling you, it's just a drawing. Probably made by some kids or something."

"Then why did your grandparents keep it, much less frame it and hang it up?"

"I don't know, Javen. I'll ask my parents about it."

Javen continued to gaze off into the middle distance with a contemplative frown.

Sigi cleared her throat and leaned back in her chair as she drained the last of her ale and slammed her mug down on the table a little too loudly. Several nearby patrons jumped, startled by the sudden noise. She ignored them, her eyes sparkling as she looked across the table. "So then. What's the plan for this evening?"

Leon squinted up at the ceiling before looking back at the group. "Maybe we could all chip in and rent an airship to Ramolay. Let Aurianna see someplace new." He leaned over to her conspiratorially. "You've never had any kind of seafood or shellfish, have you?"

"I don't even know what that means."

He leaned back, pounding his fist on the table in excitement and causing the people at the surrounding tables to glare menacingly at their group. "It's settled then. Ramolay it is."

*　*　*

Coming up with a plan had been the easy part, Aurianna realized. Getting everyone to physically act on it was a different matter altogether.

A third of the group was already in the realm of being too drunk to care. Theron was staring off into space, quietly sipping his ale as he mumbled to himself. Aurianna could have sworn she heard Sigi's name once or twice, but she couldn't be certain. No one else seemed to notice.

And Laelia . . . well, Laelia had decided tonight was the perfect time to demonstrate her Essence-given singing talent to the crowd. She was in the mood to perform, belting out tunes at the top of her lungs. The only silver lining about Laelia's current predicament was she actually had some skill, even in her drunken state.

The bad thing was the lack of a stage. Or accompaniment. She was standing at the front of the room while the audience watched on in fascination and amusement. Interestingly, Leon seemed to have become entranced, all his attention focused on the spectacle. He would probably never let her forget this moment.

Aurianna sighed and rested her chin in her hand.

Javen noticed and grabbed her other hand, pulling her up. "Come on," he said. "Let's get these jokers and be on our way."

"You think we can get to Ramolay with them in this state?"

He shrugged. "They'll sober up enough on the way." Javen gave her a lopsided grin. "I think you underestimate the fortitude of my friends."

"*Our* friends." Aurianna said the words before she thought to consider them.

Javen's smile widened. "Yes, *our* friends. Come on."

They managed to pull Leon and Theron out of the pub and into the alley outside. Sigi coaxed Laelia off her "stage" and out the door. When the six of them were all outside, Sigi suggested they all grab some coffee to drink on the way.

"That doesn't actually work, you know," Aurianna remarked.

Sigi shrugged. "It does if you ask for them to add *virtus* to it."

"What is that?"

"A very powerful kick of sobriety. No idea what's in it, but it does wonders to neutralize what hasn't already hit the bloodstream."

"That's actually impressive." Aurianna wasn't sure if Sigi was messing with her or not, but the idea seemed too good to be true.

"Yes, but the longer we wait, the less helpful it will be. Javen and I can go order us an airship while the rest of you grab the drinks."

After the two of them left, Leon led the rest of the group to an adjacent coffee shop and ordered large coffees with a shot of *virtus* for everyone.

When they all met back at the edge of town, an airship was floating at the edge of the cliff, an Aerokinetic Aurianna didn't recognize at the helm. A wide platform had been erected in the space between land and ship.

The group made their way onto the airship with little trouble. The *virtus* did seem to be a magic potion after all. Javen and—surprisingly—Leon helped Laelia cross the platform to ensure she wouldn't stumble off into the churning water below. It suddenly occurred to Aurianna to be shocked people weren't falling regularly to their deaths, particularly after a night on the town.

These thoughts soon escaped her as the ship took off, and she was once again in awe of the massive ship's ability to glide through the air with ease and relative speed. It wasn't as fast as the trains, but the route of the airship was a direct path from Bramosia to Ramolay.

Leon's hometown was across Perdita Bay diagonally from the capital, nestled between Menos and Vanito. He began regaling her and the others with stories from his childhood, though he seemed to be holding back on the details. Every time the narrative turned to some aspect of his family, Leon carefully maneuvered the conversation back to something unrelated.

Finally, Laelia—less drunk than she had been but still tipsy—interrupted him. "So, what exactly is the deal with your parents, Leon?"

His face darkened as he crossed his arms. "What is that supposed to mean?" The tension in the air warmed Aurianna's face.

"Well, I mean, you keep avoiding talking about them like it's some kind of secret." A look of sudden amusement crossed her features. "Ooh, does your father clean the Ramolay sewers or something?"

Leon froze, his gaze penetrating Laelia's obliviousness, forcing her to focus on his words. "You're one to talk about secrets, aren't you, sweetheart? Considering you have never even mentioned your parents, not even to Sigi here." Sigi threw a sharp glare in Leon's direction for involving her in the awkwardness of the conversation. But he wasn't looking at her. His eyes were still focused on the pale blonde in front of him. "And my dad is dead, for your information."

The change in Laelia was abrupt and instantaneous. Her features softened, and she lightly placed a hand on Leon's crossed arms. Surprisingly, he didn't pull away at her touch, but anger was still flashing in his eyes. Aurianna saw a trace of hurt as well, and she looked to the others as the situation became more uncomfortable. The rest of the group was pulling away to stand on the other side of the airship. She quickly followed, eager to leave them to their discussion.

The night air had a sobering quality all its own. The group stood in silence, watching the water below them as the moonlight sparkled off its surface. As she stared off into the starry expanse above the slowly approaching coastline, Aurianna thought about how it must feel to lose a parent you'd actually had a chance to know. Her pain was real, but the reality was, knowing them would have made it so much harder.

The two people behind her were engaged in some deep conversation, their heads bowed close together at the opposite end of the airship. Aurianna wondered how long it would be before they were at each other's throats again.

CHAPTER 10

LEON

The slight shudder of the air ship brought Leon's awareness back to his surroundings. He straightened from his hunched position in the corner and noticed they were docking at the upper level of Ramolay. With barely a glance thrown in Laelia's direction, he ushered the others off the ship, thanking the pilot and wishing the man a good evening.

He was excited to show off his hometown to Aurianna. The others had all been to Ramolay at some point in their lives, and they wasted no time getting to the lifts, which would take them down to the main thoroughfare. The majority of the residents of Ramolay lived in the town on the surface of the water that wound through the natural open-roofed cave carved from the cliffs. That's what made Ramolay so different from the other regions of Eresseia.

Leon had spent his childhood on the waterways of Ramolay. When his power had been discovered he'd been carted off to the Imperium. Living on the top of the cliffs had been a nightmare at first. It had taken a long time for him to adjust to the height without feeling queasy every time he neared the edge.

Energy pulsed around the wires connecting the box to the vertical tracks that took it from the top of the cliff near the train tracks down to the large pier below that separated the canals of Ramolay from Perdita Bay.

The six of them nestled within the large metal box. Both the front and back sides of the lift were open save for a waist-high wall, which made the experience both exhilarating and frightening. Leon noticed Aurianna jump when the lift started its downward journey.

He laughed without thinking, as Aurianna threw her arms out to steady herself against the metal walls of the lift, which earned him a glare. "Sorry. You just looked so completely out of your element." He hoped his sheepish look made up for his blunder.

Frowning, she risked a quick glance downward as the lift continued on its journey to the bottom. "Well, aren't I?"

"Aren't you what?"

"Out of my element."

"True, true. But we'll get you straightened out." Winking at the frightened girl, Leon gestured expansively to the town in general. "By the end of the night, you'll be swimming backstrokes down the main waterway, begging to stay."

Her skeptical look didn't dampen his enthusiasm. He was determined to make the most of the night. It was a rare thing for all of them to be out together, especially this far from Bramosia. As long as they didn't run into his brother, everything would be fine. The chances of seeing his mother were extremely low, considering she rarely left her house these days.

Feeling his mood darken as he thought of his family, Leon shook his head to clear his mind. Laelia was staring at him with a contemplative—not unkind—look on her face, and he thought about the conversation they had shared earlier.

The girl was certainly full of surprises. And secrets much like his own, it seemed.

When they reached the bottom, Leon stepped out first and turned to face the group. Javen joined him, and then Theron came to stand beside the two of them as they waited for the females to exit the lift.

Sigi was the first to speak. "So, where to first?" She and the other two girls began to walk forward. Leon found himself walking backward as Theron and Javen followed his lead.

"Well, I was thinking some food would be a good start." The women exchanged a brief glance between them, sharing a secretive smile that unnerved him. Leon narrowed his eyes as he continued to talk and back down the pier. "We'd need to catch a gondola. Hopefully my friend Emile is on duty and can recommend a good place for seafood. Not that there's any place around here that's ever bad for seafood, but I'm not here enough to be an expert on what's—"

A sudden weightlessness overtook Leon's body and then a stinging slap against his back was accompanied by a loud splash, followed by a dull roar rushing through his head. The overwhelming sensation of numbing cold inched its way across his skin and his senses were covered in a blanket of darkening stillness.

Leon's still ale-befuddled brain took a moment to understand he was underwater. Instinct took over. When his head breached the surface, the sound of uproarious laughter reached his water-filled ears. Leon opened his eyes and looked up.

Sigi, Laelia, and Aurianna were standing on the edge of the pier, looking down on him grinning. Leon turned around to look for Javen and Theron. Both males were bobbing in the water behind him, wearing confused and exasperated expressions. But Leon wasn't confused in the slightest.

"You knew!" His voice was raspy from the water that had managed to get into his lungs. He choked over the words as he swam to the edge to pull himself up the ladder. "You bloody well knew we were at the edge, and you didn't say a damn thing!"

Sigi raised her eyebrows in mock surprise. "Really? Are you sure you weren't just completely out of your element?"

"Yeah, okay, but I was joking when I said that. Now we're soaked to the skin, and the night's barely started." Leon heard the pout in his voice but didn't care. Javen had climbed back up and was sitting on the ground as he tried to catch his breath. Theron was struggling to get up the ladder but finally managed to drag himself over beside Javen.

"Oh, you'll dry off soon enough." Laelia's cheeky smile flipped a switch inside his brain.

Stalking toward her like a predator, Leon cocked his head to the side. "Well, I guess a little water never hurt anyone, did it?" She realized his intent just a moment too late. He grabbed her and spun her around, squeezing his soaked body against hers as she squealed in protest.

He stopped when he saw the odd look on Sigi's face as she stared at the two of them. Pulling away, he threw a glare in Aurianna's direction. "I'm not surprised these two would pull such a stunt, but you . . . I expected better out of you."

"Why? Because you think I'm nice or something?"

"It would certainly be a change of pace around here." He threw a glare at the other two girls. They only giggled and stepped back further from the edge. Javen helped Theron to his feet. The look Javen gave Aurianna almost made Leon sorry he had singled her out.

Almost.

His friend was clearly fuming. "I see how it is," Javen said. "And I'll remember that." He pushed past the group and marched over to the gondola area. Leon followed.

Emile wasn't by the pier, so Leon asked the other gondoliers if they had seen his friend. One said Emile was scheduled to be off duty within the hour, so Leon proposed they wait for him to return with his gondola. When the man showed up, his smile was just as infectious as always, despite the late hour.

"Leon!" Emile waved from a dozen yards out. "I see you've brought company." As he docked his boat and stepped onto the pier to join them, he added with a wink, "Good to see you've other friends besides me."

"Surprised?" Leon hugged his friend, clapping him on the back.

Emile jumped back at the wet contact with Leon's clothing, but he merely shrugged. "A little. You do tend to wallow in your own little world."

"I do not!"

His friend ignored him and turned to the rest of the group. "A night out on the town with this one, huh?" The gondolier jerked a thumb behind him in Leon's direction. "I see the fun has already somehow begun." He was staring at the bedraggled appearance of Javen and Theron.

Javen stepped forward to shake Emile's hand. "I've heard a lot about you, actually. I'm Javen. I'm probably the closest thing Leon has to a best friend. Besides yourself, of course."

Leon sighed. "Okay, if we're done playing let's-rag-on-Leon, can we make some plans? Emile, I guess since you're off duty, we'll just have to hire another driver." A light shone in his eyes. "But at least you can join us now."

Emile waved his words away. "No, my friend. I'll take you wherever you want to go."

"But you—"

"No, I mean it. It's not a problem to take a gondola, and I can still join you. I just can't be drinking up to your standards if I'm going to be back in the driver's seat after."

Leon feigned a look of hurt. "My standards? Why, friend, I'm utterly pained at your implication."

"Need I remind you of the time we had to chase that damn duck around Ramolay just because you—"

"I'm sorry, what?" Sigi and Laelia spoke in unison.

Leon glared at the man until he was sure he wouldn't speak any further. "Please don't remind me. Let's go."

"But, wait, what about the duck…" Sigi's disappointment at not getting the rest of the story was apparent, but Leon wasn't in the mood to get into *that* story. It would bring up too many questions about his life.

"I *said* let's go. Aurianna's here to try our shrimp, and they're not gonna peel themselves."

Without another word, Leon boarded and seated himself in the gondola, waiting—arms crossed—for the others to join him.

* * *

Watching Aurianna's first attempts at eating unpeeled shrimp was possibly the highlight of Leon's evening. He had wanted to let her figure it out for herself, but Sigi had insisted on ruining the fun by demonstrating for the other girl. Still, it had been entertaining.

After filling their stomachs, Leon's thoughts had quickly turned to the pubs, but Javen had spoiled that as well by suggesting they hire a boat and go fishing for a bit. Leon had never enjoyed fishing, but he reluctantly agreed if the others promised the next stop would be somewhere he could get a drink. The virtus-laced coffee had done its job a little too well, and he was beginning to feel the not-so-pleasant effects of sobriety inching their way into his system and senses.

Leon sat at the back of the boat with his long legs stretched out in front of him, watching as Javen tried to show Aurianna how to fish. Leon marveled at how little the woman had experienced in her life, and a brief twinge of guilt pressed down on his chest as he thought about his earlier words.

He was still angry about the dunking incident at the pier, but his mood lightened considerably when he discovered a cooler under his seat. Inside was a half-empty bottle of white wine. Not his first choice, but it would do.

As he pulled the cork out with his teeth, he noticed the others were staring at him. Shrugging, he put the bottle to his lips and tipped it back. The taste was overly sweet, but he wouldn't complain. Ignoring the looks Sigi continued to throw in his direction, Leon sat back, closed his eyes, and continued to enjoy his discovery.

Within moments, he became aware of someone filling the space beside him. He looked over to see the last person he expected. Laelia was staring at him expectantly.

No. She was staring at the bottle in his hands expectantly. Ah.

Who was he to judge? Feeling generous, he held the bottle out, tipping it slightly to indicate she could have some. Smiling, Laelia snatched it from his hands and took a long pull.

Leon frowned and grabbed it back, glaring at her.

She kept smiling and settled into the cushions at her back. Sighing loudly, Laelia placed her arm across her eyes as she leaned her head back on the seat. "Not a fishing man, I see."

He humphed. "No."

"Kinda funny, considering."

"Considering what?"

Laelia turned her head to the side, peering from under her arm to stare at him. "Considering you come from a town whose fishing industry is one of its major sources of commerce?"

"Oh." Leon struggled to find more to add but found the wine was hitting him harder than he had expected. The sound of a splash had both of them leaning forward in their seats. Aurianna and Sigi were yelling something over the edge while Theron was busy climbing over the edge of the railing. Emile was trying to stop him, to no avail.

What in the hell?

Leon pushed himself up, staggering a tiny bit as he moved forward in the rocking boat, Laelia close on his heels. When he looked out over the edge of the boat, he could see Javen floundering in the water. He knew the man was a competent swimmer, but he couldn't fathom how he might have fallen over the railing, considering it was waist high.

"What's going on?" Laelia's voice sounded almost concerned.

Aurianna was in tearful hysterics. "We were pulling on something—something big—and he just, he just…" Her voice trailed off as she started sobbing.

A sound out on the water pulled everyone's attention back to Javen. He seemed to be wrestling with something in the water. Something far bigger than any fish. His blood ran cold at the thought of what might be lurking in the depths, stories of underwater creatures with the bodies of humans, fins like a fish, and razor-sharp teeth ready to devour anything unlucky enough to land in the water.

Leon ran over to the lifebuoy on the side of the boat. Theron was already on the outside of the railing about to jump, but Leon grabbed his arm and shook his head violently. He pointed out to where Javen was struggling.

"Something's out there! Don't go in the water." He turned to Emile. "Help me get this lifebuoy out far enough to reach him."

Emile nodded, and the two of them worked to swing the rope out to Javen. Theron was climbing back into the boat. By that point, Javen seemed to be going under the water and rushing back up over and over. Something about his movements struck Leon as odd.

After a moment, Leon realized what was going on. Anger colored his words. "He's not in trouble, guys." Leon stepped back from the railing to look at the group. Aurianna was staring at him as if he had grown another head. "I mean it. He's faking."

Aurianna looked like she was going to hit him, but Sigi had realized the truth of Leon's words and pulled the girl over to watch Javen's shenanigans.

Why he thought it would be funny to scare the unholy shit out of all of them, Leon wasn't sure. But he was going to make his friend pay for his antics. Although Aurianna might just beat him to it.

Yelling out across the water, Leon said, "Fun's over, friend. I see what you're doing."

Javen slowly began to cease his movements, finally swimming over to bob in the water by the edge of the fishing boat. "What gave me away?" The man was grinning devilishly, like the entire situation was funny.

"Pretty obvious you were launching yourself in and out of the water. And you weren't missing any limbs, so it was a safe bet."

As Javen worked on climbing up the ladder and back into the boat, Aurianna turned to Leon with a look of wariness that warred with the anger already on her features. "What did you mean by that?"

"What?"

"The part about not missing any limbs." Her voice was laced with fear. "Is that really a thing? What exactly is in these waters?"

Leon shook his head. "Just stories."

Javen was standing on the deck, his clothing once again drenched, but this time he was smiling.

At least, he was until Aurianna walked up and slapped him in the face.

The shock must have frozen Javen, because he didn't even flinch. She stared at him, tears welling in her eyes. "That wasn't even remotely funny, Javen Ambrogetti! How dare you do that to me, to all of us!?" She stepped back and turned her back to the group as her tears started to flow.

Javen started to reach out for her, but Sigi moved between them. "She asked you a question." Her voice was eerily calm.

He frowned. "I…I don't know. It was just a joke. I didn't think… I mean, I didn't mean—"

Aurianna whirled back around. "How could you possibly think that would be funny, Javen?" She turned to Sigi, adding, "I want to know what's down there."

Sigi stared back at her friend. "Like Leon said, they're just stories. He's angry at Javen too."

Aurianna's glare went back to Javen as her breathing evened out. "Would everyone please stop patronizing me and answer my question?"

Javen's face softened as he reached out a tentative hand to brush a stray lock of hair behind Aurianna's ear. "No one is patronizing you. They really are just stories. Remember, I told you about the monsters in Perdita Bay? I was half-joking. People tell children scary tales about creatures in the water to keep them from cliff diving."

"What kind of creatures?"

"Half-man, half-fish, big teeth."

Aurianna visibly shivered. "You had no right to scare us like that."

"I'm really, truly sorry. I am. I thought it would be funny."

Sigi glared at him again. "You have a strange sense of humor, Javen."

"Agreed," said Emile, who had remained quiet up until that point.

Javen looked at Leon for help, but he wasn't getting involved in this. His friend had upset all of them, but the situation needed to be diffused. Crossing back over to his seat and grabbing the wine bottle, Leon brought it back and offered it to Aurianna. She accepted with the smallest of smiles and took a sip. She must have liked the sickly sweetness because she tipped it back and took a bigger gulp.

"I think it's well past time for a drink. Pub, everyone?" Leon rubbed his hands together, his eyes glinting in anticipation.

CHAPTER 11

AURIANNA

The entire coastline was laid out before her as Aurianna stood in the gardens of the Imperium. A setting sun hung just above the waterline, purple and orange hues reflected in jagged patterns across the water. The last vestiges of daylight blazed in their wake, chasing the colors onto the cliffs below.

A gentle breeze teased stray locks of hair from her plait, the pieces tickling across her neck and cheeks. The beauty that graced this world never ceased to amaze her, no matter how many days or weeks she woke up within its boundaries, half of her hoping to return home, the other half overjoyed at the chance to discover something new and wonderful.

Javen gently nudged her with an elbow. "Still not getting old, is it?"

"I'm not sure it ever will. You have no idea what it's like to live your entire life under an ashen sky."

Home was still a pull on her heart, an ache in her chest. But she found the only thing she truly missed was Larissa. No other faces ran through her thoughts, a fact that should, perhaps, have made her feel guilty.

Only it didn't.

"I can only imagine." A corner of his mouth quirked up with his flat words. Javen put an arm around her shoulders, pulling her closer, but Aurianna shrugged and pulled away. She could feel his eyes boring into her. "You're still mad."

She crossed her arms and turned around to face him. She knew his words hadn't been a question and didn't require a response. The twinge of pain she still felt at the reminder of the incident in Ramolay put a bitter taste in her mouth.

"I know. And I know I can't keep saying I'm sorry and expecting a different response. It was stupid. Period. People do stupid things when they've been drinking." At her pointed look, he added, "And I'm not saying that as an excuse. I'm just saying it wasn't intended to upset you or anyone else. Leon and I used to do stuff like that all the time when we were younger. Boys can be really weird, I know. And the only girls I normally hang around are Sig and Laelia. They're mostly used to us, but I forget you're still kind of new." His lopsided grin took over his face. "Plus, I've never really had a girlfriend before, so…" He shrugged.

Javen's prank upset her when she thought about it, but not for the reason he thought. After everything was said and done, it was her own reaction to the whole thing that had frightened her the most. She had been terrified and upset in a way she had never felt before, and she didn't want to think about what that meant. What her feelings might mean.

"So, what's with all the secrecy? And why am I wearing this ridiculous thing?" Aurianna asked to change the subject. She lifted her long skirts, the thin layers of sable-colored chiffon falling delicately below a beaded empire waist with ruched detailing. The bodice was the same shade of black, sleeveless and loose enough for comfort, with a v-shaped neckline and wide shoulder straps covered in light embroidery. Sigi had borrowed the dress from a taller friend, insisting Aurianna wear it after Javen had suggested she should wear something "nice" for the occasion, whatever it was. The dress was neither constricting nor overly fancy.

"You don't like it? You can wear something else. I just thought you'd appreciate the chance to dress up a little." His face looked pained.

"No, I really do like it. Sigi has good taste."

"Indeed, she does. Though I hate to think what she might try to put you in for the Yule Ball. It's coming up soon."

"I have no idea what that means."

He laughed. "Later. For now, let us be off."

"And where are we going?"

"First? Dinner of course."

"Aren't we heading in the wrong direction?" she asked as they crossed the bridge and made their way into Bramosia.

"I . . . was thinking perhaps something a bit less . . . communal. More intimate."

"Oh." That word—*intimate*—rolled off his tongue with the slightest twinge of something deeper, but she didn't have a response. This was a moment in time, a point of no return, and she felt that realization press in on her from all sides, despite the open air around them.

Aurianna was pretty sure his feelings ran far deeper than anything she could reciprocate. They barely knew each other. However, she felt closer to him than anyone else, save her aunt. Even Sigi, whom she was starting to consider a dear friend, seemed more aloof since she had returned to this life, this world.

This home.

He led her down the main street, and they strolled among vendors finishing final sales for the day and closing shop. Every familiar sight made her feel strangely full of foreboding. Unease filled her as she thought of each person who inhabited those homes in her future timeline, faces that did not yet exist and—if she succeeded in her reason for being here—might never exist. A future rewritten with uncertainty. The only thing left of that life would be Larissa, and only because the woman was never meant to be a part of that life, any more than Aurianna was.

What would happen to Larissa?

Javen stopped in front of a large building, lamplight spilling through the open doorway. The sound of voices filtered out to them, soft and easy, unlike the loud and boisterous noise of the pubs. They entered and stepped up to a woman behind a small desk. She gestured for them to follow and led them through the many small tables within the room to a table near the corner.

Intimate, indeed.

Javen beamed as he pulled out one of the chairs, standing patiently until she realized he was waiting on her to sit down in the proffered seat. These were niceties she was unaccustomed to, but she returned his smile to show her appreciation.

When they were both seated, the lady who had shown them to the table nodded as she filled water goblets from a pitcher that seemed to come out of nowhere. "Wine?" she asked.

"Of course," he replied.

Javen turned his attention to her, his face beaming once again as he reached across the table for her hand. She didn't pull away, despite her initial instinct to do so. She gazed around the room, her eyes lighting upon couple after couple seated at virtually identical tables. A small bar sat in the corner by the door, the bartender cleaning a back counter with a pass-through window into the kitchen beyond. Two women were walking back and forth between the bar and tables, serving customers at a leisurely pace. Aurianna was surprised to see a few men also waiting on tables. The pubs employed only women to serve.

"Are you happy?"

She snapped her head back to face her dinner companion. "What?"

"I asked if you were happy."

"What do you mean?"

He furrowed his brow. "I didn't realize it required explanation." When she glared at him, he hastened to assure her, "I'm not trying to trick you. It's just a simple question."

"No, actually, it's not simple. Because I don't think that's really what you're asking me."

"Oh? And what am I asking you, then?"

"You want to know if I am happy with *you*."

"Yes. I rather thought that part was implied." He pursed his lips. "But, in truth, I do want to know the answer to both. I think you know how I feel."

"I—Yes, I think I do. And to be completely frank, I don't know how to answer you. In general, I'm happy with my life right now. As you know, I'm struggling with this distance between me and the others, these feelings they have that you keep promising will go away with time. No one has said anything to my face since that first conversation, but I can still feel it. Other than that, I'm feeling better about my training. I do miss home, but not as much, if I'm being honest with myself. And as for you—"

"Us."

She nodded. "As for us, I think I'm happy enough. It's not easy for me. I've never been close to anyone, not in that way. We didn't have the luxury of going out for a fancy dinner where I'm from.

You find someone, get betrothed, have kids, and keep moving forward."

"So, you've never…been in a relationship at all?"

Looking down at their joined hands shyly, she said, "Well, I did kiss a boy once."

"Yes, I remember."

"What?" *How could he…* No, he wasn't talking about Damon. Javen was referring to the time he himself had kissed her. She shook her head, her face turning red at the memory of that day on the hilltop. "No, I mean before. Back when I was still no one and nothing. Damon was…" Thoughts of him drifted into focus as she again thought about the repercussions of her actions here in the past. The idea of erasing him from existence frightened her beyond measure. The greater good seemed not so grand when she thought about the lives she would possibly be erasing.

Her breathing became erratic, and Javen sensed her thoughts. "This boy was important to you, wasn't he?"

"No. I mean, yes. Everyone is important. It's just that I knew him, and I knew others, and all of them might not exist if I continue on this path to change the future."

One of the male servers arrived at their table with the wine and two glasses, filling them and setting the rest of the bottle on the table. He recited the menu for the evening, and they ordered. Aurianna quickly took a sip of her wine, feeling a warmth spread down through her torso. She needed to be careful, but she also needed to calm down.

She was just about to speak again when another voice intruded into their conversation from behind her shoulder. "Well, hello there, Javen. So nice to see you this evening." Belinda. *Perfect.*

Javen had a wary look on his face as he said, "Good evening, young lady. How are you?"

Belinda had stopped beside their table, leaning into it slightly as a pout spread across her lips. "Young lady? Come now, Javen. We know each other better than that." Her smile was devilish and hinted at some deeper meaning.

Aurianna tried her best not to snort. The girl was beyond obvious and far too pushy for her own good.

Belinda's smile twisted into a grimace when Javen didn't immediately respond, and she said, "Well, I guess I'll get back to my dinner companions." She turned around and practically stomped off, sitting down at a table with two other girls Aurianna recognized from Belinda's entourage.

Javen ignored the entire ordeal. "So, I was going to say perhaps we should enjoy the evening and avoid such weighty topics. Let's stick to more pleasant dinner conversation, shall we?"

Though a part of her didn't want to shove the thoughts away, she knew he was right. Dwelling on them didn't help, and right now was a good time to get to know him a little better.

"All right," she said, "tell me about your family."

He looked suddenly uncomfortable, refusing to meet her eyes as he squirmed in his seat. "What about them?"

"Sigi and I went with Laelia to Vanito a while back if you remember. We . . . got separated and went looking for Laelia. I thought perhaps your families might know one another, but Sigi didn't even know where either of your families lived."

"Laelia doesn't speak about her family. No one knows anything about them, to be honest. I get the impression she's on bad terms."

"You obviously don't speak about yours either. Are you on bad terms with your family?"

"No." His gaze was lost in some memory of long ago, his eyes burning with a fire she'd never seen before. "My family is gone."

"Gone? You mean they're dead." She reached out with her other hand to grab his, squeezing. "I'm so sorry."

"It happened a long time ago. How is the search going for your family, by the way?"

"Leon hasn't discovered anything else. I may never know."

A waiter appeared holding two platters of delicious-smelling food. Since Bramosia was the capital city and could boast of a diversity of regional cultures within its boundaries, the food offerings were always a surprise to Aurianna, though not always a good one. While Javen had ordered some sort of sautéed dish with meat and vegetables served over rice, she had opted for crab-stuffed pasta with a seasoned cream sauce and fresh mushrooms.

Their culinary adventures in Ramolay had left Aurianna with an intense love of seafood, a fact that delighted Leon to no end. But she also enjoyed the different variations of pasta often served at the Imperium. The pasta she was served that evening differed from the simple noodles at their buffet-style meals. The pasta dough was shaped into rectangular pockets and stuffed full of a crab and cheese filling.

As the server placed a large bowl on the table before her, Aurianna thanked the man and stared intently at her food. When she looked up, Javen was smiling at her.

"Everything all right?"

"Yeah. I was just thinking how lucky I am compared to my life a year ago."

His smile widened. "And we are even luckier to have you."

Unsure how to respond, Aurianna concentrated on her meal, scooping up and trying a bite of pasta with the creamy sauce. Her eyes closing of their own accord as an involuntary noise escaped her throat. Embarrassed, she looked up at Javen. His lopsided grin was in full swing, and she was tempted to throw something at him.

"I told you this was going to be a good night." His eyes twinkled in the low light from the lamp.

"Indeed."

They ate their food and drank far too much wine as their conversation continued uninterrupted well into the evening. After a dessert of something that managed to be both hot and cold, they left the building and walked back toward the Imperium.

Before they reached the bridge, he led her away to the left, in the direction of the forest that looked even more menacing at night than it had during her excursion that day she came looking for the tower. When she started to protest, he placed a finger against her lips. "Just trust me, okay?"

Nodding, she took the arm he offered her as they slowly meandered in a diagonal line leading to the cliff. The edge of the forest loomed ahead of them, and she began to shake when he pulled her beyond the first row of trees.

"Javen—"

"We're stopping right up there. I promise you'll be safe with me." He pointed to the weapon at his hip, the gun she hadn't noticed until that moment.

Javen turned them to face the edge of the cliff again, stopping at the edge. Moonlight danced across the surface of the rippling lagoon far below. He was holding her close to his side when he suddenly turned to face her, his hands lacing around the small of her back. A part of her felt trapped, but another part of her felt safer than she'd ever been.

"I love you, Aurianna."

She sputtered in her attempt to find words. "Love? You barely know me, Javen Ambrogetti."

"Again with the formalities." A small, innocent-looking smile played on his lips as the breeze from earlier softly caressed them with a swaying rhythm. Even with Perdita Bay lurking just below them, it was rare for even a small breeze to pass by, a fact she attributed to the missing god of Air, Caelum—brother of Terra and her sisters.

She wondered for a moment why she had never told anyone apart from the Arcanes about her visit from the Essence. She'd spoken to Simon, who had encouraged her to continue down "whatever path" she felt was right. The man was obviously just as clueless as she was.

Her friends hadn't brought up anything related to the prophecy or the Enchantress again, not since the first conversation they'd had when she returned. Javen said the others were still struggling with the idea of peace not being as close as they thought. Aurianna had no desire to force them to talk with her about it, so she had remained silent. Perhaps she should talk to Sigi about it, though the girl would probably think her mad. Telling Javen had crossed her mind, but she didn't want him to think she was making things up just to get his sympathy. He didn't seem to be very religious.

But Theron. Theron was a very pious man, despite the many vices he shared with his friends. He might be the only one who could perhaps hear and believe her.

"Aurianna?" Javen had been speaking to her, but she had no idea what she had missed.

"Yes?" Her face felt flushed as she chewed on the corner of her mouth in embarrassment.

"You were a million miles away, weren't you?" He sighed. "I asked if you could accept it for what it is ... for now. You don't need to say anything. I think you feel the same way. You just don't want to admit it."

She started to protest, but then she realized he might be right. Perhaps love was too strong a word, but she did care for him.

Javen pulled her closer, his hands still around her waist. Leaning forward, he pressed his lips to hers with a light pressure, moving toward something more as she returned his kiss. Aurianna opened her mouth to his, their movements growing more and more heated. His hands strayed further down, cupping her behind as he slowly backed her up against a tree.

His hands were suddenly everywhere, his breath hot against her neck and he trailed kisses down the length of her throat. One hand bunched her skirts, lifting one side up her leg, exposing her thigh.

Enough. This was too much, too fast.

"Wait," she whispered, her voice sounding small and breathy to her own ears. When he didn't stop, she spoke louder. "Javen, stop." He backed away a few inches breathing heavily as he looked at her with a question in his eyes.

Whatever answer he saw there made him nod and step away. Before he could give voice to an apology, Aurianna followed her instincts and did the only thing she knew to do.

She ran.

CHAPTER 12

AURIANNA

Aurianna had no destination in mind. She didn't even know why she had taken off like that. All she knew was she had to get out of there, and fast.

Holding her dress up as she ran, Aurianna realized how thankful she was for the practical shoes Sigi had given her to wear with the dress. Anything with heels would have been a nightmare to run in.

She could hear Javen calling her name far in the distance. The sound was ebbing away, so at least he wasn't trying to follow her.

She stopped running when she reached the stables. Her subconscious had known what she needed, even if her brain hadn't. The stablemaster directed one of his grooms to get Oracle ready for her. The man asked no questions, even though she had shown up in an evening dress.

Oracle was overjoyed to see Aurianna, the mare's nose nuzzling her until Aurianna was ready to mount up. It was quite a spectacle, she was sure, but neither of the men spoke a word or offered any advice.

When she had adjusted her skirts to cover her legs, Aurianna clicked her tongue to set the horse in motion. Oracle took off, galloping full out across the open landscape that led to the town of Menos, on the opposite side of Bramosia from the scene she had just left in the forest. Aurianna forced the mare to slow to a trot as they covered mile after mile of green but uninhabited land, and she breathed a sigh of relief. The openness of the area was comforting, in stark contrast to the ominous forest Javen had taken her to.

Nothing was actually wrong with the forest. She had been through it herself, albeit during the daytime. But it had also been the scene of the Volanti attack from several moons ago, an attack supposedly due to be repeated any day now, though no one could predict exactly where or when the monsters would arrive, so the forest held an overwhelming fear for her.

The fear she felt reminded her of her recurring nightmare, though she couldn't be sure the shadows in her dreams were, in fact, those same creatures. It was just a dream, but if she was going to admit any kind of belief in a prophecy about herself, she had to at least acknowledge the possibility of a dream being more than a dream.

Like the other dream she'd had, the one with the glowing orb. Some meaning existed, some hidden truth was in that dream, but it was out of reach. Maybe she would have the dream again and be able to explore it further.

The ride was exhilarating, but her heart was still heavy. Guilt washed over her as she thought about how Javen must be feeling. He would feel hurt, but she thought he would forgive her abrupt departure even if he couldn't understand it. Javen would give her any time and space she needed. But he didn't understand her well enough to grasp her true reasons for leaving.

His advances had been sudden, but not entirely unwanted. The truth was she was afraid of trusting him—or anyone—enough to make herself that vulnerable. What she needed was time, and perhaps more confidence in her own life—answers to her questions, information about her past, more surety of her purpose in this world.

Vague assurances from a group of enigmatic men who spent most of their time holed up in a dusty old room were not enough. Neither were melodramatic claims from a deity who gave her nothing and asked for everything. But how could she expect anything more when she herself held back so much?

She suddenly reined Oracle in, turning back to the stables. She would get her answers.

Tonight.

* * *

"And you say this orb is floating? Of its own accord?" Simon looked at her skeptically.

"It's a dream, Simon. Is it really so impossible to imagine a floating ball of light? In a world where I can make magma or water do the same?"

Of all the news she had brought to him, she had assumed her talk with Terra, the goddess of Earth—an actual goddess—would have been the most interesting to him. But he had shrugged that information off as if it were a common everyday occurrence.

Simon was far more interested in the dream, asking many questions for which she didn't have answers. "I do not doubt your words. I merely wish to verify the details." He turned to place his palms on the table behind him, putting the full weight of his body on them. His sigh echoed against the stone walls. "Aurianna, you have the ability to get all the answers you want, but you continue to ask the wrong questions."

"What is that supposed to mean?"

"Look around you," he replied. "What do you see?"

She humored him by turning in a circle, peering at the shelves around her. "Old books."

"Yes, exactly."

Aurianna frowned in confusion. "I don't understand. Even the Magnus is forbidden from reading the books in this room."

"Yes, he is, in a way. But you are not."

"Why in hell would that be? I'm no one." She raised her hand to interrupt the denial plainly written on his face. "I'm not talking about the stupid prophecy. I told you before that I chose my own destiny. I made a choice to stop the woman. My hand wasn't forced by words on a page."

"Would you have been here to make that choice, at that time, were it not for the existence of the prophecy?"

She opened her mouth to speak, to protest his words. But she realized she couldn't. If a goddess was telling her she was meant to do something, why was it so hard to believe?

Simon continued, "You want to believe your life is your own, your choices are your own. And that is precisely the point. Your choices *are* your own. You choose how this plays out. Your decisions will either lead to victory or defeat, and you have the power to lead us down either path."

"So, the prophecy isn't a guarantee?"

"Of course not. That's what I keep trying to tell you. But the only way for you to truly understand is for you to gather as much information as you can."

"Information even the Magnus isn't allowed to have."

"Not by our will. No one has ever stopped him from opening one of these tomes and reading it himself."

"I don't understand."

"He or anyone else could open these books. They would not be stopped."

"Then why does he believe he's forbidden from doing so? At least, I've been told he believes—"

"Because he was told so by his own father, and his father before him. His grandfather tried and failed."

"Failed how?"

"The pages were simply blank. He couldn't see what was written there."

"Some spell or power devised by the Essence?"

"Precisely. Only those who are supposed to see will be able to. When I showed you the prophecy that day, you could see it because they allowed you to see it."

"But Sigi, my friend—"

"Was also allowed to see it. That is how I know she is important in all of this. You should keep her close and lean on her for guidance. The Essence would not choose allies for you that could not be trusted."

Trusted.

"So, the Magnus is from a line of rulers?" Aurianna chose to ignore her churning feelings over the previous line of thought.

Simon nodded. "Usually works that way. On the rare occasion where there is no heir, the title goes to the closest living relative."

"Why aren't they allowed to speak of their Kinetic power?"

Simon looked uncomfortable. "Because there are some who could use it against them. They train privately and never use their power publicly."

"How do we even know they have any power if no one sees it?"

"The Magisters are privy to it, of course, but they are sworn to secrecy. A Magnus is required to choose a spouse who is also a Kinetic."

"Unlike the rest of the world."

"Yes, others are forbidden. It is to insure no one has too much power, other than the ruling family. Two Kinetics will always give birth to another Kinetic."

"Why? I thought it was random?"

"And now, Aurianna," he said as the corner of his mouth tugged up in the slightest of smiles, "you're asking the right questions."

* * *

She attempted to muffle the sneeze, but they seemed to get progressively louder the more dust she stirred up. The bookshelves in constant use by the Arcanes didn't suffer the same fate as these mostly forgotten tomes. Most of the ones she picked up—led to them by some unknown force or instinct—were covered in layers of dust.

Sitting at a table in a far back corner of the Arcanes' quarters, Aurianna was surrounded by piles of books she had already perused over the course of the afternoon. Though she had started yesterday after her talk with Simon, there hadn't been much time before bed, leaving her to dream about all the things still left unanswered.

Javen had been beside himself with worry when she finally went upstairs, a fact she felt somewhat guilty for, but she had assured him everything was fine between them. She just needed time—time he was more than willing to give, he'd said. He'd tried to apologize for the incident in the forest, stating he wouldn't lay a finger on her again until she said it was all right, but she had made it clear his attentions weren't unwanted—just a bit too much too fast. Her reasons were her own, and he wouldn't understand her trust issues, but he did seem incredibly remorseful.

After training was over for the day, she had made an excuse to her friends and gone back to the Arcanes. She wasn't even sure what time it was now, with no windows or access to the world outside.

These men—for indeed there were no women among them—did this all day, every day.

It was already beginning to grate on her nerves.

The book she had just opened was larger and even older than some of the others, if she understood the shelving system Simon had explained to her. She had wanted him to help her find the answers she sought, but he had insisted she work alone. He knew more than he let on but refused to help her, refused to guide her, except to say she should follow the path that draws her.

The words on the pages—some of which were written in a language she did not understand or recognize—began to blur together. Page after page, book after book. She didn't even know what she was looking for. Perhaps something about her dream. Perhaps something about the Kinetics or their powers.

Perhaps an answer as to why she was down here wasting her time.

She would much rather be in the library many levels above, reading about some fictional adventure. Instead she was down here looking over old prophecies, ancient histories, and a multitude of other mind-numbingly boring subjects.

Aurianna stood and began to pace along the row adjacent to her table. Further down, she saw the book containing the prophecy. Her prophecy.

Something drew her to it. Maybe that book contained more than Simon had shown her. It would contain other prophecies, at least. She took it down when she was certain it was the correct one. It was unmistakable and completely devoid of dust.

Taking it back to her seat, she opened the book to the first page. More vague words which elicited more questions than answers. She flipped through for a while but grew tired of looking for the page in question.

The Essence take her. She needed air.

She stood in a huff, leaving the books where they were. Walking down the row once again, she followed the back wall. As the path continued, she started to wonder where the Arcanes slept. How they ate. Where they showered. All mundane things, but still her curiosity would not let up. They were said to rarely leave their room, a fate they shared with the Arcanes in her own time.

She found no doors, no exits from the main room. It was odd. And impossible. The room was large, filled from end to end with bookshelves and tables but little else. The Arcanes were enigmatic, but they were still human. They needed to eat and sleep just like anyone else.

Near a small alcove, she glimpsed something from the corner of her eye. A tapestry adorning the wall moved the slightest bit.

No breeze blew through this underground prison of a room. Reaching out, she touched the fabric, pushing inward toward the wall. There was no resistance behind it.

No wall.

Aurianna turned to see if anyone noticed her—though she didn't know if they would stop her or not—and was satisfied she was alone. She pulled back the tapestry, revealing a large opening. A doorway.

It was pitch black just inside, but further down the passage she could see the faint light from sconces. She took another look around her and quickly stepped through the entrance into the dark beyond.

CHAPTER 13

AURIANNA

The passageway quickly began to slope downward. Aurianna wondered if she was entering the depths of the world itself, the stone the only thing between her and massive waves of magma that would rush in and melt her in an instant, no matter what power she might possess.

The paving stone seemed older than that in the Imperium, the surface smooth from wear. Aurianna continued, despite a chill in the corridor that made no sense and seemed to come from nowhere. Several times, the passage wound back on itself, spiraling down, but always leading further away from the Imperium, at least as far as she could tell.

The path leveled off and straightened along a dimly lit corridor. She noticed unusual symbols etched into the stone walls. She thought some of them looked familiar, but they were all intertwined, looping along the tunnel wall.

Eventually, the passage sloped again, but this time it slanted upward. After what felt like a lifetime in the semidarkness, she came to a door covered in the same symbols, though these were painted rather than carved. Placing a hand gingerly against one of them, she traced the lines, retrieving them from her memory in a wash of sudden recognition.

Some of these symbols were similar to those at the temples, though there were clear differences. She remembered the necklace Theron always wore around his neck, a thing precious to him above any of his other worldly possessions because it was a reminder to him of what he had almost lost and what it had meant to his parents when he'd almost died.

Closing her eyes, Aurianna took a deep breath and pushed on the door. It opened without hesitation. She peered within and was surprised to see exactly what she had been looking for.

Beds bunked three high and scattered throughout the room. Some empty, some occupied by men in dull-colored robes. The Arcanes slept here, that much was clear. But where, exactly, was here?

Several pairs of eyes opened at her approach, though none looked surprised to see her. The one closest to her sat up, staring at her oddly as he raised one eyebrow.

When he didn't speak, she asked, "What is this place?"

A voice from across the room answered, "I believe you are asking questions to which you already know the answers." She turned and saw several more of the men had sat up on their beds.

The symbols continued into the room, all the way up the walls, and across the ceiling. A heat emanated from above, but her body had gone cold, her veins full of ice and fear.

Aurianna knew that heat and what it meant. And suddenly so many questions, even ones she hadn't realized she was asking, were answered.

The room where she stood was under the Consilium, directly below the burning pit.

She could barely choke out the words. "How?"

"Which question are you asking, Aurianna?" Simon's voice behind her nearly made her jump out of her skin as she swiveled around to face him.

"Were you following me?"

He inclined his head to her. "Of course. I knew where you were going, and I knew you would have questions. And as forthcoming as my brothers here are, I assumed you would prefer a familiar face."

"Why all the secrecy? Why not just tell me?"

"You said yourself that Terra told you they cannot meddle in any of this. You must find your own way to avoid the timelines colliding. And we are merely the servants of the Essence. We do as we are told."

"How then? How are we here?"

His gaze knowing, Simon leaned forward as his voice took on a conspiratorial tone. "At the Consilium? Or do you mean something else?"

"You know damn well what I mean, I'd wager."

"Come, and I will show you."

Despite her frustrations at his secrecy, she knew this was a rare opportunity for answers. An opportunity she would be foolish to pass up. The room was circular, the outer edges free of the beds and furniture that lay scattered throughout the large chamber. Their footsteps echoed in the space as she followed Simon to a metal ladder. At the top was a metal hatch, which he opened, revealing another ladder that led up through a hole to the levels above. They climbed to just below the next level, Simon turning back to gesture with his finger to his lips.

He peered over the edge of the floor above then climbed out. Aurianna followed. The intensity of the heat made her dizzy. When she was standing on solid ground again, a wall loomed in front of her. Sounds echoed around the stone passageway that veered off around the corner to their left. To the right was a large stone door. She knew where she was, at least. In the future, the door would lead to the room where they stored drained bodies, bodies she and others had been forced to carry down the corridor and throw into the burning pit. Aurianna opened her mouth to voice her question, but he once again put his finger to his lips. Pulling her close, he whispered, "We must be silent or risk them seeing you. Look if you must, as they won't be facing this way, but you cannot make a sound, no matter what you see."

Narrowing her eyes at his words, she crept over to where the wall led down and around to where she assumed the burning pit would be. What did these people use it for? Surely nothing like what her own people had been doing—throwing dead Kinetics in after draining them and stealing their power.

The noise of the sloshing magma was loud enough to cover any small noise she might make. Peeking around the edge, she felt the heat like a wave of despair as she saw the last thing she ever expected to see. Standing guard, their backs to the pit, was a row of Praefects.

Praefects she knew and hated.

Praefects she recognized.

CHAPTER 14

AURIANNA

Aurianna felt a noise somewhere between a strangled sob and a scream bubble up inside her throat before Simon put his hand over her mouth to stifle it. He pulled her back around the corner, holding her against him as she struggled to get free.

His voice was in her ear. "You absolutely cannot make a sound, or they will find you. And you do not want that, considering what you are. Do you understand?"

She knew he was right. These men would know she was a Kinetic. She felt sure they would be able to tell. They would lock her away in one of those cells where they kept the prisoners. They would drain her of power then throw her into the burning pit.

Nodding her agreement, she took a deep breath as he lifted his hand from her mouth. He dragged her over to the ladder and pointed up. She understood and followed him. Once again, he checked before leaving the ladder, which ended at this level, the only above-ground level of the Consilium.

He offered her a hand up, which she accepted, her own hand

shaking so badly she almost lost her grip. When she straightened, Aurianna realized her entire body was shaking. In front of her was a door she knew all too well. This was where she and the other workers would enter the Consilium when their labor assignment placed them at the burning pit.

They went through the door that led outside. The fresh air was a shock to her system. The sky was darkening, the Darkness settling in for the evening.

She whirled on him, grabbing hold of the front of his robes, "What the *bloody hell* is going on?" she hissed, still wary of being spotted or overheard, despite the workers having gone for the day. Curfew was approaching, but anyone could be nearby.

Grasping her forearms to extricate himself from her grip, Simon motioned behind her with a nod of his head. He didn't give her a chance to decide, tugging her along by her arm. They skirted the main avenue, ducking around the edges of town until she saw where the edge of the forest should have been. In its place was the barren landscape she had known all her life, the gently rolling hills and promise of something beyond.

This wasn't possible. None of it was possible.

Simon pulled her far enough away that no one would be able to see them in the ever-present Darkness. He stopped, turning to her, his mouth open to say something.

Aurianna beat him to it, punctuating her words with a jabbing index finger to the chest. "How is this possible? Did you drug me somehow?"

He shook his head sadly. "No. You know I didn't."

"I know nothing right now! Explain."

"You saw those symbols in the passages. They are ancient runes, used by the Essence. We still use some of the runes in communicating and writing about the deities. In your true timeline, I mean."

"And which one would that be, Simon? Forgive me for being a bit confused right now."

"Yes, I know. The place you know as the past is where and when you were born. Your age may complicate the matter, but it is your true home." His eyes searched around them, checking for interlopers. "The symbols, as I said, are runes. Runes which hold a magic far deeper than anything possessed in this world, past or present. They were put there by the Essence to protect those rooms and passages from time."

"Meaning what?"

"Meaning time does not exist within their borders. The ebb and flow of time exists outside of them, but within them we are beyond such constraints. We can visit whichever point in time we find necessary at any given moment. The Essence entrusted us as guardians of not only those books, but also the events which transpire around the prophecies. We are the keepers of time, so to speak, albeit indirectly. The Essence merely provide us with the magic—as you call it—since we possess none of our own."

"No. No," she said, suddenly raising her voice to scream. "No! I was almost captured trying to travel back in time. Which I did twice!"

"I know what you're thinking, and I need to tell—"

"You have no idea what I'm thinking. You and your Essence conspired to turn my life upside down, to take me away from everything I know and love. And then I find out you could've just walked out your front door and invited me into the past. No need for an Aether Stone, no need to be hunted down by Carpos. No need to spend weeks missing my home, missing my aunt, the only person who has ever truly cared for me!"

Aurianna turned around in a furious rage, heading for the only place she felt safe. Aunt Larissa would be there, would be able to shield her from all of this.

Sneaking around the buildings in the Darkness was easier than she expected. When Aurianna reached the door of her childhood home, she didn't bother knocking. Walking in, she was shocked to see her aunt sitting calmly in a chair in the front room, as if she'd been waiting on her.

Rising from her seat, the older woman enfolded her in a fierce embrace. "It's good to see you again."

Aurianna began shaking again, tremors racking her body almost convulsively. "You're not surprised, are you?" she asked, backing away with small steps. She continued retreating until her back met a cloth-covered object. She turned to look at Simon, who gazed at her with pity she did not want to see. "You know. You've always known."

Her aunt didn't deny the accusation but stared at Aurianna for several moments before speaking. "Right now, I am waiting on your return, so we can't be long. I will head down to the Imperium soon, and you cannot be here."

"How do you know? How do you know what you're about to do if Pharis hasn't returned to get me yet?"

The woman sighed heavily, sitting back down in her chair and gesturing for Aurianna to join her. Simon remained standing. "Some things would take too long to explain. Other things I *cannot* explain, not without damaging the timelines. You have to return, and you have to continue your training." She reached for Aurianna's hand, squeezing. "I know it's hard to leave now that you're here, but you must leave all the same."

"Would someone please tell me what's going on? Why can't you come with me? Why couldn't I have just gone that way to begin with?"

Simon answered her. "I was trying to tell you the Darkness is what stops magic in this place. Not lesser magic, Kinetic powers and such. That is diminished here, but not completely gone. The magic controlling those doors in and out of our rooms is made dormant by the hunger of the Darkness. Arcanes can still use them because we are protected. Because we have no magic within us. But you, Aurianna," he said, his voice rising in intensity as he came to stand by her chair, "you are blessed with Kinetic power, magic that the Darkness will not allow back out. The Aether Stones are the only power that is stronger than the Darkness."

"So, I'm trapped here." Aurianna's voice quivered with laughter verging on hysteria.

Larissa gave her a sympathetic look. "You have the Aether Stone I gave you. That's the only way to get magic out of this place. Their power comes straight from the Essence, from the beginning of time."

"No, I . . ." she started to deny having it, but reaching into her pocket, she pulled out the object. She remembered placing it there that morning, an action that had merely been an afterthought at the time. At least it had felt like one. "But what good is it? It doesn't work." Indeed, its inner light was still dark. No glow emanating from the depths of the Aether Stone. Her gaze lifted from the object in her hand, and she glared at both of them quizzically.

"Aether Stones absorb power from each other," Simon said. "They're connected, so if you have a dormant Stone with you when you use a working one, it feeds off the power. Not completely, but they recharge a little more each time."

Larissa said, "You've gone through the Essence three times now with it in your pocket. It should be fully charged at this point."

Aurianna shook the object in front of her. "It's not glowing though. You said before that it stopped glowing when the magic left it."

Her aunt nodded. "The Darkness sucked the magic from it. But it is recharged, so you just have to speak the vow to the Essence like before, and it will work."

"So, you're just pushing me out—no answers, no explanations." Aurianna stood up, her body still trembling, heat rising in waves within her. "Why can't you come with me?" The heat was suddenly replaced with an icy coolness. But she was still shaking, almost violently so.

No, she wasn't shaking. The ground beneath her was.

A roar began somewhere under her feet. Larissa had risen to stand as well, reaching out to steady herself as she spoke above the noise. "I can't. Even the Stone can't help me." The woman's eyes were glassy with unshed tears, a sadness etched within them that was miles deep. "Besides, my job is here, to help you when you return, and send you off on your way again when Pharis shows up the second time."

"Am I doing this?" Aurianna yelled above the roar.

"Yes, and you need to leave. Now. Before the Carpos show up."

Aurianna looked at Simon, who shrugged. "Too late for me to get back my usual way. I trust you'll be gentle?" He smiled at her, and some part of her wanted to smile back. The tremors beneath her eased a bit as she grasped the Aether Stone, spoke the words, and waited, as sparks of Energy struck out in every direction. In the haze around them, she saw Larissa run out the front door. Simon grabbed the Stone just before they were pulled into the Essence.

* * *

They landed in the forest, a fact for which she wasn't sure she was thankful. Aurianna picked herself up, having almost grown accustomed to the effects of time travel via Aether Stone.

Simon, on the other hand, lay panting on the ground, holding his side with a grimace of pain. Begrudgingly, Aurianna held out a hand to the older man, who accepted it with a tight-lipped smile.

"That is not an experience I would like to repeat," was all he said.

Aurianna's eyes flashed in anger. "And yet you would subject me to it…four times now?"

"Yes, well, that is not our doing. It is technically not the fault of the Essence either. They cannot control the Darkness, and while they are masters over time, they cannot reconcile separate time-lines. No one has that power."

"They created the world, yet they can't control it?"

"The world simply *is*, Aurianna. The Essence created the life within it and wield some control over things, or at least they used to be able to do so." Simon shielded his eyes from the midday sun, gazing at the Imperium in the distance. "But there are powers that existed long before them. Not actual entities, but laws. Rules." He set off toward the building. "And speaking of rules, we need to determine which ones we may have broken. I don't know what day it is, or how long we've been gone."

Aurianna remembered it had been late afternoon or possibly evening when she had discovered the passage to the Consilium. The sun was bright, the sky clear. How many days had passed?

When they reached the front entrance, Sigi was outside on guard duty. When her friend realized who was approaching, she ran forward in a very un-guardswoman-like manner, hugging Aurianna and talking excitedly.

"Oh, I'm so glad they were right. We spent hours looking for you the other night. Javen was losing his mind. Then I went to speak with the Magnus, who talked to the Arcanes, who told him not to worry about you for a few days. But it's been a week, and I didn't trust them. I didn't know what to do."

"Sigi, slow down," said Aurianna. "I'm fine. Simon and I had to take a little trip."

"For a week?"

"It wasn't…I'll explain later. Right now, I should probably head to class and let Javen know I'm not dead." When her friend looked at her dubiously, she repeated, "I'm fine."

She followed Simon into the building, but instead of heading upstairs to her classes, she took the stairwell down with him.

Simon glanced at her from the corner of his eye. "I thought you were going to class."

"I am. I will. But not until you tell me everything."

"I can't do that, Aurianna."

"Why?"

He stopped. "You were chosen for this path"—he held up a hand as she opened her mouth to interrupt—"and I do realize that makes it seem as if your destiny is out of your hands. That couldn't be further from the truth. You can still make decisions along the way, both good and bad, that can affect the outcome. Victory is not guaranteed. But you are the one who has to find the correct path." He continued down the stairs. His words echoed around her as she turned and went up to the classroom level.

It took two tries before she found the right classroom. She wasn't sure of the exact time. She should have checked the giant clock out front on their way in. The first room she tried held her own group in the midst of some bookwork related to Earth training. Hilda and Sebastian stared at her awkwardly as she tried to leave without attracting the attention of Magister Garis. The woman turned just as she was closing the door, so Aurianna muttered a quick apology, saying she would be right back.

Javen pounced as soon as she peeked into the room where his class was, creating an extremely awkward and embarrassing situation. She pulled herself away, smiling shyly at his classmates as she tried to explain to Magister Martes why she had missed his class for a week.

"I am well aware of your situation, my dear." His stress on the word situation made her feel ill at ease, but she thanked him none-theless and went back to her own class.

It was the last session of the day, apart from Weapons training, which she was improving in. It helped that Javen was working with her during their free time as well.

Not today though. When the afternoon free time came around, Aurianna made excuses, causing Javen to give her his worried look.

"It's nothing to be concerned about. I just need to talk to Simon is all."

"Didn't you just get back from a week-long trip with Simon?"

"No. I actually got back from an hour-long trip with Simon. Time travel, remember?

"I really don't understand how the whole time-travel thing works. All I know is you were gone for a week, and we were wor-ried." He sighed, adding, "Yeah, fine. I'll see you at dinner?" He was pouting and trying to hide the fact. But Aurianna saw through it.

She put her arms around his neck, which lit his face up in a smile, his brown eyes glimmering with hope. "None of this has anything to do with you. I promise. I just have a lot of questions for the Arcanes."

"I could go with you."

She shook her head. "No, I need to do this on my own. That's what everyone keeps insisting above all else." She rolled her eyes, causing his smile to widen.

He leaned in, looking into her face to see her reaction. He was waiting on confirmation from her that he could continue. When she nodded, he placed a kiss on her lips, quick but soft, and left her alone in the underground tunnels.

She didn't even have to knock before the door to the room opened, Simon himself answering this time. "Come in."

"You don't seem surprised to see me again so soon."

"I'm not."

She looked up, taking in the details of the ceiling, which she had never noticed before. "So how does this time thing work exactly? I could just walk back out, and it might be the next moon cycle?"

"Exiting into whatever time we need it to be only works for us. But time is fluid in here for anyone else. Or rather, more like non-existent. When you were down here looking through the books, no time was passing upstairs."

Like the evanescence. The oneness with time the goddess Terra had spoken about. "But Sigi said they were looking for me."

"Well, at that point, you were gone. But prior to leaving through the Consilium, you could have sat here for days, and no one would have even noticed."

"So, I could go missing and no one would know?"

Missing.

Aurianna couldn't hear Simon's response over the pounding and rush of blood in her head. The man at the pub, the one she had recognized as the Kinetic who had died in her arms in the future, had said there were Voids going missing. No one had seemed concerned, but maybe that was a mistake.

Interrupting whatever he had been trying to explain, she said, "What do you know about the Voids who have gone missing recently?"

Simon's eyes lit up, but he was shaking his head at the same time. "Ask the question you want the answer to."

She glared at him, irritated he could so easily read her mind. "Why does everyone treat the Voids like they're nothing?"

"Kinetics are power. When that power doesn't manifest in the way they expect, there is shame attached—to them and to their inability to show their power."

"That doesn't explain why they're treated as lesser humans. Even non-Kinetics aren't treated—" She paused, her mind rewinding back to his previous statement. "What did you say?

"Ask the question."

"You said their inability to *show* their power. Not their lack of power. They once had something, some kind of power, or they wouldn't be here. What happens to that power?"

"People are afraid of what they don't understand. They seek to subjugate it, to make it conform to what they do understand."

"Simon, what happens to their power?"

"Nothing. It is right there within them."

"Then why can't they show it?"

"Because it's not the same kind of power. All of this was set in motion a very long time ago, before the known histories you study in your classes. The Essence are the embodiment of all Kinetic power. They each specialize in one of the elements: Pyrokinetics, Hydrokinetics, Geokinetics, and Electrokinetics. As I'm sure you know, Aerokinetics are somewhat rare these days. They each have a nickname, but their official names are all linked to the element in question, and that power stems directly from the Essence. The Aether is a realm none of us can truly understand, but it's made, essentially, of everything and every element. This is where all life originated. And so, there is Kinetic power in all of it, even time. Chronokinetic, though you will rarely hear it used, means shaping time itself. The Essence hold that power equally, or at least they used to."

"You didn't answer my question."

"I did, actually."

"Are you saying the Voids can control time?"

"No, that is not what I'm saying. I'm saying their power, like that of time and all the others, comes directly from the Aether."

"And the Aether is made of everything." *Every element.* "Are you saying . . ." The words caught in her throat. She couldn't finish the sentence.

"Some possess very specific pieces of the Aether."

"So . . ." Aurianna said, thinking it through, "instead of having the power to control the elements . . . they are essentially, a vessel holding a piece of an element. The actual element itself. The source of the power."

"The source of it, but not the control of it."

"They can't control the element they possess?"

"Think of it like a recipe card. One side contains the ingredients needed. The other contains the instructions for how to use them." He leaned forward. "We heard about your little fiasco down in the tunnels. With your Fire training."

The day she had almost blown up her teacher.

"Yes?"

"You had a third person with you that day, did you not?"

The Void. The one who had fainted when she had created the explosion. No, not fainted. What she had done to him had been far worse.

"I . . . I . . ." Her way with words today was top notch. But she couldn't breathe at the thought of what she'd almost done, what she could have done to that Void.

"Didn't you think it odd the Magister reacted as he did?" Aurianna remembered Magister Daehne had been shaken by the experience, barely speaking to her for a long time after that. After he had gotten over what must have been shock, the man had seemed far more interested and excited in her training.

"Do they know? The Magisters, I mean?"

Simon shrugged. "They have an idea. But no one wants to face it, so they ignore it."

"Has that happened before?"

He shook his head. "Not often. It takes an awful lot of power to bleed a Void like that. Most Kinetics can barely move the elements in the world around them. Plus, the Void would have to be made of that specific element."

"Fire truly is my specialty then?

"Ask the question you want the answer to, Aurianna."

"Is my power different from other Kinetics?"

"Oh, yes. Very much so."

"Why? And don't say it's my destiny. That's horseshit."

Simon winced at her vulgar language. "You are confusing the idea of destiny with some all-powerful entity controlling your life."

"Isn't that exactly what destiny is? Prophecies and all that nonsense?"

Licking his lips, Simon turned his gaze to his feet, his face scrunching up as he fought to find the words he needed. "You said yourself you choose your own destiny. You don't know how right you are. When I say I cannot tell you things or help you beyond a point, I am being truthful. I *cannot* say some things, and I *cannot* do some things. Not yet, anyway. The only person with any ability to make their own choices right now is you."

"I don't understand."

He inclined his head. "Then perhaps you should attend to your studies."

"You mean in here?"

"I mean whatever you think is best."

Frustrated with his vague answers, Aurianna spun away to stomp off to her table in the back, to return to her "studies" as he called them. A few steps away, she paused without looking back. "Simon?"

"Yes?"

"I hurt that Void. Didn't I?"

Silence for the briefest of moments. "Yes. You took too much. Drained him."

She blanched at this admission, the confirmation of her worst fears. "Then I'm no better than those in my time who tortured the Kinetics."

She felt a hand on her shoulder, a light touch followed by a squeeze. "It was an accident, Aurianna. Draining others is forbidden here, but energy exists in everyone to some extent. Even non-Kinetics. Voids just have more of it, and it flows out of them much more readily."

Turning around, she looked up into his eyes. "There is a man, a Void, who keeps staring at me. I think he might have even followed me around. Do they know? Do they somehow sense what I did?"

"They don't know what they are, what they possess." He looked too pained to continue, but he said, "Maybe you should speak with him."

She nodded, though she knew she didn't have the courage.

Walking back to the table, Aurianna looked at the book containing "her" prophecy. She glared at it, willing the book to spill its secrets to her.

"Show me what I need to know," she mumbled irritably, opening the book to a random page. It was blank, as were most of the other pages she leafed through. Clearly the Essence had not deemed those pages appropriate to be known yet. *What a stupid system*, she thought as her eyes scanned for some invisible marking, some sign of the pages hiding their contents.

Nothing. They were completely and truly blank.

The ones that did contain words felt just as empty, or they might as well have been. She stopped at a page filled with drawings, symbols like the ones in the hidden passage. She had seen some of them before, in books and at the temples, but she hadn't really paid much attention before. The picture at the bottom of the page looked like Theron's necklace. It seemed to be a combination of the symbols, a testament to some long-forgotten unity among the Essence.

A few minutes later, she came across the page with the words she had dreaded ever since she had first read them:

> *When the red sky at morning*
> *Bursts forth to cleanse the land,*
> *Beware the dragon's warning,*
> *For the end is close at hand.*
>
> *Rising up to heights unknown,*
> *Burning forth to scorch the sky;*
> *Beware the infernal stone,*
> *For the end of all is nigh.*
>
> *She will steal your life,*
> *For the world to burn and bend.*
> *Beware the silent knife,*
> *For she will be your end.*

Aurianna turned the page, hoping for something, anything to connect all the disjointed ideas spinning around in her head. On the back of the page were more drawings, along with words scribbled in the margins.

Her breath caught in her throat, the page before her swimming in her vision, the words hazy and swirling as she fought for a solid grip on reality.

She recognized that handwriting.

It was her own.

Chapter 15

AURIANNA

Aurianna slammed the open book down on the counter before her. Simon, standing on the other side, jumped briefly from either the noise or the sudden movement.

Yet he did not move. His eyes did not stray from hers. Deep pools of gray, a storm behind the clouds she saw building within his gaze.

"No. More. Lies." Her chest heaved with other words, unspoken words, uncontrollable sobs suffocating her with a blind rage. This was madness.

"I haven't lied to you. Not once."

"Omitting the full truth is the same as lying!"

Simon placed his palms on the counter to either side of the book, an audible sigh escaping his lips. "I told you there were things I couldn't say, things you needed to find on your own. I've never denied that, never hidden it."

The offending page, the evidence of something beyond her comprehension, stared up at them, mocking her. Pulling at the strands of her sanity. She pointed to the writing at the edges of the page. "How?"

"These rooms are fluid beyond time. I told you that."

"So ... I've been here before?"

"Many times, yes."

"Why couldn't you tell me that?"

"Would you have believed me? The Essence show us what they can, in the manner they choose. You needed to find the proof through the natural consequences of your decisions."

"These rooms are outside of time, yet I have somehow traveled here. Has my memory been tampered with, or is this some future version of me?"

"Neither."

"Neither?"

"It is always your twenty-year-old self who comes here, who finds those drawings and the words you wrote down."

"But I haven't written any of this. And you said it isn't some future version of me."

"Time is a very complicated mess, Aurianna. And we are in dangerous territory here."

"When did I write this? And what does it mean?" The writing was unmistakably her own, but the words in the left margin were just common knowledge, nothing world-shattering or shocking. *Symbols represent the elements: Fire, Water, Earth, Energy, Air.* Underneath those words were more. *Each element managed by one of the Essence: Caendra, Unda, Terra, Fulmena, and Caelum. Air is weak because of Caelum. Why?* In the right margin, near the bottom: *Control is key. I made a promise to Larissa. Nothing is worth my heart. Trust the right ones.*

"I can't—literally I cannot—answer your questions until you ask the right ones. When is irrelevant."

"How is it irrelevant?"

"Because the 'when' in question is outside of your current reality. That 'when' does not exist, as far you're concerned."

"Why did I write these words then?"

"To find a way to stop the singularity."

"All of you keep using that word, and I've just been going along with it. But what does it actually mean?"

"The singularity is the moment at which time itself becomes infinite. In that moment, only you can choose your path and stop it. If you succeed, we can alter the future and make different decisions. Until then, time will continue in the same pattern it always has—infinitely—resulting in the future you've been a witness to. The singularity is a precise moment when the correct path being chosen will erase the time loop this world has been stuck in for a very, very long time. Long before anyone currently alive remembers. Arcanes have this knowledge for the same reason we knew what happened on the night of your birth, and for the same reason we know anything."

Aurianna remembered the tome Simon had mentioned before, the source of their knowledge. "The Book of Histories."

"Precisely."

"I want to read it."

"I'm afraid that is impossible. Until you stop the singularity and open the loop, anything outside the prescribed chain of events must come directly from your own blind choices, or not at all."

"Or else the timelines will explode." Her tone was flat as she stared at him in mocking incredulity.

Simon winced. "Something like that. The timelines are very fragile, and only one can exist or be known at a time. At least, that's the case for most of you. Some beings exist outside of the timelines."

"Like you."

"Yes, like me. Like the other Arcanes. Like the Essence. Like . . . others. We know and see each possibility, each timeline, each direction the tree could branch. We also watch and remember each time it doesn't, each time the singularity occurs and the actions taken result in a failure to stop it."

Dizziness took over her senses again. Aurianna reached out for the nearest chair, almost missing her target until Simon came around and helped her to lower herself into the seat.

He patted her hand. "I know it's quite a lot, and I realize you're overwhelmed—"

"Me? You're saying I've done this before and failed. How many times?"

"Too many to count."

"And you've watched me fail each time, watched everything play out over and over." A sudden thought slammed her body back against the chair. "What happens to me?"

"Doesn't matter. What matters is—"

She reached forward, grasping the front of his robes, naked fear in her eyes. "Simon, tell me."

Wiping a hand across his face as he wrenched himself free of her clutches, the man seemed to age in an instant. His face became haggard. Shadows under his eyes blossomed into dark circles she hadn't noticed before. The weight of the world was on his shoulders. On the shoulders of all the Arcanes. To watch, helplessly, as the world burned. Over and over again. With no ability to change it.

Simon finally spoke, his eyes refusing to meet hers. "You die."

* * *

Aurianna stumbled into the temple, not caring how much noise she made or who might be inside. A cleric walked in to address the sounds echoing around the chamber, but the look of her—hair wild, eyes frantic—must have scared him away. He turned around and left without a word. She was kneeling before one of the altars, caught somewhere between fear and anger, her head spinning with the words *you die.*

She had been dying over and over in an endless loop, and no one had bothered to tell her she was marching to her death. Terra, goddess of Earth, had been less than forthcoming, but perhaps a chat with another deity was in order. Despite her overwhelming feelings, Aurianna had deliberately passed up the closer temples, choosing instead to visit the temple to Caendra, goddess of Fire. At least she knew some connection existed between this goddess and her own abilities. And she'd been here before.

Like the other temples, the related symbol was etched all around, altars and trays dispersed in a circle around the center. This temple had more candles than she had ever seen, scattered all around the room. A large fire, the flames of which rose to just beneath the ceiling, filled the middle of the circular space. A chest-high wall encircled the fire.

Unsure of what to say, she began a prayer of mumbled words, asking for guidance, for answers. It would be enough. It had to be.

She glanced around the altar to the flame-enclosing wall, hoping to see Caendra perched on the high edge. Nothing was there.

A moment later, Aurianna was startled enough to emit a high-pitched scream when a figure appeared right in front of her, leaning on the altar in a very un-goddess-like pose. The woman emitted the same otherworldly glow as Terra had—the same slight transparency. This goddess was just as beautiful, but with hair of light brown, several shades darker than Terra's blonde locks.

The illumination radiating outward was enough to almost blind Aurianna at so close a distance. Caendra was goddess of Fire, and that is exactly what she appeared to be made of, her glowing form alight with what looked like tiny flames.

The goddess spoke first. "I would have thought you were expecting me, what with all your muttering and praying."

Aurianna looked behind her. The enormous fire was paused in its movements. She turned back around. "Everything is stopped?"

"Of course. Can't have the locals thinking we're so available, can we?"

Caendra's words angered her. Sputtering, Aurianna said, "Yes, it would be *terrible* to give the people hope, now wouldn't it?"

A smile was still plastered on the goddess's face, widening to show perfectly white teeth that seemed to dance in the flames consuming her. Cocking her head to the side, she replied, "And why would having us here give them any more hope?"

"Because they need to know someone is looking out for them. Which clearly you aren't, or you wouldn't need me here to keep trying and failing at your little game of life and death."

"What makes you think this is a game?" Caendra's fire lurched forward as she moved closer to Aurianna. "What makes you think we have any more control over it than you do?"

"You're a goddess! You and your siblings created everything in this world. You could stop this if you wanted to."

Caendra shook her head sadly. "No, we cannot. We have been banished from this world for a very long time."

"And yet here you are."

The goddess hissed. "Our time here is limited. Our ability to affect anything has been taken away. Our silence is not our own doing."

"Then whose is it?"

Luminous eyes pierced through the flames, then turned upon the floor dejectedly. "One who stole everything from us. Stole our—" She seemed to struggle with the words, unable to speak the ones she wished to speak. "I cannot say more. We cannot enter this world for long, and we cannot do so without stopping time. It isn't a choice. Terra tried to tell you that."

"Why do I have to die?"

"There is no 'have to' in any of this. You do not have to die. You must, in fact, live. Else we will be trapped in this loop for all eternity. In your hands lies your own destiny, but ours as well."

"Why me?"

"Because you were born of a union . . . a union that changed things. You alone of all humans have a connection to the deeper magic, through a random set of events no one could have predicted. Perhaps they are not random, but that fate is not of our doing. When we were banished, it was a calculated move to strip us of any power within this world. Your parents found one another despite impossible odds, and your ability to affect change was granted the moment your curse was transformed into a protection spell. That spell provided a way out, a way to undo it. It was a spell to keep you safe and bring you back. You can break the loop and begin the journey to free us. But you have to listen to your own heart."

"That's very helpful. Thank you." Aurianna deadpanned.

Caendra's smile turned rueful as she sighed. "You've been given the information you need, the clues to help you. You've kept a record of them."

"The book?"

"Yes, and that's not a small thing. You possess more clues than you realize, but you must unlock the answers yourself. Your experiences are neither meaningless nor random. Listen to what you hear and follow what you see."

"Can you tell me if there is any meaning in these dreams I keep having?"

The goddess hesitated. "Yes and no. There is meaning in the answers. Some have not been revealed to you yet. That is the only place where our influence can reach through, albeit only in small ways."

"So, these dreams are coming from you?"

"From the Essence, yes. Collectively we can breach the wall of your unconscious mind when you sleep and push images through to guide you. But the wall is still there, even if it is hazier. Once you stop the singularity and open the loop, we can reach you more freely within the dream space."

"And then it will be over? The war, all of it?"

"No," Caendra replied, shaking her head as she moved closer. "The war will not be over. The battle will be won, and the next phase will be possible. Until then, we will never even reach the next phase. If you want answers, if you want our help, you must succeed."

"If I've failed so many times already, how am I supposed to . . . why does anyone expect me to do any better this time?"

"You were groomed for this role, as hard as that may be to hear. Larissa loves you. She knew what she had to do. Her job was to prepare you, but she failed in that. Something changed this time though."

"What changed? You said things can't change."

"You can because of what and who you are. Because of your curse, the spell, and the preparations your aunt made to ensure you were raised outside of the dangerous section of the time loop. Something made her change her tactics though, but you'll have to ask her that yourself." The figure began to fade, waves of light and half-substance swimming before Aurianna's eyes. "I'm being pulled back, so I must go. Follow your heart, and choose wisely, child."

The goddess of Fire was gone, her ethereal flames extinguished as time began to push forward once again. The sounds in the room and the crackle and hiss of flames pounded in her ears as Aurianna struggled to her feet and left the temple.

CHAPTER 16

LEON

"Ladies, ladies, please," Leon drawled, an arrogant smile playing on his lips as he threw his hands up to stop the onslaught of shopping bags being thrust his way. "I know I said I'd take you shopping, but I ain't your pack mule, all right?" They had just exited a boutique in the main square of the capital city, a small shop specializing in cosmetics.

Laelia and Sigi glared at him as Aurianna yanked her bag back with a sheepish grin. Of the three, she had the least number of packages. And she had thanked him. She wasn't the problem.

Leon glared back at the other two.

Sigi broke the silence. "And here I thought you were a gentleman."

Laelia snorted in a very unladylike manner as she rolled her eyes. "Right, yes, that's the description I'm always hearing. *Oh Leon, so polite and gentle with the courtesans.*" Aurianna tried to hide her smile behind a hand.

"I'll have you know I *am* quite gentle with any and all women."

Leon smirked in Laelia's direction—a gesture which he knew rankled.

"Any and all. Right."

He frowned, snatching the bags from the three of them. "Fine. I guess this is all I'm good for then." He shrugged. "Where to next, ladies?"

Ever since the official announcement for the Yule Ball had gone out to the denizens of the Imperium, it was all anyone could talk about. Kinetics in Bramosia and dispersed throughout the five regions also received invitations. Only Kinetics would be in attendance. The rest of Eresseia would hold their own winter festivals and celebrations. Leon wished desperately for an opportunity to sneak out and join the other festivities in town, or even back home in Ramolay—avoiding his family, of course.

That would be his own personal hell, as he'd learned in the past. He would never make that mistake again. Family was overrated. He would attend the ball for the sake of his friends, for the sake of Javen who had been hounding him about it. Even Theron seemed overly interested in what amounted to a stuffy party full of food and dancing. And drinking. But drinks were easy to come by in any pub in any town.

Sigi's voice cut through his thoughts. "There's a dress shop I like just two streets over."

Laelia said, "But Roma always has the latest styles. Her shop is right over there"—pointing at a storefront three doors down and across the street—"and she always takes very good care of her customers."

Sigi shrugged. "Sure. Plenty of time to check out more than one shop."

The girls strolled leisurely down the row of shops. Leon followed, his arms laden with bags full of feminine hair products or makeup or whatever it was the girls had spent an hour gushing over at the boutique.

As Leon went to step across the street, an ear-splitting boom rocked the ground beneath them. He was thrown forward, knocking Aurianna to the ground just before he landed on top of her. Leon barely managed to roll to the side to avoid all his weight crushing her. His vision was blurred by the tremors that continued every few seconds, but he could see the figures around them frantically dashing to the nearest wall or sturdy pillar to lean against. Some people just sat to avoid being knocked down. He hoped they'd not be trampled by the panicked crowd.

After a few moments, the shaking subsided, leaving behind a landscape of disarrayed bodies. The people slowly began to make their way to their feet. Leon got up and looked all around, trying to determine the source of the tremors, but he could see nothing.

He reached down to help Aurianna to her feet. When he turned to the other girls, Sigi was already struggling to right herself and shake the dizziness from her head. Leon hesitated half a second before offering his hand to Laelia, who surprised him by taking it without so much as a glare or snarky comment. The situation must have dulled her senses.

"What the hell was that?" Sigi asked, gazing around in utter confusion.

"It seemed like it came from over there," Leon pointed toward the entrance to Bramosia, where the cliffs loomed in the distance, "but I can't be sure. We should go check it out."

The streets were filled with curious citizens who furiously threw questions at one another. No one seemed to have the answers. Guards rushed by, impatient with the crowd and anyone in their way. Sigi led her friends to the guard station, a small building which housed the town's local City Guard members. The City Guard was made up of Kinetics from various regions within Eresseia—those who showed an affinity for weapons and wished to pursue the life of a guard.

Sigi peered within the small space. "Empty. Weapons are gone as well."

"No one came back this way. They must have gone on past here then."

They walked out of the main area of town, heading to the cliffs. Members of the City Guard, as well as other people whom Leon recognized as fellow Kinetics, stood in small groups gazing down at the lagoon below and talking in loud voices.

Leon approached a woman he knew as another Hydrokinetic. She was almost a decade older, her short dark hair blowing in the wind coming across the cliff's edge. "Fay, what's going on? What was that?"

The woman shrugged, a far-off look in her eyes. "Dunno. Looks like the irrigation channels up the side of the cliff have come dislodged."

"Dislodged?"

"Yeah, I really ... I just ..." Fay's words trailed off in the wake of her overwhelming confusion.

"You just what? What is it?"

The woman shook her head violently as tears filled her eyes. "Oh, Leon." Her lip quivered with unspent emotion. "You heard it. The explosion." Fay nodded as a look of understanding crossed his face. "It's the resistance. Gotta be. Especially after all the commotion in Eadon recently."

Sigi stepped forward, crossing her arms. "Eadon has always been an issue when it comes to Kinetics."

Aurianna looked at Sigi quizzically. "Why is that?"

"A lot of them are resentful of the Aerokinetics scarcity. Some even think we're intentionally stifling it somehow." When Aurianna started to open her mouth to reply, Sigi shook her head and held up a hand. "I don't know. It's just envy and bad feelings all around, and we can't do anything to stop it because we don't know why it's like that to begin with." Looking around the group, she let her eyes land on Fay. "Anyway, all I was saying was, those protests aren't anything new."

"Yeah, but they've become more organized," Fay replied. "Everyone seems sure the resistance movement is behind it. They've got a name and everything now. Calling themselves the Order of the Daoine."

"Day-oh-een. What . . . what language is that?"

"No idea."

Leon reached out to steady the Hydron as she wobbled, swaying on her feet. "Honey, how about you go sit down? Where's Juliet? She can walk you home."

Fay looked up at Leon, her eyes blinking in confusion. "She's gone."

"What do you mean *she's gone?*"

"I thought she said you knew. Her and Orion left a couple of weeks ago. They went to visit family, I think. Should be back any day to comply with the control measures."

"No, I guess I forgot."

"I'll walk her home." A voice behind them made the women jump. Leon turned around to smile at Javen, who sidled up to the group with a cheeky grin on his face. "Been trying to get Fay alone for quite some time now, anyway." Javen winked at the older woman, who blushed and dipped her head at his words.

Always the charmer. Leon rolled his eyes.

Leon saw Aurianna hide a snicker behind her fist, coughing out the sound before anyone else noticed. He nodded to Javen. "Thanks, brother."

"So, what's going on? Felt like a damn earthquake back at the Imperium."

"I thought you were 'busy' today," Sigi said, a knowing look on her face.

"Yeah! What was so important you couldn't help me play bag-sitter?" Leon asked, a pretense of indignation screwing his mouth up into a pout.

"No one held a weapon to your head," Laelia replied, "though I wouldn't have minded the opportunity to watch you squirm a little."

And here Leon thought the girl's switch was set to non-bitch for once. No such luck. "Just because you force all your gentlemen friends at the end of a barrel doesn't mean we all work that way."

She narrowed her eyes and threw a sardonic smile his way but thankfully kept whatever she was thinking to herself.

Since no one seemed to be answering Javen's question, Leon volunteered the only thing they knew so far. "Probably the resistance is behind it. At least that's the current theory."

A look of amusement danced in Javen's eyes. "Really? Behind *what* exactly?"

"Someone sabotaged the irrigation pipes." Sigi was looking around for something as she spoke, her voice sounded distracted.

"So, the water system's damaged? Interesting."

Javen's words were innocent enough, but the tone gave Leon a chill for some reason. He stared at his friend for a moment, unsure whether to comment or not. Making a mental note to bring it up when they were alone, Leon stepped closer to Javen, puffing out his chest. He was well aware he cut an impressive figure.

"All right, buddy. You walk Fay home, and we'll see what we can find out about what happened. Let's meet at Madam Trudel's in about half an hour or so. And afterward, how about *you* carry some of these shopping packages, okay?"

Javen gave a one-finger salute and put his arm around Fay's shoulders, leading her back into Bramosia. Leon and Sigi marched over to the nearest guard, Laelia and Aurianna trailing behind.

Sigi caught the attention of one of her fellow guardsmen. "What do we know?"

He scratched the top of his head, looking back down at the water. "Well, as far as we can tell, someone's sabotaged the water system."

"The water's poisoned?" Sigi asked, concern etched on her face. They were all thinking back to the last time the water supply had been tainted, when presumably, the Enchantress—or whatever the hell she was—had somehow contaminated the wells in Rasenforst with dragonblood.

"No, not the water supply. Or at least, I don't think so. It's the system itself. The infrastructure and irrigation channels the Hydrons use to move the water into town and anywhere it's needed."

"So, we have no water here now?"

"We have no way to get the water up here. The lagoon's too far away for even the best of us to pull it up without the channels in place. We'll have to come up with something in the interim while the system's being repaired."

"Which will take how long?" Aurianna chimed in.

The guardsman looked at her like he hadn't realized she was there until that moment. "No idea, but they'll get started as soon as possible. We sent word to the Imperium to let the Magnus know we may need to pull some workers from other regions. People experienced with this kind of stuff." He was scratching his head again.

Leon thrummed his fingers against his leg, his mind racing over this new predicament. This would mean more hours and more work for him and the other Hydrokinetics. He sighed, grumbling to himself.

Making up his mind to worry about that later, he plastered a smile on his face, displaying a happiness he was far from feeling. "Sounds like tomorrow's going to be a lovely day for me. How about we head over to the pub to meet Javen? Ladies?"

Sigi stood glaring down the cliff face, shaking her head. "Hard to see the damage from here, but part of the cliff is gone." She turned back to the group. "Nothing to be done for now, I guess. Let's head on, then."

They walked in silence, Leon leading the way.

* * *

After meeting up with Javen and stopping for lunch at a local cafe, Leon and his friends picked up where they had left off before the explosion: dress shopping.

He was *thrilled.*

But at least he had Javen to be miserable with now, and another pair of hands to handle the multitude of bags the girls kept thrusting their way.

At the first dress shop, Laelia and Sigi both were fawning over what Leon had to admit were quite beautiful ball gowns. For some reason, he had a hard time picturing Sigi in one, even though she'd gone to every Yule Ball since he'd known her. As rough and tumble as she seemed with her lean muscle and athletic build, Leon had always been amazed at how feminine she could be when it came to things like cosmetics and finery.

Neither female deigned to show them what they had bought, simply handing the packages over to the men as they walked by. He'd see them on the night of the ball.

Sigi was complaining she hadn't chosen her dress yet, and Leon wondered what was in the bags she had handed him. Knowing Sigi, probably more cosmetics. The woman ducked into yet another shop as their package handlers took a much-needed rest on the bench outside the store.

Leon and Javen lounged in the afternoon sun as they waited on Aurianna and Sigi to try on fifty-seven thousand more dresses—a slight exaggeration perhaps, but not by much.

Feeling an odd rush of nervous energy, Leon turned to Javen and asked the question that had been on his mind since their earlier conversation. "You okay, man?"

Javen's forehead wrinkled in confusion. "Yeah. Why?"

Leon shrugged, turning his gaze back to the street in front of them. "Just wondering. You've been more irritable lately. And earlier, you…"

"I…what?"

"You almost seemed amused by the whole thing." Leon looked back at his friend again.

Javen visibly bristled. "So, which is it, Leon? Am I irritable or amused?"

Sighing, Leon leaned forward on his elbows, balancing his weight on his knees. "I just meant…it seemed like something was on your mind."

"Am I not allowed to have thoughts?"

"Well, yes, of course you are. But you can always talk to me if something's bothering—"

"I appreciate it, Leon, but I really don't need your help. I was amused the resistance has gotten so bold. I admit it. I'm not sorry for what they did, but I had nothing to do with it, if that's what you're thinking."

"I wasn't thinking anything. I was just offering an ear is all."

"When I have something to say, you'll know it." The decidedly unnerving look returned to Javen's eyes, the corners crinkling in amusement at some secret thought.

Fine. Let him be moody if he wants to be. I tried.

A rustling behind them caused them both to turn toward its source.

Sigi approached, sporting a rather large bag, which she promptly handed to Leon with an expectant smile.

"You didn't find anything?" Javen asked Aurianna as she walked out empty-handed.

Laelia looked put out. "The lady who owns the shop brought out practically every dress for her to try on, but nothing seemed to satisfy her."

"In fairness, I agree with her decision," Sigi said. "None of those were right for her. Though I do love mine. Thank you for recommending this place, Laelia. It's a bit pricier, but well worth it."

"Where to next?" Leon asked.

"We can take a look in that shop I was talking about earlier," Sigi replied. "It's just a little way, and hopefully we can find her something."

When they reached the store, the girls walked in, followed by Javen. Leon cocked his head to the side and said, "And where are you going?"

Javen turned, the corners of his eyes crinkling in amusement. "It's boring just sitting outside, don't you think? At least they have cushioned seating in here."

Leon was happy to see Javen's mood seemed to have shifted. He shrugged, following his friend inside. The girls were scanning row upon row of fluffy fabrics, each one more decadent than the last. Why women felt the need to wear those monstrosities, he would never know.

Javen sat on a nearby bench, so Leon took the seat beside him. He took off his hat and placed it over his face as he leaned back against the wall. After several minutes, Leon realized he'd been nodding off as he jerked forward, his hat tumbling to the ground. He heard voices coming from the back of the store. It sounded like the girls were arguing. Javen was nowhere in sight.

Following the sound of the voices, he came upon a scene he wasn't sure how to process. Javen was holding up two dresses in front of himself, identical in style but one was pink, and one was blue.

"What the actual hell are you doing, man?" Leon whispered.

Javen gave him a sheepish grin. "Just helping out."

Sigi grabbed the pink one and held it up against Aurianna's figure. "This one." She held it out for the other girl to take it.

Before Aurianna could react, Laelia snatched the blue one from Javen's other hand. "No, the blue one looks better on her." She held the dress out to Aurianna expectantly.

"The *pink* one is prettier. Pink is *always* prettier."

"Not on her! Not with her coloring. She definitely needs to pick the blue one."

"Pink!"

"Blue!"

Aurianna was looking at her two friends, eyes tinged with uncertainty, but she wasn't moving to take either of the proffered garments. Leon watched as the two continued bickering. They seemed to be completely oblivious to Aurianna's discomfort, not to mention the commotion they were causing. People in the store—both customers and clerks—were covertly watching the scene unfold.

Leon decided enough was enough. "Look, Aurianna, which one do you like better?"

The poor girl seemed skittish and darted her eyes at him like she had forgotten anyone else was there. "Me?"

"Yes, you. It's your dress. You're the one wearing it. Which one do you prefer?"

"The blue one is—" Laelia started to say.

Leon cut her off with a jerk of his hand. "*Aurianna*, which one do *you* want? If you were here by yourself, which one would you pick?"

Her cheeks flushed as she finally whispered, "The pink one, I guess."

"Ha!" Sigi didn't bother to hide her gloating. "Like I said, pink is always prettier."

Laelia rolled her eyes, refusing to show her disappointment. "Color doesn't work on her, but whatever. Do as you wish." She turned away with a bored yawn, strolling back down the aisle as she ran a finger down the line of merchandise. Even though he agreed with her, Leon refused to say so aloud.

The shop clerk, who had been hiding in the corner, stepped forward and took the dress to wrap it up for sale. Aurianna gave the woman her name to take the credits from her account with the Imperium.

After making sure all the appropriate undergarments had been obtained—an experience that would have been the highlight of Leon's day had it not been for the frustration and boredom that was setting in—the group went to a local costume shop specializing in seasonal items. The Yule Ball was a masquerade, so each of them— the men included—would need to get a mask to complement their attire. Leon and Javen already had their formal wear for the party.

Leon was making his purchase, his mind already jumping ahead to their next stop—which included a drink or three at the pub— when the ground beneath his feet began to rumble, followed by the now-familiar sound of explosions.

All of them ran out of the store, leaving behind their purchases and bags. The sound of the store clerks' shouting was a vague backdrop to the blasts that continued to rock the area for half a minute after they reached the outside of the shop. Leon looked both ways and led them to the end of the street where most of the Kinetics seemed to be heading as everyone else ran in the opposite direction to safety.

"Do you think it was meant to go off when the others did?" Javen panted, out of breath as they continued to race to the location of the explosions.

No one bothered to answer. They came to a stop at the edge of the cliff once again. Sigi walked up to the nearest guard, speaking in low tones for a moment before returning to the group.

She was nodding as she approached, but her face was ashen. "Yeah, it looks like the first set of blasts was intended to trigger this second set almost immediately, but something went wrong." She hesitated, glancing behind her at the chaos ensuing around the entrance to the irrigation system tunnels. When she looked back at the group, Sigi's eyes were full of unshed tears. Leon reached out and pulled the tiny woman into a tight embrace, and she buried her face in his massive chest as a sob escaped her throat.

Sigi drew back, shaking her head. "They sent in a team to investigate the damage, and I guess they… they triggered the undetonated devices somehow." She crossed her arms against her chest, drawing a deep breath. "At least one person died, and the rest aren't in good shape. Someone went to get the healers already, but I don't know what all they can do."

Aurianna reached out and placed an arm around Sigi's shoulder. "I'm so sorry, Sigi. It was someone you know?"

"Yeah." Another sob from the guardswoman as she fought to regain her composure.

Laelia grabbed Sigi's hand, her face contorting into a grimace. "I'm sure the healers will do everything they can and take good care of them. There isn't anything we can do just now. Why don't we leave them to it and get that drink, okay?

Leon wasn't sure what he was more surprised by: the fact that Laelia had shown sympathy toward another human being, or the fact that he agreed wholeheartedly with her idea.

209

CHAPTER 17

AURIANNA

"Happy birthday, my darling girl." Sigi's father was embracing his daughter with a fondness that made Aurianna's chest ache with the twinge of jealousy that lurked there.

Sigi had invited her on a visit to her family home but had neglected to mention it was her birthday. "Sigi, why didn't you tell me?"

"Oh, our Sieglinde has always been funny about that," her father replied. Sigi's eyes rolled back in her head at the use of her full name, but clearly her father got a free pass. She was normally very vocal—even physical, Aurianna recalled—when someone dared to call her that. Her father didn't seem to notice the reaction. Johan Hellswarth was built like a powerhouse and was in good shape for his age. As one of Rasenforst's most talented weaponsmiths, he and his sons worked very hard to keep the family business running.

"But why?"

Sigi shrugged. "Lots of birthdays in a family this big. It's not a big deal." Sigi and Hilda were the only females and the only Kinetics of the eight siblings in the Hellswarth family. Aurianna couldn't imagine having one brother, let alone six.

"I beg to differ." The deep voice behind them echoed in the stillness of the front entrance of the home. Theron stood at Sigi's back, his hands wrapped around a gigantic bouquet of flowers, his fox winding a path around his ankles. Aurianna bent down to let Rhouth sniff her hand. She was Theron's animal companion, his helper during hunts. "Happy birthday, Sig." He handed her the bouquet and placed a chaste kiss against her temple.

Aurianna looked away, feeling awkward and uncomfortable at the display considering what she suspected about Theron's feelings for Sigi. Johan reacted with a similar attempt at throwing his attention anywhere but in front of him. Aurianna wondered if he knew.

"Well," Johan said, gesturing inside the house. "Everyone, do come in. Theron, can you stay for dinner?"

"I, uh...I don't want to impose." Rhouth gave her master a contemptuous look before gliding through the sea of legs to enter the house without a glance back.

"Don't be ridiculous, boy. Come on in." The four of them made their way to the kitchen, where Sigi's brothers—all six of them— were crowded around a table laden with food. Aurianna was surprised to see Hilda sitting among them.

Sigi seemed just as surprised. "Hilda? How did you get here?"

The younger girl smirked. "Jumped on an early train this morning. Surprise!" She held out her arms, hugging her sister fiercely. "Happy birthday, sister."

Aurianna knew better than to desire something she could never have. Still, she secretly longed for the closeness something like sisterhood could provide. She wanted to be close to people, but it never seemed to work out well.

Simon's words echoed in her head, the conversations she'd had with both him and Caendra banging against her skull, begging to be shared with someone. Yet she couldn't bring herself to do it. Did she trust anyone—even Sigi—enough to share that terrible dark secret with them? Could she bring herself to tell someone about the true nature of her destiny?

Everyone sat down to eat the evening meal. Idle chitchat took up most of the conversation until one of the brothers, Will—the eldest, if Aurianna remembered correctly—asked about the explosions in Bramosia.

"So, do they know anything else about the business with the bombs?"

Sigi sighed, putting her fork down. "Will, really?"

"I'm just concerned is all."

"Well, first, we don't know for certain they were bombs. Second, all we can do is try to fix things while also beefing up security. Shifts have been insane lately, but we don't want something like this happening again. The water channels are going to take a while to replace, so the Hydrons are on double duty as well. They have to work in tandem to get the water all the way up to the cannisters."

"What about the second explosion?"

"It's complicated, but it took out the underground sections. Or part of them at least. The Pyros are in an uproar over it because they can't get to the magma now without burning themselves. Everything's exposed and dangerous at the moment. So, no hot water, no heating systems, no ovens for cooking. At least not for most of the town. They've been able to get a minimal amount of fire up into the sections considered most vital. The main square, the cafes, the pubs, any of the public spaces."

"Everyone's having to eat out at the restaurants then?"

"No, oddly enough."

"So how—"

Sigi's head snapped up as she leaned back and crossed her arms in front of her. "They're doing it themselves."

"Doing what themselves?"

"Cooking. Starting fires. A few areas have created neighborhood cooking fires for people to come with kettles of water or pots of food to heat up."

"Huh. Good for them." Will went back to eating, a look of contemplation on his face.

"Good for them?" Sigi was seething. "You do understand these attacks totally undermine our ability to help them, right?"

"What makes you think they need you to help them?" her brother Emery asked. The rest of the family had been sitting in silence, watching the conversation thread its way along to this point.

Sigi glared at him. "Now you sound just like them."

"Like who?" Aurianna was confused.

Her friend slowly turned to face her, eyes cutting daggers at every face along the way. "The resistance group. The Order of the Daoine, or whatever they're calling themselves. They ended up taking responsibility for those explosions in Bramosia and tampering with the irrigation systems. They want to get rid of us, Aurianna. Don't you understand that?"

"Get rid of us? Like, as in *kill* us?"

Sigi shook her head. "No, but they want our power taken away. They want us to become totally useless."

"Just because the townspeople are fending for themselves doesn't mean we're not needed, Sigi." When the other girl shot her a hurt look, she continued, "I'm not defending the resistance. I'm just saying it's not a bad thing if people learn how to do some things for themselves."

"I guess."

Johan cleared his throat. "How about some cake for the birthday girl, huh?"

Sigi's face brightened a bit at his words. Anton, Sigi's younger brother, gave his sister a squeeze on the shoulder on his way to the kitchen. When he returned with the biggest chocolate cake Aurianna had ever seen, all the negativity seemed to ebb from the room in one swift whoosh of exhaled air.

When everyone retired to the family room after stuffing themselves with dessert, Theron hung back in the shadows with Rhouth at his feet. Aurianna edged over to him as the others were reminiscing over childhood memories, a conversation she felt inclined to disengage from anyway. Theron glanced at her from the corner of his eye, returning his gaze to Sigi almost immediately. He wasn't even trying to be subtle about it.

Rhouth was looking up at her owner with undisguised irritation in her features. Maybe she was jealous.

"Have you ever told her?" she whispered as quietly as she could.

He visibly jolted at her words, squirming under her penetrating gaze as he fought for a reply. "What?"

"Don't 'what' me. You know exactly what I mean."

"Not sure I do."

"Fine. Be that way. But . . . I think you should tell her."

"Why?"

"Because no one ever seems to want to tell anyone the truth around here, and it might actually be a nice change of pace. Besides, I think you might be surprised by the answer."

Now she had his attention. Theron had turned his entire body to face her, looking into her eyes with a desperation she had never seen him show before. After a moment, he shook his head, sadness replacing the brief glimpse of hope she had caught in his gaze. "I need to get Rhouth back to camp. We have an early start tomorrow and a full day of tracking to look forward to." He raised his hand to the group and said his goodbyes, leaving without even looking in Aurianna's direction. The fox trailed in his wake.

Despite his abrupt departure, she decided to follow him outside. He was halfway down the street when she called out to him. "Theron?"

He stopped but didn't turn. "Yeah?"

"You said you were tracking tomorrow. Not hunting?"

He stood for a moment, finally walking back to her. She met him halfway. Whispering, he said, "More Voids have gone missing. The Magnus didn't seem too put out before, but now it's becoming a problem. He doesn't want this to get out to the general population."

"Of course not." Her sardonic reply caused the tiniest of smiles to creep onto Theron's lips.

He tipped his hat. "Goodnight, Aurianna."

"I'd like to help."

Inclining his head to the side, he asked, "Why?"

"Because, despite what everyone seems to think, I am here for a reason. Simon—one of the Arcanes—he told me some things about the Voids. I haven't told the others yet, but I think it might be connected."

"What kind of things?"

"Let me help you track them down, and I'll tell you everything I know. We're staying here tonight, so I can meet up with you whenever you like."

Pursing his lips, Theron mulled over her words. Slowly nodding his consent, he said, "All right. But I'm starting at dawn."

* * *

"Are you sure about this?" Theron's voice cut through the early morning fog as Aurianna stood waiting outside Sigi's family home.

"Why wouldn't I be?" she asked.

His figure suddenly loomed just in front of her. "Tracking isn't the most glamorous job, nor is it likely to be as interesting as you probably think it is. Just ask Rhouth. She's not too keen on searching for things that don't fill her belly." He nodded down to the animal, who looked up at him in exasperation. She let out a sharp yelp, the sound swallowed by the dense misty air.

Aurianna knelt and held out her hand to the fox. Rhouth padded over, stretching her torso as she let Aurianna pet her orange-red fur. "She looks ready to me. Aren't you, girl?" The fox gave another quick yelp in affirmation. Aurianna stood. "Let's go."

Theron led her over to the local stables at the edge of Rasenforst. They would be taking horses back to Bramosia to allow for brief stops along the way. Aurianna hoped Oracle would forgive her for riding another horse just this once.

According to the hunter, at least five Voids had gone missing so far. In the exchange of information, Aurianna shared everything Simon had told her about the Voids. The man was normally adept at hiding his shock and maintaining his composure, but her words had a clear impact on him.

"They're *made* of the elements?"

Aurianna's attempt at a shrug was counteracted by the cantering of the horse beneath her. "So says Simon."

"Well, I mean, I guess it makes sense, but I don't understand why the Arcanes would keep this to themselves. If the Magnus or the Magisters know—or even suspect—about this, and they aren't saying anything, why would the Arcanes just stay silent? Why not tell the world?"

"I get the feeling they're under orders on just about everything they say and do."

"From the Magnus?"

"No, from … it's complicated."

"Uh huh," Theron muttered. Aurianna knew he was frustrated at her holding back, but she didn't know how to explain it all. Or if she even wanted to.

They rode in silence for a while, stopping whenever Rhouth got excited over a scent. Aurianna was unclear as to the exact nature of how she was tracking the Voids specifically, and when she asked Theron about it, he simply replied, "She's smarter than both of us combined. And she knows it."

When they reached Bramosia with no definitive leads, Aurianna was beginning to feel more desperate than ever. Always more questions, never enough answers. They dropped their horses off with the stablemaster, and Aurianna briefly visited Oracle, who gave her a look of pure condescension, as if she smelled the other horse's scent.

Aurianna and Theron made their way to the entrance to town. Just before reaching the capital city, they both stopped, stunned at the scene that greeted them. They hadn't been able to see the cliffs on their way to the stables, but now the view was laid out before them. Up and down the side of the cliff, where the saboteurs had destroyed much of the infrastructure for the water system, the stairs carved into the cliff face were filled with a line of people. They were passing container after container from one person to the next, almost machine-like in their motions.

Aurianna cocked her head to the side, turning a questioning look at Theron. "This is new."

He nodded absentmindedly, pushing his tongue against the inside of his cheek, puffing it out as he scrunched up his eyes in fascination. "Yep."

"What are they doing?"

"They … are gathering and transporting water to the city."

"Who are they?"

"Not Kinetics, I can tell you that much."

Aurianna couldn't hide her smile. "So, they're handling things. Is that what you're telling me?"

Theron's eyebrows shot up. "Find that amusing, do you?"

"Not amusing, no. But, as someone who spent most of her life fending for herself and working hard just to get by, I can't say I don't appreciate their efforts."

Theron returned her smile. "Good."

"Really?"

"Yeah. I get it. I daresay that's possibly part of the reason for the attack in the first place."

Aurianna gasped. "To force the non-Kinetics to stop relying on us so much, you mean?"

"Yep." Theron pulled something from his pocket and threw it to Rhouth, who snatched it up in her mouth before Aurianna could even see what it was. Theron reached down and ruffled the animal's head. "Let's go."

Twenty or so steps further on, Rhouth suddenly took off down the main street, making a beeline for the middle of town. They followed her, but the fox didn't stop at the square. She kept going at a steady pace, paws careening along the pavement, occasionally bouncing back to make sure they were following before taking off again. Eventually, she slowed down as they reached the top edge of town, just before the Consilium.

Turning in a circle, Theron looked around with a wildness to his eyes, frustration showing in the lines around his mouth. "So . . . I think you're losing your touch, old girl."

"Maybe not," Aurianna said.

"Meaning?"

"Meaning there's a whole maze of passages beneath us." She

shrugged. "Who's to say there aren't even more tunnels than the ones I've seen so far?"

"Fair enough, but you're talking about solid ground and stone beneath us. I don't think my little friend here is *that* good. Probably just her stomach talking." Rhouth glared at him for a full five seconds before making a noise not dissimilar to a huff.

Aurianna laughed. "No, but I think we're heading in the wrong direction either way. The tunnels are the key. I'm sure of it." She narrowed her eyes at the hunter. "If I ask the Arcanes, I'll just get the same old vague nonsense. Unless, of course, I 'ask the right question' or whatever."

"So, what now?" Theron gazed intently at her. "You giving up?"

"No, but I think Rhouth has given me another plan."

"And what's that?"

"Dinner."

"You heard her, Rhouth. Let's go." He spun around and strode back to the entrance of the town. The fox shot her tail up into the air and followed behind Theron's retreating form.

CHAPTER 18

AURIANNA

Aurianna stared at the open box sitting on her bed, biting her nails as she contemplated the unexpected container. The contents were both exciting and distressing. And there was no note.

It made no sense.

The box had been sitting there when she'd returned to her room, waiting for her like a ghost.

Tonight was the night. She had her dress and everything she needed for the Yule Ball, so why would Javen send this?

Maybe he didn't want her to know it was from him.

Still, she had to admit it was a brilliant choice, far better than anything they had looked at. The yellow-gold hue glowed with a sparkle that didn't come off as gaudy or ridiculous. In fact, it was possibly the most beautiful dress she had ever seen.

Made of satin and taffeta, the ball gown had a tight bodice and full skirt, though not overly bell-shaped. Off-the-shoulder sleeves with a thin gauzy material that swooped across the front left the rest of the arm and shoulder exposed. The décolletage was low-cut yet classy, certainly less revealing than some of the ones she had seen in the shops. The sparkle came from the satin material which took over most of the dress, rows upon rows of ruffles that held an ethereal sheen even in the low light. The bottom was exquisitely feminine, flowing in soft but voluminous waves.

And it was far too expensive. She would never have bought anything this extravagant. The cost would exceed her allowance for at least six moon cycles.

How had Javen managed it? He didn't even receive an income yet, only the base allowance given all Acolytes. She couldn't believe he would do this, no matter his feelings for her. It was just one night.

Hands trembling, she lifted the dress higher in the air and shook her head in incredulity. Maybe he had pulled some strings or something. Maybe he knew someone.

Bare shoulders were still a little unnerving to her, but this was a whole new level of lavishness. No sense wasting the effort he had made.

After taking a long shower, she approached the box again, pulling out the dress and fingering the petticoat underneath. She put on undergarments and slipped the golden dress over her head before stepping over to the full-length mirror. She threw a guilty glance at the pink dress she had bought for the occasion; it looked pitiful hanging against the wall. Hopefully, she'd be able to return it. She'd never been certain about the color, and Laelia had seemed to think the same. The blue had been a somewhat better match for her coloring, but this...

Staring at her reflection in the mirror, she was hit full force with the brilliance behind the color choice.

The image before her was stunning. Her amber eyes had a natural glow to them, especially in low light. Now they were competing with the light of her bedroom, and the golden dress managed to pull the luminescent streaks from her amber eyes and put them on display for the world.

She looked down, smoothing the skirts as she tried not to cry. It was such a silly thing to cry about, especially with everything going on in her life. But standing there, entranced by the glow emanating from her own eyes reflected in the gown, she couldn't help wondering if this night was somehow bigger than she realized.

Turning slightly, she looked back over her shoulder to stare at the word branded into the skin on her right shoulder blade, right near the top. *Effugere.* This would be the first time anyone here would see it, but she knew she shouldn't be worried. Plenty of others had tattoos, and according to Sigi, it was a personal choice, not a punishment as hers had been. The word was written in the old language, something she had always been told was as ancient as the world itself, far older than anyone—other than maybe the Arcanes.

And even though they most likely already knew about it, the Arcanes wouldn't care about her having been marked with a word meaning *runaway*. They seemed to always know far more than they were willing to acknowledge about everything.

Perhaps they even knew something about the missing Voids. Her hunting expedition with Theron and Rhouth had turned up nothing. Nothing useful at least. Exploring further in the underground tunnels was the next step, but it would have to wait until after the Yule festivities were over. Kinetics from all over the land were here to join in the celebrations. Too many people asking too many questions.

A buzzing sound interrupted her thoughts and signaled Sigi's arrival. The girls had agreed to meet up early to help each other finish getting ready. Laelia had a fellow Vanitian helping her. She declined Sigi's offer to help her with her cosmetics, stating the other girl was better at helping with her ivory-pale skin, which was probably true even though Sigi knew at least as much about cosmetics as she did about weapons and fighting.

With a final glance down at the change in attire, Aurianna realized Sigi was probably going to squeal. Preparing her ears for the onslaught, she opened the door and beamed at her friend...

...who did indeed squeal, right on cue.

Dragging the other girl into the room before she could alert the entire dormitory, Aurianna stepped back and threw out her arms. "I know. But let me explain—"

"Where did you get that? And how much did it cost?"

"I didn't. And I don't know. It was sitting on my bed when I came back to shower."

Confusion warred with the excitement on Sigi's face. "So, wait. How then?"

"I guess Javen changed his mind about the pink dress?"

"Well, clearly, but that's not what I meant. How did he get into your room?"

"Cleaning crew maybe?"

"Maybe." Sigi frowned. "Not that I don't love it, but we got all the accessories to match the pink one. Which I will gladly take off your hands. If you don't want it." A fierce grin still covered her face, and she waggled her eyebrows.

"It's all yours. I appreciate your opinion, but I think Laelia was right. Pink is more your color."

Sigi held up a small handled case she'd been holding at her side. "Shall we?"

They spent the next hour finishing the process of getting ready. Sigi, despite her love of pink, had chosen a champagne-colored dress for herself, with a mask in a light shade of cream that looked lovely against her russet-colored skin. Sigi's tattoo climbed down her neck and shoulder to the top of her right arm, the thin lines fiercely elegant, whatever the design was meant to represent.

Sigi turned her back to Aurianna, looking over her shoulder as she held up her long hair. Aurianna stepped forward to lace up the back of the other girl's dress. Clearing her throat, she asked, "What do your markings mean?"

"It's something from my mother. She used to draw a lot when she wasn't helping my father or taking care of us. I was really young, but I remember evenings when she would sit on a chair in the family room and sketch out scenes, or portraits of us, or anything that came to her mind. This was one of her abstract drawings. It was probably her favorite one, I'd say. Helps me remember, you know?"

"Yeah." Aurianna's voice was barely a whisper. She turned to let Sigi lace her up.

She'd forgotten about her own branding until Sigi lightly ran her finger across it. "What's yours mean?"

For a moment, Aurianna didn't answer. People would naturally ask about it, so shying away from the truth was pointless. "It's in the old language. Means *runaway*."

Aurianna expected her to focus in on the meaning, but instead Sigi said, "What old language?"

"I don't know. That's just what the Praefects and Consils called it. It's ancient and hasn't been used in a very long time, whatever it is."

"Huh. Nice."

Nothing else was said about the marking as they worked on each other's hair. They discussed the evening ahead, what hairstyles were best, and which color lipstick to wear. Aurianna was staring at herself in the mirror far more than she was want to do. She hated her freckles, so she chose to focus on the aspects of herself she did like. Her eyes weren't bad, she had to admit. Their unique golden hue had always given her a small feeling of pride, and the dress had only improved that feeling. Her cheeks were rosy with excitement.

Aurianna's copper-brown hair was pulled back, Sigi braiding it into an intricate series of swirls, the bottom half cascading down her left shoulder in a loose, wavy plait.

Sigi had opted for a full updo hairstyle, with loose pieces curled around her face.

They found a pair of golden slippers within the folds of the packaging in the box, along with a golden mask decorated with sequins and crystals that bounced the light around the room.

"Oh my Essence," Sigi whispered.

"I was about to put on the white one we bought to go with the other dress."

"No. This is infinitely better."

"Agreed." The mask was simply exquisite, and Aurianna shook her head. "He shouldn't have done this."

"Well, he did, and you must humor him. As unbearable as it may be." Sigi giggled. "Oh, poor you."

"Right." Aurianna returned her friend's smile as they smoothed their dresses out and sauntered down to the main hall.

* * *

Everything was lit up like something out of a dream—the wall tapestries overrun with holiday cheer in honor of the Yule Ball, a celebration of the solstice and the winter moon cycles that led into spring.

The weather near the Imperium was typically warm, but a slight chill pervaded the air during this part of the year. It was nothing compared to the cold Aurianna had lived with for most of her life, or the chilly frost of Rasenforst and the northern areas of Eresseia. But here in the southern portion, nestled between fields of green and the dense forest, the climate felt almost perfect.

The entire main level of the Imperium was decked out for the occasion, including the grounds and gardens outside the main entrance of the hall. The Yule Ball was a time for food and drink, fun and laughter, or so Aurianna had been told. The length of the enormous room was lined with tables laden with foods of every kind, sweet and savory, along with drinks in every color imaginable.

Literally every color imaginable, in various shades of each.

As Sigi and Aurianna entered the crowded hall, they quickly spotted Laelia standing back from the throng, an equally pale girl at her side. When they approached the duo, the other girl whispered something to Laelia and walked over to the food table. Laelia wore her new red dress with a black sash, complemented by a shiny black mask edged in lace and black satin shoes with the tallest heels Aurianna had ever seen. The girl didn't need any help in the height department, so the shoes made her look like a giantess.

Everyone else must have been having the same thought. Aurianna could feel every eye in the room looking in their direction. It wasn't until they were standing directly in front of the walking tree of a girl that Aurianna realized Laelia wasn't the center of everyone's attention.

She was.

Laelia was gawking, staring openmouthed with a look bordering on obsessive fascination with a side of intense jealousy. "What. The. Actual. Hell." Crossing her arms in front of her, she added, "Girl."

Sigi, thankfully, came to her rescue. "It was a last-minute, surprise gift. *Someone* left it in her room."

Laelia raised her eyebrows. "Someone meaning Javen?"

"We assume so, yes—"

Aurianna interrupted her next thought. "But I'd rather you not bring it up. It may be that he doesn't want anyone to know, so don't mention it unless he does."

"I really don't think it's an avoidable topic of conversation." Laelia scoffed, a look of mild amusement on her face. "Everyone— and I mean, *everyone*—is currently staring at you like you grew an extra head." Her smile faltered slightly after the words left her mouth. "But in a good way," she hastened to add.

Aurianna blushed at the girl's words, though she knew they were true. Everyone was staring at her, and she did look amazing. Like she'd been dipped in gold and sprinkled with sunshine. Instead of responding, she asked, "Speaking of which, where are the boys?"

"Who the hell're you calling *boys*?" Leon's deep drawl boomed above the din echoing throughout the room. He wore black pants and a black tunic, with a sleek matching jacket trimmed in thick silver thread woven into the lapel and edging.

"Nice mask," Sigi said.

"Why, thank you," Leon said as he laid a hand against the side of his silver mask. He took a long, not-so-subtle look at Aurianna before adding, "Though I do believe I've been outdone tonight."

Aurianna wasn't sure if Leon realized she was wearing a different dress from the one she'd bought on their shopping trip, but either way, he was drawing even more attention to her attire. Theron stood just behind him, dressed in dark brown and green with a matching green mask. Javen wasn't with them, a fact which Aurianna was grateful for considering the current context of the conversation. She changed the subject. "Where's Javen?"

"He . . . well, he was right behind me," Theron said. Other than looking over his shoulder for his friend, he hadn't taken his eyes off Sigi since they'd walked up. He had barely even noticed Aurianna, a fact which spoke volumes. Aurianna gave him a knowing smile, which he also ignored.

"Who was?"

Javen sauntered up behind the girls as Aurianna turned around to face him. Dressed in pure black from head to toe—including his mask—he stopped in his tracks as he saw her face, but only faltered for a brief second. After an awkward moment, he smiled at her and offered his arm. "And it looks like I've got the most beautiful girl in the room as my dance partner."

"If I'll have you," Aurianna teased, smiling into his deep brown eyes and all the warmth they held.

Javen reacted with a pretense of shock before leading her off to the dance floor.

Just before they reached it, she realized she wasn't ready to embarrass herself like that just yet. Tugging on his jacket, Aurianna gently led him over to the refreshment table with a sheepish smile. Grabbing two glasses, he handed her one with a smile. "Whenever you're ready." Lifting his glass in a toast, he said, "To a little liquid courage then." They clicked their glasses, and Aurianna downed half of her drink in the first gulp.

They watched as a few couples were tentatively beginning the night's festivities with a dance that looked somewhat familiar to her, based on the practicing she had done with Javen. They watched for a while and, after a couple of drinks, Aurianna felt somewhat better about going out on the floor. More couples were joining in, so blending in with the crowd would be easier. The last thing she wanted was to draw more attention—but of the wrong sort—to herself.

As she set her glass on the table, she looked up to tell Javen she was ready. She was aware of a sensation on the back of her neck of being watched. She immediately began to worry the Void who had been stalking her was at it again. However, she dismissed the thought when she remembered no Voids would be in attendance at this celebration.

The thought still plagued her as she waited for Javen to finish his drink. She turned her attention to the dais where the Magnus sat looking out over the crowd. To his right stood his son. And Pharis was staring straight at her, although it was impossible to read his expression from this distance, especially through a mask.

She was relieved to know the source of her discomfort, even if it meant it was the Regulus. Feeling emboldened by his unabashed staring, she decided to stare right back. Although, she doubted he would care that he'd been caught staring.

His attire for the evening was midnight blue trimmed in a deep gold, with a blue and gold capelet draped over one shoulder and an indigo-colored mask also outlined in gold. The Magnus wore a deep shade of plum purple, also trimmed with gold, accompanied by a solid gold mask.

Even as she pointedly returned his gaze, the Regulus continued to stare—the decidedly bold, bordering on rude gesture making her feel oddly exposed.

Finally, pulling her gaze away, she looked around the hall and tried to take it all in. The decorations were beyond anything she could have imagined. Many of the Acolytes had helped in preparing for the ball, but the Youngers, even who had worked on the decorations, weren't allowed to attend. They would have their own activities going on in other areas. The ball was for Olders and adult Kinetics only. Presumably, Kinetics were in attendance who lived and worked in the various regions across Eresseia and only came to the capital city when it was time to check in.

Despite the vastness of the hall, a plethora of bodies crowded the space, and the air was almost stifling. More and more were heading to the dance floor, so Aurianna looked to her date and nodded to let him know she was as ready as she would ever be.

Javen had been practicing with her for weeks—sometimes into the wee hours of the morning—to at least familiarize her with some of the more common dances. A few were somewhat familiar to Aurianna. Although very little dancing occurred in the future, occasionally, small celebrations would bring out the human instinct for dance and song.

But some of these dances were far more intricate. A large group of musicians sat together, playing instruments of all shapes and sizes, most of which Aurianna had never seen before. They would all be Kinetics, but she had no idea where and when they learned to play music.

Javen placed a hand at her waist and one on her shoulder as she did the same to him, swallowing the lump in her throat. She allowed him to lead her around the floor, managing to swirl and twirl at the appropriate times—for the most part. After a few songs, she began to lose herself in the movements and enjoy herself. The drink had probably played no small part, and Aurianna realized she would need to be careful and not indulge in it too much tonight if she wanted to keep her head.

Feeling sweat begin to settle on her skin, Aurianna felt overheated by both the dancing and the crowd of people swarming closer and closer. As the song came to an end, she was about to ask if they could take a break and have another drink—though water was more on her mind than anything else—when a hand lightly tapped her shoulder. She saw the look of utter disgust on Javen's face, so when she turned, she wasn't shocked to see Pharis standing there, bowing slightly and holding out his right hand in a gesture that seemed to indicate he wanted her to join him. Throwing a look at Javen, she fumbled to find the right words, unsure of how to respond.

Aurianna turned back to Pharis, struggling to hide her shock. "Can I help you?"

The Regulus wore a teasing smile, his eyes never leaving hers.

"Well, this is typically a gesture asking if you'd give me the honor of a dance."

Aurianna heard Javen growl behind her just before he muttered, "Get lost." The words were low enough not to attract attention but loud enough to reach the other man's ears.

The anger rose on Pharis's face, and hoping to prevent an all-out fight in the middle of the dance floor, she placed a gentle hand to Javen's chest and leaned in to whisper, "He may have an important message for me from the Magnus or maybe the Arcanes. Just one dance. I'll be right back. I promise. I was just about to ask about getting something to drink. I'm so thirsty. Could you please get me some water?" She leaned back to look at his face. Javen was gritting his teeth and glaring over her shoulder, not even looking at her. "Once the next song is over, okay?"

She could feel Pharis behind her, waiting patiently for her to join him. Aurianna raised her eyebrows and nodded to Javen with an encouraging smile. "It could be important, you know?"

After a tense moment, he returned her nod. Straightening his spine, he walked away in a huff. Aurianna turned back to Pharis, who was still holding out his hand. She gingerly placed her own in his palm, and he pulled her toward him, placing a hand on her waist as he slid the other up her arm. She silently prayed Javen wasn't watching them.

The Regulus was clearly trying to stir up trouble.

With a devilish smile, he led her in dizzying patterns around the sea of bodies cramping the dance floor. These were moves she was not prepared for, nor accustomed to. The heat she had already begun feeling from the night's exertions increased as the upbeat tempo of the song echoed in her ears. It was already winding down, so she knew she still had another full song before he was done with her. The speed of their dancing made it difficult to speak with him.

As the music slowed, she narrowed her eyes at him. "You did this on purpose. I'm guessing no one sent you, and you're just trying to piss him off."

Pharis laughed, the corners of his eyes crinkling with genuine amusement, more mirth than she had probably ever seen him display. "Perhaps I did enjoy that more than I should have. But no, that wasn't my main intention."

"So, you do have a message for me?"

"Message?"

"From your father. Or the Arcanes."

"Well, no, actually. I just thought perhaps—"

Before he could finish his sentence, the music trailed off and a new song filled the hall. It was a tune much slower than any they'd played so far, and her feet struggled to find the rhythm. Javen hadn't practiced anything this slow with her. Finally, she gave up and let Pharis lead.

Everyone on the dance floor had shifted their hold on one another, so she wasn't surprised when Pharis wrapped his arm further around her waist. He pulled her in closer, the side of his face pressed against her temple, the fingers of his other hand interlocking with her own.

"What . . . what are you doing?" she asked, even though the answer was obvious.

His entire body seemed to stiffen, and his movements froze for half a second. "This is just . . . I mean, it's a slow song." He pulled back after a moment of silence and looked at her quizzically. "They don't dance in the future?"

"We did!" Aurianna was indignant, though his tone hadn't seemed mocking. "I mean, some. And we have practiced over the last several weeks, but nothing like that."

Pharis pulled her in close again. "You mean lover boy didn't teach you how to slow dance?" His breath was hot against her ear, sending shivers down her spine as he spoke.

"He's not my . . . no, he didn't." A heavy sigh echoed in her ear, but her dance partner didn't respond. She frantically searched her mind for a topic of conversation as they slowly swayed to the music among the remaining couples on the floor. This kind of dancing didn't involve much footwork, which should have made it easier for Aurianna. But the *closeness* left her mind fuzzy and her head light.

Grasping for anything to keep her thoughts occupied with something other than the man pressed against her, she suddenly remembered he never finished his sentence before the song started. "What were you going to say earlier?"

"Huh?"

"When the last song ended, you said you didn't have a message for me, but you started to tell me why you came over."

"Oh." His voice was raspy, almost a whisper. "Doesn't matter." After a moment, he added, "I just . . . I mean, you look . . . this dress. It really is perfect on you. You belong up there standing next to my father. Honestly, with the dress, you look like my sister."

"I look like your sister."

"No, not like that! You don't look like my sister. I'm just saying . . ." He sighed again, shaking his head. "You look amazing. The most beautiful girl in the room by far."

Any words she had been about to say slid off into an abyss of silence.

The silence lasted for a full half of a minute. Then, "Was that a compliment?"

He laughed, letting out a breath he'd been holding for far too long, by the sound of it. "Yeah, I guess it was. I'm not a complete ass, you know."

"Perhaps not. But telling me I look nice one evening doesn't exactly make up for your previous behavior."

"In case I didn't make it clear, 'nice' doesn't really describe it. You look like an angel in that dress. I'm very glad you wore it."

"So, this is all about my dress?"

"No, that's not . . . I wasn't . . ." He growled, the sound a deep rumble in his chest that resounded in her own due to their proximity. The sensation started a flutter that made her head swim. "The dress accentuates your eyes. It accentuates you." His head dropped a fraction of an inch toward her shoulder. "Your eyes have this thing about them, this glow. Especially in the dark. I've never seen eyes like yours. It was the most defining characteristic the Arcanes gave me to help me find you."

"They knew my eyes were amber-colored?"

"Yes." They swayed to the music in silence. "And I'm not trying to."

"Trying to what?"

"Make up for my previous behavior. I've had every right to be angry with you on multiple counts."

"Do you just get off on holding grudges against people for perceived slights against your royal person?" She was, of course, referring to his accusations against Javen, and she hoped he grasped her meaning.

Instead of yelling or storming off, he surprised her by laughing. "My royal person?"

"You do have an unusually high opinion of yourself."

"What makes you think that?"

"You came over here and asked me to dance with the full certainty I would say yes."

"And you did."

"Yes, but only because I hoped you might have news for me."

"All business tonight, are we?"

"When it comes to you, yes. I'm sure your father is bursting with joy seeing us dancing together."

"Told you that ship has sailed."

"Not if he thinks he can get us to do it voluntarily. The Consils couldn't do anything about it if it's our choice, I'm guessing."

"Are you proposing?"

She pushed against his chest, her mouth open in incredulity as she met his mocking eyes. "What? No!"

His devilish smile had returned. "We could go right now and make it official."

"You *are* a complete ass."

Laughing loud enough to attract a few stares from the dancers around them, Pharis pulled her back into a close embrace. "I was joking of course."

"It wasn't funny. That's the sort of thing that's going to get Javen into a fighting mood. Considering you're the Regulus and if he touched you, he'd probably be arrested, I'm guessing that is exactly your intent."

"Or maybe I was just trying to lighten the mood."

"I didn't realize the mood needed to be lightened."

"Too many things are weighing on my mind these days. I've often been accused of being too serious, too solemn. Sometimes—and only sometimes—you make me feel like I can think about other things and perhaps laugh a little. I'll admit I was angry when you left to go back."

"You were angry at me because I was going home?"

"No, Aurianna. I think you know why I was angry."

"I really don't." She could hear him grinding his teeth, but she didn't know what to say. At the time of her departure, they had barely spoken since the night of the train incident. What could she possibly have done to upset him?

"Then it doesn't matter."

A note of sadness in his words carved a small hole in her heart.

She decided to change the subject. "I guess you know about the missing Voids by now." Why had she chosen that, of all things, to discuss? He was already moving into a sour mood.

"Yes. Apparently, you do as well."

"Well, it's not exactly a secret."

"It would be if my father had his way." His voice dropped even lower as he spoke the words.

"Really? So, he doesn't like people knowing about this. But I mean, why does he care if they're just Voids? Nobody seems too concerned about what happens to them."

"Nobody? You're painting with an awfully broad brush there, don't you think?"

She closed her eyes. "No, you're right. I know you're not your father. But it's not like I see you trying to free them or anything."

"Free them? Like their slaves or something?"

"Aren't they?"

"Of course not. They aren't able to join the Kinetic community in the normal types of jobs we do, so they help out in other ways."

"Help out? They do your cooking and cleaning, and they take care of the place. They do all the stuff it takes to run everything around here but don't get paid. No allowance or bank account for them, right? And relationships aren't just frowned upon for them. Simon told me it's absolutely forbidden for them to be with anyone who isn't a Void. Sounds like slavery to me."

"Who's Simon?"

"One of the Arcanes. He's told me quite a bit actually. For an Arcane, that is."

"So, this...Simon. He's a friend of yours?"

"I don't know that I'd use that word. But he occasionally answers my questions, which is more than most people around here do. Seems like everyone else is either avoiding me or hiding something from me."

"You've got friends here. That's more than I'll ever have. I suggest you not forget that."

"Don't throw your self-pity in my face. My friends are the ones who are avoiding me these days."

"They seemed to be talking to you when you arrived at the ball." Had he been watching her the whole time?

"About unimportant things, yes. But when I bring up anything of actual significance, like the Enchantress or why I'm here, they change the subject or ignore me."

"Hmmm," was his reply.

For a while, they just danced.

Finally, in a quiet voice he said, "I never thought about it like that. It's just the way things are for Voids. It's not like they don't have food and shelter. Besides none of them have ever complained as far as I know."

"Who are they going to complain to, Pharis? I don't think your father would take too kindly to that. I'm not saying I know they're unhappy. I really have no idea. I'm just saying the system seems highly skewed toward those who are in the position of making the rules. Those without power have no one to represent or advocate for them. The non-Kinetics have the Consils. The Voids have no one."

"I wish I could hate you as much as I want to," he whispered, his voice so soft she wasn't sure if she'd heard him correctly. He tensed as soon as the words left his mouth, making her think he probably hadn't meant to say them out loud.

She nodded but didn't speak. She couldn't trust her voice anymore as a strange feeling swept over her. She didn't want to think about it or acknowledge it, but there it was all the same.

No matter what that feeling was, she knew it wasn't right, and her feeling of guilt confirmed it.

The song was winding down. It had felt like ages since they first began dancing, and she needed to get away. Pushing back from Pharis, she said, "Thank you for the dance, but I need some air," and walked off before he could respond.

CHAPTER 19

AURIANNA

When she walked over to the refreshments table, Javen was nowhere to be found, but Laelia was standing by the drinks sipping on something bright red in color. As Aurianna approached her friend, the other girl's smile widened as she waggled her eyebrows. "So…" Laelia had her feline smirk on full throttle.

"Don't. Please don't." Aurianna had subconsciously put her hands on her hips.

Laelia looked her up and down. "Don't what? I just said 'so.'"

"Yes, but there are a million questions in that little word."

"Are you going to answer any of them?"

"Not even a little bit." Aurianna sighed. "There's nothing to answer. Just bad timing on the song and too many assumptions on my part."

"And what exactly were you assuming?" The girl's smile wasn't going away.

"I just thought there might have been something important he needed to tell me or something. I don't know."

"Did you really think that, or is it just what you told Javen?"

Laelia's words were not what she wanted to think about. Her cheeks reddened with a twinge of guilt. She didn't have an answer for that, so she reached behind her friend and grabbed a glass, downing the contents and not caring what they were. She still needed some water, so she walked down the length of the table until she found some.

As she was relishing the cool liquid, Laelia rejoined her. Glancing at the girl out of the corner of her eyes, Aurianna said, "In case it wasn't clear, I was done with the conversation."

"Yeah, fine. I just wondered if you had seen Sigi."

Aurianna laid the cup back on the table, icy fear clutching at her heart. "No, why? Is she missing?"

Laelia laughed. "No, you idiot. I meant have you seen her out on the dance floor?" Laelia spun her around to face the throng on the dance floor. Aurianna's jaw dropped.

The song playing was a little faster than the earlier one, the couples' footwork forming intricate patterns. On the far-left edge of the area, Sigi's champagne-colored dress could be seen amid the twirling before she was pulled back to her partner's arms. The man didn't look familiar, but Sigi seemed to be having a good time. And her dancing skills were very good.

Aurianna gaped for a moment before something at the end of the table attracted her attention. Theron was watching the spectacle, his face so crestfallen she couldn't fathom how no one else seemed to notice. His expression was one of utter defeat. She couldn't understand why he refused to say something to the woman.

As if he could sense her eyes on him, Theron looked over at Aurianna, a flush creeping up under his mask before he quickly turned away. He was making his own choices, and she had no right to interfere.

Aurianna went in search of her date, aware that he was most likely very angry, especially if he had seen even a portion of her time with Pharis.

Stepping out onto the nearest balcony, Aurianna breathed in the fresh air as the coolness of the evening brushed in waves across her overheated face. She chose to place the entirety of the blame for her current condition on the exertion of dancing. The sweat on her skin quickly chilled in the night air and caused her to shiver. She closed her eyes as her mind tried to avoid thinking about the last several minutes.

"Got that out of your system, have you?"

At the sound of the familiar voice, her eyes flew open. She threw a sharp glare to her right where the speaker stood, his back against the balcony railing and his arms crossed. A barely concealed wrath radiated off him in waves.

"Excuse me?"

Javen hesitated before responding. He looked down at his feet, licking his lips and taking a deep breath. "I'm well aware of the effect that man has on women. Everyone knows his reputation."

"I'm perfectly capable of taking care of myself."

The smallest of smiles tugged at the corner of his mouth, but he refused to give her any more than that. "I'm sure you are. In fact, I know you are. But it doesn't take a genius to see what he was doing. That was supposed to humiliate me, and he did it intentionally."

She sighed. "Yeah, you're probably right. But if I had let the two of you get into an altercation, things would've gone very poorly for you, considering who he is. His father would not have let you get away with anything. Especially not tonight, in front of everyone."

"I know." He turned around, placing his elbows on the railing and looked off into the darkness in the distance. The back of the Imperium offered no views apart from the wide, open waters leading to nowhere. "So, did you at least learn something interesting at the expense of my dignity?"

"I thought he might be able to shed some light on the whole thing with the missing Voids, but he mainly spoke about his family."

"I'm really getting sick and tired of his accusations—"

"No, he wasn't talking about you or anything like that. He was just talking in general. He needed someone to talk to. It was just a bonus that talking to me riled you up."

His head jerked in her direction. "That's not funny."

"Come on. Why don't we go back in now?"

Javen reluctantly offered her his arm, leading her back into the ballroom.

Sigi and Laelia were on the other side of the room talking to a group of people Aurianna didn't recognize. Theron was nowhere to be seen. After a moment of searching, Javen spotted Leon on the dance floor and pointed him out to Aurianna. The man was dancing with two different girls and seemed to be having the time of his life.

Javen turned to her with a question in his eyes. She nodded her agreement and let him lead her back into the sweltering mass on the dance floor.

* * *

They danced and laughed for hours, it seemed.

Dancing was easier with Javen, comfortable and less anxiety-inducing. Belinda made several appearances, trying to lure Javen to dance with her. Her gestures weren't subtle in the least, and her juvenile behavior began to grate on everyone's nerves. The girl didn't seem to notice or care, and she continued, although Javen flat out ignored her.

A shout rang out, echoing across the massive hall. The musicians, one by one, stopped playing until silence filled the room. Silence except for the sound of an argument quickly heating up on the other side of the room. Aurianna left Javen behind and pushed her way through the crowd.

The scene before her was so very ordinary to her mind. She had expected some magical or frightening entity, another incident, another disaster. But the reality in front of her was mundane by comparison.

Pharis was shouting into the face of a slightly older man who looked like he was moments away from punching the Regulus in the face. Yelling and getting angry seemed to be a go-to response for Pharis, and she was glad to see she wasn't the only recipient of his rage.

A woman stood just behind the other man, her face streaked with tears and what looked to be more than a little fear. The question was, who was she afraid of, the man in front of her or the Regulus?

The answer quickly became apparent as Aurianna caught the gist of the argument between the two men. The older man was telling Pharis to "mind his own damn business" as Pharis shouted at him about showing respect for others.

"Who I do or do not show respect for is my private concern, not yours!" Spit flew from the man's mouth.

"It's not a private concern when you behave this way in public. And there is never—and I mean never—a reason to raise your hand to a woman like that. You are clearly drunk, and I suggest you leave. Now." The voice of the Regulus had gone cold. A phantom icy breeze swept through the hall.

"You and your father think that just because you sit up there," he pointed to the dais where the Magnus was glaring at the scene with contempt as he whispered into the ear of one of his guards, "you can push everyone else around and always get what you want. The needs of others be damned!"

Pharis took a step forward, putting his finger in the man's face. "That has nothing to do with the fact that you tried to physically harm this young lady. What about her needs, what she wants?" He was speaking through gritted teeth, and Aurianna could hear the grinding noise from where she stood. "I'm pretty sure she didn't come to this party expecting to have her night ruined. Not to mention everyone else's. I tried to keep this between us, but you refused to listen when I asked you to step away from her. Now everyone knows what you did, and that's on you."

The other man grabbed the offending finger in his face. But before either of them could act further, two guards stepped up behind the stranger, pulling his arms behind his back and ushering him away from the crowd. The man was screaming threats until they managed to get him out of the ballroom and away from the scene.

Everyone was looking around at one another, then to the Magnus for instruction on what to do next. The musicians were waiting patiently for the cue to continue the music, but no one seemed inclined to resume the festivities.

Pharis stormed off, not heading for the dais, but instead making a beeline for the staircase leading to his and his father's rooms. Aurianna raced after him, unsure of what she wanted to say or why she was following him.

He opened the stairwell door and disappeared. She reached the door right after him, stopping it from slamming closed as she entered the space. She looked up as the door shut behind her. Pharis was looking down at her with a mix of shock and…something else.

"I'm sorry. I didn't mean to startle you, especially since you're probably already on edge."

"On edge? Why in bloody hell would I be *on edge*?"

"I just meant you seemed really upset about what that guy did and said."

"And what? You came to check on me?"

"Well, yes. And to thank you. For stopping him."

"What was I supposed to do? He was yelling like a damn fool, obviously had too much to drink, and she was crying. They were making a scene, and I tried my best to handle it quietly. He wasn't having any of that. And his words simply proved my point about everyone painting me as a being just like my father. They don't even—"

A multitude of voices on the other side of the door rose as one to cry out in fear. Aurianna and Pharis looked at one another, shock and fear paralyzing them for only half a second before they rushed back into the hall.

People were running to the balconies on the front side of the building, the ones that faced Bramosia and the rest of Eresseia. The two of them followed the crowd, catching snippets of conversations as they pushed their way through the throng.

. . . can't believe it . . .

. . . hope no one's in there . . .

. . . not tonight . . .

As they reached the open air, Aurianna looked into the distance for the disaster she had been expecting earlier. But the problem was much closer.

The forest near the capital city was on fire.

* * *

The night breeze brought with it a faint smell that tasted familiar on Aurianna's tongue and brought an acrid harshness to her nostrils.

The forest is on fire.

Without thinking, she turned and raced to the front doors of the Imperium. People were running in all directions, seemingly unsure of where safety was. Only a handful of City Guards were on duty.

The rest were attending the ball, dressed in their finest and running past her to the weapons storage rooms.

But Aurianna knew no weapon would stop the raging inferno. It needed water. Lots and lots of water.

The forest was a flaming torch in the distance and, as she followed the small crowd across the bridge, Aurianna realized she had no plan whatsoever. She wasn't even sure what made her think she *could* do anything.

Delusions of grandeur. She grunted in self-derision.

The Order of the Daoine had knocked out the irrigation systems, and repairs had not been completed. Putting out the fire would take an enormous amount of water.

Aurianna came to a halt, wincing when the blazing heat reached her skin. She could see several Hydrons working as hard as they could to pull water up in assembly-line fashion, much like the non-Kinetics had done the day she and Theron had been tracking the missing Voids.

This was no less impressive, simply because the Hydrons had no need for buckets, and they could maneuver far more water in less time. The townspeople stood by, willing to help but knowing perhaps this wasn't the time to exert their independence over their Kinetic neighbors. In that moment, they were all aware of their common goal.

Pushing past the growing line of Hydrons, Aurianna made her way down to the bottom of the steps. Not wasting another thought on what she was doing or how it would look, Aurianna dove into the chilly waters. She prayed to the Essence for a repeat of before, hoping for the bubble to form around her as it had that day with Pharis.

But the surface tension of the water gave and moved down with her, encircling her and enabling her to continue to draw air into her lungs. Concentrating on moving the bubble straight up, Aurianna tried to retain as much water as possible. The thicker the exterior of the sphere, the more it would help.

She felt the moment when the bubble broke the surface of the bay. She saw the shocked faces but silently willed them not to stop doing what they were doing. It was going to take all their efforts to stop the inferno.

As she reached a height that seemed well above the treetops, Aurianna willed her bubble to move toward the forest, trying her best to keep all the water pulled against the outside surface until she was ready. She had no way of knowing for sure just how thick the bubble was.

When she felt she was over the edge of the flames, she took a moment to contemplate the sheer lunacy of what she was about to do. If she didn't bring enough water to extinguish the patch below her, she would most likely not survive. A burning death. She shivered.

If she couldn't manage to slow her fall, the ground would kill her. Perhaps she might survive the impact from this height, but it seemed unlikely. Aurianna had never trained the limited air powers she—like all Kinetics—should have had. Although she had never tested her theory, she felt certain that was how she was moving the bubble. Pharis hadn't been in the mood to discuss any of it that day.

Aurianna looked down, drew in a deep breath, and braced herself for whatever might happen. Even if it did work, she would have to do this multiple times to reach enough of the flames to make a difference. She reached out and touched a finger to the inside of the bubble, simultaneously willing her body to float gently down to the ground.

A sharp snap accompanied the bursting bubble, water plunging down past her feet. She could see some of the brightness ebbing away below her, but Aurianna had to concentrate on her landing.

It was no use. She was plummeting far too swiftly, the ground closing in so fast her head began to swim.

Suddenly, Aurianna felt an indescribable sensation take hold of her body, and her free fall slowing down a bit. The inexplicable miracle was enough to bring tears to her eyes. The forest floor was, thankfully, no longer on fire in the circle below her. A tree loomed, and she began to see the flaw in her plan.

She fell past the top of the nearest tree and through the foliage that remained. As she was falling past a large branch, Aurianna reached out and grabbed it with both hands, wrapping her arms across the top to stop her fall.

The impact with the bark scraped her side and took her breath away—and perhaps bruised some ribs—but she slowed enough to avoid any major damage. Aurianna made her way down the tree, branch by branch, using tiny bursts of air to help her progress. None of it compared to that last bit of power she had felt just before she landed in the tree. Maybe the Essence had found a way to help her after all.

As she reached the bottom of the tree, Aurianna looked around to survey the area now fire-free. It was even larger than she had hoped, and a path to the edge of the cliff was now clear so she could make her way back to the steps. All she had to do was repeat her exact movements over and over until the fire was out. And hope she could land safely each time.

Easy.

Follow the path that draws you.

She shook her head to herself as she walked through the trees to the open air by the side of the cliff. A crowd had gathered there, some helping with the water, others just gaping at her with open mouths.

A sudden thought made her look down. Aurianna had known

she must look a mess, but a brief glance at her forgotten attire told her she would never be wearing the beautiful golden dress again. Soot and ash stained her clothing and skin. A few rips and tears could be seen in the fabric near the bottom, probably a result of the tree. She let a moment of regret wash over her before shrugging her shoulders and heading back to the steps to dive into Perdita Bay once again.

A hand reached out and grabbed her arm as she passed the crowd. She turned to see flames flickering in the reflective depths of sapphire-blue eyes.

Pharis put his hand on the opposite shoulder and looked her up and down, a mixture of rage and confusion on his face. "What the bloody hell are you doing? Are you insane?"

Aurianna stepped out of his grip. "I'm trying to help put out a fire. If you'll excuse me." As she turned back to the cliffs, another set of hands reached around her and pulled her close. Sigi wrapped her up in a tight embrace. Behind the woman stood Aurianna's other friends, all of them staring at her with fear in their eyes. When Sigi finally let go, Javen grabbed her face in his hands and furrowed his brows. "What were you thinking? What…what…" His voice trailed off. He planted a harsh kiss on her forehead.

A feeling of intense certainty came over her—a surety of purpose—and Aurianna pulled away to look at the others. She quickly explained what had happened the day she had tried cliff diving and what she had done with the fire. "I have to get back, or it might be too late." Without stopping to answer any more questions, Aurianna sprinted to the steps, people dodging out of her way as she ran down the steps on the side of the cliff.

A raging inferno awaited.

PART THREE

THE WORLD ABLAZE

This fearful dance will set the world ablaze;
Embers ignite, dreams fading into dust.

Chapter 20

LEON

Leon hesitantly rapped his knuckles against the door. Still no answer.

Weird.

"Is there a reason we're standing out here instead of heading to the pub?" Laelia had her arms crossed and her lip stuck out in an obvious pretense of a pout. It was almost cute.

"This is important." Leon could feel his anxiety rising, the trepidation in his mind bleeding out into the air around him. The sun was lowering on the horizon. It was past time to hit the pub.

Theron placed a hand on Leon's shoulder. "More important than a drink? Are you feeling okay, friend?" The hunter grinned, but Leon couldn't bring himself to return the gesture.

Instead, he shook his head sadly. "No, I'm not. Orion has been gone for far too long, and someone said they thought there were lights on in the house last night. It's dinnertime. They should be here. I was worried about them the night of the fire, but no one's seen either of them since they supposedly left to visit family."

Internally, Leon raged at all the questions looming over them, with no answers in sight. The fire that had destroyed part of the forest—though less than it might have, thanks to Aurianna and so many others—was still a mystery. Who had started it, and why? Leon leaned against the door and crossed his arms. "I didn't think they would have left without telling me. This whole thing has been—"

His words were cut short by the sound of the door rattling open on rusty hinges. Leon turned around to see his friend standing in the doorway with a look of absolute joy on his face. Orion gestured for him to come inside. "Come in, friend. I have something to show you." He suddenly realized the others were there as well. "Um, well, hello again. Perhaps you could all come back later?"

Leon frowned. "What's going on? You know my friends. Why are you being so rude?"

"Not—" Orion lowered his voice before continuing. "Not here. It's just…" He sighed and pursed his lips. "Can they truly be trusted? I mean… *truly*?"

"What? Of course they can!"

"Where's the short one? The City Guard?"

"She's on duty right now. And Javen had something to do for a class, I think. Why? Orion, what is going on? Where have the two of you been all this time?"

"Shhhh! I said *not here*." Orion sighed. "Come on then. Inside. Hurry." He motioned them all in and closed the door.

Leon surveyed the room, looking for some sign as to what the hell was going on. He turned in a circle, spreading his arms as he said, "Okay, spill it. Why all the secrecy?"

Just then, a shocking noise erupted from another room, stilling all their movements. It was an unexpected sound in those parts, but still so very recognizable.

The wails of a crying infant.

Shit. Shit, shit, shit.

His mouth agape, Leon pointed behind them. "What is that?" The others were staring in shock as the truth seemed to hit them all at once. Aurianna just looked confused, and Leon could sympathize.

Orion was smiling. The man was actually *smiling*. He shrugged. "My son."

"You have got to be kidding me. Is this a joke to you?"

A soft voice behind him answered. "No, Leon. Not a joke. Meet our child."

Leon turned to face Juliet, who was holding a bundle of blanketed pink skin in her arms. She held the baby out to him as if she expected him to take it without a thought or care.

He didn't move, couldn't move. "Your child? How the hell did that happen?"

Juliet couldn't hide her amusement at his bewilderment. "Do you really need me to explain to you how babies happen?"

"What? No, no. No. I just . . ." No longer able to stand on his trembling legs, Leon sat down on a nearby chair. "No."

Laelia moved in his direction instinctively before stopping herself. "Perhaps you should start at the beginning."

"Before we do so, you must all swear to keep our secret. You cannot share this with anyone, especially your friend the guardswoman."

"What do you have against Sigi?" Theron's voice held menace.

"Nothing. But obviously this could get us in serious trouble. She works for the Magnus. If you weren't such a good friend, Leon, we wouldn't even be having this conversation." He walked over to put his arm around his wife protectively. "I won't let anything happen to Juliet or Levi. This is my family, Leon. I love you like a brother, but nothing is more important to me than these two people right now." Orion squeezed his wife's shoulder.

Juliet looked up at him in naked admiration. "Everyone should sit down so we can explain." The rest of the group obliged her. "The last time you were here, you probably thought we were acting a little strange. Orion was being a bit overprotective, of course, but he had good reason. I was pretty far into my pregnancy, and we were struggling to keep it hidden."

"That's why you left." Aurianna was staring at the woman with a contemplative look on her face. Leon wondered what she was thinking about this whole situation. His own thoughts were a jumble inside his head.

"How?" That was his most pressing question. When Juliet looked like she was going to make another snarky comment, he said, "I mean, how did you bypass the birth control?"

Orion shrugged. "We managed to strike a deal on some bottled water."

"Wait, you were *trying* to get pregnant? Why?" Laelia's high-pitched quip and look of horrified confusion almost made Leon laugh. Almost.

Juliet answered her. "Because we wanted to start a family. Yes, it's against the rules, but the rules are wrong, are they not? Why shouldn't we be able to have children just because we were born with abilities we had no control over?"

"I understand what you're saying, but you can't expect to hide this forever. You may not like the rules, but they're still the rules." Leon was getting agitated at the weight of responsibility this secret was already placing on all of them.

"We just have to hide it until we finally get our transfer to Menos approved. That's where we've been all this time. Orion's sister, sadly, had a stillbirth recently. No one knows she lost the baby. She's going to pretend little Levi here is hers, at least while others are around. It's a good cover. We put in for a transfer when we first found out, but it takes a very long time."

"I just can't understand why you would take the risk!"

"I can." Aurianna's voice was quiet, but the room went silent at her words. She looked around the room in surprise as if she wasn't aware she had spoken aloud. Looking sheepish at her outburst, she continued, "I just mean, I don't think it's fair to expect people to live their entire life under unnatural circumstances. Having a family is a reasonable dream."

"That's not the point!" Leon knew he shouldn't be yelling, and the baby started wailing again to remind him of this fact. The child's screams rent the air, and Juliet quickly began to feed him to keep the noise from attracting the neighbors. "You see what I mean? This is a disaster waiting to happen. There are rules, and we may not always understand them, but we are supposed to follow them. Who knows what the consequences could be?" He was panting in his frustration, so he took a few calming breaths to cool down.

"Do you always follow the rules?" Aurianna was staring at him pointedly.

"What? No, but—"

"And have you ever thought about the fact that the Magnus is allowed to have children with another Kinetic? It can't be that disastrous if they can do it, can it?"

The room felt stifling as everyone stopped to consider her words. Leon realized in that moment there were probably a great many things he had never questioned.

"Well, I'm just concerned that—"

A thunderous boom shook the room. The noise had come from outside. Theron jumped up to look out the door. Juliet ran into the other room with the baby.

After a moment, Theron turned back to face them, a look of frantic worry on his face. "We're under attack."

"What? By whom?" Orion's fear for his family was etched plainly on his features.

"Volanti."

"What are we going to do?" He noticed Aurianna was looking more than a bit nervous at the thought of fighting the creatures once again.

But Leon was used to these interruptions and never allowed himself to be caught unawares. "Well, my first suggestion would be to kill these assholes."

Theron rolled his eyes in Leon's direction. "Obviously. But considering where we are and how many I'm seeing out there, I'm not really sure what you're suggesting. We can't get to the Imperium without walking right through the middle of them."

"What I'm *suggesting* we do is fight them."

"Completely outnumbered and with no weapons?"

"I can't really help with the numbers, but I like to be prepared." Snatching open the door to the alleyway, Leon peeked out and saw the disaster just a few streets over. Two of the creatures were rampaging through the middle of a now-empty marketplace. If the Volanti followed their normal pattern, there would only be one or two more of them somewhere close by the others. Judging by the cacophony of noises in the distance, however, normal was an empty hope at this point.

Leon sighed, steeling himself for the battle ahead as he stepped into the evening air. He skirted the corner of the building and walked purposefully up to a dilapidated refuse bin that looked as if it hadn't been touched in years.

Opening the lid of the bin, he turned to see that, despite the danger, everyone except Juliet had followed him.

"Where did these come from?" Orion's eyes were wide with confusion as he looked at the stockpile of weapons and ammunition laid out inside the container. He wiped his arm across a sweaty brow.

Holding a finger to his lips, Leon said, "You keep your secrets, and I'll keep mine."

Laelia looked both shocked and impressed. "Nice," she said with a tone of grudging respect. A little twinge in his chest thumped against his ribcage.

The monsters could be heard roaring and stomping their way around Bramosia, far closer than was comfortable. Leon motioned for everyone to take whatever they needed. He was already as prepared as he could be, his trusty arm cannon already on his arm. Pulling a cigar from his front shirt pocket, he expertly bit off the tip as he fumbled around for his lighter. He placed the cigar between his lips and lit the end, relishing the first draw as he rotated it around to get the smoke going.

The bin was practically empty, everyone having loaded weapons into any available place on their person. Aurianna had a double holster with a handheld gun on each side. Laelia had a rather large gun in her hands and another smaller one shoved into the side of her boot. The males got inventive with stowing weapons on their persons, trying to arm themselves in every way possible... because by now they had all seen what Leon already knew.

This was no ordinary attack. An entire horde of Volanti had arrived in town.

Chapter 21

AURIANNA

Aurianna was panting by the time they reached the middle of the main square in Bramosia. She had no time to catch her breath, however, as the creatures straight out of a nightmare loomed just ahead.

The Volanti towered over most of the buildings, their sharp claws and teeth glinting in the evening light. Their elongated hands and feet seemed even more surreal than they had before, with the barest hint of a human-like form twisted into something completely horrifying. Their heads, with pointy ears and a wide angular face, sat directly atop bunched shoulders. The membranous wings of several Volanti were splayed out, flapping a beat here and there as they rampaged about the city.

But nothing compared to the horror of those claws and teeth. The curve of claws held an almost graceful beauty compared with the death awaiting anyone who got too close to those razor-tipped fangs.

Orion glanced behind every few feet, and she knew he was worried for his new family. A year ago, Juliet would probably have been out there with them, helping to fight the creatures and protect her home. But now she had something more important to safeguard, and Orion would ensure she got the chance to do that.

Crowds of people lined the streets. At least the Kinetics among them had weapons they could use, even though they had little effect on the creatures. Kinetic powers didn't work directly on the Volanti, but the guns were fired using Kinetic power. Unfortunately, that meant they were useless in the hands of a non-Kinetic.

Aurianna spotted Sigi with a group of other City Guard members, all of them trying to fight the creatures while simultaneously urging civilians—Kinetic and non-Kinetic alike—to seek shelter away from the disaster laid out before them. Vendor stalls were damaged beyond repair and strewn all down the main thoroughfare. Five Volanti clustered together, but Aurianna could hear more in other parts of Bramosia. She knew this was unusual. Something was going on. Why were there so many this time?

She looked around, hoping to find Javen, but she didn't see him anywhere. He had been back at the Imperium, studying for some test. He was most likely still there if he hadn't already joined the crowds gathering to fight the creatures. The other time she had witnessed a Volanti attack, Javen had been eager to fight them. But perhaps they had sealed the exits of the Imperium.

Leon, Theron, and Orion ventured further into town, well to the right of this group of creatures, looking for the ones they could hear but not see. Laelia signaled to Sigi, who responded by pointing behind her. She wanted them to stay behind the City Guard, but Laelia shook her head and joined a group attempting to flank the creatures. They slowly crept forward and to the side, aiming and shooting their weapons the entire time to keep the Volanti distracted from their true purpose.

Aurianna felt lost. She stood where she was, firing both of her weapons simultaneously. Breathing deeply and purposely, she thought back to all her training. As long as she could keep up her strength, the guns would continue to work. She mustn't expend all her energy at once.

A shout to her right broke her concentration. She saw Pharis struggling to shake several guards off his arms.

What the hell is going on?

Keeping alert to the Volanti as she sidled up to the commotion, Aurianna raised an eyebrow to the Regulus when she caught his eye.

Pharis huffed. "These…imbeciles won't let me go. They seem to think I am a child, or worse, completely inept."

One of the guards spoke. "Sire, you are supposed to be inside the Imperium. The Magnus ordered the doors locked and everyone still inside to stay there. This is no ordinary attack. At least a dozen Volanti are in the area."

A…dozen? Aurianna's head swam.

"And that is exactly why I need to be out here! If there are that many of them, you need as many able bodies as you can get to fight them."

As if fighting them ever does any good. Although, if there are over a dozen of them, not fighting them would be akin to volunteering for death.

He managed to wriggle free, but the same guard put his hand against Pharis's chest to stop him. Anger and disbelief flared in the eyes of the Regulus. But the guard didn't seem to notice. "Please, Regulus. The Magnus will not—"

"Hang the Magnus!" Pharis pushed the offending hand out of his way and motioned for some of Sigi's group to follow him. He traipsed off toward the edge of town, well out of reach of the Volanti. Sigi shrugged at Aurianna across the crowd between them and pointed at Pharis. Apparently, she intended to follow orders. Several others went with her.

Where, exactly, is he going?

Aurianna stood frozen for half a beat before following the Regulus's thudding steps. She passed Sigi and her group, ignoring the frown her friend gave her as she walked by. When Aurianna caught up to him, the Regulus glanced sideways at her and rolled his eyes. "What do you want?"

"I want to know where you're going."

"A small group of them are at the top of the hill, near the Consilium." He drew his weapon, pointing the barrel at the ground as he continued walking up the hill.

"And how would you know that?"

"I was on the roof. You can see them from the Imperium. And there's no one heading them off in that direction. A fact I tried to tell my father, but he, of course, never listens."

"What good do you think you can do on your own?"

"The cliff is steepest there. It should be a simple act of luring them off the edge and into the outer waters."

"You do realize they can fly, right?"

"Yes, I realize that, but if we distract them with these stupid, useless weapons, maybe we can get them to back up over the side before they have a chance to save themselves."

"That's a mighty big *maybe*. It's a long drop. Something tells me they'll just fly off, either before or after they hit the water."

"Fine then. They fly off. Problem solved either way."

Aurianna shook her head. "No, not solved. They'll either fly back now, or later. And they might end up just heading to another region, somewhere not so heavily guarded. You do care about your citizens, do you not?"

Pharis sighed, stopping mid-step at her question. The group

behind them was catching up, but Sigi signaled them to stop and wait. He turned to face Aurianna, his hands resting on his hips as he licked his lips and let out a big breath in frustration. "And what would you suggest then, savior?"

That word rankled more than she cared to admit. But Aurianna ignored his sarcasm and repeated her question. "Do you care about these people, Pharis?"

"Of course I care!"

She nodded. "I know you do. You wouldn't be out here otherwise."

"Okay, great. So, what's your plan?"

"I don't . . . I don't have one. I just—" A sudden thought flashed inside her mind. "Wait, I do."

"You do what?"

"Have a plan. Remember what I did with the forest fire?"

"Yes, but we're not trying to quench their thirst, now are we?"

She shook her head. "No, I'm saying maybe I could put *them* in water bubbles and send them over the edge."

"For the love of the Essence, how is that any different from my plan? They still might fly off as soon as the bubble bursts."

"Not if I make sure the bubble isn't a bubble at all. Maybe I can fill it with water instead of air."

Pharis stepped back a pace from her, a look on his face that might have resembled admiration—albeit grudging. "That's . . . actually a really good idea." He turned to face Sigi and the other guards. "Listen up. There are at least four or five Volanti near the hill where the Consilium sits. At least, there were." Pointing at Aurianna, who stood behind him, he said, "Here's the plan. I'm going to have her try to trap them inside solid spheres of water while we distract the other ones. The hope is the water inside the sphere will, in effect, drown them. Then we simply drop it down into the outer ocean."

Aurianna stood with her mouth agape, staring at the back of his head like he'd grown a second one. *He's going to* have *me try to…he's making it sound like it's* his *plan, the ass!*

Pharis spun around before she could say anything and continued up to the Consilium. Rooted to the spot, Aurianna glared after him as the guards began to pass her by. Sigi stopped to check on her, but Aurianna shook her head and plastered a smile on her face.

"It's nothing." And it was nothing, for the moment. Arguing over whose idea it was wouldn't solve the problem at hand. People's lives were at stake.

She and Sigi walked side by side up the hill, neither of them speaking. Sigi kept glancing at her out of the corner of her eye but didn't say anything.

When they reached the building, Aurianna found Pharis and the first of the group already engaged in battle. Three Volanti roared and squawked at the group as weapons were fired and bullets went astray as they bounced off their targets. The rest of the creatures Pharis had spotted must have taken off to other areas.

Time was a key factor in this plan. She would have to do it quickly, or else the rest of the creatures might catch on before she had a chance to trap them, one by one.

The one closest to her would be the test. Sneaking by to get closer to the edge, Aurianna concentrated on the water below, despite being unable to see it. She immediately realized the flaw in her plan.

The Volanti were gigantic. She had known that when she came up with the plan, but with the monster looming within reach, the enormity of the task was overwhelming. Forming a ball of water that size seemed impossible.

Still, she had to try. Aurianna could feel the ball forming, but this time, she wouldn't be inside of it. She had to shape and create the bubble with no way of knowing if she could control it from the outside.

She willed water to enter the empty space inside, creating a perfectly filled sphere that she brought up to where they stood. When the top of it rose above cliff level, she breathed a sigh of relief. The sphere was clearly large enough to fit the creature. Without hesitating, and before it could think about what was happening, Aurianna rushed the ball toward the first Volanti.

The impact was so sudden, so swift, the creature didn't even have time to react. It began to thrash around, claws and wings reaching out to save itself. But Aurianna kept her focus on pushing back against the pressure from the inside, trapping the creature in the water as its movements began to slow. After a few moments, the thrashing stopped.

Moving swiftly again, Aurianna yanked the ball over to the edge, frantically trying to dodge the fighting. One Volanti had a guardsman in its grasp, shaking the man violently in its outstretched hands, claws almost cradling the poor victim's body. Or what was left of it.

A spray of blood flew out and over the top of the bubble, sliding down in a silky-smooth cascade of red. Aurianna fought down her horror and revulsion to focus on her task. When it dipped over the side, she simply let go, running over to the edge to survey the results.

The lifeless body of the Volanti was hurtling toward the waters below. Breathing a sigh of relief, she gathered her strength to repeat the process. She had nearly formed the size of the next sphere when she heard a cry behind her. Losing all concentration, she turned around and saw red eyes peering up at them from lower down the hill.

Two more Volanti were advancing on their group.

Sigi and another of the guards were shouting orders at the others to split off into two groups, half of them heading down the hill to face the new threats.

Suddenly, the waning sunset was blotted out as a whooshing sound filled the air. Three more creatures dropped down from the sky, their wings completely unfurled and flapping in a steady rhythm as the Volanti landed on the ground between the other two sets of creatures.

They were trapped.

Correction. Each of the two split-off groups was now trapped between sets of creatures.

She and Pharis were trapped between a swift death on the crashing waves behind them and the two Volanti still on the hill with them. Water wasn't going to help them now.

Time was up.

Out of the corner of her eye, Aurianna watched as Pharis raised his weapon. They could do nothing else but try to push back against the creatures and hope they could regroup with the others after pushing through.

She had both of her guns out, firing as fast as she dared. It was no use. The monsters were steadily advancing, and they had the benefit of sheer size. Aurianna's heart was pounding, fear enveloping her in a cold sweat as the impending reality of their situation loomed in her vision.

Pharis, inching backward as she did, occasionally threw a glance behind them at the cliff. Whatever he was thinking, it wouldn't work. Even with her newfound Water powers, the drop was far too steep. Only death lay behind them.

But death was before them as well. Bit by bit, the Volanti were forcing them closer to the edge, the irony of which wasn't lost on Aurianna.

They were out to avenge their fallen brother. She knew she couldn't fool them with her bubble trick again. Both of them had been on the hill when she had murdered one of their own. They would not let her leave this place alive.

Aurianna turned to look behind her, unsure what she was looking for but hoping for some sort of miracle. Without warning, a blinding pain ripped across her back and she almost stumbled over the edge. Falling to one knee, she doubled over as she heard Pharis shouting at her. Placing a hand on her shoulder, his other still firing at the Volanti, he asked, "Are you okay?"

At first, she couldn't speak through the agonizing burn creeping up her spine, but finally she nodded, getting back to her feet and turning to face the enemy once again. "Yeah, I think so. Hurts like hell." She looked over at Pharis and saw a look of immense guilt on his face.

"I'm so sorry. One of them lunged at you. I only saw a blur of claws then it jumped back."

"Cheap shot."

"Yeah, well, it definitely needs to be looked at."

"Kinda busy at the moment, Sire."

His jaw clenched at her sarcasm. "Right. Let's keep ourselves facing them from now on. No surprises."

Pharis and Aurianna reached the apex of the cliff and stood with their backs touching, afraid to let the enemy get the jump on them again. The dark forms of the creatures moved like shadows up the hill as the other groups continued to wage their own battles.

The further back the Volanti pushed them, the harder it was to stay in their back-to-back fighting stance. The edge of the cliff loomed just behind them. Thoughts of its sheer face flashed through Aurianna's mind as a repeating image. A fall from this height would mean sure death. The finality of the thought brought tears to her eyes.

"This isn't working. There're too many of them!"

"Yeah."

She was shocked by his flippant response. "That's neither helpful nor reassuring."

"Do you trust me?"

"Not even remotely."

He smiled. *Smiled.*

"I'm sure I don't know what the hell is so damn funny!"

The lopsided smile was still plastered to his face, some hidden joke she wasn't getting.

"Aurianna, do you trust me?" He held out a hand as if expecting her to take it.

"No!" *Had he lost his mind?*

"Good." Without warning, he grabbed her hand and shoved himself into her, hurtling them both backward and over the edge of the cliff as her screams rent the night air.

Chapter 22

AURIANNA

The screams were snatched from Aurianna's throat as gravity took both her breath and her voice away.

Falling.

Falling.

Falling.

Then the world turned upside down in an instant. The feeling that she was shooting up into the sky like a falling star in reverse completely overwhelmed her. Down became up, and up became down, her soul and physical body wrenched apart as a vision of death passed across the inside of her tightly closed eyelids. Aurianna wasn't sure which half of herself her consciousness was grasping onto.

But considering she could distinctly feel her insides trying to claw their way outside, her bets were on her corporeal half.

All other awareness—apart from overwhelming fear and shock—fell into the nothingness below them, the numbness cutting off most of her senses.

The first to return was smell. The air smelled of . . . nothing. No smell of smoke or trees, no stench of blood or death.

Next was hearing, though the only sound reaching her ears was the roar of the wind in her ears.

Aurianna's stomach took a nosedive through the soles of her feet as the wind pushed against her frigid body. The dizziness made it impossible to tell which end was which. But arms. She felt arms around her, holding her in a fierce embrace which was all she could feel or understand or care about at the moment.

The vertigo could have lasted seconds or hours. She had no idea. She knew she needed to open her eyes, test her sense of sight and make sure she's wasn't actually lying dead at the bottom of the sea.

Opening her eyes gingerly, she realized something in an instant. She must be dead.

All she could see was the coastline far off in the distance, the twinkling stars overhead . . .

And the shoulder she was currently holding onto for dear life.

Looking up slowly—the alternative being out of the question, if her senses were correctly assessing the situation—Aurianna recognized the face that went with the shoulder, and the eyes that were staring at her with an intensity that held both fear and relief within their sapphire depths.

Pharis opened his mouth as if to speak but faltered. His eyes held the promise of an explanation, but perhaps conversation wasn't the best idea while they were . . .

What exactly were they doing?

Aurianna resigned herself to the fact that she would have to fight against her sense of self-preservation and look . . . down. She had to know what was below, though her mind had already answered that question. She just didn't like the answer.

Slowly—*ever so slowly*—she tugged her eyes away from his as she bent her head back. A look of panic crossed Pharis's face, registering her intention. He shook his head at her violently, but she was already intent on her course of action.

She had to look. She had to see.

She had to know.

It was too dark to make out much, but the roaring waves were far below, the coastline speeding past them like a train.

Only it wasn't the land that was moving. It was them.

It was Pharis.

He was...flying.

Flying.

She felt her consciousness slipping away and her body growing limp as she fought to keep her head up. Pharis had anticipated her reaction, gripping her tighter and readjusting one of his arms to wrap under her thigh to keep a solid hold on his passenger.

When she was able to hold her head back up and look, Aurianna could see the town of Rasenforst sweeping by in a blur of images and firelight. She only recognized the place because of the multitude of fires and the architecture of the buildings she glimpsed.

Pharis was circling back around to the edge of Eresseia furthest from the site of the Volanti attack. At least, she hoped he was. All other thoughts were impossible to sift through now. The wind was making her eyes water, so she closed them, praying to the Essence she would touch solid ground again.

And in one piece.

Feeling a decrease in their speed, she risked a glance out—not down—and saw they were coming up behind the city of Vanito, Laelia and Javen's hometown. A dark and unwholesome-looking forest lay behind the town, and for a moment, Aurianna was terrified Pharis meant to drop her into the wilderness and leave her there alone.

The thin air must have been affecting her brain. Pharis might be many things, but he would never, ever do something like that.

Of course, an hour ago she would have sworn he couldn't fly, but here they were.

She expected the landing to be slow and soft, a gentle drifting to the landmass below. In reality, they landed with a ground-shaking quake that jolted her insides and made her teeth rattle slightly.

Setting her down and stepping back, Pharis was visibly anxious, his hands twitching and his eyes roaming the surrounding area in quick back-and-forth motions. She had never seen him this nervous. Was he afraid of what might be lurking in the woods, or…?

"Go ahead." It was the last thing Aurianna expected him to say.

"Go ahead?"

He nodded but couldn't meet her eyes. "Yell. Scream. Freak out. I should probably regret this, but to be honest, I'm just glad someone else knows."

"What exactly is it that I know? What is going on? Did I miss something in training?"

He grimaced at her tone. "No, you didn't miss anything." He ran his fingers through his windswept hair, sighing. "I'm a Zephyr."

She blinked. "A…a what?"

Closing his eyes, Pharis let out another long sigh. "It's just what we call an Aerokinctic."

"Aero…" Bewildered, Aurianna opened and closed her mouth a few times. "Pharis, I've seen what Aerokinetics can do. That…that is beyond anything—"

"Yeah, I know it's… That's partly why it was kept a secret. The Magnus doesn't want anyone else to know the heir to his title is that powerful. He's worried it'll make people uncomfortable. Not to mention jealous and angry."

"You think?" Her incredulity flowed like ice through her veins.

Her face felt cold and uncomfortable. Maybe she was finally going insane … or was about to faint. This was all just too much.

"I didn't ask for this. My mother was from Eadon. She was always so proud that I had taken after her. Surpassed her really." His expression showed regret—and something else.

"I'm trying to understand what just happened." Lightheaded and dizzy, Aurianna sat down on a nearby bolder. In the distance, the faint sound of singing reached her ears, but the sound wasn't coming from the town of Vanito.

"Is there a town in that direction?" she asked, pointing into the dense darkness of the forest.

A distressed look crossed his face. "No. Why?"

"I thought I heard …" Her voice trailing, she realized the singing had stopped. Or perhaps she had imagined it. "Never mind."

Changing the subject, Pharis said, "I think I should take a look at your back."

"What?"

"Your back? The gash across your shoulder blade. I could feel the blood soaking your back."

In all the chaos of the attack and the ensuing—*journey? flight? ride?*—Aurianna had almost forgotten about the injury. The mention of it brought back her awareness of the pain, the dull but persistent throbbing a brutal reminder of what could have been. What almost was.

"Shouldn't we be going back to help?"

"What do you propose we do? I think they're onto us with the bubble thing."

"Well, we can't just sit here and do nothing while the others are under attack!"

He stared at her, shaking his head sadly. "I can't go back just yet." His tone held a slight edge of apology. "Not until my power recharges. That takes a hell of a lot out of me." He stared at the ground. "I'm sorry. I was only thinking about getting somewhere safe at the time."

Aurianna chewed on her bottom lip as she thought of a reply to his news. "Okay."

Raising his head to stare at her, Pharis squinted an eye. "Okay? That's it?"

"I mean, we don't have a choice, right?"

"Right. So, should I look at your injury now?"

She nodded. Pharis moved to sit behind her. Turning her back to him, Aurianna gingerly removed her overcoat as he helped her to peel the garment from the wound. They were careful not to rip away any skin that might have stuck to the blood already beginning to dry.

She realized she couldn't easily show him her back without loosening her bodice. A sudden shyness hit her, and a flush crept over her skin. Aurianna worked at the laces, loosening the shirt enough to pull it down over her injured right shoulder.

With her shoulder exposed, Pharis inspected the wound. His hands were surprisingly soft, his touch making it hard to focus.

She tried to distract herself from the sensations at her back, both the painful ones and the lighter, more delicate examination. "Thank you, by the way. For saving my life back there. You might have warned me though."

"Didn't I?"

She couldn't see his face, but she could hear the amusement in his tone. "No. You didn't."

"Well, it's bled quite a bit, but it doesn't look horribly deep, so I think it'll be okay once we get you some medical attention. Probably gonna leave a bit of a scar though."

Aurianna let out a sound halfway between a snort and a growl. "I'm used to it."

His fingers trailed softly across the top of her shoulder blade, a feathery light touch just above the wound. He let out a soft breath and whispered, "Does this mean something?"

She felt his exhalation against her chilled skin, the sudden warmth spreading downward. Her head felt light again. Closing her eyes to regain her befuddled faculties, Aurianna took a moment to respond. "That's what I'm told."

Effugere.

"You didn't pick it out." It wasn't a question.

"They didn't exactly give me a choice when I was being branded with a red-hot poker."

The finger on her back stilled its movements, the body pressed against her tensing. "Who?" Pharis's whisper was soft but held a note of violence in its depths.

"The Consils. My Consils, in the future."

"I don't understand. Why would they force you to get a tattoo?"

"In my time, it's a form of punishment to deter people from doing things the Consils don't approve of. In my case, it was because I tried to run away. And it's not really a tattoo—not like you're used to, at least."

"Run away from what?"

"Home. Them. The *known*." Aurianna shrugged. "It's not like I didn't plan on coming back. Just got tired of being told where we could and couldn't go, what we could and couldn't do. My actions wouldn't have hurt or affected any of them, except for Aunt Larissa." The one regret she had from the experience. "I wanted to see what was out there." She finally turned to face him, the memory of her rebellion emboldening her. "I don't think you understand how lucky you are to live in a world where not only does the sun rise into the sky to light up everything around you, but you can actually *travel* to those places freely without any retribution."

Pharis looked down at the ground. "So, they caught you?"

"Only because my so-called friends got scared and decided, instead of coming with me, to report me." She realized her bottom lip was becoming sore from her subconscious habit of chewing on it when she was anxious or upset. Right at that moment, she felt both emotions welling up inside of her, threatening to flow out either through tears or an angry outburst. Desperate to reign it in, she continued speaking as if her insides weren't in turmoil. "I was caught and arrested and punished. I spent an entire moon cycle in a cell while they tried to 'reeducate' me. Then they burned that word into my skin because it means 'runaway' in the old language, and they wanted everyone to remember the consequences of disobeying the rules."

"Your friends." His tone of voice, hard and judging, when he said those two simple words summed up everything she was feeling.

She nodded, tears spilling down her cheeks in spite of her determination not to cry in front of him. "Yeah, that's the worst part of it. Completely changed my relationship with all of them, but at least I knew from that moment onward people couldn't be trusted."

"That must have been a lonely time for you."

"I've felt alone for most of my life. You get used to it."

"No one should ever get used to being alone. Not when there are people who care about them."

"I'm not sure those people exist in my case. Except for Larissa." Thoughts of home always pained Aurianna, but the idea of returning to Larissa was the only thing that mattered.

"I think maybe you aren't looking hard enough." His gaze was penetrating, but she refused to examine his meaning.

When she didn't respond, Pharis said, "For what it's worth, despite how you got it, I think it's quite pretty."

Grateful for the change in subject, she replied, "I'm surprised you didn't notice it at the ball. My dress made it really obvious from the back."

"That dress showed . . . yeah." A lopsided grin and a faraway look crossed the man's face for a moment. "Your eyes though. They're uncanny and certainly a defining feature. That and your freckles."

She turned red. The freckles that peppered her cheeks and nose had always annoyed her. "My freckles?"

"The glow from your eyes—the amber and gold just sparkle or something. It lights up your cheeks and makes your freckles stand out."

"Thanks?" Her voice flattened, trying not to sound offended.

"I didn't say it was a bad thing. The opposite, in fact. It was just the first thing I noticed about you when I came to get you."

When he came to get me. A sudden thought occurred to her, and she was anxious to change the uncomfortable subject. "Wait. Back up a minute. If you can do . . . that," she gestured to the open air behind them, "it means when you came to get me—"

"I could've avoided a great many things? Yes, believe me, I know. When I arrived, I fell directly into the bay and couldn't do a damn thing about it. The subsequent icy cold swim I took was just a bonus." His lips twisted into a grimace. "But surely you understand why I couldn't use any more of my power there. Too dangerous."

"So only you and the Magnus know about this?"

"And now you. Plus the Arcanes. And the Magisters, all sworn to secrecy. The Air instructor is the only one of the Magisters who knows how strong my power is. The only other people who knew were my sister and my mother." He grimaced with pain she could only guess at, his sapphire eyes glistening with unknown memories.

"I never even knew my mother." Aurianna didn't know what else to say.

"What makes you think you would've wanted to?" His words were biting, his tone sharp.

Taken aback by the sudden animosity of his statement, she gasped. "Why would you say that?"

His jaw clenched, and his nostrils flared. A deep growl resonated in his chest as he raked his hands through his hair. Pulling at the strands, he took a deep breath. "Look. I need to tell you something, and I should have told you a long time ago. Part of it isn't my fault. The Arcanes … you of all people know how things are with them." Shaking his head, he turned his glare back to the ground beneath him. "But part of it … Deep down, I know it's stupid of me to hold it against you, but I can't help it."

"What is it?"

His eyes darted back up to her, the pain in their depths shooting daggers through her chest. "It's just … every time I look at you, all I want to feel is rage, and all I can see is my mother's face."

"Your mother? Why would looking at me make you think of your mother?"

"Because your mother killed my mother."

CHAPTER 23

AURIANNA

Stunned, Aurianna stared at Pharis, shock and confusion freezing then numbing her from head to toe.

Her brain tried to puzzle out a meaning from the string of words he'd placed together, end to end, but to no avail. The words didn't make any sense. And her mouth refused to open, to work in a normal fashion, to ask the question she needed to ask.

She was dreaming again. The flying . . . it had to all be a dream. A horrible dream.

But Pharis wasn't speaking either, just staring at her, waiting on a response she was unable to give. He looked simultaneously angry and frightened.

The climate was chillier here, a crisp bite to the breeze she could only sense from the movement of the trees surrounding them on two sides. The sky was dark, the forest even darker in the evening moonlight. Aurianna remembered stories of the unknown wildness that lay beyond, stories filled with rumors of ancient beings. Stories meant to scare the Youngers, most likely. But here she was, immobile, mute, and the very nearness of those woods made her tremble. That was all she needed.

Then feeling came back into her body, slowly, piece by piece, and her thoughts became words. "What?"

Well, one word. But an infinite universe of questions lay in that one simple word.

He pointed to the boulder they had vacated. "Perhaps you'll want to sit down for this."

"I'm not even sure I can move right now. Start talking."

He nodded, but his attention seemed to be on anything but her as he began his story. "A long time ago, my father fell in love with another woman. She was a Kinetic, so she lived at the Imperium for most of her childhood like other Kinetics. I don't know for certain when it started, but she was at least twenty years younger than he was, only a few years older than me."

Resentment and unadulterated hatred flashed across Pharis's face, but Aurianna wasn't sure whom his ire was aimed at in that moment.

"For years, he obsessed over this girl, doted on her, gave her things. I don't know the details, but I know she ended up pregnant by someone else—a Kinetic. Obviously, that was a massive disaster considering how strict the rule is."

Aurianna's thoughts fled to Juliet and Orion, and the newborn they were forced to keep hidden in Bramosia. The sheer joy they felt at what they had, no matter the cost. *Their happiness should be celebrated*, she thought.

"So she ran away," Pharis continued, "but my father couldn't let her go. He was haunted by his feelings for her, as unhealthy as they were. And she had broken the law. He had people tracking her for several moons. She locked herself in a tower when it was time to have her child. No one could get in without her permission." Pharis stumbled over his words, his eyes narrowed in anger. "She had somehow put a spell on the tower—"

"A spell?"

"It's—I don't know. The Arcanes say it's ancient magic of some sort. You know how they are about giving out information." He ran a hand over his ruffled mane. "So, she locked herself in with . . . whatever the magic was . . . and locked everyone else out. My father tried everything he could think of to get to her, but the only ones ever allowed in were the midwives. And then, she . . ." His voice trailed off and his shoulders slumped as he finally looked her in the eyes with a gaze of utter despair.

"Anyway." A brief rustling in the trees stole his focus for half a second before he brought his attention back to his story. "My mother knew. I don't know for how long, but she had known for a while. Maybe even the whole time. It wasn't like he was especially secretive about it. He was pretty blatant at times. And my mother suffered for his selfishness. Her health began to deteriorate a few years ago. I watched her as everything weighed her down, made her more and more frail. She wouldn't eat half the time. I knew that she knew. And her grief is what killed her."

There were too many factors to think about, too many threads woven into the story's fabric. More questions instead of answers. But yet . . .

"You're saying the . . . the woman your father was in love with was . . ."

"Your mother."

"But that means . . ." The next words choked her as she tried to force them out, wrapped a pale hand around her throat and squeezed until she felt a pulsing behind her eyelids. She closed her eyes. Aurianna wouldn't—*couldn't*—believe he had kept such vitally important information from her.

Now those words came tumbling out in a flurry of anger and confusion. "You lied to me! You've known all this time, and you never told me where she was."

"And that's the part I don't take the blame for. The Arcanes made me swear by the Essence not to tell you until after the Yule Ball. I know I should have said something the moment it was over, but to be honest, with the fire and everything that's happened, I just … No, there's no excuse. I realize that. But you must know the only reason I agreed to it is because they promised it would make all the difference for you to know after, and not before. I have no idea why. You know how they are."

"I thought I knew a lot of things! I thought I knew you wouldn't lie to me. I thought I was on a path of my own choosing. I thought *my mother was dead!*" Loud sobs were already racking her chest, the forceful spasms making it difficult to get the words out. An inhuman noise screeched from her throat, her body collapsing in a sobbing heap on the ground where she stood.

Pharis ran to her, wrapping strong arms around her as each tiny convulsion jerked the breath from her lungs. Her mind was clouded, an ache resounding in its furthest reaches as she tried not to focus on the *other* things, the things she hadn't said.

Aurianna couldn't face them, couldn't give voice to those thoughts. They clawed into her soul and dashed her spirit against the walls of her heart. The pain was unbearable.

He continued to hold her as her anguish wrung every last tear from her body. She was lost, lost in a sea of confusion, drowning in sorrow she could not run away from. Not this time.

As the sobs began to calm, the *other* things hurtled to the front of her mind before she could stop them. She couldn't ask. She had to ask. She didn't want to know. She needed to know.

"Pharis?" she whispered.

"Yeah?"

"Who put the curse on me? When I was born."

"I don't—"

"Don't lie to me."

"They said… they said your mother was a very powerful Kinetic. Too powerful, from what I understand. She was capable of doing unspeakable things, and many were afraid of her. That's what my father said." He sighed. "We've never really discussed it, and I never wanted to ask. But I think he was attracted to her power more than anything." Running his hands down the side of her face, Pharis wiped the dampness away, trying to get her to look at him.

"Tell me." Amber and sapphire gazes locked, neither willing to look away.

"Your mother is the one who invoked the curse on you. She must have resented all the trouble getting pregnant had caused her. Even before that, she was feared for her power. She was angry, and spiteful, and wanted nothing more than revenge against the Magnus and all those who hunted her down. Now she wants to destroy this world by creating a hatred for Kinetics in the minds of everyone else."

The woman she had tried to destroy on the train was the woman who had given birth to her. The woman who had cursed her. Just because she had been born. The pieces of her soul that were still intact burst into flame. In her mind, she saw those twin orbs of fire lying nestled in the hands of the woman they called the Enchantress. No one had told her. They had let her attempt to kill her own mother.

And yet, the Enchantress had tried to kill her. A killing curse, Aunt Larissa had called it. It was her aunt who had been able to change the curse into a sort of "sleeping" spell, a spell to keep her hidden from her enemies until the time was right. Larissa had smuggled her out of the tower. She had been one of the midwives during the birth. Pharis said they were the only ones allowed to enter past the locking spells the Enchantress had enacted on the tower.

Ashes. That was all she had left. Embers of who she had been . . . or thought she had been. The remnants were just a reminder of everything she had lost, everything she would never have.

The last vestiges of dusk gave way to the darkness of night. Aurianna knew what she had to do, but the thought ate away at her insides like a ravenous Volanti.

Still, betrayal was a keen motivator. What loyalty did she owe to the woman who gave birth to her and then cursed her to die? She thought of the necklace she had placed such a high sentimental value upon, the only piece of her mother she ever imagined she would ever have. Her aunt had kept so much from her, far more than she had admitted or even alluded to.

Yet she knew she would never completely blame the woman. As angry and resentful as Aurianna felt, the idea of having to tell a little girl her mother had tried to kill her was beyond anything a person should have to be responsible for, no matter the cost of withholding the truth. Larissa had been protecting her, probably more than she should have, but her aunt had raised her and loved her. She was all the family Aurianna had left.

Except.

Except for what lay behind the walls of that enigmatic tower. Perhaps another spell could be broken.

Suddenly very aware of the closeness between them, both physically and emotionally, a surge of guilt passed over her. Yes, Pharis had saved her life, and the conversation had been very emotional. But she realized she did care a great deal for Javen, who would be livid if he could see her at that moment.

And she really couldn't blame him.

As she stood up, Pharis caught her arm in a firm grip before she could step back. "Where are you going?"

His touch was warm but gentle. She snatched her arm back. "To do what I came here for."

"That's . . ." The color drained from his face as her meaning registered in his mind. "You're going to kill her." It wasn't a question.

"Yes, Pharis. I am. And you're going to help me." The look of shock that met her words was enough to tell her he wasn't completely on board with her plan. "I don't need a lecture, and I don't need to think about it any longer."

"How do you propose we get into the tower? It's locked with what seems to be a very powerful enchantment."

"She gets out, doesn't she? And no one sees her leave. So there must be a way in that isn't obvious. I'm inclined to believe there's more to the underground tunnels than we've previously explored."

"I don't know. We've explored quite a lot."

Don't think about that kiss, she told herself. Too late.

Pharis continued speaking, unaware she was lost in her own thoughts. "You know, we should get your back tended to before we go anywhere."

Refocusing her attention to the task at hand, Aurianna insisted, "No time. I want to do this now. We need to find a way into the tunnels without anyone seeing us."

"You don't think people will already be worrying about you?"

"Far more likely there are guards losing their minds right now, trying to explain to the Magnus how they lost his heir. The kingdom wouldn't be the same without their handsome Regulus."

The corners of his mouth turned up as he folded his arms across his chest. "You think I'm handsome." Arrogance poured off him in waves.

"No, the kingdom thinks you're handsome." Chewing on her bottom lip, she muttered, "The female half at least. And probably more than a few of the other half."

Staring at her with a look of mild amusement, he remained silent as his smile widened. A flush crept up her face. Pharis had a way of making her feel exposed, even when he said nothing. His gaze was intense, but his grin made it even worse.

"Well, you do have quite the reputation, you know?"

The smug grin faded. "What is that supposed to mean?"

"I think you know what it means. My friend Leon has a similar reputation, only he usually pays for his recreational activities. I guess being the handsome heir works in your favor."

"Did you just compare me to someone who pays women to sleep with him?" He cocked his head to the side, looking simultaneously offended and amused.

"If the shoe fits…"

"You weren't complaining that night you kissed me."

"The night I… you can't be serious. I don't understand why you did it, but that was all you."

"Why *I* did it? *Me?*"

"Yeah, pretty sure it was you who kissed me. Not like anyone else was there. I mean, it was dark, but I feel pretty confident in my assessment."

"Wrong, sweetheart. *You* kissed *me.*"

"I can't believe you would actually deny it."

Pharis turned sullen as pain flashed in his eyes. "Whatever you say." Walking over to her, he put an arm around her waist, and for a second, she was convinced he meant to kiss her again. Instead, he said, "Yeah, so I think we both need to put in an appearance. Find your friends, let them know you're okay, and get a healer to patch you up. We can meet up once everyone has gone to bed for the night. You ready for this?" He was referring to the flight back home she realized with a start.

Aurianna nodded slowly, reluctant to put herself through that again. Pharis agreed to meet at the entrance to the tunnels around midnight. She braced herself for the return journey, closing her eyes and forcing herself not to think about his body pressed against hers.

* * *

Aurianna lay in bed, staring up, counting the dots of plaster on her ceiling. The exercise was far better than the alternative— entertaining the thoughts that tried to plague her heart and mind.

The first place she had looked for her friends was Bramosia, considering the scene she and Pharis had left behind. The trip back had been frightening... and exhilarating. But flying was something she would probably never get used to.

Not that she planned on spending enough time with Pharis to test out that theory. She was willing to trust him to help her defeat the Enchantress, but only because he was also personally invested in this situation. That was the only reason, she kept telling herself.

Aurianna had let her guilt sway her into reentering the capital city alone. Pharis had tried to protest once they had landed in the forest a good way from the town, but she had convinced him entering together would provoke more questions about how they had disappeared. She hadn't said she also wanted to avoid upsetting Javen, but from the look on Pharis's face, he had probably suspected her real motivation.

Everyone had been understandably worried but dealing with the aftermath of the Volanti attack had taken up most of their attention. Part of Aurianna was hurt they hadn't been actively looking for her, but she was mostly relieved no one was asking questions.

After the City Guard had mobilized, the creatures had finally been fought off, but not before taking a young woman and her son with them. The damage to the city was extensive, but restorations would begin the following day. When she arrived, everyone had been either tending to the injured—Aurianna had someone tend to her wound as well—or helping to sort out some of the more manageable catastrophes of the night.

Before returning to her room, Aurianna decided she wanted confirmation of Pharis's story. Not that she didn't trust him, but it just seemed too insane to be true.

The Enchantress—the woman who tried to blow up Bramosia, who spiked the wells with dragonblood—was her mother?

Perhaps she should take a step back and think about how ridiculous it sounded.

Aurianna was already knocking on the door when those thoughts finally began to subside. As terrible as the idea was, she knew it was true. All of it.

Before she could back away and change her mind, the dim light from inside the room was spilling out onto the ground at her feet. A bespectacled older man was holding the door open for her, beckoning her inside.

The man led her into the middle of the room, to a narrow aisle between two shelves of books. Simon seemed to be counting them.

She cleared her throat, causing him to turn and look at her. A face full of weariness gazed at her. "I take it he finally told you."

"Pharis? How do you know what he told me?"

"Because you always have that look on your face when he tells you."

"I…what?"

"It is a heavy burden you must bear for a time, but it will soon be lifted."

"Lifted how?"

"By the truth."

"I thought it was the truth. Are you saying Pharis lied to me?"

Simon shook his head and returned to his odd task of counting. "The Regulus isn't lying to you. But, as you well know, the truth is often more complicated than a lie could ever be."

"What is that supposed to mean? Can you just speak plainly for once?"

"You know I can't. Just keep doing what you're doing and—"

"Follow the path that draws me?"

Simon beamed at her. "Yes. Exactly."

Aurianna fumed for a moment, then turned and stormed out of the room, slamming the door as she passed. The man was infuriating.

And calm. He was way too damn calm about everything.

She was too keyed up to feel her exhaustion, despite the events of the evening. Not bothering to shower, she lay down atop the covers of her bed to await the agreed upon meeting time.

It wasn't till midnight that the halls grew silent. Slowly, she crept past the other rooms and down the stairwell to the bottom level. The only specific places she had visited so far were the rooms dedicated to the Arcanes and the Voids. She knew there must be other areas, but Pharis was right. The two of them had explored so many passageways, it made her head hurt to think about.

And the idea of secret tunnels didn't make sense if just anyone could stumble upon them. There must be something they were missing.

A shuffling behind her startled Aurianna from her thoughts. She turned around as Pharis strolled up, a seriousness etched into the corners of his mouth and eyes.

"How's your back?" His concern seemed genuine, at least.

"I'll survive."

He reached out and grabbed her wrist with a gentle but firm grip. "Aurianna, I need you to understand that I don't hate you. Not really. It just feels like it sometimes."

"That's … wonderful to hear, Pharis," she deadpanned.

"No, I just mean I … I'm angry, and I take it out on you because it's easy."

"Again, thanks." He opened his mouth as if to respond, but she waved him off. "It doesn't matter. You should be angry. Be angry all you want. But direct your anger at the woman in the tower, okay?"

"She's not the only one, you know. I guarantee you my father didn't bring you back here to help anyone but himself. He might be obsessed with that woman, but there's nothing in this world he would ever love more than himself and his power. I don't know why he wanted me to marry you, but it's all tied into whatever schemes he's concocting. Whether it's revenge or power or … I don't know. Let's just be careful, okay?"

She nodded and led the way forward.

They began walking in a random direction without any purpose or plan. The tunnels they chose were different from ones they had used before, but after a while they all began to look the same.

"This is hopeless." Aurianna stilled her steps, throwing her hands up in the air in frustration. Exhaustion crept in from every corner of her mind and body, the surreal events of the entire day a dead weight on her shoulders. "It's like a never-ending maze down here."

Pharis stopped just ahead of her and turned around with a glint of amusement in his eyes. "Or maybe that's just what they want us to think."

Her eyes narrowed. "Not funny."

"I tried," he said. "So, what do we do now?"

"Why are you asking me? This is your home, remember?"

"You're the girl with the destiny, right?"

"Again, not funny."

"Come on. It's a little funny."

"I still haven't forgiven you for lying to me."

He looked genuinely pained. "I didn't exactly lie. But I did apologize for holding back the truth. I am truly sorry. Despite what the Arcanes said, it was a terrible thing to do."

"Still, you might want to be careful. We're not too far from the place where I almost blew up that Void."

"You…Wait, what?"

"Remember Magister Daehne telling all of you about it after the train explosion? We were training, and he brought a Void in to help in case…" Her words trailed off as she remembered a conversation she'd had with Simon.

"Aurianna, there's a difference between giving the man a scare, and *blowing him up.*"

"Yeah, yeah, I'm exaggerating. But listen," she announced as excitement bubbled up in her chest, "there's something else too. Simon—the Arcane—told me the Voids aren't what you think they are. They're not devoid of power. They *are* the power."

"What does that mean?"

"Don't you see? It's like pieces of a puzzle, two sides of a coin. As Kinetics, we can manipulate elements. But Voids—they *are* the elements. Their bodies hold some small piece of the element. And when I created the explosion, I think I was…draining him."

Pharis's eyes widened in horror at her words, but something else was there as well. A tiny spark of amazement, of hope. "Are you sure about this? Can you trust what this Simon says?"

She nodded. "He's irritatingly vague and cryptic most of the time, but he was definitely being sincere. And he said the Magisters suspect it to some degree. Maybe they know. I'm not sure."

"Bloody hell! The train!"

"What about it?"

"Aurianna," he replied, his voice filled with excitement and trepidation, "if this is all true, then you drained your…the Enchantress that night on the train. That's what caused the explosion."

"That would explain a lot." Perhaps it wasn't the answer she wanted, but it was a start. Yet so much about the Voids…

The Voids.

"I think I know where we might find what we're looking for."

"Where's that?"

"The Voids. Clearly there's so much we don't know or understand about them. Does anyone ever visit their rooms down here?"

"No, I don't think so. But Aurianna, they might not take too kindly to a Kinetic and the Regulus just strolling through their home."

"Okay, well, then we have to be really careful." She smirked at him, batting her lashes.

He sighed. "Why do I feel like I'm going to regret this?"

Aurianna realized they had wandered far from the last known area she was familiar with, "Any idea where we are?"

"No, but I can figure it out."

At the next intersection, Pharis went left and took a sharp turn around a corner. Following closely behind, she looked around at the walls of the tunnels. "I've always meant to ask, but who keeps all these lights powered? I mean, they're everywhere. We haven't reached a tunnel yet that didn't have them."

"In case you haven't noticed, we have a *lot* of Kinetics. Plenty of Sparkers need a job and have nothing better to do.

"Hmmm." Aurianna reached out a tentative hand, her touch inches from one of the fixtures.

Pharis snatched her hand back, looking at her like she had grown an extra head. "Have you lost your mind?"

"No, I . . . It felt like . . . Never mind."

Glaring at her like she might suddenly lunge for the ball of Energy again, he started walking again, turning back every few seconds to check that she was still behind him. After a few moments, his lowered voice trailed back to reach her ears. "You are quite mad sometimes. But also, very brave. No one else would have done what you did."

"What is that supposed to mean?" She continued to follow him, their soft footsteps somehow echoing down the passage.

His shoulders sagged as his head slumped forward a fraction. Pharis sighed then spoke quietly into the stone corridor. "The night of the Yule Ball. You freaked me out, freaked everyone out. But you were . . . radiant."

"Yes, I believe you mentioned something about freckles and glowing eyes. Makes me sound like a creature from another world to be honest—"

"No, I mean after that. When you came waltzing back to the edge of the forest like you owned the damn place, it was like . . . like . . ."

"Like I *owned* the damn place? I had a lot of things running through my mind that night, but I'm pretty sure that wasn't one of them." Aurianna paused, crossing her arms and adopting a defiant stance.

After a few unshared steps, Pharis looked back over his shoulder and stopped. His eyes locked on hers, daring her to look away as his next words took her breath. "You didn't have to think it. You lived it. You *did* own it that night. You looked like a goddess. A dangerous and beautiful creature. From another world, as you say." He looked ahead of him again and shook his head. "You saved so much, and you didn't even stop to think of your own safety. A true savior." He smiled at her, the slightest hint of amusement reaching his eyes.

"Don't call me that. I have tried my best to do what I can, but I am no one's savior. I was covered in ashes and bits of tree because I couldn't even manage to land on my own."

"Who said saviors don't need help sometimes?"

Narrowing her eyes, Aurianna felt a wave of astonishment wash over her. "That was you, wasn't it? You slowed my fall and saved my life. I thought maybe it was … never mind."

Pharis's only answer was an even bigger smile. Without another word, he went on.

Aurianna recognized the door as they approached it, and looked around to make sure no one was in the tunnel near them. When she'd been here with Magister Daehne, the door had been open, and Voids had been busily at work. However, it was now well past midnight, and even though there were always some Voids on duty during the night, most would be asleep.

Probably. If they were lucky.

The closer they got to the door, the less sure she felt about this plan. She was still certain there must be something of interest, but whether they could find it without being caught was another matter. It wasn't that she was afraid of the Voids, but considering several of them had already gone missing, sneaking around in their rooms probably wouldn't go in their favor if they happened to startle someone.

Pharis laid a hand on the doorknob, looking at her before he turned it. This was her last chance to back out.

She nodded, and the silence was filled with a soft creaking as the door swung open. They both winced at the noise, frozen in the doorway as they waited to see if anyone or anything within stirred at the sound.

When nothing happened after an agonizing moment, Pharis led the way into the main room. Tables lined the area, surrounded by benches and chairs that had seen better days. Aurianna searched the edges of the room, locating the exits. Two doors led off to the right and three to the left. The rooms to the right were closed. Aurianna prayed to the Essence those were the bedrooms. Any Voids who were working tonight could come through at any moment though.

Upon closer inspection, only one of the passages to the left led directly into a room—what appeared to be an enormous pantry. Shelves of food and other items lined the walls down both sides of the expanse. A light was on in the room, but the space appeared to be empty.

They continued to the next doorway and followed the passage within, which seemed to go on forever. After a minute or so, however, the pair discovered the path terminated at a massive kitchen. Several Voids were busy stirring pots and rolling dough out on the counters, most likely in preparation for the following morning's breakfast.

Creeping carefully back on silent feet, they took the last of the three left-hand doors.

* * *

After they'd traveled a long while in the semidarkness, Pharis picked up the pace, whispering, "I think I see a door up ahead."

When they reached it, he approached and gently pushed against the wood. It didn't budge, so he pushed harder, throwing his weight into the endeavor. Aurianna looked down and noticed a small handle on the side. Pulling on it, she motioned Pharis out of the way as the door opened. He grinned sheepishly then chuckled. "Handle. Got it."

Stepping through the doorway, she encountered a solid wall of foliage. Above her head, the vegetation continued to grow all the way back across to the Imperium's outer wall, creating a natural roof for the small enclosure. When she turned to the right, she realized she was looking across Perdita Bay to the regions beyond. They were standing on a precarious ledge on the side of the island the Imperium sat upon.

"Well, this looks like a dead end." Aurianna couldn't hold back her irritation.

"Yeah, but why?"

"Why what?"

"Why have a door that leads to nowhere but a swift death or at best a very cold dip in the bay?"

"How should I know? You people do some really weird shit around here."

Pharis raised an eyebrow. The corner of his mouth twitched slightly. "You people? You still don't think of yourself as one of us, do you?"

She frowned thoughtfully. "No, I guess I do. Mostly. It's just some things are hard to get used to." To her left, the massively tall expanse of shrubbery wound around behind them, leaving them enclosed between greenery, solid stone, and the sheer drop to the water below.

Back inside, they closed the door behind them and continued along the dim passageway. Aurianna made a mental note to investigate the strange door when she wasn't working on tracking down her birth mother or saving the world.

Sigh.

After a while, the passage started branching off into side corridors on both the left and right—the spaces both narrow and dark, two things Aurianna was not overly keen on exploring. The main passage they were following was spiraling down further and further into the depths. Aurianna was at a loss to explain how this whole place wasn't filled with magma. The deeper they went, the more perplexed she became.

Looking down one of the side tunnels on her right, she was sur-prised to find her feet following the narrow space. She heard Pharis curse before following.

She couldn't seem to stop walking in that direction. Suddenly she realized why.

Aurianna recognized this place. In her dream, the glowing orb had guided her here, had taken her to the room where it had transformed into a giant crystalline shape. She had been irresistibly drawn to the orb itself, and then to the jagged spikes of crystal. Her fingertip had been inches from one of the sharp tips before she'd woken up.

Pharis was muttering behind her about traps and falling to their deaths, but she couldn't seem to stop following the passage. Instead, she started telling him about her dream. When she finished, they were approaching what appeared to be a doorway with no door. A faint light emanated from the area to the right of the doorway.

When she stepped into the room, her eyes immediately trailed over to the source of the light. She gasped.

It was just as it had been in her dream. A giant structure of glowing amethyst, myriad jagged spikes and peaks protruding from the middle, from the top, from everywhere. Suddenly she realized what it looked like, and Pharis spoke in unison with her.

"Aether Stone," they both whispered.

"But how? What is this?" she asked.

Pharis shook his head. "It must be the source. The Arcanes never tell us where they get it from. I'm guessing they break off pieces of this thing." He gaped in wonder at the light that shone across the surface.

"Larissa said…" Aurianna sighed. "There's a lot we don't know, and I feel like far too many people could give us answers if they wanted to."

"There's a doorway on the other side." Pharis pointed to the opposite wall. A slightly darker space indicated where the passage continued. "Just there."

They left the giant Aether Stone behind and continued through the opposite door. Aurianna was grateful the downslope seemed to level off somewhat. They might have to double back to the original passage, but something told Aurianna this was a situation where she needed to follow the path that drew her.

It wasn't long before another doorway stood ahead of them in the tunnel. This one led into a lighted room with a staircase at the back. But try as they might, they could not pass through the entrance. No barrier was visible, but nonetheless, something was blocking the door from the other side.

Pharis put out a hand to block her attempts. "I think this is it, Aurianna."

"What?"

"This is the entrance to the tower of the . . . of your mother."

She turned a sharp gaze to stare into the room within. It was sparsely furnished, but a steep winding staircase wound up the wall at the far side of the room and traveled up out of sight. Her mother might be just around the bend, and she would never know because the doorway was most definitely sealed by some sort of magic.

Pharis stared into the interior, scratching his head.

Backing away from the entry, she shook her head. "There has to be a way in." She continued backing up, contemplating what her options were.

Aurianna felt a cold hand cover her mouth before she could scream. She was dragged down a small side tunnel. A strong odor filled her nostrils. Her head began to feel light, and her eyes closed against her will. Consciousness faded, and the world disappeared into a dream.

CHAPTER 24

AURIANNA

Silence greeted Aurianna as she swam back into consciousness. Her eyes still closed, she listened for any kind of sound that might clue her in to her current location.

Nothing.

Slowly, she opened her eyes to a room with a dim light that cast shadows on the low ceiling above her.

She was not alone. A man dressed in the dark-gray robes of the Voids was sitting in a chair several feet away, his golden-brown eyes fixed on her, a look of wonder on his face. His dark brown hair had the smallest hint of gray at his temples.

Aurianna knew him. He was the creepy Void she had caught staring at her multiple times.

"I've seen you watching me, and you've obviously been following me. And you drugged me."

Nodding sadly, he clasped his hands in his lap. "I have, but I need to explain." His voice was soft, but his words held a strength of purpose.

"Was it the Magnus or the Arcanes who put you up to this? Or someone else?"

"No, it's nothing like that. I'm not working for anyone. This is personal."

She sat up slowly, looking around the sparsely furnished space. The only items in the room were a chair, a small table, and the thin mattress she was lying on. "Where's my friend?"

"I imagine the Regulus is right outside the door. I tried to get away, but I heard him following me the whole time. I think he's waiting on me to leave so he can sneak in and rescue you, but he might as well come in and listen to what I have to say."

A noise to her right caused Aurianna to turn her head too quickly, the motion blurring her senses again and making the room spin. A hazy form moved closer, and she heard Pharis ask, "Who are you?"

"My name is Ethan. I'm going to explain everything, but I'm a Void here at the Imperium."

"So, we're back at the Imperium now?" Aurianna's vision had returned, but her head was pounding.

"Yes. This room is unoccupied for now. I thought it best we have some privacy for this."

"Says the kidnapper."

"I'm not kidnapping you, but I knew you'd run if I tried to approach you. I was aware you'd noticed my attention, and I could tell I made you nervous." Throwing his hands up, the man named Ethan sighed. "That wasn't my intention, but here we are."

"What is it you want?" Pharis was standing against the door frame, his stance clearly ready to grab her and run if need be.

"Simply to talk. I want to explain everything. I should've done it a long time ago, but for the longest time, I wasn't sure it was you. Just wishful thinking, I kept telling myself."

"Me? What about me?" Aurianna's attention was suddenly piqued, and all thoughts of escaping the room cleared from her mind.

"When I saw the necklace, I was so sure, but it seemed so impossible. I just…" Ethan's eyes lit up with an intense longing. "You look just like her."

"If you're talking about my mother, I've heard enough about her already—"

Ethan shook his head. "I don't know what you've been told, but I can assure you no one knows her better than I do."

"And why is that?"

"Because I'm in love with her."

The room stilled for half a beat before Aurianna found the words she was grasping for. "Apparently you aren't the only one. I don't know what hold this woman has over men, but I wouldn't be surprised if it's some sort of enchantment."

"No, definitely not an enchantment. We love each other very much and have for quite a long time."

"Each other? Are you saying…?"

"I'm saying—trying to say—I'm your father."

Pharis took a step forward but stopped himself. "No. No, no, you're a Void. That's impossible."

Ethan turned to him and bowed his head. "Forbidden perhaps, but not impossible."

"Aurianna, we should leave now. This man is clearly up to something."

"I recognized the necklace you were wearing before. It was hers—your mother's. She never took that thing off, so I thought I must be mistaken. But it's so unique, and then there were all the rumors about why you were here. For a long time, I had thought… I thought you were dead."

"Yeah? Well, I almost was thanks to the woman you call my mother."

A look of shock flashed across Ethan's face. He looked both horrified and confused. "No, child! No, Syrena didn't do that."

Syrena.

Pharis had moved forward and backward several times, uncertainty clouding his movement. He was practically in the other man's face when he yelled, "Don't try to protect that evil woman! Everyone knows what happened." He was panting in his anger, bits of spittle flying from his mouth as he reached out to grab the front of Ethan's robes.

The other man tried to respond, but he was having difficulty speaking as Pharis shook him. Ethan finally pulled himself away and stood on the other side of the room. He straightened his robes and took in a deep breath. "Everyone might think they know what happened, but they weren't there."

"And you were?" Pharis's face was still red, but his voice had settled down.

"In a way. I couldn't actually get in because of the locking spell they had placed on the tower, but I saw enough."

"What did you see?" Aurianna couldn't deny her curiosity any longer, despite the source. She needed answers.

"You're not actually listening to this, are you?" Pharis asked her heatedly.

"What harm is there in listening?" she bit back.

"Regulus," Ethan interrupted, "you know what your father did. He had no business going after a woman twenty-five years younger than himself. Her powers far exceeded those of any other Kinetic, and Darius—the Magnus—became obsessed with the idea of creating offspring with her and ruling the land."

"How do you know that?" Pharis's voice had gone quiet.

"He wasn't shy about telling her! I guess he thought she would be flattered, because in his mind anyone with power would want to use it like he would. But she was disgusted by all of it. So I suggested we run away, hide somewhere until he got bored and left us alone. But he didn't. And being away from here for so long, without the contraceptives, is how she got pregnant. Despite the risk, we were happy and excited to start a family. I thought we could somehow escape from that madman."

"You are speaking of your Magnus, Void!"

"And saying nothing more or less than you yourself utter when you think no one is listening."

The glare the Regulus shot him was nothing short of murderous, but he didn't respond.

Ethan shook his head, staring at nothing, as if he were in a trance. "He sent his best trackers after us, and they took her straight to the Magnus. I had already known about the secret passage to the tower from here, so when I found out where he was hiding her, I rushed down to the entrance you discovered earlier. I found it in the same condition you did, a completely impenetrable barrier blocking me from entering.

I was desperate to see Syrena again, desperate to make sure she was okay, that the baby would be okay. I tried screaming her name, beating on the wall with my bare fists, but no one came. I started visiting the door every day, spending every moment I wasn't required to work sitting there waiting for a glimpse of the woman I love."

Tears shone in his eyes when he looked back at her. "After about a week, she finally came down to that lower room, and I was . . . I was so relieved to see her, to know she was okay. I called out to her, but she couldn't hear me. Whatever magic that had the tower closed off kept her from hearing or seeing me. It broke my heart to be so close to her, to be able to reach out and almost touch her but never being quite able to do so. I needed her to know I was there somehow. I needed her to not lose hope, so I gave her the only gift I could. She always loved roses."

"That was you? How?" Aurianna had seen those roses, their vines twisting and twining up and down the tower and the surrounding ground. Not even a Kinetic could have pulled that off with power alone.

"That is perhaps a more complicated story, but suffice it to say, your mother taught me a thing or two about how to really use our powers."

With a sharp burst of acidic laughter, Pharis said, "But you're a Void. You don't have powers."

"You don't really believe that, do you?"

Aurianna stood up, putting herself between the two men. "I know about the . . . The Arcanes told me you can't control the elements, but you do contain elements within yourselves somehow. But that's not the same thing as being a Kinetic."

"No, it's not the same thing, but it's just as important. The Magnus refuses to acknowledge it, and you're right that most Voids can't do anything with it. But that's only because they don't know how."

"You expect us to believe you're Aurianna's father?" Pharis piped up behind her.

Ethan smiled. "You don't have to believe me. Ask Syrena yourself."

Aurianna felt her resolve harden, and she knew what her next step was. "Oh, don't worry. I plan to as soon as I figure out how to get into that tower."

"You won't be able to just walk in. The enchantment they placed is bound to her. Only she could get in, and absolutely no one can get out."

"What do you mean *they placed*?"

"The Magnus. He's the one that had her locked up in the tower."

Pharis started forward again. "Wait. You're saying my father locked her in there?"

"That's exactly what I'm saying."

Pharis shook his head. "Why would he lock her in there, and then tell everyone else she locked herself in?"

"Are you telling me your father isn't capable of being dishonest to get what he wants?"

Pharis glared at the man, and Aurianna felt a sudden wave of giddy amusement at the irony of the situation. The ordeal was making her delusional, but Pharis's next words brought her back to reality. "Fine. But what would he stand to gain from that?"

"To have someone to blame when bad things happen. To make her look like the bad guy. You know your father better than anyone. The Magnus isn't used to not getting what he wants. I think you're well aware your father is the reason we had to run away. He was completely obsessed with her."

"No, the reason you had to run away was because you broke the rules. Not only did a Kinetic get pregnant—which was bad enough—but she had a romantic relationship with a Void, That's unforgivable."

"She wasn't pregnant when we left. And yes, we couldn't risk someone finding out she was with me. But Darius wouldn't leave her alone. That's why we had to leave."

The rules of this world were often confusing for Aurianna, but most Kinetics seemed to be totally oblivious to the things that didn't add up. Frustration marred her interactions with others, and Pharis was no exception. "Pharis, why do you think they have rules like that? Why is it so important Kinetics not have children? I mean, if it's so important, why does it not apply to the Magnus?

He can have children, so why should it matter? And why are they not allowed to be with a Void if they want to? If Voids are so unimportant—as they are treated—then why should anyone care who they're with?"

"Because . . ." he growled at her, "because of this! Exactly this mess we are currently in!"

"But we're only in *this mess* because they had to hide it."

"So now you don't think the Enchantress is to blame for the train? For you almost getting killed? For the dragonblood or plotting to start a civil war?"

Crossing her arms, she countered, "No, that's all on her. Two separate issues."

Ethan stepped around her, his eyes darting between the two who stood face to face in a standoff. "I'm telling you, she cannot leave the tower. That's how I know she didn't do the things you think she did."

Aurianna whipped her head around to look at the man who called himself her father. *Father. Dear Essence.* "Oh, she most definitely *can* get out. I saw her myself, on that train. Red hair. Crazy fire powers. I know it was her."

"There has to be another explanation. She would never, ever hurt anyone. I can't believe she's the person everyone says she is. A bit of a temper, perhaps, but I love how passionate she is. From what I've heard around here, I think you got that from her. She was bold, but kind."

"You're painting a far different picture of her than anyone else has. As much as I would love to believe you, as much as I would prefer my mother not be the horrible person everyone thinks her to be, to not be the woman who put a killing curse on her own baby—"

"Aurianna, I swear to you it couldn't have been her."

"You said yourself no one can get in. Who else could it have been?"

"When the pains came, and it was time for you to be born, the Magnus allowed midwives in to help with the birth. I hid when they showed up, but I saw them enter the tower through the barrier . . . like it opened just for them. I stayed down by the door through the night. I couldn't see anything since they remained in an upstairs room, but I heard much. I heard her screaming in pain. I heard her call out my name, and it ripped my heart to shreds not being able to go to her." Ethan's eyes had taken on a faraway look. "I prayed every day that she would look down and see the roses and know I was with her in the only way I could be." His voice trailed off.

"So, what happened?" Aurianna asked pointedly to snap him out of his reverie.

"A little while later, a man showed up—one of the Arcanes. He just nodded at me and walked straight in without a word. Once I heard the first cries of my child—of you, Aurianna—I thought somehow everything would be okay. But something was wrong. I heard the voices getting louder, and then two of them started screaming. It was just chaos. I could distinctly hear your mother crying, saying *please don't hurt my baby*. A terrible crashing sound erupted, followed by more voices, more screams. A few moments later, a woman came running down the stairs holding a bundle of blankets. She looked through the doorway and seemed to be staring at me like she could see me. I didn't understand what was happening, and I didn't know what to do. Then suddenly she ran right through the barrier like it wasn't even there. She didn't stop, but she spoke to me as she hurried past, something like *don't worry, I'll make this right*. I was in shock for a moment, but then I took off after her, realizing that bundle of blankets was probably you."

"You just let a strange woman run off with me?" Aurianna knew it must have been Aunt Larissa, but how would this man have known whether a stranger's intent was good or evil?

"No, of course not! I felt odd for a moment, like I couldn't move or think straight. Then I tried to chase her down, but she was just… gone. Like she'd disappeared."

"Like she went through a time portal with an Aether Stone?" Out of the corner of her eye, Aurianna saw Pharis throw a sharp glance in her direction, but she ignored him.

"Maybe, but she couldn't have had more than a half a minute head start, and she was carrying a baby."

"I think you underestimate my aunt."

"Your…your what?"

"Nothing. What about the other midwives?

"I don't know. They could have left at any point while I was chasing down that woman."

"That woman's name is Larissa, and she saved my life. You know nothing about her."

"And there's still so much you don't know about Syrena."

"You mean like how she taught you to make plants grow from nothing to completely surround the tower?"

"That, and other things. She could do things no one else could, things no one else even knew about. Not even Darius."

"How?"

"What?"

"How could she do things no one else could?"

"It's all connected: the elements, the powers, the control. Kinetics were never meant to be limited in the ways they currently are."

"What do you mean *limited*?"

"Like with the roses. Geokinetics can do more than just move around a bit of stone or earth. If they were properly trained, they could control just about anything growing in the ground."

"Maybe having that much power isn't a good thing."

"Perhaps, but maybe you should find out more about our history—about Eresseia—before you make any judgment."

"I know power can do great things, but I also know power can cause people to get hurt. Your own people even." Aurianna noted the look of fear in the man's eyes at her words. "Ethan, the Voids that have gone missing . . . Do you know something we don't, or am I right in thinking they've been taken, and it has something to do with the fact that they're basically walking elemental power? I mean, it seems like they're basically concentrated sources of Fire, Earth, Water, and Energy."

"And air," Pharis added in a near whisper.

Ethan nodded. "Yes, I think that's exactly what happened, but I think the problem exists because no one talks about any of this. No one wants to give up the power they have, so they smother any knowledge concerning a different type of power."

Pharis leaned back against the wall, picking at his nails. "Not all Kinetics would feel that way."

"They haven't been given the chance one way or the other, have they?"

A cold chill swept across Aurianna's exposed skin. She sat down in the lone chair Ethan had vacated. "What do you know about the Aether Stone?"

He shrugged. "I know it's ancient, but I don't know where it came from."

"Ethan, where are you from?"

"Ramolay. Both of my parents passed away a few years ago. Syrena—she's from Menos. Her mother passed away as well. She never knew her father."

A dense silence expanded in the small confines of the room, making her ears ring with the sound of the nothingness she was feeling. Leaning forward, Aurianna placed her elbows on her knees and cradled her head in her hands. She began to shake from the combination of exhaustion and hopelessness permeating her mind and soul.

After a few moments, Ethan's voice broke the silence. "I hope I've convinced you Syrena isn't who they want you to believe she is."

Peeking up through the spread of her fingers, Aurianna breathed out a sigh of frustration. "I'm not convinced of anything. I don't know a thing about this woman apart from what people tell me." She shot Pharis a meaningful look. "And none of you can seem to agree. My necklace was the only physical piece of evidence linking me to her, and that's gone now."

"Gone?" Ethan's face was pained.

"It fell into Perdita Bay the night the train exploded." Aurianna's agitation flared. "But even that means nothing! It doesn't prove anything."

"Your eyes."

Ethan's words caught Pharis's attention. He looked up with a questioning stare. "What about them?"

Ethan nodded in Aurianna's direction. "She has her mother's eyes."

Pharis looked pensive, but Aurianna spat out, "So? Lots of people have similar eyes and aren't related." The words fell flat as they dropped from her lips. Even she heard the ridiculousness of the statement.

Pharis was still looking at her. "Aurianna, no one has eyes like yours. And you know it."

"And your temper." Ethan was smiling now.

She wasn't amused. "Excuse me?"

"What I mean is, you're a very emotional, passionate person from what I hear, and so is your mother."

"I fail to see your point. Are we just throwing insults now?"

"It's not an insult. That's one of the things that drew me to your mother." The bastard was still smiling at her. "Syrena cares. Too much. But it can also manifest in negative ways, like when she would get angry. Things would…happen."

Aurianna sat back up, narrowing her eyes. "What kind of things?"

He shrugged. "Fires getting out of control, lights flickering, things like that. Sometimes worse. But training never really helped her much." The man hesitated, holding onto something he didn't want to share. Finally, he shrugged again. "She didn't … need to train, not in the traditional sense. The powers came to her so naturally the Magisters were somewhat afraid of her. She never did anything intentionally, and she never hurt anyone—" Ethan's eyes implored her, beseeching for her faith to match his own— "but her emotions fueled her powers. She had to learn to control them."

Pharis shot back, "From what I've seen, that day never came."

"From what I've heard, our Aurianna here has the same obstacles to overcome."

Hearing his words, she exploded. "I'm not *your* Aurianna, or your anything! You, sir, are a stranger to me. How old are you?"

"Thirty-three."

"You're barely more than a decade older than I am, and you want me to look at you as my father?"

"I don't want you to do anything you don't want to do. That's not why we're here. I realize how odd all of this is. Of course I want to be in your life, now you know the truth. But I understand how confused you must be right now."

"I don't think you understand at all. I don't think anyone can. Why are you just now telling me this? Why wait, if you've known all this time?"

"I didn't know for certain, but I suspected from the first. And it's difficult to get to you without attracting the suspicions of those who wouldn't want me speaking with you if they found out who I was."

"Like the Magnus? Or do you mean the Arcanes?"

"The Arcanes know who I am, but the Magnus does not. He doesn't know what I look like, not really. Do you think he would allow me to live if he knew I was the one your mother chose over him? When we were tracked down, she gave herself up so I could get away." Tears shone in his eyes. "I begged her not to, but she wanted to give me a chance to sneak back and avoid the wrath of the Magnus."

"And yet, the Arcanes know."

"I have no idea how, but yes."

"Oh, I have a pretty good idea."

Ethan spread his hands in supplication. "You're not my hostage, Aurianna. I'll admit there's a part of me that wants to keep you here—to keep you safe—and to make up for so much lost time. Well, it's lost from your perspective. As far as I'm concerned you were born less than a year ago. You would still be a baby if none of this had ever happened. You would be with your mother and me. We would be a family."

"Don't start getting any ideas about family with me! I don't know you, and I don't even know how much of what you're saying is true. But the only family I've ever truly had is waiting on me to fix all of this. Larissa—even though she's kept so much from me—is the only person who truly cared about me."

"That's not true. When your mother found out she was pregnant—"

Ethan stepped forward like he was going to reach out to her, but Aurianna sidestepped his advance. "Stop calling her that!"

He stilled his movements. "I just want you to know that you were wanted and loved. I promise you that. And we love each other very much. I need you to know that too. I can't lose her. I can't lose either of you."

Bile rose in her throat. "I need to go."

Pharis hurried over to her as she stood up from the chair, wrapping his arm around her waist and walking her to the door. All her emotions were on high alert, alarms going off in her head as she thought about Ethan's words: *Her emotions fueled her powers. She had to learn to control them.*

The familiarity cut through her like a knife. Larissa had been right all along.

CHAPTER 25

AURIANNA

Aurianna allowed Pharis to lead her back up to the main levels of the Imperium. When he attempted to continue up to the dorms, she shook her head and pulled away from his grasp.

His eyebrows furrowed at her sudden distance. "What's wrong?"

"Are you really asking me that?"

Pharis pursed his lips and cocked his head to the side. "You know what I mean."

"I . . ." Aurianna's voice trailed off as she struggled to find the words. "Pharis, I have to speak with him."

"Who? My father?" His gaze was wary as he began to realize her intentions. Shaking his head, he reached out to touch her again but let his hand drop suddenly with a slight widening of his eyes, as if he realized what he was about to do. "It can wait. I'll go with you tomorrow, I promise."

"I've been waiting for *years*. I'm not waiting any longer. Everyone's been lying to me"—she threw a pointed glare in his direction—"so I think I deserve the truth for once."

Pharis hung his head for a moment before looking back up at her. He ran his hands down his face in frustration. "All right, all right. But he's not going to be happy about being woken up." At Aurianna's fiery gaze, he threw his hands up in the air in defense. "Not that that matters right now. But I'm just warning you."

"If I were you, I'd run ahead and warn *him*."

"Duly noted. You don't want me to walk up there with you?"

"No. Go on ahead and wake his royal ass up, so we can get this over with."

Groaning, Pharis opened the stairwell door and walked through into the main hall. Aurianna decided to give him a few minutes to reach the guards and request an audience. In the meantime, she sat wearily on the stairs and let the events of the day and night wash over her.

Trying not to think about any of it was useless. No matter what was true, all of it was far too big to ignore. She was trying to leave the more personal aspects aside to emotionally sift through later.

But it was no use. The family she'd been looking for—the main reason she had left her home to begin with—was within her grasp. Yet it wasn't in the neat little package she had hoped for, dreamed of in her most vulnerable moments. She had accepted the death of her parents a long time ago. She had accepted the *specifics* of her mother's death only recently. And now she had found out that none of it was true.

Accepting that they were alive was much, much harder. Facing the idea that they were only slightly older than she was? Next to impossible.

An image of her aunt flooded her mind, reminding Aurianna of what she had left behind to come here. Larissa was the physical representation of what Aurianna thought a mother should be, but it was more than that. Her aunt was a kind person, a good woman.

The female in the tower . . . well, whatever else she was, no one, apart from Ethan, saw her as anything remotely kind or good. Was it possible she wasn't the woman from the train?

But Aurianna knew what she had seen that night. The hair, the flames, all of it pointed to the Enchantress. It didn't matter who or what she was to Aurianna. The woman was a murderer and a monster.

Aurianna shook the sinister thoughts from her head. She stood and marched up to the throne room to speak with the man who may have created that monster.

She stopped just in front of the guards posted at the door. They nodded to her and motioned for her through. As she crossed the threshold to the room, she saw Pharis standing off to the side, staring fixedly out the window and deliberately ignoring her entrance. The Magnus was looking directly at her as she approached. Darius's face was a mix of confusion and irritation. He never took his eyes off her as she marched determinedly up to his not-a-throne, his seat of power in the world he was desperately trying to create.

Refusing to be intimidated, Aurianna glared back at the Magnus without saying a word. Finally, he broke the tense silence.

"What is it you want at this time of day? It must be important if my *son* was made to come and fetch me from my bedchambers. Got him wrapped around your little finger already, do you? It certainly shouldn't surprise me."

Aurianna allowed the slightest of smiles to tilt the corners of her lips. "Pharis has nothing to do with this. He happened to be up early and roaming the halls, and I asked if he would request an audience with you."

"And what is the purpose of this audience?"

She knew rushing straight in and asking about the tower

wouldn't lead to any answers. Not any good ones, at least. Aurianna decided on a different tactic. The only way to get the truth would be to get the Magnus so flustered he let something slip.

"I want to know what your angle is."

"Excuse me?" Darius raised his eyebrows, his head jutting forward in consternation.

"You have the ability to change people's lives for the better, yet you don't."

"I have no idea what you're talking about." His eyes had narrowed suspiciously.

"I just don't understand how you could have access to all this power, yet you use it for such mundane things. You could do so much for this world, but you're over here heating up my shower and irrigating crops."

"And what makes you think those things aren't important, aren't vital to our society?"

"Well, as much as I enjoy the hot showers, I don't know that I would call them vital. The crops I can understand, obviously. But these are all things that people—just regular people—could do for themselves. Why do they need you—need us—at all?"

"We provide things they couldn't have without our help. Think about Energy, the electric power running through every town, every city. Could they survive without it? Sure. But why should they if we can provide it?"

"But you're not providing it. You're simply transporting it. And that's only because you're hoarding here at the Imperium. If you built a generator like you have here at each town, they could run it themselves without having to touch it or move it."

Darius spat back, "But then what would be our purpose, Aurianna? What would they need us for?"

"Exactly." At his sharp glance, she went on. "That's it then. That's what you're afraid of. You're worried the non-Kinetics will one day realize they don't need you. And what will you do then? You might have to actually work for a living."

"This is my kingdom, Aurianna. I take care of these people, my people. Without Kinetics, they would be helpless." The Magnus kept glancing over at his son who stood in the corner of the room, impersonating a statue. Pharis looked uncomfortable, like he was waiting for Darius to discover his role in everything that had happened over the last twenty-four hours.

Aurianna wasn't about to drag him into it any further than he was already. Ignoring his presence, she kept her eyes on the Magnus. "Only because you and your predecessors have taught them to be so. You enable their helplessness. I think you underestimate how that makes them feel."

"If they didn't like it, they wouldn't allow it."

"Perhaps they won't for much longer."

"Is that a threat, my dear?"

"No, sir. Just an observation."

The man squirmed in his seat—the chair designed to look like every picture of a throne she'd ever seen in books. Aurianna had begun to realize everyone's perceptions of the dangers of the Magnus wielding that much power were based on an extreme lack of knowledge and, experience, and perspective. She had been reading since she was little, something most of these people rarely did outside of required reading for school. They couldn't imagine how bad things could turn out because they had never experienced it, either in their own lives or in books.

"Why are you here, girl?"

"What do you mean?"

"I mean, why are you really here? You didn't come here just to have a philosophical debate with me."

"It's not philosophical when the people—"

"Enough!" he shouted, standing up to tower over her. The man was as tall as his son, an impressive and imposing figure, but Aurianna wouldn't allow herself to be intimidated.

She held her head high. "Fine. I'm here to ask you to release the lock on the Enchantress's tower."

The Magnus fell back a step, almost tripping over his chair. He reached a hand up to absentmindedly fondle the silver pendant he always wore around his neck. "What are you talking about? Why would you want that tower unlocked?"

"So, you admit you're the one who had it locked, not her?"

He looked uncomfortable, his face ashen. Sinking back into the chair, the man appeared defeated but said, "I admit no such thing." His grip on the necklace had tightened, and suddenly, Aurianna knew.

Whatever magic had been used to lock the tower, it wasn't Kinetic power. This was deeper and older, maybe Fae if the stories were to be believed. She wasn't sure how the spell had been performed, or who had done it, but she was certain about one thing.

That necklace was the key.

Cocking her head to the side, Aurianna narrowed her eyes at the Magnus as she plastered an amused smile on her face. "That's a lovely pendant you have around your neck." Any color remaining in the man's face drained the moment those words left her mouth. More certain than ever, she continued, "I used to have a necklace I wore all the time. It belonged to my mother. Very old. Ancient. But mine had a dark sapphire stone in it, almost black."

Darius was visibly shaking. "Guards! Take this girl to her room and post a guard outside until further notice. She is not to leave the room until I say otherwise."

Well, I guess I should have expected that.

As rough hands gripped her on both arms and began to drag her from the room, Aurianna thought detachedly about how indestructible she had begun to feel over the last few moons. Having powers—more than she had been told were possible—had given her a dangerous sense of purpose and self-assurance. Regret washed over her with a heavy dose of reality. She wasn't above the law. She wasn't all-powerful.

She was just a girl with a vague sense of a plan who had gotten in way over her head.

The thought almost made Aurianna cry, but she refused to let a single drop fall in the presence of the men who marched her to her room and closed the door behind her. The metallic noise of the locking mechanism was normally comforting, but now she knew it wouldn't protect her.

This was now her prison.

She finally let go of the sobs threatening to engulf her and let the tears flow. She cried into her pillow until a numbness took over. Deciding to take a hot shower, Aurianna was almost done when she realized with a start that she was a hypocrite, enjoying the luxuries she had just vilified to state her case to the Magnus. But the soothing warmth of the water did help to calm her down.

Once she was dried and dressed, Aurianna sat back down on the bed to try to formulate a plan for getting out of her room.

She must have leaned against her pillow and dozed off in her exhausted state. A buzzing sound echoed in the small space, startling her into consciousness, and it took her a moment to realize someone was at her door.

Probably the Magnus himself, come to announce I'm to be thrown into the outer ocean as punishment for my crimes.

Ignoring it was useless. If he wanted in, he would simply have the door opened if she refused to open it from the inside. With a bravado she certainly didn't feel, Aurianna stabbed at the button to open the door as she squared her stance and stared straight ahead.

Sapphire blue stared back. Confused, she hesitated before speaking. "Ph-Pharis. What are you—"

"That's Regulus to you, girl. Now step aside and let me in. The Magnus has sent me with a message."

"But I—" Aurianna felt herself tearing up all over again. This wasn't the man she thought she knew.

"Move!" he roared and shoved his way in. When he pressed the button and the door closed, Aurianna found herself slapping the back of his head before she realized what she was doing.

She had *slapped* the Regulus.

But the man before her turned around sharply as he placed a hand gingerly against the place where her hand had made contact. "Ow! What the hell was that for?"

"What do you mean *what was that for*? You bloody swine, I thought we were friends. I thought—"

"You thought I'd choose my father over you?"

"Well, yes. I mean no. I mean…" She didn't want to think about the implications of that statement.

Amusement flickered in his eyes as he reached into his pocket then held up his hand. Something shiny sparkled in the dim light of the room.

"Is that…?" Her eyes flicked back and forth between his grinning face and the dangling pendant. Aurianna couldn't form the words.

"Yeah."

"But how did you … I mean, what did you do? Does he know you took it?"

"Hell no. Do you think I'd be standing here if he did?" Pharis waltzed over to her bed and sat down. A jittery feeling wiggled down her spine, but she sat down beside him, leaving as much space between them as she could. What if one of the guards walked in right at that moment?

"After your pre-dawn audience, he went back to bed," he continued. "That's the only time he takes it off. I thought maybe it was something my mother gave him, considering he's always wearing it. I never dreamed..." Sighing, he dropped the piece into her outstretched hand. "Well, there it is. Do what you need to do."

Aurianna went into the bathing room to wash the sleep from her face but spoke through the half-open door. "But won't you... I mean, the moment he wakes up and sees it gone, he's going to know you were the one who took it, won't he?"

"Most likely. Or he'll figure it out soon enough. I'll worry about that. You go talk to your mother."

"Please don't call her that. And I don't know about talking. Am I not here for the purpose of stopping her? Shouldn't I be going in guns blazing, as they say?" She sat back on the bed.

Pharis laughed quietly. "I think talking is more prudent, at least until she gives you a reason to do otherwise. Keep your guns on standby though." He patted her leg, then immediately realized what he had done. Snatching his hand back, he stood up suddenly.

Without thinking, Aurianna reached out a hand to grab his arm before he could go. "How did you get them to let you in?"

He shrugged. "Exactly what I said when you opened the door. Said I had a message for you straight from my father. They didn't even question it." A pensive look crossed his face. "Guess that should worry me actually." Pharis shrugged again and made for the door, promising to distract the guards long enough for her to sneak out.

Aurianna had doubts about his plan. It seemed too simple and too ridiculous for the guards to fall for it. Yet when Pharis stopped a few paces away from the end of her hall and grabbed his chest before slumping to the floor, both guards ran over to him without a thought. She silently cursed him for being right, giggling to herself as she crept out and closed the door behind her. Hopefully they wouldn't check the room right away if they thought she was still in it.

* * *

Javen's eyes lit up as Aurianna explained everything she had learned over the past day—about her mother and the man who claimed to be her father—and explained to him what her plan was. She left out any mention of Pharis being directly involved because she knew how Javen would react.

At least, that's why she told herself she did it.

They were sitting on his bed as she recounted her story. Aurianna kept glancing to the door, convinced the Magnus would find out she was gone and come here looking for her. Javen sat close, his arm around her while she talked about her discoveries and the fight with the Volanti.

When he asked how she had managed to escape them, Aurianna knew she couldn't divulge Pharis's secret. But she hated lying to Javen, so she simply said, "We used Air to avoid the water." She failed to mention who the *we* included.

"How did you get your hands on the pendant?" Javen narrowed his eyes in suspicion, and she couldn't tell if he knew more than he was letting on.

Aurianna hesitated, but she knew she couldn't outright lie. "He doesn't wear it when he sleeps. I had Pharis grab it." Wincing internally, Aurianna felt a gnawing guilt eating at her core.

"What? Why would he do that?"

"I went to talk to the Magnus, and they were fighting"—another partial truth—"so Pharis was already mad at him. I told him I needed the pendant, so he got it."

"Just like that?"

"I told you. I think he was just trying to piss off his father."

Javen's eyes bored a hole into hers as he stared at her, his scrutiny almost unbearable.

Dawn was probably already on the horizon, and the little amount she had slept wasn't doing her any favors. This was not how she wanted to spend her time.

Reaching out a hand to brush a stray hair from the side of her face, Javen let his touch linger there. The gesture was comforting, but Aurianna's mind was cluttered with all the pieces of her shattered life. She was trying desperately to fit all the pieces together, but the picture kept rearranging itself and was no longer recognizable.

Slowly, he leaned in closer as his hand slid behind her back. The wound from the Volanti flared up for a moment, and she involuntarily flinched. A question in his eyes turned to sudden realization. "The creature? This's where it hurt you? I'm so sorry I wasn't there to protect you."

"It's okay. I know the Magnus closed everything off. Besides, I had others there with me. I actually was lucky." Aurianna smiled at him, hoping to lighten the mood and change the subject.

Javen returned her smile, but a wildness lingered in its depths. He leaned in again, his lips brushing against hers in the slightest of touches. His eyes found hers as he said, "I'm still sorry. For everything you had to go through, everything you learned." He pressed his lips to hers again. "I care about you, Aurianna. I do. And I'll help you do whatever you need to do with that necklace."

He kissed her again, this time deeper, but still soft and gentle. His free hand lightly brushed against her leg, his other still wrapped around her torso. Pulling her close, Javen whispered, "I want to show you I care."

She knew what he meant. She wasn't going to pretend she didn't. This was new territory for her, a fact of which Javen was well aware. But he had been so patient with her, so kind, so gentle through everything. Even the night of their first date when she had run away from him in fear, he hadn't shown any anger or frustration with her. Only understanding.

And she felt guilty. Guilty for all the details she was leaving out, all the things she didn't want to think about. Javen had been there for her through everything. Her lack of experience was simply a product of living in a village where nothing was done for pleasure. Everyone had a purpose, survival their common goal.

But here, everything was different. She wanted for nothing, and no one would judge her for doing what she wanted to do.

A few weeks ago, Javen had practically proposed to her. It had made her feel both terrified and comforted to know someone cared that much about her. She could trust him to keep her safe.

And this was all she had ever wanted. Someone she could trust.

CHAPTER 26

AURIANNA

Aurianna stood facing the edge of the cliff, her insides melting into a pool of jelly. Javen held her hand as she stared at the pendant in her other hand.

Follow the path that draws you.

Destroying it had seemed like the thing to do. It was going to take some of her fancy Fire work to get the stupid thing hot enough to melt.

And Darius could find them at any moment, a fact which weighed heavily on her heart knowing what Javen was risking by helping her. But he had insisted on supporting her in this final stage—presumably—of her journey to fulfill her destiny.

Whatever that destiny was supposed to be, she had never expected it to look like this.

"Ready?" Javen squeezed her hand in encouragement.

She nodded, swallowing the lump in her throat as the reality of the situation began to press down on her chest with a force that threatened to bring tears to her eyes.

Argo, the Aerokinetic who had flown the ship that had taken her to the Imperium for the first time, was waiting close by with his airship floating well below the level of the cliff. They were hoping to keep him hidden until the last moment. He was risking just as much as she and Javen were, possibly more. Argo would fly her up to the top of the tower where the sides of the upper platform were open to the air.

Aurianna had insisted she could use a water bubble to send herself across Perdita Bay to the tower. Javen had argued she would lose the element of surprise if she did that. Airships flew by the tower all the time. That's also why she was waiting until the last moment to melt the pendant.

Still, she regretted having to involve any more people. Argo had readily volunteered when they had gone looking for an airship captain. Something about him had always made Aurianna feel at ease, so she had confided a small portion of her mission to him. Whatever the man was, Argo was clearly not a fan of the Magnus.

Just before signaling for Argo, Aurianna tried to wave to Javen but received a gentle kiss instead. The exchange was somewhat awkward considering everything that had happened between them since she had entered his room in the early hours of dawn, but she didn't regret one moment of it. Her innocence had left her the moment that dying mage had called out to her for help in that place she used to call home.

Javen had been just as gentle and understanding as she had expected. No regrets whatsoever.

When she finally gave the signal, Argo brought the ship up just enough for Aurianna to jump in. Her ability to use Air had increased somewhat, so she glided down as gracefully as she could. She smiled at her captain, and he returned the gesture. Argo was kind, and Aurianna hoped he would not suffer for aiding her.

The ship swiveled back around and flew toward the tower.

When they saw it looming in the distance, Aurianna looked down at the pendant in her hand, worrying her powers were not as ready for this as she had thought. No Voids around to drain—not that she would have done that again—and no magma in sight. Yet she had been making great strides with her Fire powers, unbeknownst to most. Magister Daehne had started treating her like his star pupil, which was both reassuring and somewhat creepy.

She had managed to conjure up some small flames, but it didn't always work. All of this was a wasted gamble if she couldn't melt the damn pendant.

Holding out her hand, palm facing up, Aurianna concentrated on the silver and what she needed to do to it.

For the love of the Essence, please work. Please, please work.

Tiny sparks shot up in her palm, but it wasn't hot enough to affect the metal. Focusing all her energy on her hand, Aurianna stilled her mind and closed her eyes. After a moment, a small whooshing sound filled the utter silence. Opening her eyes, she saw the pendant being caught up in the smallest fire she had ever seen, its edges curling like a piece of paper. The effect was odd, and she still wasn't sure how she avoided being burned by either the flames or the burning metal.

But it was working. Aurianna willed the fire to grow hotter and the metal to melt faster, as they had almost reached the top of the Enchantress's tower. At her request, Argo was keeping the ship just below the open level, so as not to attract attention until the last possible moment.

When the pendant was gone, she closed her palm, extinguishing the flame. Her gaze lingered on the water below before she turned to look at Argo. He nodded at her, a smile still on his lips, no trace of doubt in his eyes.

She could do this.

Raising her hands—she wasn't entirely sure why—Aurianna felt the power behind the water in the bay as it came up at her command. She willed the waters to surge well above the level of the airship, then she spread her arms apart to mimic what she wanted next.

And the water obeyed. It spread out to create a wall of liquid. Next, she formed a way up to the platform. The water cascaded up like a set of stairs. Glancing back one last time, she nodded to Argo before leaping onto the bottom of the liquid staircase and taking the steps up to the top.

The landing was softer than she expected.

The woman standing across from her on the other side of the platform was nothing like she expected.

Flaming red hair floated out from her head as the air whipped around them. She was close in size and shape to Aurianna, though perhaps her hips were slightly more rounded. Her scarlet skirt and bodice left little to the imagination, an odd choice of clothing for someone trapped in a tower. From a distance, Aurianna couldn't confirm the woman's eye color, but they did seem to glow like her own.

Any last hope of Ethan being either wrong or a liar was shot, though the fact that she was able to do what she had just done should also have left no doubts.

She had wanted them all to be wrong. Despite everything, the idea of destroying her own mother was almost more than Aurianna could bear.

Focusing on the negative emotions, she reminded herself that this was the woman who tried to kill her when she was just a newborn infant. A woman who could do that to her own child didn't deserve mercy or pity.

As if from nowhere, the space on either side and behind the

Enchantress was suddenly filled with the fiery outline of something out of a nightmare.

Aurianna knew it was a dragon. She could see through parts of it like she had with the Essence. Was it an illusion, or a spirit? The woman swished her hands, and it headed straight for Aurianna.

Instinctively, she threw her hands up in front of her. The stone around her feet began to rumble before it warped and stretched in front of her like a barrier.

Had she done that?

Lowering her arms, Aurianna stared at the solid wall of stone in front of her just before it crumbled to the floor of the platform.

"Impressive." The Enchantress's voice was deep but light. It didn't fit the figure standing there with a magic dragon curling its translucent self around her. "They finally decided to try to get rid of me for good, huh? I won't make it easy for you."

"No, this is just you and me. And whatever the hell that thing is."

"This? Oh, he's harmless. Unless I don't want him to be." The woman tilted her head, a fiendish look curving her mouth into a semblance of a smile. "And who exactly are you? Who do I have the pleasure of disappointing?"

"I think you know who I am, though you wouldn't recognize my name."

"I'm afraid I don't. Try me."

"I was named Aurianna by the woman who raised me."

"Hmm. Interesting. *Dawn*, right? My mother used to teach me the old language before I was taken away by your master."

"My master?"

"Darius. He so enjoys seeing the new recruits being brought in every year, new little soldiers for his Kinetic empire." After some thought, Syrena asked, "This woman who raised you . . . what was her name?"

"Larissa." Might as well jump right into it.

The other woman's eyes bulged, her mouth opening and shutting a few times before she managed to whisper, "What did you say?"

"Do I have your attention now?"

"What is the meaning of this? Who sent you here?"

"No one sent me here. I'm here on my own to confront you for what you've done and to stop you. Again."

"Again? I'm afraid I haven't had the pleasure of meeting you before, dear."

Aurianna bristled at the woman's condescending tone. "See, that's just not true, and you know it."

"And where would I know you from then?"

"The first time we met . . . well, I was a bit younger then, so you wouldn't recognize me."

"I see. And the second?"

"Just a few moons ago. When you tried to blow up the train and take half of Bramosia with it."

Syrena's laugh echoed against the stones. "I'm afraid you're mistaken. Can't say I remember being involved with that, though the spectacle was quite the show from up here."

"Why the hell are you lying? I would have thought you'd be proud, considering your goal."

"While I don't think I could ever resort to killing innocent people, I almost wish I could take credit for something that memorable. But I'm afraid I can't. As I'm sure you know, Darius doesn't exactly let me out for recreational time." Furrowing her brows, she said, "I'll ask again. Who are you?"

Aurianna was sick of the games, sick of the woman's flippant tone, sick of everything that had brought her to that point. Irritation lacing her voice, she said, "You mean, you don't recognize me . . . Mother?"

Syrena's face blanched. She stood frozen for half a second,

stumbled back, then rushed forward in a flash of movement, her hand reaching out in front of her as if to touch her, to convince herself of something. Aurianna stepped back out of her reach, the Enchantress staring into Aurianna's eyes with horror and shock burning in her own.

"I realize how much of a disappointment this must be to you, considering I'm still alive and all. Thanks to Larissa."

"Larissa," Syrena whispered. "You . . . You really have seen her?"

"Seen her? The woman raised me. She's been the mother you never wanted to be."

Confusion dulled Syrena's expression, a distant look in her eyes. "I don't understand. Larissa was . . . she was here when . . . But I thought . . . I thought she was killed."

"Well, I guess you missed us both then. Lucky for us."

"Missed? I didn't . . . What is it you think I did?"

"You mean apart from trying to kill me? Twice?"

"You can't be . . . my child is dead!"

"Like I said, sorry to disappoint *you*." The pain came anew as she heard the words spoken aloud.

"No! I saw it curse the child. Larissa took off with the baby but that . . . that monster was right on her heels. I thought . . . I thought . . ." The woman was becoming hysterical.

"What monster? The only monster I see here is you."

"You can't seriously think I would murder my own baby!" Her sobbing intensified. "I loved that child, and she was taken from me before I even had a chance . . ." Pursing her lips, Syrena's focus shifted. "Your eyes . . . they're—"

"Like yours? Yeah." A touch of light green around the edges was the only difference between Syrena's eyes and her own.

The sudden silence stretched on between them, expanding and collapsing at intervals. Aurianna's anger morphed into something less tangible, the pain and loneliness of the truth of her life nearly suffocating her.

Syrena's words ripped through the empty air like a knife. "The night my—you were born, I had three attendants, three midwives. Two of them were very old, very dear friends of my mother. The third—her name was Amara—was … she was not herself. I should have known something was off, but the birth pains were already well upon me when they entered the room. They told me Darius had allowed them to enter the tower to help with the birth." She winced at the memory. "I didn't really question it considering how far gone I was with the pain. Plus, I had known Larissa for most of my life, and I trusted her implicitly.

"A few hours later, a messenger from the Imperium arrived. Azel was an Arcane. I recognized him, so I assumed Darius had allowed him in as well. But there he was, holding a book, spouting off some nonsense about a prophecy. Stuff about the red sky at morning—" Her jaw dropped open. "Dawn," Syrena whispered, understanding finally slamming into her. "He also mentioned a dragon, but no one but Ethan knew about my ability to conjure one."

"I guess you're going to tell me you had nothing to do with the dragonblood incident? All those people you poisoned." Aurianna felt her face flush with anger.

The woman's gaze turned pensive. "Poison? How do you think I could have poisoned people? As I've said, I cannot leave this tower."

"The same way you were on that train the night I found you trying to blow up Bramosia."

"I wasn't on the train!"

"I saw you with my own eyes!" Heat crept up the back of Aurianna's neck as her breath came in pants, the anger overtaking her senses.

Syrena shook her head. "Don't you get it? They can make you

think whatever they want. My dragon isn't real. It's an illusion." To accentuate her point, she waved her arm in a circle, and the phantom-like outline of the dragon disappeared. "I've never even seen a real dragon. Before tonight, and your mention of dragonblood, I would have said they no longer existed." She stepped forward, closing the distance.

Aurianna tried to move away, but she realized the parapet was almost at her back. "Why should I believe you?"

"Because something very sinister happened that night, and I would guess it's somehow connected to the things you're telling me. That Arcane walked in and read out the prophecy like I wasn't sitting there screaming in pain. I don't even remember most of it. I thought the 'she' he kept going on about must have something to do with me, but at that moment, I really didn't give a damn. Then he started stammering about something needing to be awakened and a fire in the blood—though again I was just thinking about me, so I assumed he was referring to Fire powers."

"And then what? He just conveniently vanished before chaos ensued?"

Syrena's face morphed from revulsion into a mask of regret. "Something like that, only much, much worse." Her face took on a gentler appearance. "You came into this world only to be a victim of something I cannot truly explain. The midwives told me it was tradition in my mother's family to bestow a blessing on a newborn infant. Hermia blessed the child with strength of mind. Amara was supposed to go next, but something strange happened. Suddenly she wasn't herself anymore. Her shape changed. Everything about her was different, even her voice and height. Suddenly she towered over everyone. It looked like her, at first. But that wasn't Amara." Syrena's gaze swept the stone floor between them before she looked up into Aurianna's eyes.

"Larissa was trying to keep . . . that thing away from the baby. Whoever or whatever it was, it . . . it cursed the child with death."

"Cursed *how*?"

"I'll never forget those eerie words." The other woman visibly shivered, her voice barely a whisper. "I was still in shock from the pain, and we all thought she was going to give her blessing. The voice was . . . it was not human, but it said . . . *Before the Darkness comes to stay, the child will grow upon the day. And when the years have come and gone, touch the thorn and die at dawn.*

"Then it turned on Hermia and killed her without a second thought. She crumbled into a pile of ashes before my eyes." Her cheeks were wet as the tears rolled down her cheeks. "Azel too. He was there, and then he wasn't. Just a pile of ash. I don't know why it didn't kill me too, or you, in that instant, or why a curse was necessary.

"Larissa grabbed the baby and spoke some words. I didn't really hear or understand. I was too focused on the thing in front of me, and I think I was screaming, begging it to stop. Larissa ran off with the child, and the monster followed her. That was the last I saw of either of you."

"I don't understand this whole blessing and curse thing. Is that some Kinetic power I'm not aware of? I never questioned it when Larissa told me, but it doesn't make sense with what I've learned since then." Aurianna paused, crossing her arms as she leaned forward. "Of course, she tends to keep a lot of things from me."

"That sounds like her. But I have no idea. The midwives insisted on the blessings, but I just thought it was a gesture, a ritual. I never thought it meant anything."

"If it wasn't for Larissa's blessing or spell or whatever it was, I wouldn't be here now. She used hers to change my death sentence into . . . something else. She had to take me through the Aether, into the future. A future that is nothing like this world. A hundred years from now, Kinetics don't exist, and we fought just to survive. The sun was blocked by the Darkness at some point."

"The Darkness?"

"I wish I could explain it better, but that's just what we call it. No blue skies or sun visible by day and completely pitch black at night. You can literally feel it in the air, something ominous and overwhelming."

"And Larissa willingly took you there?" Syrena's eyes were wide with shock, horror etched into her features.

"It's not like she had a choice. That was where the Essence took us when she cast the spell. She raised me for twenty years. Then I was brought back by the—a man—who said he'd been sent from the past to fulfill a prophecy." Aurianna thought it best to leave Pharis out of the story for the time being.

"The prophecy was about you then?"

"I don't know what to think at this point. I didn't believe in prophecies at first."

"And now?" A slight smile tugged at the corners of Syrena's mouth, the wetness on her face already dry in the airy breeze sweeping through the tower's top level.

Aurianna shook her head. "I have no idea. None of this makes any sense. Ethan told me basically the same thing as you, but I don't know either of you. How do I trust people I don't know?"

"Even if we really are your parents?"

"That's irrelevant. You're what? Five to ten years older than me. Kinda weird." A wave of nausea hit her with the force of speeding train as her mind contemplated the ramifications of the bizarre conversation.

"Perhaps. But I—" Syrena's face paled as she pointed off into the distance behind where Aurianna stood.

Still wary of some trick on the part of the other woman, Aurianna turned around slowly. Flashes of light flickered in the distance. At first, she thought it must be lightning. But the night sky was calm and clear. The bright lights were coming from the roof of the Imperium.

"Perhaps someone is taking advantage of your absence. Who knows you're here?"

Instead of answering, Aurianna whispered a desperate plea to the Essence as she ran to the edge of the platform. Raising her arms in the air, she summoned the waters once again. They instantly shot up and leveled off, providing a flat surface for her to stand on.

She looked back at the woman. Their eyes met, and an unspoken promise was made. This conversation was not over.

Breaking her gaze, Aurianna climbed over the short wall. Heedless of how dangerous it would be if she lost control, she pulled the waters beneath her and guided her unorthodox transport back to the Imperium.

The distance was great, but the forward motion of the water made it seem as if it was almost nothing. The edge of the Imperium grew closer within moments.

As she neared the building, Aurianna could see there were several people on the roof, none of them moving. Six were dressed in gray robes and were staring straight up at the sky. Inexplicably, they were the source of the blinding flashes of light.

Voids. Were these the missing people?

Aurianna put all her concentration into forming a small waterfall to guide herself onto the building. The moment her feet touched the rooftop, she rushed toward the Voids, only to stop in frozen terror at what she saw.

Javen.

His eyes blazed, and his mouth curved into a smile of cruel satisfaction.

A smile she had never seen before.

CHAPTER 27

AURIANNA

Disgust. Shame. Regret. All slammed into her in one massive wave of self-loathing. Memories of the previous night bathed her in a sheen of sweat and humiliation.

A small voice in the back of Aurianna's head told her she should have known, should have trusted herself over the lying serpent which stood before her instead of slithering away like the monster he clearly was.

A monster who had taken advantage of her, manipulated her into believing in someone else just one more time.

Aurianna felt as if she were losing her mind, imprisoned inside her own thoughts. She was heartbroken, haunted by the ghosts of what might have been. What never should have been.

Bruised. Broken. Betrayed.

Despair bit into her with a sharp realization that Javen had robbed her of her innocence. There was simply nothing left of herself to give.

Drained.

Yet here were others far worse off, suffering at the hands of the man she had trusted implicitly. The man who had burned her alive in more ways than one.

Aurianna knew she was becoming hysterical, her grip on sanity loosening with every uneven breath she managed to pull into her lungs. The person responsible for her suffering was also responsible for whatever was happening to these Voids. And then she noticed the crumpled form of a girl nearby. Was it Belinda?

Green eyes stared back at her with amusement and satisfaction, watching her crumble. Javen said nothing, just stood there with his hands folded casually in front of his body as if the end of the world were not upon them.

Aurianna shook her head in confusion and horror. "No. No." His eyebrow shot up, daring her to voice the words she couldn't say. Her voice was barely a whisper. "What are you doing?" She had already answered the question in her heart.

"You claim to be such a smart girl, always figuring things out. Go ahead, then. Figure it out."

His gaze bored a hole in her brain. Her thoughts were tumbling around without focus, without purpose. Too many lies. Too many truths. All mixed together in a symphony of information she was ill-equipped to sort through without breaking into tears.

Instead, looking down at Belinda, Aurianna asked, "What's wrong with her? Did you … did you do something to her?"

With the tow of his boot, Javen kicked the body lying on the floor in front of him, flipping the girl over onto her back. A noticeable roundness protruded from Belinda's torso.

Pregnant.

Bile rose into Aurianna's throat, a sickening sensation beginning in her toes and moving upward at a rapid pace. She shook her head in disbelief. "I don't understand."

"See, I think you do. You just don't want to admit maybe you were wrong."

"About what? I've clearly been wrong about a lot of things." She glanced back to the line of Voids standing with their faces to the sky, unmoving, their bodies covered in a patina of Energy that radiated and sizzled with a high-pitched sound that made her ears hurt. "Those are the missing Voids."

"Fantastic powers of observation, Aurianna. What else?" Javen's smile was cruel and condescending.

"Don't talk to me as if—"

"As if what? As if your judgment of character has failed miserably?" He smirked at her reaction, and his tone was mocking. "Come on, Aurianna, savior of Eresseia! Let's hear your brilliant explanation for what I'm doing."

At that moment, the sound of several pairs of footsteps thundered across the space behind her. Leon's voice pierced the night air. "People are downstairs screaming about Voids, and we…" His voice trailed off. "Javen, what's going on?" His tone was wary, incredulous.

"Why don't you ask her?" Javen replied.

Aurianna looked behind her. Leon, Sigi, Theron, Laelia, and a few other Kinetics she recognized were standing there, including the one she had spoken to at the pub that night. The one she had watched die in the future. "I don't…" she began, unable to finish the thought. Turning back to Javen, she repeated, "What are you doing to those Voids? What did you do to *her*?" She pointed to the girl lying on the ground.

"Belinda has proven to be very useful, both as an albeit meaningless distraction and an adequate vessel for my plans."

"Your plans? Do you realize what you sound like?"

Javen laughed, the sound echoing off the rooftop. "Oh, but I *am* the villain."

"Your plans were to get her pregnant?" Aurianna heard a few audible gasps behind her as her friends took a closer look.

"That was certainly part of it. It's only because of you that any of the rest of this is necessary."

"Me? This"—she waved her hand around at the spectacle in front of her—"has nothing to do with me!"

"It has everything to do with you. Had you just died when you were supposed to, I wouldn't even have this opportunity." Bowing, he said mockingly, "So, thank you."

Her eyes narrowed. "What do you know about that?"

"I know about anything and everything—far more than you will ever learn in your insignificant little life, especially considering it's about to end."

Sigi's voice shook with emotion. "Javen, what have you done?"

"Friend," Leon said, "you and I both know you've got nothing against those Voids. If you're upset about the system, if you're upset about the Magnus, I understand. I've always told you that. But this isn't the way, man."

A flash of rage lit up Javen's eyes. "You think I give a damn about your system, or your leaders, or even these pathetic beings behind me? You call them Voids for a reason. They have no power. They are utterly useless. I am giving them a purpose, the only purpose they'll ever know."

Aurianna asked, "And what purpose is that, Javen?"

"Why, to give *you* a purpose, my dear. You wanted to save the world. Here's your chance."

"I don't understand why you're doing this, or even *what* you're doing."

"I am giving you your destiny, Aurianna. Your reason for being here. Your singularity."

She was beginning to hate that word. "What *is* the singularity?"

"You are."

A pain exploded behind her eye sockets. "What do you mean, *I am?*"

A sigh escaped Javen's tightly pursed lips. "Well, you're the cause of it, at least. Without you, there is no singularity. Look, we've been here before." He almost sounded bored. "We've done this before, and frankly, I'm getting quite tired of it."

Another set of footsteps pounded across the roof behind her. A hand gently touched her arm, and she looked over. Pharis was standing beside her, but he only had eyes for Javen right then. Unadulterated hatred seethed through every muscle of his trembling body.

Javen merely smiled at the Regulus. "Well, since we're all here now, let's get this show on the road." Before anyone could stop him, he walked up to the nearest Void and whispered something in the man's ear. As if in a trance, the Void reached out a hand to grab that of the Void next to him. One by one, each of the Voids took the hand of the next, creating a chain of Energy and locking them together in a solid line of pulsating power.

Javen looked thoughtful before he spoke again. "You have two options. You can either let all this power do its job and say goodbye to half the town. Or you can try to stop it and be responsible for the disaster yourself. Either way, the outcome is the same, and everyone left in Eresseia will believe Kinetics are responsible for it." A devilish smile parted his lips as he said, "War is inevitable. The future is inevitable. No matter what you choose, you cannot win."

The flashes of Energy formed a sphere around the Voids. The circling bursts of heat and light began to expand. A rumbling sound joined the high-pitched whine of the electricity spinning around and around, faster and faster, as the bubble of Energy grew exponentially.

The heat was intense, almost unbearable as the expanding orb drew closer. Aurianna's gaze was fixed in its core, her mind refusing to acknowledge the reality of impending doom—for herself, for her friends, and for many other innocent people. She heard voices beside her, behind her, around her, but none of the words registered. Through a haze, she saw Sigi and the others running for the door. Laelia was yelling something at her, but Aurianna couldn't hear her. The buzzing energy from the chain of Voids was so loud it was impossible to focus on anything else.

When Pharis grabbed her arm, attempting to pull her toward the stairwell with the others, Aurianna made a decision. Doing nothing was out of the question. Running wouldn't stop it from killing them all. Javen had said it wouldn't make a difference. Hell, hadn't Simon mentioned the exact same thing? The end result was always the same. She would die. But maybe she could prevent the deaths of others.

Wrenching herself from his grasp, Aurianna planted her right foot behind her. The glowing monstrosity before her was large enough now that she had to lean her head all the way back to view the top. At least a third of the roof was covered by it, and it continued to expand.

She held her hands out to the ball of Energy, feeling the searing heat but refusing to stop. Pharis was screaming her name. Others were as well, but she needed to keep her attention on what she was doing.

What *was* she doing?

The blazing light was rushing up her arms, across her chest, filling the space around her. Aurianna was absorbing the Energy. With no idea how or why, she was pulling the power into herself, the sphere moving to encircle her as it slowly left the chain of Voids. One by one they collapsed to the ground, but some of the Kinetics had run over to help them up. Aurianna wasn't sure if they were still alive, or if their bodies or minds could even survive the ordeal. But some were getting up and others were carried away.

Aurianna succeeded in pulling all of it away from the Voids as she stood cocooned in the warmth. Oddly, it didn't seem to burn her skin, but the heat was intense. Her hair was flowing out on all sides, and she could feel a prickling sensation on her scalp. When she looked behind her, she was surprised to see the scene had changed in what had seemed a small span of time.

Several airships were docking up next to the roof as dozens of Kinetics and Voids were pouring out of the stairwell and getting on board. Leon and Theron were helping those who needed assistance. Sigi was directing people onto the ships, trying to balance the crowd among the vessels. More ships arrived, and Laelia was trying to help Sigi maintain some semblance of order with the swarm of bodies pushing their way through.

Pharis was staring at her, horror written on his face as he shook his head.

But where was Javen? She suddenly realized he was no longer there, yet she hadn't seen him leave.

Pulling air into her lungs became a chore. Anger and betrayal battled for dominance within her. She had trusted him above all others. She had given him everything she had to give. But it had all been a lie.

Why? Did he hate the other Kinetics so much? Was he working for the resistance? The Order of the Daoine had attacked systems, blown up infrastructure. Were they capable of killing innocents to further their cause?

Aurianna was too far gone to stop now. Her emotions raged on, feeding off one another. She felt control slipping from her grasp, her anger a runaway train that would soon explode just as surely as the one she had blown up.

The one she had blown up.

Pharis had suggested she must have pulled the power of Fire directly from the woman on the train. The woman who insisted it wasn't her, but none of that mattered now. She had felt lost and helpless in that moment, upset that so many would die if she couldn't stop it.

And she had blown up the train.

You can try to stop it and be responsible for the disaster yourself. Either way, the outcome is the same.

Aurianna suddenly realized what Javen had meant by that statement. He had known what she was capable of, had known she would be hurting and angry. Had known she couldn't control her emotions if she was pushed too far.

She could finally admit to herself what her plan had been all along, ever since she made the decision to free the Voids. Knowing it deep down and admitting it to herself were two different things.

Sacrificing herself had seemed like such a simple choice in that moment. Aurianna had made it without a thought for what it would mean for her. Somehow, she had always known this was the result of all her attempts at heroics. It was simply a desire to protect her friends and all the other people in the area, Kinetic and non-Kinetic alike.

But her rage was getting the better of her, and Javen had known it would. Had counted on it.

Instead of saving everyone, she was going to blow up the Imperium, and Bramosia along with it.

It was inevitable. Simon had warned her. It had always happened this way.

Two faces in the sea of people stood out like flashes of lightning to her frightened mind. Both Kinetics she had met in the future, neither of whom she'd been able to help.

Both men who had been terrified at the sight of her. And now she knew why.

If this was the last vision they had of her before they jumped to the future at some point, it was no wonder they had looked at her with such despair and fear. She was about to destroy everything they knew.

She was the reason for the eventual civil war. She was the reason why so many Kinetics took a chance by traveling into the future to escape a horrible fate, only to find themselves at the mercy of an even worse one.

Bile rose in her throat as a wave of dizziness swept over her. Her breathing became more erratic. The Energy flying around her body was moving faster than ever, whooshing in circles as the sound grew again.

Disgusted at the role she had been tricked into playing, Aurianna looked around her in a sudden fit of longing to see her friends one last time. If those two Kinetics made it out of the area safely, then maybe her friends would too. They would hate her for what was about to happen. Maybe they would understand it hadn't been the outcome she wanted, but the deaths would be the same, no matter her intention.

She hoped Javen found himself at the mercy of those goddesses when all of this was over. That is, if *she* didn't track him down in the afterlife first.

Suddenly remembering Pharis, she glanced back to where he had been standing. He was just a few yards away from the edge of her electrified enclosure. Tears welled in his eyes, a mirror of her own. Why was he still standing there? Why wasn't he getting on a ship?

Trying to project her voice over the ear-piercing sound of the Energy, Aurianna screamed, "Go!"

But Pharis seemed to realize what she was doing. Maybe he had known the whole time. He shook his head.

She repeated the word, but he shook his head again. Crazed with grief, she said, "You'll die if you don't get on a ship." She could only hope the others were getting themselves to safety as, out of the corner of her eye, she saw the first of the airships flying away from the roof and into the darkening sky.

"I'm not leaving you!" His voice was hoarse and rough with unshed tears.

No one should ever get used to being alone. Not when there are people who care about them.

Pharis was right. She did have people who cared. Despite Javen's betrayal, there was no reason to believe her other friends didn't care. She realized now that he had lied to her, deliberately created a wedge between her and the others. But they had always been loyal and true to her, even when they had disagreed.

Pharis had tried to tell her. *I think maybe you aren't looking hard enough.*

Her breathing evened out as everything else vanished. She focused on the man in front of her, a sense of weightlessness edging her closer to the ball of Energy surrounding her.

No, the edge was coming to *her*. The ball was shrinking.

Intense heat flooded her veins. Aurianna looked down at her hands. They were covered in trails of electricity, but the flashes were directly touching her skin now. After a moment, even those tiny lines began to dissipate.

She was absorbing the power. But the telltale sensation she was about to implode never came. The Energy was simply flowing into her body. The heat in her veins was cooling off as each second passed.

Finally, light and heat vanished. Silence echoed in the night air.

Pharis was staring at her in wonder and delight.

Shouts rang out behind her, and Aurianna turned slowly, afraid of what disaster she might witness or be a part of next. But the voices were cheering, and she smiled despite the tears threatening to overwhelm her.

She had found her control.

Friends and strangers alike ran up to her, shouting and clapping her on the back. Hugs came from every direction. She saw no sign of the two Kinetics from the future. They must have left on the airships that had already flown away.

As things began to calm down, Sigi raised her voice to the crowd, telling them they should all still take precautions and board the remaining airships, just to be safe. No one was going to argue with that.

Most had already left, so it didn't take long to empty the roof of bystanders.

"I should have killed you when I had the chance." The voice was filled with disgust. *Javen.*

Aurianna, along with everyone still left, turned back to where the circle of Voids had originally been standing. The monster had indeed returned, his face filled with fury and bewilderment.

And he was aiming a weapon directly at her.

Before her, a wall of protective stone rose up from the rooftop, gaps every few feet and Javen on the other side.

Her friends ran for cover behind the walls of stone as they threw curious glances her way. She would have a lot to explain to them once this was all over, providing they made it out alive.

But first they had to stop Javen. He wouldn't give up easily. Aurianna knew he needed to stand trial for his crimes, but she had no idea how to get to him without being shot. At least they all seemed to be carrying their weapons.

Leon looked like he was about to collapse from grief. Aurianna knew he couldn't be counted on to help if it came down to it. Sigi's face was resolute, as were the others.

Pharis was standing behind the barrier next to hers, staring at her across one of the gaps in the stone, his weapon drawn and ready. Aurianna knew he wouldn't hesitate to shoot Javen. She shook her head at him.

He raised his eyebrows, giving her a look that said *he did just try to kill us.* Yes, he had tried to kill them—plus a lot of other people. But she knew deep down that a part of her still harbored feelings for Javen. She shouldn't, and she knew it didn't change anything. However, she also knew she didn't want to kill him. He needed to be punished, but that wasn't their job.

Maybe she could talk him into listening to her. Maybe she could convince him to turn himself in rather than face the possibility of being killed. He had to know Pharis wouldn't hesitate if given the chance. She couldn't give Pharis that chance.

A storm of gunshots drew her attention. Javen's superior skill with a gun was reflected in the ease with which he shot round after round in their direction. Sigi and Theron fired back in quick succession, their initial hesitation gone in the heat of self-preservation. Still, something was odd.

Javen seemed to be firing from behind an invisible wall. Their bullets simply bounced off the air in front of him, pinging in every direction, none connecting with the intended target. Yet Javen faced the same issue as his bullets hit nothing but stone.

Sigi's training as a City Guard kicked in, an intense focus pulling her into the fray. She seemed almost unaware of those around her as she popped around to aim and shoot, then ducked behind the stone barrier.

Laelia crouched on the other side of Sigi, her weapon out but unused. It was clear that her need for self-preservation warred with her feelings of friendship. Aurianna thought suddenly of the fact that all these people—not just Leon—had known Javen for most of their lives, had taken meals with him and trained with him. Grown up with him in a world that threw them all together and forced them to make sense of their lives in a short span of time.

Leon hadn't made a move to draw his weapon. He simply stood with his back to the stone, his shoulders hunched over, and a look of absolute despair on his ashen face. Theron kept glancing over at him, worry making him clench his jaw. He, at least, was shooting over the barrier every few seconds. Theron could hold his own with a weapon, but this was a different kind of prey, a friend-turned-enemy in the space of a few minutes. Still, he seemed to sense the danger in not taking the offensive.

Shouldering his weapon, Pharis stuck his head out, yanking it back just as a bullet came whooshing through the gap between them. He pointed his weapon blindly around the edge of the rocky shield and fired a few times before returning to a position of safety.

"We can't do anything until that shield—or whatever he's got—comes down!" Pharis yelled over the blasts of hot metal rending the air and bouncing off stone and…whatever Javen's barrier was.

She nodded. This would have to end now. They would run out of ammunition soon, and she had no idea if Javen had another weapon or not. Sigi might, but the issue was that their weapons were useless against someone their bullets couldn't reach.

Aurianna glanced down to the weapon in her hip holster as she assessed her determination and contemplated how to perform the basic functions she had trained for. What should have been second nature by now felt hollow, foreign—something some other version of herself had done in some other life.

At first, the ice cold of the gun shocked her. But the fire within her was heating up like a fissure of boiling lava, ready to burst forth. Something else was there as well, a sizzling buildup that made her feel…alive.

Aiming the weapon at the ground, she looked to her left. Leon was running his hands through his hair, his body rigid as his eyes darted around in dizzying circles. He looked like he was about to be sick. Laelia held her weapon around the cover, shooting off a few rounds at a time, but most of her attention was focused on Leon. She kept looking back over her shoulder at his rigid form, saying something to him Aurianna couldn't hear.

Aurianna let her gaze wander as she contemplated what to do. There had to be a way to get him to surrender without further violence. Whatever his reasons, whatever his motives, somewhere deep down, he had to care. If not for her, then for one of the others. Leon was, after all, his best friend. Maybe if she shot Javen in the leg, they could somehow restrain him. All she knew was this chaos could not continue.

The wind became a whisper, and Aurianna let it settle on her heated skin. A few beads of sweat dripped into her eyes. She rubbed her hand across them to alleviate the burning and clear her vision. Her heart rate peaked. Breathing, she tried to remember her training amid the racing thoughts in her mind.

Her training took over. Pulling the weapon in tightly to her shoulder as she leaned into the gap, Aurianna quickly flexed her arm around the stone and took a quick aim at Javen's leg. The recoil knocked her slightly back, and the percussion joined the rest, reverberating in her ears and far across the town below.

But the invisible shield swiped away her projectile like it was made of air. The shot bounced back in her direction. Aurianna reeled back as a high-pitched sound indicated it had hit the other side of the wall she hid behind.

Whatever was protecting Javen would continue to be in the way as long as they kept to their current position. Aurianna made a split-second decision, running past a gaping Pharis as bullets whizzed by her head. She tried to throw up more stone for protection as she made her way around to flank the man she had given everything to: her mind, her body, her heart.

Her trust.

The man who was now trying to kill her without a second's hesitation.

Sigi seemed to immediately understand what Aurianna's plan was, so she reached over and grabbed Leon's weapon from its holster. Laelia looked over and saw she was needed as well. Both of them, along with Theron, began to release a barrage of bullets on their enemy.

Just the distraction she needed.

When Javen turned to her friends, Aurianna didn't hesitate. She needed just the right angle to get past whatever was protecting Javen, so she took the risk and leaned out from behind the stone barrier, exposing herself in that brief instant as she took aim at his leg once again.

But she couldn't take cover fast enough. Javen had always been the best shot—and the fastest.

His weapon was aimed at her heart and, as if in slow motion, she watched his finger pull the trigger, a slight smile touching the corner of his mouth.

Somewhere to her left, she heard a deep rumble, then a blur of dark blue and black slid into her vision, filling the space between her and the death that awaited her.

The world was silent, as if holding its breath.

A gunshot simultaneously fractured the air and ripped apart her world.

CHAPTER 28

AURIANNA

The echo of the gunshot hung in the air. Rosy shades of sunset lavender swam at the edges of her vision.

An incremental slowness—like swimming, yet without any water—had control of her as she looked to her left and then to her right, the movements a surreal blend of reality and dream.

Somewhat dispassionately, her head turned back to look at her friends. Sigi looked horrified, her face frozen in shock. Laelia had managed to bring both hands up to cover her mouth before everything had gone still, her eyes wide with the same fear. Theron's face was grim, all color drained.

Utter heartbreak was chiseled into every line and crease on Leon's face as he watched his best friend become someone none of them recognized.

Belinda lay in a crumpled heap on the far side of the roof.

Aurianna was aware of these impressions in a detached way.

Breathe in, breathe out. Were they only words in her head? Was she still breathing?

The world around her seemed frozen and silent, and yet, no deity appeared. No Terra. No Caendra.

Two things she couldn't bring herself to look at, two things her mind was blocking out. Trying to protect her heart, her eyes looked everywhere but where those two things were.

Why did he do it?

Aurianna wasn't sure which *he* she was even referring to: the one who had destroyed her life, or the one who had sacrificed his own? Did it even matter?

This was… This was *not right not right not right.*

She lifted her head, forcing reality back in as dark hair, still mid-motion, floated out behind the body that had flung itself in front of her own… *not right not right not right.*

Aurianna allowed the numbness to possess her. She stepped around Pharis's frame, refusing to look at his face. Her eyes went to the bullet hovering in the air inches from his heart.

His heart, her heart. *What difference does it make?*

She would have to look at his face. She owed him that. She owed him her life.

She owed him her heart, yet here he was offering up his own.

The idea of death had always bothered her, but she had never feared it. Not like this. Not until now. Not until it wasn't her own life she was terrified of losing.

A hesitant glance up revealed the face Aurianna had grown to know so well over the previous moons, despite pretending she wasn't memorizing every inch, from the dimples at the corners of his mouth to the way his forehead creased whenever he grew frustrated. Usually about something involving her. Yet, even if she had been ignoring the secret words behind Pharis's outward actions until now, this moment was everything he had ever tried to tell her. He had always held his feelings behind his eyes, if only she had looked harder.

Now those sapphire orbs held nothing but resignation and a shred of fear. He had been afraid, yet he had acted on instinct. No denying it anymore: Pharis was in love with her.

The simple statement was powerful in that moment of her darkest hour. Darkness was creeping in from all sides. Love no longer mattered. Love was dead. Knowing it was useless, Aurianna pushed with all her might against his frozen form. He didn't budge.

Anger. Hurt. Betrayal. She had shoved it all down deep to save everyone.

Yet she couldn't save the one person who mattered most. Mattered most to whom? To her or to Eresseia? Perhaps both.

She had shoved it all down. Now it was bubbling up to the surface. Narrowing her eyes, Aurianna slowly turned her gaze to the monster who had taken everything from her. Her love, her innocence, the tiny part of her that had wanted to trust again.

She could trust herself. She could trust the man who was inches from death beside her. She could trust the friends who had shown up when she needed them most.

But she couldn't trust her judgment.

For a moment, she just stared at the creature a dozen yards away, saw the look of triumph in green eyes that held only contempt for her. The joy in those eyes was a light she longed to extinguish, but a part of her was resisting. Her heart was in two places at once, and both were about to be destroyed. One by love, the other by hate.

She glanced back to her friends, frozen in various states of distress. Memories of a conversation with Simon floated into her conscious mind. The goddess Terra had described the state she had held Aurianna in as evanescence, a oneness with time. This felt the same, yet no goddess was present.

But Simon had used a different word: Chronokinetic. Kinetic power was specifically a mortal power, at least for those who could wield it. That meant Chronokinetic actually described a type of Kinetic power. The power of time. Power *over* time.

She was in the Aether somehow, passing through the realm of the gods as she had when Pharis had pulled her through time. Only no stone was being used, no simple portal through from one side to the other. No goddess to create the stoppage of time.

Aurianna finally understood that no one was coming to rescue them. This wasn't the work of the Essence. This was her own doing.

The Aether surrounded her, cocooned her. The only movement was her own. Tears began to well in her eyes and threatened to spill over. *Not yet. Not yet.*

One foot in front of the other, right, left, right, left. Eyes focused downward, watching feet move forward, closer to the place where she didn't want to go.

Needed to go. Had to go.

The distance was brief, but the journey took a lifetime.

She didn't want to look into his eyes—didn't want to see joy or pain in those pits of raging jade fire. She simply didn't want to see.

If she looked up, she would see the now motionless puff of smoke at the end of the barrel.

But the heart has a will of its own. Without conscious volition, her gaze lifted to stare into those soulless eyes. Pain flared in her chest, but Aurianna knew she didn't have the luxury for feelings just then. Her hand was moving at her side before she could think, before she could change her mind or stop the inevitable.

With the barrel of her weapon pointed just at the side of Javen's temple, she aimed, and the world shrank to no more than what she could see in her narrowed sights. Nothing but the weight of the weapon in her hands. Aurianna inhaled as time refused to progress, and she could no longer hear over the sound of her own rapid heartbeat in her ears.

Then even that sound faded away as she slowly exhaled and turned her gaze back to the ground beside her, unable to bear witness. She squeezed her eyes shut as she squeezed the trigger.

Three things happened simultaneously.

She felt the weapon fire, but the sound never reached her ears.

Time came back to run its normal course, but still—no sound came with it at first.

The tears finally slipped over and rolled down her cheeks just as a heavy rain began to fall, quickly drenching them.

Still, she felt nothing.

Her eyes now open, Aurianna refused to turn and look behind her. Instead, she looked up at the others as the numbness of shock took over her body.

Sigi's mouth was open in a wide pantomime of horror. A faint mumbling in the distance that sounded like a muffled scream. Leon ran forward, stopping just behind where Aurianna stood as the sudden storm around them raged on, bolts of lightning crashing dangerously close. She saw him drop to the ground in the corner of her vision.

But Aurianna felt nothing.

As her sorrow caught up with her, the tears intensified, as did the rain now falling in sheets. The storm was escalating rapidly, a torrent of rain mixed with jagged flashes of lightning that blazed across the sky and booming claps of thunder that shook the ever-growing darkness around them. Darkness that was…intense and…*familiar*.

Arms wrapped around her shoulders, tugging on her, as Sigi's face appeared beside her. She was yelling something at Aurianna, but the words were just mumbles in her ears. She couldn't make meaning out of them. Even the lightning cracking the air sounded faint to Aurianna's ears.

Sigi continued pulling on her, trying to move them away. But

Aurianna couldn't fathom where they would be going. Here was everything. Here was life. Here was death. She couldn't leave the pieces of her heart behind.

Laelia ran past to drop down beside Leon. Aurianna watched as the same scene played out between the two of them, Laelia trying to pull Leon back, and Leon refusing to budge. Aurianna was careful not to turn too far in that direction. Seeing what she had done would be her complete undoing. But she could see Laelia yanking on Leon's arm as the biggest and strongest of them all sat on the ground weeping over his dead friend.

Dead. Javen was dead.

Not now.

She gasped in a deep breath and held it. She couldn't handle that line of thought right now. Deep down, she knew her friends needed her, but her mind and body were in a state of shock that numbed her to everything except the body lying on the ground just yards in front of her. Dark hair lay nestled across the front of his face, his body sprawled out like he was asleep.

But Pharis wasn't asleep.

No.

Dead. Pharis was dead.

No.

The word echoed in repeated booms across her thoughts.

Slowly, her body inched forward in his direction. Sigi was still guiding her, but when the other woman realized Aurianna's intended destination, she tried in vain to ease her away to the safety of the roof's stairwell door. Aurianna wrenched herself free of her friend's grasp, shoving her off again when Sigi attempted to grab her shoulders again. Sound was returning slowly, so she understood the faint but muffled words the girl screamed at her.

"We have to get out of here! There's nothing we can do for him!"

Theron was crouched over Pharis, checking his pulse and holding a hand on the Regulus's chest. Detachedly, Aurianna realized Pharis was probably bleeding out.

She couldn't watch.

She had to watch.

Over to the side, Belinda's crumpled shape still lay in a motionless pile. As Aurianna dropped to the ground at Pharis's side, she looked over at Theron and nodded at the pregnant girl. He hesitated, then nodded back in understanding before lifting himself up. Before walking over to pick up the unconscious form, he stopped and said, "The bullet went straight to his heart, Aurianna. His heart …stopped almost immediately." Aurianna didn't watch to see where he went, but she assumed he was working on helping everyone get to safety.

Her eyes were only for the man who lay unmoving on the ground beside her. Compared to what she had been expecting, very little blood stained the front of his tunic. Theron was right. His heart had been stopped dead.

Dead. Pharis was dead.

CHAPTER 29

LEON

Leon looked up from the ground at his feet. His eyes tried to focus on whatever was hovering over him, tugging at his arm.

Bright blue in a sea of creamy ivory. Concern was written there. Concern for him.

Dazed, he tried not to think about what lay behind them on the roof of the Imperium.

A broken, bloody body. His friend. His best friend.

A traitor to his own kind. But why? What had possessed Javen to betray them all?

She had stopped him.

Aurianna. She had killed Javen. Killed his friend.

His friend.

All his energy seeped out into the air around them as he slumped further forward. Laelia was yelling something at someone, but he couldn't be bothered to care. A crack of thunder rent the air, so close he could practically feel his hair stand on end.

Suddenly, a rough set of arms was tucked under his own, and

Leon felt his body being lifted from the ground. He didn't want to leave his friend. What would happen to his body? Confused, he turned to face his tormentor.

Theron stood him on his feet then slapped a strong hand on Leon's shoulder. "I am hurting with you, brother. But right now, we must protect the rest of those we love. You've got to snap out of it, friend!"

Hesitating only a moment, Leon nodded. The man was right. He watched as Theron lifted the unconscious girl from the ground at his feet and ran to the door leading from the rooftop. Glancing to his right, he saw Laelia still standing there, dripping wet but waiting as patiently as she dared in the hellstorm that had become their reality.

The airships that might have been their saving grace were long gone. The damage from the battle was apparent everywhere, but they needed to focus on getting off the roof.

Aurianna and Sigi were standing over what appeared to be a very dead Regulus. Leon couldn't be bothered to care about that, not when Javen was equally gone from the world.

Laelia reached out and grabbed his hand. He allowed her to guide him through the door and down the stairs. Shouts were ringing up the stairwell—a mix of panic and fear. He heard hollered orders, most likely guards who wouldn't be stopping to ask questions.

Besides, who would believe them if they told the truth?

Their Regulus lay dead, as did another Kinetic. A Kinetic with connections to Leon and his friends. How much had those who had escaped on the ships actually seen? Did they know who had truly been at the center of the treachery?

Leon and the others would be imprisoned without a doubt, especially considering how many witnesses had seen Aurianna wielding that deadly ball of Energy. She would be accused of the sins on that rooftop—especially considering her volatile reputation—and they would be perceived as accomplices.

The Magnus was now their enemy.

Theron was just below them, struggling along with the pregnant girl as Sigi came up behind him to help guide the way. Despite her status as a guardswoman, she could do nothing to help them. She had been a friend of Javen's as well. Leon saw the pain of it on her face when she glanced back to him and Laelia. Laelia . . . who was still gripping his hand tightly. He could feel the tremors racking her body, a mirror of his own fear and shock.

The voices shouting orders sounded closer, and Leon began to realize there might not be another ending to this ordeal. How could they fight their way through a throng of guards while trying to walk right out the front door?

Leon and Laelia had caught up to Sigi and Theron with his unconscious burden, the four of them running as fast as they could down the winding staircase. They were nearing the main hall entrance level, Sigi pushing forward to open the door for Theron, when a voice yelled from behind them to stop.

CHAPTER 30

AURIANNA

No. No. No. No.

Sigi had long since stopped trying to pull Aurianna away from Pharis's still form. Her friend now silently stood over them as Aurianna felt fresh tears spilling over, mingling with the drops of rain pelting her skin and clothing. Another crack of lightning rent the air and sizzled down in a solid line of bright white to the rooftop, yards from where she sat bearing witness to the end of everything.

Pharis's blue eyes stared up into the endless darkness of the night sky. The lightning lit up his features, for a moment breathing life into the scene. But Aurianna wasn't fooled. A burning chunk of metal had torn into his flesh, taking his life. At least his heart had stopped, saving him from a long and painful death.

Needing to feel something, anything, Aurianna leaned down to his face and pressed her lips against his. They were still warm, and she remembered the quick yet rough kiss he had given her in the tunnels beneath the Imperium so many moons ago. It had been over before she could even respond, and it wasn't the kind of kiss she wanted to remember him by.

A sudden strong surge of pain and loss filled her up, and she pressed her mouth harder against his, trying to drown out the rage she felt at having her heart ripped in two. The remnants left in her chest burned with a fire she couldn't control, but something else was crackling deep in her core. She felt, rather than heard, a humming. It vibrated inside her, filling the empty spaces, forcing a shudder across her body. She was dimly aware of Sigi whispering her name, but she was too far gone in her grief and whatever was currently happening to her.

A sensation like a spark flickered in and out within her, like a candle in the dark struggling against the wind. The storm around them raged on, but a tempest inside her battled for dominance. Still she held the embrace, a strange excitement creeping into her thoughts. Her scalp began to tingle as she felt pieces of her hair floating up to stand on end. Sigi's voice grew more insistent, a note of fear and awe in her tone as the Darkness surrounding them began to thrum with Energy, expanding and taking on a life of its own.

Then Aurianna's insides snapped like a tree branch in a storm, and power like she had never felt before awakened within her and began to flow out in flaring waves of heat and light. Her fire had never felt quite like this. This was like . . . like power itself. Through her closed eyelids, she could sense an intense light flaring across her skin and through her touch.

A single soft motion fluttered against the hand she had pressed against Pharis's blood-stained chest. Shock forced her eyes open.

The empty gaze of the dead that had pierced the sky above was replaced with sapphire, pure brilliant sapphire, staring back at her—into her soul.

Pharis's gaze was locked on her, confusion and wonder warring on his features. His forehead creased, and Aurianna wanted nothing more than to kiss that wrinkled bit of flesh. A startled laugh erupted from her as she continued to hold herself against him. Streaks of light still flashed against her skin, but the remnants were fading. A voice cut into her reverie.

"Did you just…I really don't want to think about what I just saw. Right now, I think we need to get the hell out of here." Sigi's raspy whisper barely resonated above the sound of the torrential wind and rain, the thunder rolling ominously overhead. She looked like she wanted to add something else, but her stunned silence spoke volumes. This was a conversation for later.

"Go on," Aurianna said. "We'll be right behind you. Make sure the others get to safety."

Sigi looked as if she might argue the point, but instead the girl just turned and ran to the door. Aurianna turned to see that the others were already gone.

A touch against her cheek brought her back to the man she had thought was gone forever. Pharis was running the back of his hand down the side of her face, his own visage completely free of any pretenses. No mask, no hiding. His feelings for her were dancing in his eyes, but his smile spoke of things yet to come.

That simple gesture was a ray of sunshine in the gray world surrounding them. "I know you kissed me first that time."

Before she could respond, Pharis leaned up and kissed her, his elbows straining against the ground until he tilted his body up into a sitting position and grabbed the sides of her face, deepening the kiss. Despite her body's protestations, concern forced her to pull away slightly. "Pharis, you just *died*. I don't think this is the time."

"Did I? Well then, I think this is the perfect time to celebrate. Besides," he said, raising an eyebrow, "I believe you kissed me first."

His smile was both alien and completely familiar to her, and it was her undoing.

Pulling her back to his lips, Pharis wound his hands into her rain-slickened hair as he brought the two of them up to a kneeling position. One hand slid down her wet overcoat and maneuvered inside to grab her by the waist, drawing her in closer.

Aurianna could feel every inch of him against her. She lost herself in his kiss as it became more and more desperate. A nagging thought in the back of her head told her they needed to run, to leave before guards showed up or the lightning chose to come closer.

But this was no natural storm, and the thought both terrified and excited her. Still, the guards would be a very unwelcome addition to the scene, especially if they tried to arrest her. *Tried* being the operative word.

She was power incarnate now. The idea was heady, and she felt dizzy. Pushing Pharis away, she looked into his eyes. They both gasped for air as she struggled to get the words out.

"Guards" was all she managed to utter. His gaze traveled down to her lips once more, but he looked back up and nodded. He tried to get to his feet, almost falling over in the process. Aurianna caught him, wrapping his arm around her shoulders as she made her way to the door.

CHAPTER 31

LEON

At the sound of the familiar voice, Leon turned to see a soaked Aurianna rushing forward, her movements awkward because…

Because she was holding up a very pale—but very much alive—Regulus.

Could that mean…?

But no. No one else was with them, no other forms brought up the rear. Leon felt his chest drop all over again. The hand that held his squeezed once tightly, then let go, as if its owner could read his thoughts.

Everyone stared at Aurianna as she caught up to them. Laelia looked the most shocked, her face filled with terror at seeing the dead man before them. Her mouth flopped open and shut a few times before she whispered, "I don't…I don't…"

Aurianna pushed past her, pulling the Regulus with her and continuing down the stairs. "Questions later. Right now, we get to safety. Keep going down." She turned back to see if they were following.

Leon pointed at the man at her side to punctuate his words. "Why are we still running if *he* is standing here, alive and well? They have no reason to follow us now!"

"They'll assume you've kidnapped me," the Regulus stated matter-of-factly.

"Then stay here!"

Aurianna paused for a moment, chewing her bottom lip as a frown pulled down the corners of her mouth. "He can stay if he wants, but I think it's best if he comes with us."

"Best for whom, darling?" Leon glared at her. Without the Regulus, they would be safer. Surely she could see through her selfishness to realize that?

"I don't . . . Look, it's his choice. But the Magnus is up to more than we know, and eventually he's going to come looking for my parents. Too much is at stake here, more than you understand. And Pharis is on *our* side. But it's his choice."

"Our side? How convenient!"

"He just took a bullet for me, Leon!" Tears welled in her eyes, but she stopped speaking to regain control of her emotions. Leon saw the war raging inside her mind, and he knew he was being unfair. Pain was making him irrational. His heart was still on the rooftop, still staring at the dead eyes of the friend she had shot and killed.

And he wasn't sure how to cope with that just yet.

"Look, I'm sorry. I am. But don't ask me to trust the son of the man we're running from."

"Fair enough." Those words came from the Regulus himself, surprising Leon. "I choose to follow you. I realize you have no reason to trust me. But I am not my father."

Not my father.

Oh, but we are our fathers. There is no escaping it, Regulus.

Shaking the crushing thoughts from his head, Leon looked back to Aurianna. "We can't stand here forever. What now?"

"Besides Pharis, there's also…*that* issue." She nodded at Theron. Leon knew she meant the girl in his arms. A Kinetic who was pregnant by another Kinetic. It seemed to be a growing epidemic in his world.

Aurianna shook her head before nodding resolutely. "Follow me." She pushed on without waiting for any of them.

Despite the layer of confusion enveloping the rest of the group, everyone followed her sudden burst of confidence, picking up speed as they heard more voices above them.

Panting, Laelia asked, "Where exactly are you taking us?"

Aurianna didn't waste words. "Just follow me."

Not that we have any choice right now.

Guilt gnawed at him, ate away at his insides, as he thought about all the little things he had missed. All the flippant remarks, the resentful comments Javen had made. All the seemingly incongruous behaviors he had overlooked when all he had needed—all he had wanted—was a friend. Someone to care whether he existed or not.

Perhaps his mother was right after all. People seemed to have a tendency to die around him. Maybe it was all his fault. If he had just paid more attention, stopped drinking and screwing around so much, maybe he could have helped Javen through whatever it was that had made the man miserable enough to do what he had done.

Up ahead, Aurianna was struggling to open a door. Sigi jumped forward to hold it open for the rest of the group. As he passed her, Leon shared a look with Sigi, a mutual sadness permeating the space between them.

She had been close to Javen as well.

They entered the underground tunnels, the area the Arcanes and Voids called home.

"Why are we here?" Leon asked angrily.

Aurianna flinched noticeably, and he immediately regretted his tone. A little. She let go of Pharis, who seemed to be standing just fine on his own now—a giant question mark amid all the madness.

Later. They would get those answers later.

Instead of Aurianna answering him, the Regulus piped up, his voice raspy and quiet in the stone corridor. "She's taking us to the tower." He looked over at Aurianna, as if looking for confirmation.

She nodded. "Yeah. My ... my parents are there. They can help us. At least, I assume they're still there. They may have figured out I broke the locking spell, so they may have left already. I'm really not sure. No one will look for us there, at least not right away. Maybe we can figure out a way to lock it again ... or something." The woman looked like she was about to start crying, and Leon wasn't sure he could handle anything of the sort at the moment.

The Regulus reached over and put an arm around her. Leon felt his blood boiling at the intimacy of the gesture. Javen hadn't been dead an hour, and here was this bastard—

"So, I take it Ethan was telling the truth, everything about your ... the Enchantress." The Regulus's eyes were full of concern and a sadness Leon didn't quite understand.

The conversation left too much unsaid, and Leon felt some answers were needed in that moment. He looked at Aurianna and asked the only thing his mind had managed to grab ahold of during the exchange. "So, you found your parents?"

She nodded, but her hesitation was apparent in the gesture. "I did, but I haven't fully digested all of that just yet. My father ... is a Void. I know it sounds crazy to you guys right now, but we can get into longer explanations once we're safe. The real issue is the other thing."

"What other thing?" Sigi's voice was almost a whisper.

Aurianna's gaze traveled to the Regulus as she spoke. "My mother. I don't really know of an easy way to say this, or even how to explain it." When her voice trailed off, the man at her side nodded in encouragement as Leon waited with bated breath for the rest of the revelation. Aurianna continued, her voice even softer than Sigi's had been. "The Enchantress is my mother."

Time stopped, or at least Leon thought it did. No one moved, no one spoke, and the air itself seemed to pause in anticipation of the aftermath of that one simple sentence.

Laelia's deep laughter broke the stillness. Leon turned to stare at her, as did the others.

How was any of this funny?

When the sound died out, she had the decency to look slightly abashed, but the laughter was still dancing in her crystal-blue eyes. "Come on, seriously? The levels of irony here are more than anyone could handle. Poor Aurianna here is facing some sick joke from the Essence. Honey, the only thing you can do is laugh. Beats crying, anyway."

Aurianna's face lit up slightly, and she did almost seem like she was about to smile, but a deep sorrow still shone in her eyes. Maybe the others couldn't see it, but Leon could. He was sure it was mirrored in his own.

"I don't know what to think about some things that have happened, but I do think Ethan was telling the truth about most of it. The woman—her name is Syrena—insists she couldn't leave the tower and wasn't on that train, but I know what I saw. However, I also know the tower was locked by Pharis's father, so she couldn't have gotten out on her own. Perhaps she was being used and somehow was made to forget, some kind of Fae spell or something. The lock on the tower was something old, something ancient like that. There are more questions than answers, and I'm sorry I don't have more to give you. She and I left a lot of things unanswered when I had to rush back, but I think we can trust them to keep us safe. For now. And if not, we'll move on to somewhere safer."

"We'll figure it out," the Regulus said, looking into Aurianna's eyes with a knowing look. She smiled back at him. Leon turned away to avoid losing his temper and saying something he might regret.

Laelia spoke up. "Okay, let's go then." She had let go of Leon's hand when he'd turned around, but when he looked back, her eyes were only on him. "We'll sort through all this once we get there."

"Right," Sigi chimed in. "Lead the way." She gestured for Aurianna to walk ahead of them. The Regulus was right by the girl's side. Leon fought down his anger, reminding himself nothing made any sense right now.

They journeyed down tunnel after tunnel, ending up at the entrance to the Voids' area. When they walked in, many faces looked up at them, most immediately going back to their work. A few rushed over to a corner of the room, running back with towels in hand for the bedraggled troupe that had entered their space without a word of explanation. They took the proffered towels, nodding their gratitude.

Aurianna continued their journey by exiting through a door and down a passage. As they trudged along many winding passages, Sigi asked, "Why did those Voids back there look completely unfazed by our showing up?"

Aurianna shrugged without turning around. "Don't know. Maybe my...Ethan told them to expect us. Or me at least, I guess? He couldn't have predicted I'd be bringing an army with me."

The words rang with an odd truth in Leon's ears. They were an army. He wasn't entirely sure who all their enemies were, but the battle was most certainly not over.

* * *

The man Aurianna called "Ethan" looked just like any other Void.

But he looked incredibly happy to see the girl. As did the woman who stood beside him in the doorway of the underground entrance to the tower.

The tower of the Enchantress.

Syrena, Enchantress, mother. Whatever she was—whatever Aurianna was calling her—Leon certainly didn't trust the woman. From the looks on the rest of the faces in the group, neither did anyone else.

The woman was barely older than the rest of them, and the man was only slightly older than that.

The weirdness of the situation wasn't his issue, though.

Safety was the important thing, and this arrangement was only temporary. They would need to understand what in the Essence was going on and formulate a plan.

Theron had placed the pregnant girl on a table in the room as they had entered the tower. *That* was another mystery needing to be solved. Had Javen really impregnated the girl? Used and manipulated her?

Leon couldn't believe his friend was capable of that. But he wouldn't have thought him capable of a multitude of things he had watched the man do that night. If Leon couldn't trust the man who had been his closest friend for years, how was he supposed to trust anyone else? Here they were, aligning themselves with a rogue Void, the Enchantress they'd thought was their enemy, and the son of the man who would most likely want them all dead by tomorrow.

How the hell is this ever going to end in anything but disaster?

Leon flattened his lower back against the wall behind him as he slumped forward. The others were talking, but he couldn't bring himself to listen or care in that moment.

Theron walked up and joined him against the wall. Pursing his lips, the man threw a glance in his direction. "You need some sleep."

"I guess."

"Come on. They said there're rooms upstairs. Let's go take a look while the grown-ups talk."

Leon followed Theron's leisurely pace, not bothering to say anything as he passed by the others. He felt a certain pair of blue eyes on him, but he kept his gaze to the stairs as he ascended. At the top, Theron hesitated and finally turned left. Leon followed him up to a random door. It looked like no one had entered the room in ages.

"I'm guessing one is as good as any. She—Syrena—said all the rooms have bedding but if we needed more, or extra towels, to let her know."

Leon shook his head, his nostrils flaring. "I'll be fine." He turned to head into the room but stopped a few feet away. "I don't know that I trust these two."

Theron nodded. "I got you, brother. Trust me. I don't think even Aurianna trusts them completely. Sigi and I will probably take turns keeping watch."

"You need sleep too, friend."

"Don't worry about me. I'll make do." Theron tipped his hat as he reached for the handle to shut the door. "Goodnight."

Leon stood in the middle of the room, staring at nothing for the longest time. Eventually, the exhaustion of emotion and the letdown after the rush of battle began to weigh on him, so he trudged across the room to fall ungracefully on the bed. After a while, he sat up and pulled off his wet jacket and boots, throwing them on the floor before emptying his pockets and holster onto the table by the bed.

He was just contemplating whether he had the energy to light up a cigar when a soft knock sounded at the door. Grimacing in frustration, Leon stood up slowly, making his way over to the door. Theron better have a good reason for—

Bright blue eyes greeted him as he opened the door. Laelia was a whir of movement as she swept into the room without a word.

"Well, why don't you come in?" Leon drawled sarcastically as he pushed the door closed.

As he turned to face his uninvited guest, Leon's senses were accosted by a flash of pale skin and hair as it rushed at him. Lips were pressed against his own, soft and warm and everything, everything, everything…

A dizzying wave of newfound energy crested over him as he pulled her closer to him. Laelia intensified the kiss, pushing his back up against the door with a sudden forcefulness that bled over into the movement of their mouths. Hungry, insistent, heated. The sheer force of her cleared all else from his mind, and he welcomed the complete absence of anything but what felt so right, so natural.

So like home.

Leon didn't stop to contemplate the wisdom of the decision he was making, didn't stop to wonder just what the hell he was doing with *her* of all people. He didn't stop to think at all.

He just felt. Felt her. Felt her soft creamy skin. Felt the small curves of her body beneath his roaming hands. Felt her smooth lips keeping up the steady but insane pace he could barely match.

Laelia was a whirlwind, a force of nature. No, she was the eye of the storm, the storm that had become his life over the past few hours. He almost laughed aloud at the sheer irony of his current predicament.

Bloody hell.

Suddenly, the woman grabbed his arms and pulled them around the back of her upper legs. The only warning she gave him was the movement of her right leg as she raised it up and wrapped the appendage around his hip. He tightened his grip on her and helped her lift herself into his arms. Wrapping both legs around his waist, Laelia locked her ankles and grabbed the back of his head as she deepened the kiss.

Bloody hell.

Easing the two of them closer to the bed, Leon took small steps and adjusted his grip on her backside. Little moans were escaping her mouth, which spurred him to his destination. He squeezed her bottom before attempting to softly place Laelia's small form on the bed behind her.

But she was having none of it. Wiggling out of his grip, she pulled back into the mattress just enough to grab ahold of his shirt front with both hands. Leon was too stunned to fight it as she flipped him over onto his back. Before he could gather his wits, her knees were sinking into the mattress on both sides of his legs as she leaned back down to kiss him again.

And he wondered if he had only imagined falling back onto the bed, for his body felt like it was floating, weightless in a dream. Above him, a form both angel and demon worked the buttons on his damp shirt. Every time he reached up to return the favor, she slapped his hands away and continued her ministrations with his clothing. Once she had divested him of his shirt, she briefly leaned back to pull off her own.

Maybe he was dreaming. Exhaustion had overtaken him just minutes before, so perhaps he had fallen asleep on the bed and was merely dreaming of Laelia…straddling him.

Certainly a new dream if that were the case.

But she felt too warm, too real for his senses to truly believe it was anything other than some strangely wonderful thing happening between them. This wasn't the time to analyze.

What Laelia wanted, Laelia usually got. So he let her set the pace and take him away from his sorrow, if only for a while.

CHAPTER 32

AURIANNA

Aurianna recited the words of "her" prophecy for Ethan and Syrena. She doubted she would ever forget them, she'd read them so many times.

"And that's all it says?" Ethan's voice held a note of unease, but Aurianna almost felt like laughing. Nothing had panned out the way she had been told it would. The whole thing was ridiculous. The prophecy, the Arcanes, all of it.

The words could mean anything, especially now. Aurianna wished she could talk to the Essence again, or Simon for that matter.

Mother, father, parents. These were words she couldn't think about just yet. Ethan and Syrena sat next to one another at a small table and hadn't stopped touching since she'd arrived with her friends. They barely looked away from each other when they spoke to her. Aurianna couldn't deny the love she saw there, the longing and the overwhelming relief at finding one another again.

But Syrena had been on that train, and Aurianna had fought her. And yet the woman insisted on denying it. Had she experienced some strange spell or memory loss? Were they all being played by another force—something yet to be identified?

The Essence could have been lying to her all along. In the Fire temple, Caendra had told Aurianna her birth had been the product of "a union that changed things." A relationship between a Void and a massively powerful Kinetic would certainly fit that description, but why not just tell her the whole truth? She couldn't even trust the gods after what she had seen and experienced.

And Javen.

Javen was gone, she reminded herself, forcing back the tears yet again. She would not let her grief run rampant in front of these strangers, or even in front of her friends. Pharis was standing behind her, giving her space to speak with Syrena and Ethan. Sigi stood close by, her eyes never leaving Aurianna. Theron seemed to be observing everything at once, his keen hunter's eyes darting around the room in the bottom level of the tower where they had all congregated.

Rhouth was curled up at his feet, fast asleep. Somehow, the crazy fox had followed his scent all the way down into the tunnels. How she had managed to get through the stairwell door, they would never know. But there she was, both companion and protector, loyal to her master. Animals were clearly more dependable and trustworthy than people.

Syrena had been speaking to Aurianna, but she had been too distracted to catch what the woman had said. "I'm sorry?"

"I asked if you'd like to finish this in the morning after you've had a decent night's sleep. You can have your pick of any open rooms on the next level. This tower used to be something, I'm sure. Maybe City Guard barracks at one point."

Sigi looked up at those words. "How long ago was this?" she asked.

"Oh, I don't know. I'm just speculating. A lot of the décor in here looks military, but I doubt it's been used in many years." Syrena smiled sardonically. "At least, until my incarceration, that is."

Sigi didn't return her smile, and Aurianna understood her concern. No one trusted anyone right now. Syrena and Ethan didn't trust Sigi or Pharis. Sigi didn't trust Syrena or Ethan, but she was treating Pharis almost as if he himself were the Magnus. Pharis didn't trust anyone but Aurianna, it seemed. He just followed along and did whatever she asked. It was actually grating on her nerves a bit.

And then there was the issue of the very pregnant Belinda. They'd covered the girl's wet form with a blanket and tried to position her comfortably on a padded bench in the corner. They'd checked her for injury, but she didn't seem to have even a bump on the head, so it was anyone's guess why she was still unconscious. And somehow, impossibly, her swollen belly seemed even larger now than it had on the rooftop.

How was getting Belinda pregnant related to anything Javen had been planning? And how would that play out now that he was gone? How had they even managed it with the birth control herbs in the water?

Belinda hadn't woken through any of the journey, and Aurianna walked over to check that the girl was still breathing. When she got closer, Aurianna could see her chest moving. Theron moved across the room to stand beside her. Rhouth yipped at the sudden movement, yawning and stretching before following him over. Aurianna glanced from her up to Theron. "Is it weird having a shadow following you around all the time?"

His eyes crinkled in amusement. "We all have our shadows. Some of them we just can't see."

His words sent a chill across her skin. She nodded at the girl. "Thoughts?"

"About what happened? Or what to do now?"

"Both. Either."

"Well, I have no idea what happened. Well, I mean, *clearly* we all know something happened." A knife sliced into Aurianna's heart, and Theron noticed her pained reaction. He reached over and pulled her into a tight embrace. She laid her head on the thick lapel of his coat as he patted her head. "We'll get through this, friend. When she wakes up, we'll have to face the truth of whatever she has to say. But as for the future... only time will tell. Whatever needs to be done to fix things moving forward, we will handle it. Together."

Aurianna wished she could share his confidence in their future. Her destiny seemed to be constantly changing, no matter what some stupid prophecy said. Everything was different now.

Exhaustion crept into her soul, pushing out rational thoughts and bringing with it an overwhelming sense of numbness. Aurianna raised her head, giving Theron a look of thanks for his words of comfort. She approached Sigi, and her friend reached out and squeezed her hand. "We'll be down here keeping an eye on things."

Aurianna looked the woman over. "You need sleep just as much as I do."

"Theron and I already discussed it. We'll take turns keeping watch. We'll be fine." Hesitation flitted across Sigi's gaze. She opened her mouth but abruptly closed it again. Finally, she whispered, "Did you... Did you..."

"Did I what?"

"Did... I mean, the Energy. The storm..."

"Spit it out."

"When you were containing that ... thing, did you somehow absorb it? Is that where the Energy went? Is that what you did to ..." Sigi glanced over at Pharis awkwardly. Raising her eyebrows, she whispered, "to him?"

The question only increased Aurianna's exhaustion. She couldn't think about those things right then, not when she didn't really know or understand, and it just brought up painful memories. She drew in a deep breath and let it out in a whoosh. "I don't know." Irritation laced her tone. She couldn't help it.

A look of guilt crossed her friend's face. "We'll talk later. Go." Sigi pushed her along. "Get some rest."

Nodding to Syrena and Ethan as she trudged up the stairs, Aurianna made her way up the spiral staircase with mumbled thanks and goodnights all around. At the next level, she took a right and walked around almost to the opposite side of the circular rooms of the tower before stepping into an open bedroom. There were no windows, of course, but a few sconces seemed to give off a minimal amount of light in the small room.

Before she got two steps in, a presence at her back made her turn around. Sapphire glowed at her in the near dark. Pharis grabbed both sides of her face as he pulled her close. His gaze dropped slowly down to her mouth as she felt his hot breath on her skin.

Aurianna whispered, "Pharis, we can talk tomorrow, but remember you just, you know, died and all. Let's not tempt fate."

"To hell with fate," he replied before crushing his lips to hers, almost knocking her off her feet.

A rush of heat filled her, but part of her mind wanted to remain rational. In between the kisses, as they briefly parted every few seconds to breathe, she pulled away just enough to say, "This isn't …" But she couldn't finish the statement, her thoughts flowing out like water through a sieve.

The sound of his boot nudging the door closed filtered through the fog in her head. A blind flurry of movement had her pressed against the wall as the kiss deepened.

Comparing would be her undoing. This wasn't Javen, she

reminded herself. This was raw passion, but this was also Pharis. And she knew he wouldn't hurt her.

Didn't she?

As he pushed off her sodden jacket, a brief flash of pain echoed at the place on her back where the Volanti's claws had torn into her skin. The healers had smothered the jagged gash in something that had smelled terrible but had soothed and closed the wound. The pain was gone in the next instant.

Pharis's lips traveled across her jawline and down her neck, sending a wave of fire across her heated skin. His breath tickled the inside of her ear when he whispered words she wasn't sure she had heard correctly—wasn't sure she wanted to hear at all.

I love you.

Her body began to shake from the pure emotion behind his whispered admission, but she couldn't acknowledge it, couldn't return the words. He didn't seem to notice or mind, for he placed his hands on her backside and lifted her up onto a small wooden dresser that stood against the wall.

Aurianna watched as he pulled off her boots and socks. This was becoming real, and a raw fear washed over her. Pharis leaned back in to kiss her again but must have seen her emotions written on her face, for he froze and asked, "He's...Aurianna, I'm not—"

Fear turned to horror in an instant. "Please don't say his name!" Aurianna whispered, her words raspy and dripping with fear and panic. She frantically pulled him in closer to wrap her arms around his neck. She pressed her mouth to his, willing her mind to forget— to forget about that night, to forget she had given all her trust to one who had betrayed her.

Betrayed them all.

She didn't want to think about him now, didn't want to think about anything. She lost herself in the kiss again. Pharis initially hesitated, confused by her sudden emotional outburst and probably worried about her mental state. He tried to pull away, but she held on tighter. After a moment, his hands returned, his touch neither gentle nor rough, but purposeful and skilled.

And oh, how skilled he was. His hands roamed, but the intention was always clear as he slowed and sped up with an increasing fervor. When his lips found the space at the side of her neck again, she gasped and leaned her head back against the wall. His mouth traveled back up to her earlobe, biting softly.

Pharis reached back up her legs to divest her of her trousers, struggling for a moment as he tugged the damp material. His breath was silky and hot, sending shivers down her spine when he whispered, "This was so much easier with a dress."

"What?" came her breathless reply.

Instead of responding, he made a final pull and succeeded in removing her pants.

Dizzy with heat and passion, Aurianna was overtaken by her senses as she allowed the moment to override her pain, if only for a while.

Tomorrow the pain and heartache would return, but for tonight she would revel in the fact that someone loved her enough to give his life for hers.

It almost felt like home.

Excited for More of the Awakened Series?

The story continues in book three. Discover the shocking truth of Eresseia's past and future with Aurianna and her friends in *Midnight Descending,* the final installment in the Awakened series. Visit *lisamgreen.com/awakened* for information and links to retailers.

Turn the page for more information about the next book.

* * *

Expand the World of Eresseia with a Free Ebook

Sign up for a free ebook copy of *Daylight Burning,* an Awakened prequel novelette starring Leon Bouchard. You'll also hear about new releases and other updates from Lisa M. Green. Go to *lisamgreen.com/newsletter* for your free copy.

* * *

Enjoyed the Book and Want to Show Your Support?

You are an amazingly awesome person! Thank you! Please take just a moment and post a review of the book on Amazon, Goodreads, Barnes & Noble, or anywhere you normally post reviews.

Once again, THANK YOU!

Awakened ~ Book Three

Broken by betrayal. Surrounded by destruction. United by hope.

Aurianna must live with the consequences of her heartbreaking decisions in the aftermath of a betrayal too devastating to face.

She and her friends have no idea who is trustworthy and who is scheming for power. Their only option is to seek assistance from two groups: one that no one thought to ask, and one that no one thought existed.

The fate of Eresseia lies in the hands of those whose power is far greater than it seems, and whose leaders are not always what they appear to be. To protect the ones she loves, has she merely traded one monster for another?

Aurianna is now—irrevocably—a key player in a world that needs her as a leader, as a hero, and as the face for their emerging resistance movement.

With so many sides, choosing the wrong one could lead to the destruction of everything she has begun to think of as home.

For more information about this book and others in the series, visit *lisamgreen.com/awakened*.

LISA M. GREEN

MIDNIGHT DESCENDING

AWAKENED ~ BOOK THREE

Glossary for the Awakened Series

Kinetics: those born with the ability to control or manipulate the elements, usually with an affinity for one element in particular based on their region of birth

Arcanes: a group of men who oversee the records and history books for all of Eresseia; they advise the Magnus on a multitude of issues but are loyal to the Essence (deities) above all

Consils: political delegates and representatives for the six regions of Eresseia

Magnus: leader of the Kinetics and the sixth Consil (representative for Bramosia); the other Consils are elected officials, but the title of Magnus is always a hereditary position

Regulus: the eldest son or daughter of the current Magnus and heir to the title

Magisters: teachers at the Imperium who specialize in training Acolytes in different elements

Acolytes: Kinetics who are still in training and haven't yet reached their twentieth birthday

Voids: those who are sent to the Imperium to train Kinetic powers which never manifest; they are shunned by others and end up working at the Imperium after failing to show any power

Praefects: people in Aurianna's future timeline who are chosen to do the bidding of the Consils (do not exist in the past)

Carpos: a special group of Praefects charged with tracking down, detaining, and torturing Kinetics who manage to travel to the future

Order of the Daoine: a resistance group that opposes the Kinetics

Volanti: nightmarish creatures who attack the towns and take captives every few moons but are impervious to Kinetic weapons; they are as tall as several humans, with spindly talons for hands and feet, sharp fangs and claws, long pointed ears, a wide yet angular head, and membranous wings

Aether Stones: amethyst-colored stones of unknown origin that allow the bearer to travel through time via the Aether

LOCATIONS

Eresseia: the known world

Bramosia: one of the six regions and the capital of Eresseia; home to Kinetics and non-Kinetics alike

Imperium: school and home for Kinetic Acolytes, as well as home to some other Kinetics who work nearby; located in Bramosia

Consilium: political building for the Consils, located in Bramosia

Rasenforst: one of the six regions, connected to the element of Fire

Menos: one of the six regions, connected to the element of Earth

Ramolay: one of the six regions, connected to the element of Water

Vanito: one of the six regions, connected to the element of Energy

Eadon: one of the six regions, connected to the element of Air

Perdita Bay: the body of water within Eresseia's inner coastline

Mare Dolor: the ocean surrounding Eresseia (*Sea of Sorrow*)

The Aether: the realm of the Essence (the deities)

KINETICS/ELEMENTS

Fire: Pyrokinetics (nickname Pyros)

Earth: Geokinetics (nickname Dusters)

Water: Hydrokinetics (nickname Hydrons)

Energy: Electrokinetics (nickname Sparkers), the name for electric power

Air: Aerokinetics* (nickname Zephyrs)

*Aerokinetics are comparatively rare, though no one seems to know why. They are in high demand due to their scarcity.

DEITIES

The Essence: the collective name of the deities

Caendra: goddess of Fire, one of the collective group of deities known as the Essence

Terra: goddess of Earth, one of the collective group of deities known as the Essence

Unda: goddess of Water, one of the collective group of deities known as the Essence

Fulmena: goddess of Energy, one of the collective group of deities known as the Essence

Caelum: god of Air, the only male sibling among the collective group of deities known as the Essence

Acknowledgments

This particular book holds a special place in my heart. While *Dawn Rising* was the genesis of the series, *Darkness Awakening* contains many of the scenes I was so excited to write ever since I created them in the outlining stage. Second books can either make or break a series, and this sequel flies above and beyond (in my own unbiased opinion, of course).

My husband bears the brunt of all my hard work, through countless delayed dinners and sleepless nights as I tried to work out a plot hole or an answer to a question I was struggling with. He still puts up with it, so I guess that's good. I did write that one scene just for you, honey. You know the one.

Thank you once again to Kathryn Schieber at BFF Editing for helping me to find all the little inconsistencies that time travel (and two a.m. writing sessions) inevitably creates. I have found someone who loves grammar more than I do, and that's saying a lot.

And, as always, my heart reaches out with all the digital hugs I can muster to everyone who has supported and followed me along the way. There's plenty more where this one came from.

Lisa M. Green writes stories of myth and magic, weaving fairy tales into fantasy. She enjoys reading, writing, cooking, traveling, hiking, and playing video games that girls aren't supposed to like.

lisamgreen.com
facebook.com/authorlmgreen
instagram.com/authorlmgreen
@authorlmgreen